MIDNIGHT WALK

MIDNIGHT WALK

EDITED BY LISA MORTON

Darkhouse Publishing
Los Angeles

MIDNIGHT WALK

Darkhouse Publishing
www.darkhousepublishing.com

Cover by John Palisano and Armand Constantine
Book design and layout by Rick Pickman

FIRST EDITION

ISBN: 978-0-578-02162-1

CONTENTS

INTRODUCTION

LISA MORTON

The book you now hold in your hands is a themed anthology.

That won't be immediately apparent from reading the stories. Indeed, this *Midnight Walk* will take you down diverse paths, in terms of setting, characters, and themes. You'll find everything herein from an Indian ghetto to the wealthiest of American communities, with protagonists ranging from a nineteenth-century British noblewoman to a modern-day female arson investigator to a futuristic scientist laboring in obscurity. Certainly these tales depend on many of the genre's favorite topics—vampires, ghosts, zombies, serial killers, monsters, mysterious cults, ancient Indian curses, cannibalism, black magic, and Halloween all lay waiting in these pages—but these zombies are part of the nineteenth-century Zulu uprising in Africa, and the hero combating this Indian curse is himself a Native American.

No, what ties the fourteen works in this anthology together is the background of the contributors, all of whom are from either western or midwestern America. Many of the writers are native Southern Californians, born and raised in one of the world's great melting pots. All of us are urban and interact daily with a variety of other cultures: During a typical day, we might exchange a greeting with a Spanish-speaking neighbor; order Thai food for lunch; buy stamps from a Chinese postal clerk; and shop at an Armenian market. We may speak more than one language, be well versed in the cinema of another country, or celebrate holidays that aren't officially recognized in the U.S. Life in any big city is also fraught with metropolitan perils, everything from increased numbers of violent crimes and gangs to higher costs of living; the great single urban sprawl that is now Southern California has its own peculiar dangers, including smog and attendant health problems, traffic (and road rage), persistent drought (and the ensuing wildfires), the threat of earthquakes, and city and state governments perpetually on the brink of bankruptcy.

All of which makes for some pretty interesting worldviews among local authors.

What you won't find in *Midnight Walk* are any examples of some of the worst, most overused horror tropes of the genre's last twenty years. There are no stories here about a middle-aged writer returning to his small hometown to fight the ultimate evil; there's no backwoods mutant running down prey, no rapist gleefully and gratuitously stalking women to engage in prolonged and gratuitous torture porn.

And that's a good thing.

Because, frankly, those stereotypes haven't done the genre any favors in quite a while. We all know that the horror boom of the '80s has led to the nadir of the '00s, with only a handful of major publishers still putting out horror and daring to call it such. The big chains have eliminated horror sections, most agents won't even consider the stuff, and authors have resorted to calling their work everything from "dark fantasy" to "thriller" to "paranormal romance." There's been a lot of brow-furrowing and hand-wringing and declarations that "horror is dead" (which is always followed with a hearty round of "but it's coming back!").

Maybe part of the genre's problem is that it's trying too hard to cling to the old ways.

While other genres have expanded thematically (look, for example, at mystery, where authors like Megan Abbott and Christa Faust have created a new sub-genre of hardboiled female crime fiction), a lot of recent dark fiction still seems stuck in those same 1980s. Ever since Stephen King declared the suburbs to be the real home of horror, most mass market horror novels have situated themselves firmly in a nice three-bedroom house on a cozy side street. The lead characters are typically middle-class heterosexual WASPs, with the occasional foray into the realm of the redneck; they're confronted by some vile thing that (gasp! shudder!) dares to threaten their idyllic and all-American way of life.

Fortunately, horror short fiction has been somewhat more adventurous, and I'd like to think that's where *Midnight Walk* comes in. Put most succinctly, these stories really aren't more of the same old crap. Hey, when's the last time you read horror fiction about Chinese children or elderly Latinas? You'll also see cross-genre stories here, including horror/science fiction and horror/historical adventure. Cross-genre horror stories have in the past often been relegated to the shadowy corners of small press *very* specifically themed magazines and anthologies, but maybe it's time for them to come out into the moonlight. Just as horror elements have cropped up in more and more mainstream novels over the last decade, perhaps these genre mashups need to be openly embraced.

Obviously what I'm suggesting overall is that horror needs to start exploring some new directions, and that's one of the reasons I'm particularly proud of the contents of this book. The authors of these stories have been shaped by a world that's not reflected in horror literature often enough, and they seem determined to change that. The fact that all of them are talented and care about their craft and know how to spin a compelling tale certainly doesn't hurt.

So, can horror survive unless it changes? Is the kind of diversity found in *Midnight Walk* really the future of horror?

Maybe not … but at least it's not more of the same old crap.

MONSOON DEVIL

ARMAND CONSTANTINE

HERE AND NOW. The murderer sat in the café, a glass of beer before him. Wicker ceiling fans stirred the sweat-stinking air but brought no relief. It was a malignant place in a malignant part of Old Delhi, populated by flies and the sort of men who look for backroom deals. Beside the murderer sat his old friend Rajiv and a youngster. The tang of rain filled the air a heartbeat before the roar of a sudden downpour that sluiced over the throngs of pedestrians, auto-rickshaws, and motorcycles outside.

"Another bloody monsoon season," complained the youngster. He sat to the murderer's right, juvenile and full of bravado. He fancied himself a gangster. The murderer ignored him.

"So your devil's gone home," observed Rajiv.

The murderer nodded. He opened his coat. A tiny pin held a neatly folded lotus leaf against his lapel. The murderer plucked it off and studied it absently.

The youngster scoffed. "You don't believe all that monsoon devil rubbish?"

Rajiv chuckled and answered for him. "Every year before the monsoon season, he pays some holy man a bloody mountain of rupees so he can have this devil on his side. He's like an old woman with his superstitions. Just don't question them."

The youngster sniffed. "I question what I feel like questioning."

Presumptuousness, the murderer thought. He considered slapping the cocksure smirk off the youngster's face, but instead he looked at Rajiv and said, "It worked, and you know it. No trouble came from that business with the American woman."

"True enough," Rajiv agreed.

"What American woman?" the youngster asked. "Tell me." He raised his beer glass to his lips.

The murderer slammed his palm into the bottom of the youngster's glass, smashing it into his mouth. Teeth broke, and broken glass lacerated lip and gum. The youngster shrieked and clapped his hands over his bleeding mouth, his eyes wide and frightened now. As they should be, the murderer thought. "None of your business what woman," he growled.

Rajiv laughed appreciatively. "I told you not to question him."

A few customers glanced over, but a fearful quiet reigned. For a time there was only the sound of the rain.

BEFORE. Aaron picked his way timidly through the crowded streets of Old Delhi. The traffic roared, un-muffled and stinking of gasoline fumes. Buildings tangled with exterior wiring wept long streaks of sooty tears. The crowds pressed in like suffocating bedclothes on a hot, sleepless night and rumbled in many-voiced Hindi. As far as he could tell, there were no other white faces in the crowd.

The door to the basement was shouldered into a small alcove behind a shop selling wedding decorations. From outside he could see the shopkeeper drinking from an outsized bottle of beer, looking like a surly, drunken groom among the strings of marigolds and cheap tinfoil streamers in oranges, reds, and pinks.

He tried to concentrate on his surroundings. The neighborhood was not a safe one. Less than a year ago he and his wife had left Los Angeles for India, their hearts filled with idealistic intent, wanting to spread awareness of AIDS among the red-light districts. But his last six months here had taught him more pragmatic lessons. Walking carelessly in a neighborhood like this was an invitation to pickpockets, robbers, and worse. Try as he might, however, he could not focus. His mind was a runaway train, roaring through the litany that filled it night and day, unrelenting memories of his now-dead wife.

. . . soft skin, angelic blue eyes, loves crab but not lobster, loves narrative poetry but not lyrical, has blond curls that look like strands of warm sunlight . . .

Endless strings of minutiae. It was driving him mad. These

lists filled his mind like a stubborn song that would not go away. For six months now, helpless in this strange city, he had felt a scream building in him.

A young man squatted beside the basement door on one hand and one foot. He held one leg canted upward at an impossible angle, and his head reclined on its side as he stared at Aaron. At first Aaron took him for a contortionist. As he drew near, however, he recognized the young man's twisted posture as the ravages of polio. He wore clean white linen, and his hair had been meticulously parted and slicked.

In a voice thickened by an ill-working jaw, he bid Aaron good morning in Hindi. He introduced himself as "the valet."

Aaron stammered something about not having an appointment, but the valet only studied him wordlessly, noting the lotus leaf on his lapel.

"I was told I could come here to meet a man. A holy man." When the valet still did not respond, he added, "I have money."

The valet's eyes narrowed, and Aaron wondered if he had made a mistake. In the wrong neighborhood—and this one struck him as precisely that—such an admission might earn him a knife in the ribs.

But the valet only nodded and turned away. He led Aaron down, negotiating the narrow stairs in his peculiar gait—first foot, then hand; foot then hand. Below, in a cramped room lit only by two naked bulbs, Aaron met the man he'd come to see.

THE HOLY MAN. The holy man looked like a salesman. Razor sharp creases lined neat khakis and a blue button-down shirt. Wavy black hair swept back from his brow, and a smile of porcelain and sunlight flashed from his handsome face. To Aaron he looked dangerous. Nothing was as it seemed in this city.

The holy man sat among a pile of colorful cushions that might have come from the wedding shop upstairs. Those bright oddments stood in stark contrast to the bare brick and dim light of the basement. It smelled powerfully of rain and urine.

"What brings you here today, friend?" the holy man asked pleasantly.

Suddenly Aaron did not know what to say.

The holy man nodded at the lotus leaf. "You know something

of our customs, it seems."

"Not really," Aaron said. "A friend told me to put this on. He said . . ."

"Yes?" the holy man prompted with an easy smile.

"He said I could speak to a devil. The monsoon devil."

The holy man's smile didn't falter. He only asked, "Because there is something you want?"

"Yes."

"You have money?" It sounded like pillow talk.

"Yes," Aaron said again.

Again the smile.

"I want to forget," Aaron said.

"What would you like to forget?" the holy man asked. Then with a sly look, he guessed, "A woman?"

Aaron nodded. "I want to forget my wife."

THE DEVIL HAD COME FROM AFAR. The devil came from the Nile among the lotuses, the holy man told him. Not recently, he explained with a friendly laugh, but over the generations as the world changed hands from one people to another. Wars were fought and won; priests went into hiding and kept their secrets. The holy man's devil spread into Persia, into the secret temples of ancient Herat and the homes of believers who defied their kings with their furtive prayers. From Persia he came, after a timeless time, to this land.

The holy man told Aaron these things as a father might tell his child the family history: with purpose, but with no real hope that he would understand the significance.

The devil's fee would be everything he had. Six months ago, after Isabelle's death, Aaron made a choice to stay in this country and find her killers. He was not a man of means. He ran out of hope and money. He took a job shaving beards and clipping hair for pennies at Mr. Gopal's barbershop. Finally he had saved enough to fly back home, but if he paid the devil, he would be destitute again.

"But you will forget," the holy man said. "My devil is a patron of things revealed and hidden. He is the serpent that sheds its skin."

"Where is this devil of yours?" Aaron asked.

"Inside." The holy man unbuttoned his neatly pressed cuffs and rolled up his sleeves. His brown forearms writhed with sinuous tattoos, serpents looping and twisting on themselves. They glided over his skin, alive, each one slithering independently in a way that made Aaron's eyes ache.

Aaron could hear the traffic of the street above, could smell the piss in the dank basement, could see the delight and cunning in the holy man's eyes. All was stark and real. But his mind rebelled at the living tattoos. Still, he told himself, things are not always as they seem.

"Things are not always as they seem," the holy man said with a smile.

Aaron stared at him, afraid. But he wanted to forget. He gave the holy man his money.

THE DEVIL. The holy man smelled of cologne and laundry soap when he placed his hands on Aaron's temples. The sinuous serpents on his arms whipped into a frenzy. They crawled from his skin onto Aaron's, their electric bodies itching his cheeks and eyelids. With slippery ease, they slid into the aperture of his pupils. Itching and cold and tugging nausea from his gut.

THE BEGINNING. The red-light district was very poor. It was a place of sadness, a place where three or four generations of prostitutes often clung together beneath the same roof. The tenements there crumbled slowly under the weight of moist heat.

Aaron and Isabelle carried clipboards and free condoms. They resolved not to leave any one building until they had taught someone from each home about the transmission of HIV.

In one shabby hallway, Aaron paused. From the corner of his eye he caught a girl of perhaps nine or ten staring at him from a doorway. He rounded on her in mock ferocity. "Boo!" The girl giggled and ducked inside.

Her name was Jaya. The apartment was small, its windows covered with cardboard. Her *naani* sat preparing rice at a hotplate on the floor. She waved them in with a smile.

Aaron and Isabelle had only begun their talk when the door burst open. Charu, Jaya's mother, tottered in and collapsed.

"*Maataa!*" Jaya cried.

Blood slicked both legs beneath her sari.

"Oh my God," Isabelle said. "We need towels or something. To put pressure on her. And we need to get a doctor." She looked at the girl's *naani*. "Doctor? Do you understand?"

"Yes, doctor," Jaya's *naani* said. "Doctor."

Two men barged in without knocking. Charu moaned and tried to back away. They looked like toughs. The first, a man with wiry hair and the white line of a scar slashing from hairline to eyebrow, had blood on his pants.

"We paid for a fuck already," the man growled. "She did not finish."

"You brutalized her, you assholes!" Isabelle yelled. "She needs a doctor!"

The man only sneered, but Aaron saw the danger in his eyes.

Aaron said, "I think you guys should just leave."

"We will be getting what we paid for," the man said. Jaya's *naani* nodded and began struggling to her feet. "No," the man said. "Not the old woman. The girl."

Jaya stood up slowly. Charu moaned, "No, no, no . . ." The scarred man grabbed Jaya roughly by the arm.

Aaron had never before seen such rage in Isabelle. She rose up like a banshee awhirl with kicks and scratches. He pulled her away from the men, but not before the scarred man slapped her viciously and spit a wad of frothy saliva into her face. Aaron was not a violent man, but a dangerous force swelled in him. He shoved the scarred man with all the strength he could muster. The man stumbled and sat down hard with his mouth rounded into an idiot "O." For a moment nothing happened. And then, incongruously, Jaya giggled. Perhaps it was the accumulation of fear that broke something loose. Perhaps it was a child's strange knack for seeing a glimmer of humor amid the gloom of menace. But whatever prompted it, Aaron saw rage and humiliation spark in the scarred man's eyes.

A knife appeared in his hand. "You Americans," he growled. "You need a lesson in respect." Aaron's breath caught in his throat.

"Police!" Isabelle cried. She dashed to the tiny balcony and thrust her face through the door. "Help! Police!"

The scarred man sneered. For a terrible moment Aaron

wondered if the police would come in time. Or would come at all. But then the man's compatriot was pulling him to his feet, murmuring, "Not now. Not here."

They left. The police did not come, even after Isabelle placed several telephone calls. All the while Aaron stood staring out the window, looking out at the writhing sea of humanity but seeing only the violence in the scarred man's hooded eyes.

Later Jaya stood outside on the crumbling balcony, staring down into the alleyway. Laundry lines crisscrossed the alley. Between the flapping clothes Aaron could see the ambulance below. Two men loaded a bagged body into the back.

"I'm so sorry," Aaron said.

Jaya said nothing. She held a lotus leaf in her hands. He watched as she folded it and pinned it to her lapel.

"It's the Sign of the Supplicant," Jaya explained. She told him of the monsoon devil.

"So you want to ask him for a favor?" Aaron asked.

Jaya nodded.

"For what?"

She looked at him with young eyes made old. "To kill the man who killed my *maataa*," she said quietly. With that, she turned and walked back inside.

THE HOLY MAN'S PROMISE. Aaron opened his eyes to the slow revolutions of the ceiling fan above his bed and the buzzing noise of traffic outside. An outhouse stood below his window in the shabby courtyard, and he could smell that someone had recently shat into it.

These things penetrated his consciousness as he moved through the hazy no-man's-land between sleep and wakefulness. A paradox: he remembered wanting to forget something . . . He probed his memory like a sore tooth. Immediately his mind began moving through its regular catalog:

. . . doesn't realize she wears blue so often, always ties double knots in her sneaker laces, smiles without knowing it when she reads . . .

Hot anger bubbled up in him. Memory of his exchange with the holy man came to him, clear and strong. No, not a holy man: a charlatan. Somehow Aaron had been taken in by his trickery, the profound persona and the living tattoos that must surely have been some sort of illusion. He had been a fool to put his trust in a man like that. And like a fool, he had been duped.

Aaron tried to calm himself. He crawled out of his tangled sheets and dressed in his sweat-stinking shirt from the day before. When he banged his toe against the end table beside his dresser, the rage boiled over. He stomped and stomped until all that remained was split wood spotted with the blood from his lacerated foot.

VENGEFUL. The man in the decoration shop was brooding among his gaudy wares, still drinking beer. The rickety door down to the basement stood unlocked but darkness shrouded the hallway. Worse, the basement itself was empty. For a moment, Aaron saw slithering movement in one gloomy corner, but when he peered closely he saw only dust and crumbling concrete.

"Who can say?" said the brooding merchant when Aaron asked about the holy man. He stared past Aaron without interest.

WHISPERS. "The holy man comes some time before the monsoon," Mr. Gopal explained. His broom swished as he swept hair clippings into a pile. "No one knows exactly when or where. Rumors start. Whispers overheard by a friend of a friend of a cousin. Some few manage to find him and seek favors. And then, when the monsoons come, he is gone."

"You forgot the part where he screws you," Aaron muttered.

Mr. Gopal blinked at him through his spectacles. "Things are not always what they seem, Aaron."

A VISITOR ARRIVED. Mr. Gopal's barbershop sweltered. Beads of sweat spattered onto the barber's chair as Aaron hovered over it. Mr. Gopal, amazingly composed in his tight vest and oiled hair, clicked the music of costs and revenues on his abacus.

The wooden door-chimes clacked. A burst of traffic noise rumbled in. Aaron did not care enough to look up.

"May I help you, sir?" Gopal asked as his abacus, blessedly, fell silent.

"I need a shave," came the answer in Hindi.

Something in the man's voice drew Aaron's attention. He turned. The world tilted dizzyingly. It was Isabelle's murderer. The man's mouth pursed sourly, a petulant little hole in his sloping head. His brows knit below a greasy tangle of wiry hair, and a faint scar above his left eyebrow whitened faintly, the ghostly line Aaron had seen while the man's cronies held him down that night.

The murderer glanced at him. Aaron looked quickly away. His breath sounded suddenly too loud in his throat. He tried to find something to look at, but his eyes kept sliding back. He began to strop his razor with shaking hands, trying to appear uninterested.

"That we can manage, sir," Mr. Gopal said, returning his attention to his books. "Aaron can help you right away."

EYES. The murderer's eyes met Aaron's. Did they narrow briefly? Was there recognition in that look? If so, he gave nothing away. The barber's chair creaked as the murderer sat down before him, but Aaron barely heard it through the rush of memories from that night.

THAT NIGHT. They are eating dinner, the two of them seated at the kitchen table in their tiny Delhi apartment. Isabelle laughs good-naturedly at dropping a piece of curried lamb from her fork into her wine.

The men enter the house, swift and confident, locking the door behind them and rushing the table. Isabelle laughs no longer. Soon they have her, have Aaron. He notices her wine running over the tablecloth, lamb and all.

There are three men, rough and strong enough to hold Aaron down. The blows start raining down on him, and a fist bunches in his hair. And then he recognizes one of them. He is the man who killed Jaya's mother, the animal who had blood on his pants that day.

They wrestle Isabelle and him to the floor. For some minutes he hears one of the men rummaging in the other rooms, picking over their meager possessions like an old maid at market. Aaron's head rocks under a blow from a toughened fist. He can feel fists pummeling at his back and kidneys. He catches only glimpses of two of the men tearing at Isabelle's clothes. The blouse he had bought her, the white silk piece he had spent too much on at Harrods of London on the journey to this nightmare land. He can't see her face because it's turned away.

She screams. She screams again. The neighbors must hear. They'll be here shortly.

RAZOR TO THROAT. The murderer sat in the barber chair, staring up at the ceiling in that way men do, never meeting the eyes of the man who holds the razor to their throats.

Aaron's hand shook as he scraped the razor over the man's soapy throat. He wanted that shaking to be the righteous rage of a man who deserves justice. But it was not. His tongue felt dry as a sock in his mouth, and his throat worked noisily to swallow the bitter chalk of fear. The delicate skin of his neck was weathered and thinned by middle age. It would be so easy to slice through it, to end this animal's life. But Aaron only scraped, wiped, tilted his head, scraped and wiped again. The faint scar on his brow, that ghostly line from hairline to eyebrow, drew his eye continually.

Afterward the murderer examined himself in the mirror with a grunt. For the first time he looked Aaron full in the face. Aaron saw no recognition there. He wanted to scream. Could the murderous animal really have forgotten? It was madness, wasn't it? It had been six months, yes, but could the man really have cared so little about his actions that night that they would pass out of his memory as if they were no more important than picking up dry cleaning or filling a gas tank?

Or was the man toying with him, knowing Aaron didn't have the courage to act? A chill tickled his spine at the thought.

And then it was over. The murderer was standing and dropping a few rupees on the counter. Voices screamed in Aaron's head, demanding that he act, that he not let this monster go after fate had dropped him in Aaron's lap. But he stood frozen. The door opened, letting in another rush of traffic noise, and then shut again with a dull thud, ordinary and heart-wrenching. Aaron's mind wheeled crazily, banishing all but the terrible images, *that night* . . .

THAT NIGHT AGAIN. The men don't laugh or joke. They do their work wordlessly with a hollow detachment in their eyes.

Aaron thinks he must be able to make some appeal to these silent beasts, ask them about their wives or children, about their bosses or jobs, about what they ate that morning or whether their children are expecting them home soon—anything to remind them of their humanity. He tries to speak. He tastes blood.

The neighbors must hear the screams. No one comes. And now only one of them matters, only one man exists in this universe: the man with the white scar. He leans close to Isabelle. His pink tongue darts out like some fleshy animal creeping from its tide pool lair. Aaron struggles, putting all his desperate will into breaking free, just enough to slip one limb from the hands holding him, just the smallest purchase so that he might have a chance, that Isabelle might have a chance.

He fails—he fails.

And suddenly he sees Isabelle's breasts, her hips, and he struggles more frantically. He can't move. He can't turn away. He cannot do anything but watch. His throat hurts him, from screaming he realizes. Where are the neighbors? The scarred man's pants are down now. He can't look away. He's suffocating under a mountain, vast miles of rock and earth that smother him while horrors tear at Isabelle.

And then darkness.

INERTIA BROKE. Aaron hurried to the door. He knocked over the glass of antiseptic holding his barber's scissors, and it smashed to the floor, scattering broken glass and pungent liquid everywhere.

"Aaron! Where are you going?" Mr. Gopal stood scowling at him, hands on his hips.

He forced himself to think, to speak clearly and unhurriedly. "I've forgotten my lunch. I'll only be a few minutes, Mr. Gopal." He didn't wait for a reply.

PURSUIT. Aaron followed the murderer street after street, by turns fascinated and sickened by his seeming normality. Aaron kept his distance to avoid being noticed, but it was not necessary. The streets were thick with people, and the murderer never glanced back. He walked with his shoulders slumped and his head bent beneath the heat. Aaron thought of a devil crossing a desert amid swirling sands.

Eventually the murderer turned into a narrow street lined with industrial shops and decrepit warehouses. He unlocked the door of a motorcycle repair shop.

Aaron's mind continued its catalog, chunking through item by item, like the endless cogs on some vast and ill-begotten machine.

. . . sips wine with the delicacy of a doll but can chug beer faster than he can when she wants to, gets self-conscious and looks at her feet when she laughs in public, likes simple jewelry but only wears it rarely . . .

The murderer pulled on a set of coveralls and disappeared through a narrow door at the rear of the shop. A glimpse through the doorway showed a yard full of disassembled motorcycles and auto-rickshaws.

The empty gulf in Aaron's chest yawned with the familiar sadness. But today a bitter anger tempered it.

THE REEK OF GREASE AND SWEAT. It was silent when Aaron entered, with only the clink and clatter of tools against metal coming through the little doorway at the back. A broken desk and some boxes occupied the tiny shop. He locked the front door and walked into the rear yard.

The murderer had his back to him as he squatted over the bent frame of an ancient military motorcycle. He banged at the frame with a hammer, straightening a bend. A makeshift forge burned in the patch of dirt between the mounds of decrepit motorcycle parts. He could smell the man's sweat, could hear the damp rattle in his panting. Aaron imagined the breath rushing along the fleshy channel of his throat, passing over the pink tongue that he had pressed to Isabelle's cheek.

The murderer suddenly turned his head to spit and froze when his eyes found Aaron. He spoke in Hindi. "You startled me," he said. He squinted at Aaron. "You're the fellow from the barbershop."

"Yes," Aaron said, forcing what must have been a grotesque smile. He felt wooden, unreal, like one of the Rajasthani marionettes tourists liked to buy. Oddly, the list-maker in his head was silent, whispering only *Isabelle. Isabelle. Isabelle.*

"I know I paid enough," he growled.

A part of Aaron that seemed to float in some far off place

wanted to laugh at that. But he managed a nod nevertheless. The movement made his head ache.

The murderer peered at him, puzzled. Aaron finally knew this was no show of innocence. The murderer truly did not recognize him. Here, the two of them alone in this deserted motorcycle graveyard, there could be no reason for a charade. Nausea churned his stomach. The brutality of that night, the destruction of Aaron's entire world—meaningless, it seemed. Aaron felt dizzy.

"I know you from somewhere," Aaron said.

The murderer's eyes narrowed, but he only shrugged. "I don't remember. Should I?" Without waiting for an answer, he put down his hammer and turned back to his makeshift forge to heat the motorcycle frame.

Aaron thought of the aftermath of that night. Isabelle's body, bleeding, naked after the murderer and his compatriots had gone.

"Yes," Aaron said. "You should remember."

COMING ALIVE. A jagged metal rod lay at Aaron's feet. Before he could think, he snatched it up. For an instant the murderer's face registered fear. And then Aaron swung. The murderer flinched back. The rod only struck a glancing blow above his ear, but it was enough to lay him flat. His legs twitched and convulsed, and his eyes stared unfocused at the dirt.

. . . Pink tongue darting out from under a hooked nose, Isabelle's screams as rough hands clutch at her breasts, and oh-God-oh-God a glimpse of his phallus as he lowers himself . . . a glimpse of his, a glimpse . . .

Aaron gave a strangled cry, something bestial, a blackened lump of ancient instinct carved up from some forgotten corner of his soul. He hit and hit and hit, slamming the rod into the murderer's thighs and back, wanting to hurt but not kill too quickly.

Isabelle. Isabelle. Isabelle. Isabelle.

Aaron stopped. He panted and watched as the murderer tried to crawl away. His breath wheezed and whistled, and the sound of soft weeping nearly eclipsed a whisper of speech.

Aaron leaned close to hear him.

"Why?" the murderer sobbed.

"Why?" Aaron asked. "*Why?* You did this! You did this to yourself when you raped and killed my wife, you son of a bitch!"

Aaron hit him again, a savage blow that snapped a femur. The murderer shrieked.

"Come here," Aaron hissed as he dropped the rod in the dirt. "Let me show you something." Aaron tore at the man's pants, ripping at his belt and fly. He yanked at the trousers and rolled the murderer over so that he lay on his stomach, dusty and naked from the waist down.

He took up the jagged rod. "Let's see what it's like, huh? From rapist to raped. Let's see what it's like."

The murderer's face twisted into a wide-open scream, silent, paralyzed with agony and unable to make a sound. Aaron strained with the effort. The writhing body scuffed through the dirt with each thrust. When the screams began, they were ragged and terrible. Spit dribbled down the murderer's chin. The scar on his brow seemed to glow with a surreal brilliance as Aaron toiled. The rod grew slick in his hand.

Finally the screams stopped. Aaron dropped the rod and sat down hard. The tears came, swift and bitter. He did not want to look at the murderer's face again, but he forced himself.

He froze, the tears stopping instantly.

. . . Vacant eyes and a terrible coldness, the pink tongue, the ghost line of a scar passing from hairline to eyebrow . . .

The scar—there was no scar. No scar. The realization sparked like a miniature sun. He did not dare move—did not dare breathe—because there was no scar. Only wrinkled skin browned from years in the sun.

His throat constricted, and a strange clarity made him aware of everything around him. Flies lit with manic brevity on a pile of dog shit nearby. A cypress jutting up from somewhere behind the yard loomed overhead, its somber limbs slashing the white-hot sky with silhouette blackness. A tremor shook the murderer's legs.

Aaron rolled the body over. The nose was wrong. Here was not the hawkish thing he remembered, but a mass of crinkled dough, bulbous and round. And the hair; while it was wiry and black, it was shot with too much gray. And, God, *there was no scar.* It wasn't him. This wasn't the murderer.

Aaron vomited. He scrambled away from the body and stared in disbelief. He could not think how he could have made such a mistake. Finally, after a long heart-hammering time, he remembered the rod. It got him moving. He quickly wiped at it with the tail of his shirt, hoping to erase his fingerprints.

From the corner of his eye, Aaron thought he saw a snake slithering between the tangled mounds of motorcycle parts, sinuous and busy with movement. He thought of the holy man's tattoos.

He ran.

A BEGINNING. He was more than a mile away before he dared slow to a walk and catch his breath. He noticed his hands shaking violently. His mind sensed weakness and seized on his distraction by resuming its regular list-making.

. . . blond hair, her grandmother called her Izzy, she didn't like eggplant, never painted her toenails, eyes . . . eyes . . .

He stopped abruptly in the street, stunned. What color had her eyes been? Isabelle's face came quickly and easily to memory, but her eyes eluded him. Green? Brown? Blue? He tested the possibilities but none stood out. He had forgotten.

And then, something strange. He felt the sudden blossoming of hope. Things are not always as they seem, the holy man had said. The writhing serpents on the holy man's skin no longer smacked of chicanery, his promises no longer empty.

There were many people about, and his path crossed with thousands as he made his way numbly back to Mr. Gopal's barbershop. In a flower booth on the west edge of the market he saw the murderer again, this time hawking bunches of marigolds. Aaron pretended not to notice him. Just one man among millions in this city. When at last he returned to his chair at the shop and began stropping his razor, he could not help feeling *eager*. Eager to do the monsoon devil's work again. Eager to forget one more piece of his wife, and then another after that, until the pain was finally gone.

HERE AND NOW. The youngster cradles his lacerated mouth. Rajiv chuckles again and claps a friendly hand on the youngster's shoulder. "Keep asking questions and he'll send his devil after you next."

The murderer drops his Sign of the Supplicant into what's left of the youngster's broken beer glass. He is finished with this conversation. He grabs his coat and steps outside into the rain.

HERE AND NOW. A short way down the street, a little girl stares despondently up into the rain. It is Jaya. A figure crouches down beside her, a handsome man with a brilliant smile and sinuous tattoos visible beneath his shirtsleeves. The holy man.

"Child, do you like the rain so much that you'd stand in it so?" he asks her.

She shrugs. A Sign of the Supplicant droops on her lapel. She plucks it. "My *maataa . . .*" she starts, then trails off. "I've been waiting for someone who never came," she says instead. "And now the rains have come and he's gone away." She begins to cry softly.

"Look at me, child." The holy man gently takes her by the chin and lifts her gaze to his. "Do you like music?" he asks.

She sniffs, and after a time she nods.

"Music is a strange thing. If you listen to one note or two, it seems a paltry sound. But when you listen to all the notes—in their order, in their rhythm—we can find in those paltry sounds the most beautiful symphony. Life is much like music, little Jaya. Things happen in their own time, with their own order and rhythm. And often . . . things are not as they seem."

For the briefest of moments, serpents come alive deep in the holy man's eyes, whipping and lashing at one another. Understanding passes over Jaya's face as she realizes the monsoon devil crouches before her. He has heard her pleas, and now he has come, a dark force living inside this handsome man.

The holy man glances at his watch. He stands abruptly and turns around. The murderer is there, pressing through the crowd and not paying attention. It is as if the holy man knew he would be there.

Recognition dawns, and the murderer stares with surprise. "*You*," the murderer says. "What do you want?"

"To make a little music," says the holy man. A gleaming knife appears in his hand. Quickly, efficiently, the knife strikes, sinking into the soft place under the murderer's arm. The blood is brilliant, arterial.

The murderer gasps. He sits down hard on the street, pedestrians and rainwater parting around him with equal disregard.

The holy man turns back to Jaya, and she takes a fearful step back.

"I don't think you'll need this anymore, child," he says, and he takes the Sign of the Supplicant from her. "All right?"

Jaya looks at him strangely, then nods. With that he smoothes her rain-soaked hair with a gentle hand and smiles. And then he's gone.

Jaya stares at the murderer as he topples into the gutter, face down and lifeless, his blood mingling with the rain. A time passes. And then, her expression unreadable, she turns and scampers away and is soon lost among the crowds.

THE TENNATRICK

JOHN PALISANO

After a sultry Southern California summer filled with fire, the charred chaparral plants appeared lifeless, black and forgotten. Deep within the dry, scorched, grey earth, countless heavy seed shells cracked. They needed fires to splinter them and cast their seeds into the dirt. Nourished and pollinated by the carbonized vegetation, the chaparral secretly flourished. Underneath the growth, an undiscovered species also found its way from its own fire-split shell.

Reborn within highly flammable, slippery oils, the Tennatrick burrowed toward the topsoil layers. It stood in the light after countless years, awakened only after an extraordinary wildfire burned the previously pristine mountainside down to blackened roots.

White ash fell like snow and Jen tasted smoke from the burn. It'd been the thirteenth such fire to start in the Los Padros section of the Angeles National Forest, and the fifth she'd been assigned to investigate. It wasn't a very large fire, and everyone she spoke with believed they'd snuff it out within a day. The department always sent her out on the small ones—the fires no one else wanted. There were no movie stars' homes to save, no photo-ops, no news crews. Instead, there was a free campsite and a small public lake with a waterfall, frequented exclusively by the working poor.

She'd been leaving a message for her ex, Stuart, when someone tapped her on the shoulder. Turning to see a thin man, she put up a finger, finished her message, and turned to him.

"Hi, sir. Can I help you?" she said. The fire trucks and police cars were stretched across the access road, and she'd have put money on him asking her how long they were going to be.

Instead, he pointed up to the top of the hill. "You see up there? That's where the fire started."

He was soft-spoken, and she had to lean in to hear him. "Say again?"

"Tennatrick," he said.

Jen leaned away from him.

Had it all come to this again? Monsters.

"So that's what this is about?" The locals had started reporting seeing strange monsters starting forest fires. Every time she questioned witnesses, someone claimed to see them.

"It's true."

"What's your name?"

"Oswald Rodriguez."

Jen briefly scribbled it down, then looked up at him again. "Mr. Rodriguez, who are you hiding? A gangbanger? Environmental activist? What were you, just camping? Just happen to be in the area when all this went down?"

Jen was tired of playing good cop. She'd been trying to get to the bottom of these fires for months, with little progress. People just wouldn't cooperate. She believed that someone must know something.

"I was just taking a walk this afternoon, same as always," Oswald said. "The Tennatrick's real." He looked away for a second, and then back. "I didn't believe in it either, until tonight. Just thought it was some stupid thing the kids made up."

"If what you're telling me is true, then why aren't you running home? I'd be scared to death. And I really wouldn't be standing here, cool and calm, in the middle of a forest fire."

Behind Engine Three, Jen spotted someone she recognized from the Fire Investigation Unit—Brian Riggs. She waved him over before turning back to Oswald. Jen didn't believe him. She rubbed at a piece of ash in her eye as Brian made his way over.

"How's everything over here, Jen?" Brian said as he put his hand out. She shook it, but Brian eyed Oswald.

"You have great timing," she shook Brian's hand. "We've got another monster eyewitness."

Brian nodded. "Oh, isn't that marvelous."

Oswald pointed over her shoulder. "The Tennatrick started burning up on top of the hill."

"Did you happen to take a picture with your phone? Anything like that?" Jen asked.

"I don't have a cell phone," Oswald said. "I was walking back to my house when I saw the Tennatrick on top of the ridge. It looked like it was pouring fire onto the ground."

The hot dry air settled in Jen's throat. "With what? A bucket?" She turned to Brian and smirked. "This is a new detail."

Oswald looked toward the top of the mountainside and shook his head. "Its oil poured from its bottom. It starts the fires."

"Oh, come on. You really believe some kind of *creature* started this fire?" Jen asked.

"I do," Oswald said. He looked completely convinced.

A tunnel of flames exploded up on the hill—Jen ducked down and covered her head with her jacket. "Jesus," she hollered. "Let's get moving."

Jen looked up toward the towering wall of fire moving down the opposite side of the road. They were still far enough away from the fire that they could be relatively safe. Three other police officers, a sheriff, and a canine hiked up nearby.

"Do you believe him?" Brian asked.

"He didn't even look scared," she said. "Wouldn't you be terrified?"

"I'm not sure if I'd be able to do much of anything," Brian said. "I've seen people who couldn't stop smiling after watching loved ones killed right in front of them. Part of the survival instinct."

"I think he's buying into this myth about some monster causing this. Either that or they're covering up for someone and trying to get us to chase our tails."

They continued up the hill for a bit without speaking. As they stepped closer to the fire, Jen sensed the air getting thinner and thinner. Smoke surrounded them.

"How many acres are gone?" Jen asked. "Did Forestry Services give us any estimate?"

"Last I heard we were at about a hundred acres." Brian kept his eyes locked on the fire. "Looks like it'll jump the line soon." A small tower of flame broke past the rail to their right. An aircraft flew overhead. "Kind of late in the day for Air Ops to take their final run, eh? It's way past dusk."

The canine unit hurried past. "She's got something," someone said from behind. "Follow Cassie."

Jen rushed up the hill toward another level of road toward the top. The fire raged.

Cassie swerved left and jigged sideways before she crested the hill onto the higher road.

"Where'd she go?" Brian said.

"Bet we just got our suspect cornered." Jen breathed heavier with each step.

Jen peeked over the railing on top of the hill. The small access road in front of her stretched around an overhang to her left, before curving back downward to her right. She saw another railing lining the opposite side. She recognized the signs that identified Santoro Lake.

"There's nobody up here," she said. "Where'd they go? This is a dead end."

"Maybe our suspect made it down to the lake?" Brian said.

Jen shook her head. "I doubt it. That's a straight drop down."

She nudged him to look to their left. Cassie pointed toward a steep mountain ridge above the road.

"What's she barking at?" Jen swung her legs over the rail and stood on the other side. She put her hand against her left side, ready to withdraw her nine-millimeter.

"I don't see anything," Brian said. He looked behind them. "Where'd everyone go?" He nudged Jen.

She followed Brian's gaze, seeing only one police officer who scurried backward. He cupped his hands. "You better get back down *A-sap* or you're going to get trapped."

Jen scanned the inferno. It grew as she watched. "Shit," she said. She turned to Cassie. "Come on, girl. Let's go."

Cassie didn't register her command. Instead, she growled and focused on the mountainside.

"Forget the damn dog!" Brian said. "She'll follow us. Let's go."

"Right," Jen said and swung her legs back over the rail. As she landed on the other side the flames spread upward and arched right over the road, touching a small packet of brush on the lower side. The fire had jumped.

"Situation's real bad," Jen said, "and getting worse."

The fire rose in a blink, consuming a hundred feet of ground cover between Jen and the cop. Heat from the fire baked her cheeks.

"Get back up on the road!" She checked the ground. Dried vegetation. "This is going to burn fast as hell!"

Flames arched up and over the road, and they found a small pocket of safety near the rails on the access road where there was only dirt on one side, and road on the other. No fuel. Jen kept to the roadside. She knew if there was a break, she could at least follow the road down the hill toward safety. Brian ran behind her onto the road.

A large shiny shadow descended from the mountainside above the road. Cassie stopped barking and back-stepped toward Jen and Brian. She whimpered. Jen watched the fire, knelt, spun round, and scaled back over the rail.

Brian knelt, too. "Something big's up there," he said.

Large spiral flames reached over the rails beside them, blocking the downward path of the road. They both withdrew their pistols.

The shiny shadow crept down the hill. "What is that?" Jen said.

"I don't know," Brian said.

The animal reached the bottom and stood a few car lengths away. A long, sectioned head rose ten feet high. Seven eyes glistened. Some were red, some were blue, others were black. Their colors seemed to change subtly while Brian and Jen watched.

It balanced on several black fin-like appendages, each with small pointed burrs at the tips. The SUV-sized oval body balanced gracefully on top of the fins. The creature shuddered and stretched its jaw, speaking through several vocal clicks.

Tenna. Tenna. Tenna.

They both smelled the raw, oily stench of the Tennatrick's breath just before its long neck lunged and snapped toward Cassie. The dog rushed back several steps, escaping the creature's jaws.

Brian and Jen saw every detail of the Tennatrick's horse-shaped head, right down to the way Cassie's face reflected on the creature's shiny skin.

"This isn't happening," Jen said. "It's a hallucination from the smoke, right?"

Brian shook his head. "Sure," he said, his voice high pitched. "Whatever you want to think."

She thought he was trying *very* hard to keep his cool.

The animal made more clicking sounds.

Trick. Trick. Trick.

"What is that noise it's making?" Jen said. Despite standing in the middle of a burn, Jen's veins felt filled with ice. Her right leg shook. She willed it to stop but it kept wobbling. *Use the adrenaline. Make it work.*

"That sound?" Jen said. "That's how they came up with the name."

"The Tennatrick," Brian said.

"Yeah," she said.

The Tennatrick inched toward Cassie, then leaned back on two rear fins. In an instant the Tennatrick's front fins scooped up Cassie. She yelped as the burrs punctured her body. The Tennatrick pulled the dog toward its head.

Brian clicked his gun's trigger several times. "Fuck!" he said. "This thing's not working."

Jen aimed at the Tennatrick.

"Shoot it!" Brian said. "Fast!"

Jen swerved her aim squarely between the Tennatrick's eyes and squeezed the trigger.

The gun recoiled and the Tennatrick squealed. A small red hole appeared. Black fluid spilled out and smoldered on the road.

"Shoot it again," Brian said. "Kill it."

The Tennatrick tossed Cassie to the side, shaking the dog from the end of its fin. Cassie landed against the railing with a yelp. Jen saw several large gashes.

She squeezed off two more shots.

The Tennatrick screeched—more of its awful noises.

Jen spotted a hole just over the creature's mouth dripping black oily blood . . . then the hole shut. "It's like shooting into quicksand," she said. "It's not taking any hits."

Brian crouched behind her. "There's no way out. It's going to get us. Like it got Cassie." He looked over at the wounded dog.

Jen looked, too. Cassie didn't seem to be whimpering any longer. Smoke trailed from her wounds.

The ground moved. The Tennatrick stepped. It burrowed its fins in the ground like an ape resting on its knuckles. Its head moved slowly from side to side. It watched them with its eyes, which changed color from an oily greenish to a bright blue.

The thing sounded more percussive clicks, the smell of its breath stunk up the air between them like old sterno.

It swung with one of its fins. Jen hopped out of the way.

"Uh," Brian groaned.

She twisted round to see him laying on his back. She looked down—he looked down—they both screamed.

A large triangular slice smoldered from the top part of his left thigh. There was no blood.

Their eyes met. "Move," he yelled.

She did. Just in time. She looked at her waist and saw the fin swish right in front of her. If she hadn't moved she would have been cut in half.

She raised her gun and looked right up into the Tennatrick's eye. She shot. The Tennatrick screeched as its eye turned into a black empty hole.

Jen looked left and right and behind her. There was a break in the wall of fire. She leaned down to Brian. "Can you walk?"

"I don't know," he said back. He went to move his legs and threw his head back. Brian grit his teeth. "God damn."

The Tennatrick regained its ground and stood on its back. It towered as high as the burning treetops. She knew she had only a moment, so Jen hurried behind Brian, grabbed him under his arms, and pulled him to his feet. He cried out, but was able to stand.

The Tennatrick charged as soon as they moved. Jen pulled off two shots. Both vanished inside the creature's hide.

"That's not doing anything," he said. "We better run." He limped backward.

"Where?"

He pointed toward the right side of the road, where there was a gap big enough for them to run through.

"There's only a few feet of ground over there," Jen said. "We'll get trapped."

Brian stood, winced, said, "There's no choice," and turned tail.

"Shit!" Jen followed him, but not before getting another good look at the Tennatrick. It recoiled when their eyes met and Jen imagined it was about to whip out one of its flippers.

She ran and heard the creature make several sharp cries that were different from the clicks. The earth shook as the monster dropped down onto the road, each limb making contact.

They reached the other side of the road and hopped the rails. She wondered how Brian could be standing with his wound and thought either it wasn't as bad as she'd feared, or his adrenaline had kicked in.

Fire surrounded them on the three sides. They had to put up their arms to shield themselves. "I hear something," he said.

Jen heard it, too. "The undergrowth's burning."

The fire had spread and chased them. Jen felt the skin on her hands and face bake. "This was a bad idea."

"Now what?" Brian asked. There was barely room for them to stand safely.

"We've got to jump in Santoro Lake." She nodded at Brian. "It's now or never."

The fire closed in. From the road, the Tennatrick charged toward them, stopping only a dozen feet away. It swung one of its flippers. Jen hopped out of the way. As she jumped back, she saw Brian cowering beneath the creature.

Jen yelled his name. As she did, the animal was on him. It moved too swiftly for Jen to react. Brian's body lifted off the ground. She pointed her gun at the Tennatrick, but couldn't find a clear shot.

"Let him go!" she screamed. "Drop him!" She was sure she'd hit Brian if she fired.

Before Jen found another chance, the Tennatrick retreated backward. She couldn't see what it was doing: Flames blocked her view. A moment later two halves of Brian flew forth and splattered on the road. They landed only a few feet from her. She could see the legs, twisted, his toes pointing toward her, his innards glistening.

Her throat dried and her entire body felt numb. He hadn't just been torn in half in front of her eyes by some animal, had he? Where was the thing? She raised her gun. *Let me get another shot. Take out another one of your fucking eyes.*

Jen stumbled and saw Brian's head; his eyes were wide open. *Don't look at his face. You'll never forget it.* She looked at her feet for a moment and tried to catch her breath, but the heat was making it hard.

The Tennatrick charged forward, clicking, swinging its flippers and limbs, its head lowered, ready to do to her what it'd done to Brian.

Think!

Water. The lake. It's just a few steps, a quick fall, and I can live . . . there's fire there, but I can hop through it and I should be able to make it past . . .

She turned from the Tennatrick, put her forearms up, and charged through the fire toward the lake. The skin on the tops of her hands singed, but before she could think about it, Jen felt her feet fall out from under her. She dropped for several seconds before hitting the lake.

She felt freezing water all around her. It made the burns on her hands and forearms sting. Jen pushed her way up and out of the water. As she did she sensed something brush past her hip. *Probably a fish or plant or something.*

A thin layer of ash coated the top of the water and smoke drifted across the lake. She looked left and saw fifty-foot-tall walls of fire soaring near the top of the hill.

She glimpsed the Tennatrick through the flames, above her. It spotted her, froze for a moment, and backed fully into the inferno. *It knows I'm down here.*

Jen was starting to make her way through the ash-filled water when the Tennatrick impossibly appeared on the shore in front of her. *How could it get here that fast?*

She spun and found a flat rocky slab of what looked like granite jutting from the water to form a small island.

Hope this thing doesn't like water. She swam back to the island, keeping an eye on the creature's progress all the while. The flames lit the entire lake.

The Tennatrick raced around the perimeter and kept watch on Jen. She saw the creature turn its head toward her every few moments, seemingly tracking her progress. *The fire isn't burning the thing. It really is just running right through without getting hurt.*

Jen turned and climbed up onto the rock island. *Hope that thing can't get here. Where the hell are the relief ops?* As she horked herself up on the slab, she realized she was still holding her gun. She shook water out of it, hoping it would still fire.

She spun round and sat. Her chest felt like it was made of fiberglass. She covered her nose and mouth with the neck from her T-shirt. It was wet and would serve as a filter, she hoped. *Better than nothing.*

The trees and vegetation around the perimeter of the lake burned. There was no sign of the Tennatrick. *How long until this area burns out? It won't have fuel here forever.*

The water on the lake went still; the layer of ash on top made it look just like a normal stretch of flat land.

She looked up toward the spot from which she'd jumped, where she'd last seen Brian. *Santoro Lake. There is a waterfall here, after all. I know this place. I came hiking through here a few years ago . . . back before Stuart left. Before he found someone with a job that didn't call her away in the middle of the night. A new girlfriend who won't be too tired to . . .*

Jen leaned against the rocks. *What can I say when they ask what happened with Brian?* Her mind turned blank for a moment. *Maybe I can just say we pursued the suspect up the hill and got trapped by the fire. There was no way out. Nobody has to know about this monster thing. It was probably something else, anyway. Can't be real. Just can't. But what about his body? They'll see that it was torn in half . . .*

Something moved across the lake on the small shoreline. The Tennatrick peeked through the fire and spotted her on the rock island in the center. *You reading my thoughts? I was just thinking how to explain you away.*

Jen gulped. *This thing's huge. What the hell is it?* She reached for her gun. She coiled her hand around the butt, which made her feel better.

She stood and checked out the area in back of the island. *Water on all sides. At least fifty feet. It'd have to swim to get me.*

She turned back around in time to see the Tennatrick approach the waterfront at the beach. The creature lowered a single fin to the water, then lowered its head.

The damn thing has fins, she thought. *Of course it's going to go into the water. Look at it.* She curled back upon her rock and watched the Tennatrick. *Okay. Where's there to go? Back in the water? If that thing can swim, then that's it. I have to at least try to get out of here.*

The Tennatrick snapped back from the water as though it'd been stung. It screamed and coughed fire.

Something dripped from the flipper it had used to touch the lake. Black goo oozed onto the sand.

Jen kept her eyes glued on the Tennatrick. The creature bobbed its head up and down and seemed to be looking toward one side of the lake at something.

A second clicking voice came from somewhere else.

Toward the Tennatrick's right, fifty feet above, a second, lighter colored Tennatrick peeked through the fire. It opened and closed its jaw, sucking the fire, which changed from bright red and orange into blue and then white as the creature consumed it.

Once it got its fill, the paler Tennatrick walked onto the beach. The first Tennatrick twittered around and faced the new arrival.

Without hesitation, the second Tennatrick jumped on top of the first. It clamped its fins around the other, who tried shaking off the attacker.

Now's my chance, Jen thought. *While they're busy killing each other I can get the hell out of here. And I won't have to waste a shot from here. I might hit it, but it seems to not be too bothered with me right now.* But when she watched them a moment longer, she noticed the creatures weren't hurting each other.

A white round appendage dropped from the rear of the top Tennatrick. The appendage curled and hardened and found its way inside an opening underneath its mate. As they worked their organs together, a pinkish fluid dripped from the opening.

For God's sake, Jen said. *Is that all they can think about at a time like this?*

But she couldn't look away.

The animals' rutting became faster and more intense, each thrust more violent than the last.

Finally, the top Tennatrick stopped after four slow jerks. Its appendage slipped out, flopping like a dead snake, and dribbled pink goo on the sand. It crawled off its mate and lowered toward the sand. *Tired, aren't you, you son of a bitch? All that and it's over in five minutes. Guess some things are the same whether you're a person or a firebug.*

Jen kept still.

The darker Tennatrick crawled on top of the resting creature. At first Jen believed that, somehow, it might return the favor and drop its own appendage down. As soon as she saw the creature's jaw open she knew differently.

Ripping mouthfuls of rubbery flesh from its spent mate, the Tennatrick spit them onto the sand as fast as she'd ripped them away. The pieces smoldered and small flames sparked out in places.

Good girl. You show him.

The wounds dripped the dark viscous fluid, which sparked and flamed when spilled.

The Tennatrick tore and tossed several more pieces. For its part, the mate sounded no protest. It willingly accepted its fate.

Now why would it do something like that? Why would it just lay still while being murdered like that? And then she had an idea: *It's old. That's why it's lighter than the other one. It probably knows it's ready to die, I bet.*

Then the Tennatrick climbed off its mate, faced the opposite direction and walked backward until its hindquarters stood over the dying creature.

The Tennatrick looked out and spotted Jen. It opened its jaws, looked behind at its own rear and spread its fins outward. The back of its sectioned body split open slightly.

From the split at the back of the Tennatrick, a dark, obsidian egg slid out. The animal pushed and cried as the egg dropped onto the smoking, torn flesh of its other parent. *This is impossible. It couldn't gestate an egg that quickly. Nothing on Earth can do that.*

A second egg slid out, although it seemed to only take half as long. The Tennatrick finished, stepped forward, and lunged headfirst into the corpse, tearing out a piece of flesh, which she tossed on top of the eggs. She did this several times, each flap hissing and steaming as she ripped it free.

The Tennatrick kept working until the ground seemed covered in black fluid and torn tissue. She chomped and pulled and rubbed the pieces on top of her eggs until the sparks turned into flames. Then the Tennatrick lugged bits and pieces of chaparral plants from the beach perimeter and added them onto the fire.

The pile caught fire while the Tennatrick dropped down onto her hindquarters like a dog waiting for a snack. She watched the pyre rise and fall, all the while monitoring her eggs with the occasional prod.

Is she cooking them? Jen watched, fascinated with the ritual.

The mate's corpse smoldered. Deep within the dry, scorched, grey pile, the heavy seed-like shells cracked. Thick black fluid spilled out and sparked. Baby Tennatricks unfolded. *They look more like spiders when they're small. They needed fires to splinter them.*

Nourished and pollinated by the fire, the newborns found their way from their own fire-split shells. They rose in the flickering firelight.

This can't be happening. How could it get pregnant and give birth in a few minutes? Maybe the eggs were ready and this was just the last step? Maybe it was already pregnant . . . could be that it was just helping to lubricate the eggs and get them out of there? She shook her head. *I can't even believe I'm thinking of all this—it's insane.*

Ash from the burnt corpse blew across the lake toward Jen. She shielded her face with the neck of her wet shirt, but it was not enough to keep all of the particles out. She gulped and did her best to suppress a tickle inside her throat.

More ash sprinkled off the heap and landed on top of the already heavily soiled surface of the lake. In places, clumps of ash that became too heavy dropped down into the lake. She looked down and saw ash covering her pants, shirt, and hands. Jen looked up through the polluted grey air. Most of the ash had blown onto the lake from the ridge over the beach. *Backwinds. The fire's moving downhill and all the air's sucking the ash up to the lake.* She looked over at the Tennatrick.

She couldn't see the babies. They'd vanished. The Tennatrick regarded Jen one last time before sliding back up over the hill.

Jen watched it disappear almost as quickly as she'd seen it first appear on the shore. The backwind from the fire blew harder and faster. The remains of the mate decomposed bit by bit and its ash blew across Santoro Lake.

Jen lowered her head, turned her back to the blowing ash, and thought about climbing back into the lake. When she put her feet into the water, something spongy and hard bounced off them underwater. She pulled her feet up from the water. *It's the babies.* But she was wrong.

It's a fish. Just a fish. She looked at the large lower lip of the fish and the dark color. *Just a good old California trout. But if that fish is dead in here, then there's something really wrong with this water. Those fish are real hearty.* She curled back up onto the granite island. *Better if I just sit here and wait it out. The water's probably really toxic right now from all the ash.*

She shivered for long periods of time until, finally, the first rays of the morning sun peeked over the ridge from the same spot she'd last seen the Tennatrick.

As the dark night sky slowly turned into orange morning light, Jen heard a distant thumping sound. *Air Ops resuming. Only a matter of time until they find me.*

Within the next hour, a small team of firemen crested the perimeter around the lake and she waved to them. Two paddled out to her in a small canoe. They asked her name and if she was all right. She nodded and they helped her sit because she found she had little strength left.

"Any word on Brian Riggs?" Jen wondered if they'd found his body. She hoped that she wouldn't have to explain to them how he'd been ripped in half. If they never found his body, if the Tennatrick had taken it, eaten it, she might not. She knew that any story she'd concoct would come under scrutiny, and if she told them what she'd really seen . . .

"And what the hell took you guys all night to get here? I can't be more than a mile from home base."

"We haven't found Brian," he said. "And the fire was too intense all night. We couldn't break through until just now. It's still raging on the northern and eastern sides."

"Really?" Jen said. She wanted to say more, but none of it seemed real. She zoned out and stared at the dead fish floating throughout the lake. Jen felt empty and sad, and knew that she'd been lucky.

"You were in the elements all night. We should probably get you to ICU and have you checked for smoke inhalation and shock."

"Okay," Jen said. "I think I could just use a little sleep is all." She heard her own voice as though she were a thousand miles away.

Jen looked for the remains of the burned Tennatrick. There was nothing left other than a large indentation and a thick layer of ash. She saw no sign of the eggs or the babies. She pictured the Tennatrick digging itself back underground, leaving her with nothing but its myth until the next fires came. She'd be there, she knew, looking for it, listening for it, forever searching.

As she sat down in the backseat of a cruiser, she spotted Oswald at the perimeter of the road. Their eyes met, and she nodded. She should have listened. He had been right. The Tennatrick was all too real.

THE GUIXI SISTERS

JODI KAPLAN LESTER

一

The first name I ever had was 丽丝, but Mommy calls me Moon. Every year since I was a baby, I wear a special dress for the Chinese New Year. It is already chosen, one of the many pretty dresses Mommy brought home with us from China. By the time we left, she had one for each year until I'm thirteen. Mommy sews my Chinese name into the design of each dress. She uses gold thread. That makes it lucky. Only me and Mommy know it's there. That makes it lucky, too.

Tonight I wear my fifth dress, my favorite so far. It is made of red satin, "pomegranate red" Mommy calls it, with two phoenixes embroidered into the front panels. Every year it is something different. Mommy said she would put my hair in a twist and fasten it with a beautiful lacquered hair stick, the way the older girls do.

This morning, we go to the nail salon. The lady paints a phoenix on each of my big toes. With my new dress and the special stick in my hair, maybe this year I'll shine like the princesses. Maybe I'll get lucky and win the raffle.

Tonight, we go to the big party with the lion dance. It is exciting and scary at the same time. This year I hope I am brave enough to look under the lion's head.

After the lion dance, a lady spins plates on her hands and feet and then on a glass rod that she stands on her nose. I get nervous, especially when her face starts to get shiny. I wait for a crash, but it never comes.

In my room I put books on my head to balance like her, but they always slide off. Mommy says everyone has their own talent and that's why she teaches me so many different things. I don't think I've found my talent yet.

My orphanage sisters and I have our own private celebration for *chunjie*, the Spring Festival. We have a room every year in the same big restaurant. We eat *dim sum* and give each other gifts and dance and play. This year I have many gifts to give. After the party, me and my *meimei*, the two very closest of all my Guixi sisters, will go back to my house for a sleepover. But that party, the good party, is not for two more weeks. Instead, tonight is the big party.

Mommy calls out to me, "Moon, I'm ready for your hair." I run down the hall to Mommy's deep closet where she has a chair facing a mirror. I sit down and wriggle with excitement.

"Mommy, why does Mrs. Foo have to come tomorrow?"

"I told you, Moon. We need someone to help out and we want them to teach you Chinese."

"I already know Chinese."

"Real Chinese," Mommy says, speaking to me in the mirror. I see her in the mirror, too, and she has that look on her face, so I don't say what I was going to say.

"Mrs. Foo is from Jiangxi, the same province as you. And she won't even be living in the house. She'll be in the cottage. She sounds like a nice lady."

I still don't want a nanny.

Mommy traces her finger along the birthmark behind my ear. I feel her warm breath as she whispers my name.

"There you go, baby. How's that?"

I jump off the chair and stand in front of the mirror. Everything matches. My dress and nails and shoes. Even the stick Mommy put in my hair. I do my happy dance to make Mommy laugh and then I hug her.

It's a long trip to the party. I nap and dream. I see the moon and stars and they follow me. A face pushes through. It stares at me and I laugh. I don't recognize myself. I look older.

Some people don't remember when they were a baby. I remember. Some things. Mommy says I was never breast-fed and that's not true. I know it because that's one thing I do remember. Before Mommy and Daddy came to get me. Before they knew I was their daughter.

I want to go to China with my orphanage sisters. We can play there together like we do here. Mommy said it's not like that at the orphanage, the playing part. But she promised someday.

We drive through the fields. A strong breeze ripples through the grass, its fringe sparkling in the moonlight. My eyes fall sleepy and I think about all the things I'll do when I really am older.

Sound reverberates across the room and back. It wobbles through me.

Right now, the light becomes dark. The room is gray and murky. Right now, just before sleep, other babies stare at their fists as they twist them back and forth. Hand shadows flit across the ceiling and walls, giant moths chasing the dimming light.

The fluttering makes me giggle.

I roll over and Lu Xiao-Qing faces me. I roll the other way and Lu Yanyu grabs her toes. She looks at me and smiles. Other babies make noise and I look for them through the metal bars. But as far as I can see, it is just us three. It has been this way since we were newborns. I gesture to one. Then I turn to the other and gesture to her. Back and forth, we pass time until darkness swallows light and we are sleepy.

Footsteps shuffle in the hall. Auntie Foo comes to check on us for the last time before next light.

I wiggle my fingers at Xiao-Qing and then Yanyu and pass along what each of us said. They giggle and gurgle.

Auntie Foo walks down the rows, checking each baby. She stops at our row, then leans back into the shadows. She discovers us talking to each other and watches us, thinking she is hidden. Then she runs away.

I tell Xiao-Qing and Yanyu to be asleep before she returns.

Now, she is with Mama Lu whose angry whispers could be heard over her shuffling feet.

With my eyes closed, I listen.

Auntie Foo insists, "No, Lu Ma. Listen. The three babies in the corner. They talk to each other. With their hands. But it is more. They have understanding."

At the crib, Mama Lu stands over us. She smells like tea. She watches our still, sleepy forms. I hear her walk away angrily.

"How much will you remember, little ones? How much?" Auntie Foo whispers, standing over us.

The other babies fall asleep. Tiny hands drop back to their bodies. The shadows paw at Auntie Foo and chase her out of the room.

Smiling, I roll over and fall asleep.

Noise awakens us. It is dark. All our orphanage sisters, all the sounds I could not see, are being removed from their cribs by Mama Lu, Auntie Foo, and Auntie Zhang. They move swiftly until all I hear is their feet. Light barely shows itself. Running steps sweep across concrete, then slow. Auntie Foo's face appears above me. Her black eyes are sad. She reaches slowly for me. She hears Mama Lu's quick footsteps and pauses.

"These girls do not go," Mama Lu says.

"But, Lu Ma, why not? They are all ready."

"They will be better older. Three more months. They go at one year."

"Were they not already assigned? What about the families?"

"Never mind. Everyone will get their babies. No more worry." She swipes a thumb across Auntie Foo's wrinkled forehead.

"I'll go back to the buses then." She dips her head in a bow, then glances down at me and smiles. I hear her brush past Mama Lu who stands by our cribs for a few moments longer.

When Auntie Foo comes back, it is almost dark again. She wipes down the cribs and the bars. She scrubs the plywood boards vigorously. She works long into the dark. She looks in on each of us before she leaves.

I am almost asleep. The room is quiet. I hear Xiao-Qing and Yanyu breathing.

I smell hot tea leaves. Mama Lu stands above me. A smile of satisfaction crosses her lips. Her teeth are small and yellow-gray. There are no shadows beating on the walls.

Mama Lu hums softly, almost in a whisper. She sings a song. She picks me up from the crib and rocks me.

> *. . . hmm hm-hmm hmm . . .*
> *No longer a queen, a peasant now,*
> *the ferry takes her away,*
> *across the river, along its edge,*
> *a thousand flames await,*
> *flickering light on this dark eve,*
> *her evil cannot flee.*
> *Hmm hm-hmm hmm . . .*

She sings and runs a finger along my neck and behind my ear. She gasps. My head tingles. I close my eyes. The music fills me and I fall asleep in Mama Lu's arms.

At first light, Auntie Foo's heavy sounds wake me. I see other cribs, empty ones that had been moved out of place. Auntie Foo drags herself from crib to crib. She flips the wood boards she scrubbed so hard the night before.

"Foo A yi! Here, drink this. Lu Ma made it."

I inch closer to the bars. It is Auntie Zhang.

Auntie Foo takes the cup. Her hands tremble and spill some on the floor.

"You are clammy and pale. Wait here," Auntie Zhang says and runs out of the room. She returns with a wet towel, brushing it gently across Auntie Foo's brow.

"You do not look so good," Auntie Zhang says.

"Headache. I had such horrible dreams," she weeps.

"You will be okay, *jiejie*. You go to bed. I will stay with you." Auntie Zhang takes the tea and leads Auntie Foo out of the room.

Mama Lu moves us into new cribs in a smaller room. We have been here all day. No Auntie Foo until it is almost dark. There is commotion in the corridor.

Mama Lu holds Xiao-Qing and rushes out as Auntie Foo rushes in. She sees the baby, then looks down at me and Yanyu. Her panic dies down, but she is confused.

Mama Lu puts Xiao-Qing down and holds her hands out to Auntie Foo.

"Shhh. It is quieter here." Mama Lu gestures to the cribs around them. "They are good babies. I moved them here."

This room is better. I see and hear more. In the back of the nursery is a cot with a pane of glass above it. On the other side of the window is an office. There are three empty cribs in addition to our three.

"You feel better now? No more headache?" Mama Lu sits Auntie Foo at the desk in the office. She pours her a cup of tea. She returns to the cribs and checks on us.

The only light comes from a lamp burning on the desk in the office. It makes Auntie Foo's face golden. She inhales steam from her tea.

Mama Lu falls back into the darkness of the nursery.

Auntie Foo sighs. She stretches her back. She sips her tea and listens as Mama Lu continues the lullaby.

The song is sad. She sings with her head lowered. She is shrouded by dark. Her fingertips rest along her brow. It looks like she is praying.

> *. . . hmm hm-hmm hmm . . .*
> *Taken from the ferry boat,*
> *raised for all to see,*
> *stripped of her title and her name,*
> *the queen nevermore would be,*
> *a hollow soul of unrepented deeds,*
> *she will walk the earth a ghost,*
> *her name shall never again be spoke,*
> *or her evil will rise once more.*
> *Hmm hm-hmm hmm . . .*

When the song is over, Auntie Foo calls out in a loud whisper, "Lu Ma? What is this?" She holds up a flat square and a small pouch.

Mama Lu takes me from my crib into the office. "It is a turtle shell, the breastplate."

"And these words etched into it?"

Mamma Lu shrugs.

"But the language is strange."

"No, just old."

"It looks like oracle bone."

"Yes, I thought so, too," Mama Lu points to some black markings and a crack in the shell.

I grab at it. Mama Lu teases me, yanking it out from under my clumsy hands.

"The writing is so small," Auntie Foo says, "and that mark looks like a crescent moon."

Mama Lu nods.

"Where did it come from?"

Mama Lu shifts me in her arms. She hands me to Auntie Foo and pulls my ear away from my head, then draws a finger behind it. Auntie Foo looks closer.

"It came with one of these three. I did not know until I saw the birthmark last night. The sack was strapped around her when these three were brought in. Zhang A yi found it and, in rushing to show it to me, forgot which baby it belonged to."

Auntie Foo says nothing more. She studies Mama Lu's face further.

"I do not know what I will do with it," Mama Lu says. "I will finish up here and take the cot tonight. You finish your tea and get some rest."

"Thank you, Lu Ma." Auntie Foo looks over the shell some more and then slips it into the small silk pouch. She finishes her tea and, with a quick bow, excuses herself to Mama Lu and leaves.

At next light, Auntie Foo comes with our bottles. Instead of setting them in the cribs for us, she takes us out one at time. She cradles and talks softly to each of us while she feeds us.

Mama Lu brings Auntie Foo some tea. She closely studies Auntie Foo's face and eyes. "Bad sleep," Mama Lu says. She shakes her head disapprovingly. She pats Auntie Foo's cheek just hard enough, a slap.

While Xiao-Qing is being fed, Mama Lu stops to play with Yanyu. She pokes and pinches. She laughs an old lady laugh.

Auntie Foo and Mama Lu are in and out of the nursery, very busy with us today.

When darkness comes, Auntie Foo stays with us. She sleeps on the cot. Her moaning wakes me up. I roll over onto my stomach and watch her through the bars.

She sits up fast. She looks around her, then drops back down to her pillow. She tosses and turns, bucks back and forth. She groans and gets twisted in her sheet. She sits up again and gets out of bed. She walks around the room shivering. Her face is shiny and when she looks in on Yanyu I see her face is pale and gray. It is scary. I close my eyes before she reaches my crib.

I hear whimpering and open my eyes again. Auntie Foo sits on her cot with her head in her hands. She moves her hands away. Two large wet circles slowly spread across her nightshirt. She stands before the mirror and, with shaky hands, raises her shirt. Her breasts are slick with moisture. She grabs them firmly. Liquid drips from them down her belly. She moans. She muffles her cries with a fist.

"What is wrong, girl?" Mama Lu demands as she rushes into the room, shushing Auntie Foo with her hands.

"I am leaking," Auntie Foo cries and points to the front of her shirt, the dark circles of moisture now bubbling white through the material.

Mama Lu unbuttons her shirt. She examines Auntie Foo's breasts closely. She cradles them in her hands, weighs them.

"They are bigger now," Auntie Foo says, her voice wavering.

Mama Lu inspects the nipples. She flicks them, then roughly pinches and twists them between her fingers. Mama Lu leans out of the way, avoiding a stream of liquid. She dabs at Auntie Foo's nipple with her pinky and then touches it to her tongue. She nods and drops the shirt.

"Milk. It is good," Mama Lu told Auntie Foo.

"But how? I am not pregnant."

"No, you are not. Go to sleep. Tomorrow, no bottles. Breast milk is better. Even for you."

Auntie Foo's face falls.

"Go back to bed. No more worry." Mama Lu points to her own eyes again, then to the circles beneath Auntie Foo's.

The big party ends and we drive home. It is very late. I didn't win the raffle, but I danced a lot and I chased the lion. I peeked underneath the mask. There was blackness and then a pair of red eyes flashed at me. I dropped the mask and as it fell into place, the lion came alive again. I ran back to the table.

Mommy saw. She said it was good that I looked. I "faced my demons."

During the firecracker stomp, I closed my eyes so I wouldn't see the bubble wrap when all the children run and jump to pop the bubbles. I put my fingers in my ears because it was so loud. In my mind, colorful fireworks lit up the room.

I am very tired. We wake up early to get ready for Mrs. Foo's visit. She travels a long distance to meet us and will stay the night in the guesthouse, which is where she will live if she takes the nanny position. I help Mommy dust and clean and put fresh linens on the bed. We open the windows to air out the rooms. Sunlight floods the house.

I pick up my toys, clean my room. Mommy and Daddy are pleased that she is from Jiangxi and want to make a good impression on her.

I still don't want a nanny.

The tractor starts up. I look out the window. Far down the dirt road, where our property ends and Mr. Beyer's begins, there is a tiny, black stick figure. Daddy turns onto the road and inches his way toward Mrs. Foo, the tractor churning up dust clouds behind him.

When he reaches her, he stops and gets out. Daddy takes her bag and loads it on the tractor. They talk for a while, gesturing a lot. I can tell he is trying to explain where to sit.

I laugh because there is only Daddy's seat and no more. He must have forgotten about that. I always sit on the console when I ride with him but I'm small. From here she looks like she would fit just fine. Daddy takes her other bag and helps her in, then gets in himself. When they start up the road, I duck out of sight.

I play with one of my turtles, turning it over in my hands, pressing the secret button that makes its shell pop up. This one is empty. It seems like a long time has passed since they got back, then finally:

"Moooon! Could you come down here a minute."

I put my turtle back on the shelf, taking my time, making Daddy call again. Then I walk downstairs and slink out, hiding behind the corner of the wall. I lean out and they are both watching me, waiting. I think this is what Daddy means by "trying his patience."

Dragging my feet, I join them in the family room. Daddy introduces Mrs. Foo to me, "Or, what did you say? 'A yi'?"

"Yes. A yi. Foo A yi." She nods.

"Ni hao, Foo A yi," I sing.

"Ni hao," she says, pleased with my Chinese. Daddy sends us to my room to get acquainted. Mommy and Daddy want Mrs. Foo to like us. They say it is very important.

I lead Mrs. Foo into my room and she follows. She is old. Older than Mommy and Daddy that's for sure. She notices my turtle collection on top of the bookcase. She gently runs her fingers along the backs of all my favorites. A pair of tiny pill cases, one gold, the other silver, others studded with turquoise, red stones, coral, some with jewels and some made out of seashells. And still more with little triggers that pop the lid open, like the one I was playing with just a few minutes ago.

"You like turtle?" she asks. She waits for me to answer, but I don't.

I just stand there.

"*Gui*. Chinese for turtle. *Gui*. Now you say." She pokes me in the shoulder. "Eh?"

"*Gui*."

The lady asks me where I got them.

I shrug my shoulders, pretending not to understand. *My first one was from China, a bracelet with a turtle carved from jade.* Instead I say "*gui.*" I go back out to the front room. She follows me. I pretend not to notice that she is right behind me, quiet on her feet. But I smell her.

I walk into the family room with my hands clasped behind my back. Daddy watches the game with the sound turned down.

Mommy takes Mrs. Foo to the guest cottage so she can freshen up and rest from her long trip. She will stay the night and catch the next bus home tomorrow.

"How'd it go, kiddo?" Daddy asks me.

"She smells like *congee*," I say and stick my tongue out, "Blech."

"But you love rice porridge," he teases, tickling me, and I can tell he is trying not to laugh. I hate when he does this, not taking me seriously, and I feel like I am going to throw up from the smell.

"Why don't we keep that between you and Mom and me? Deal?"

I run off to my room.

I put my hands on my hips. I look at my turtles and scream, "*Gui!*"

Mrs. Foo does not leave in the morning as planned. At breakfast, Mommy and Daddy explain that they are hiring her on a trial basis since Daddy will be home for most of the next month.

Two weeks and Mrs. Foo is still with us. It is now time for the good party, the Spring Festival celebration with my orphanage sisters.

I bring wooden figurines. "Little barbarians" is what Mommy calls them. Gifts for Katie and Jessica, my two special *meimei*. Our parents say that at the orphanage our three cribs were right next to each other with mine in the middle.

We are in front of the restaurant where there is a giant oak tree. It is hot. The sun is very bright. Mommy forgot to bring sunscreen and sent us to stand beneath the tree while we wait for our dining room to be ready.

Standing in the shade, I am excited and give my *meimei* their gifts now.

"One for each of us," I say and let them pick their own. Katie takes the soldier with the sword and Jessica the one with the bow and arrow. Mine is the soldier with the axe. They are small enough that they fit perfectly in our hands.

We sit at the base of the tree, its roots big and thick so we can perch on them without getting our dresses too dirty. I look into the canopy of the great oak. The foliage is so dense that barely any light comes through and it casts a giant cloud of shadow over us.

Mrs. Foo comes toward us now, so we switch to the quiet language.

Mrs. Foo smiles at us and slowly makes her way down to our level, weaving like a stiff cobra, until she is on her knees. She asks the other girls their names. When they tell her, she shakes her head.

"Chinese name."

Katie, "Xiao-Qing."

Jessica, "Yanyu."

She tells them to call her "Foo A yi," just like she had told me to do. She takes our dolls and turns them over in her hands. They are stamped on the bottom, each with a different Chinese character.

"Ah, sound only," she explains, pointing to the characters. She looks up as if searching the branches for the right word, then says carefully, "In-can-tation."

She pauses and looks the three of us over as if admiring us. Her face seems full of pride and I see that her eyes are wet.

She clears her throat. "No word meaning, only sound. One day I teach you. But for now, I tell you, never speak what you learn. Bad luck," she says. "On full moon, you say sound. One time. More time. Very good luck." She brings the three dolls together in front of her and clutches them to her chest with both hands. "When all doll together, you three say sound, bring good luck. Yes?"

We all nod.

"Full moon, yes?"

We nod again.

"Tonight I teach you sound." She smiles then inches back down the base of the oak tree, like a scrawny frog.

"I have a story to tell. Would you like?" she looks to each of us.

We nod.

First she gives us back our ancient soldiers, closes our fingers around them, and then grips our hands tight before releasing them.

"Many years ago, almost three thousand years, Shang dynasty, Emperor Wu Yi was most important man of the East. He was angry man and did not believe in gods. This made gods very mad, especially when he angered them on purpose.

"People feared him. Word spread fast and the street emptied when he came to town. He always carry leather bag. Inside bag, he kept many heart inside. Heart from his people. When bag is full, he tie it to the long branch on big tree." Mrs. Foo looks up and points at the branches overhead, their shadows making her teeth look gray.

"Heart so fresh, you see them beating beneath the leather. When he come, everyone pray his bag is full."

"Why?" Jessica asked.

"If bag is full, he need no more. He take bow and arrow, aiming for the beating heart. He shoot over and over until heart stop beating and bag start bleeding. Peasant blood."

In the darkness of the shade, me and Katie and Jessica huddle together. We stare at her while she pauses to take a deep breath. Our mouths hang open and we hold onto each other tightly. Even with Mrs. Foo's broken words, or maybe because of them, I am too scared to move. We wait for her to go on, hanging onto her last word.

Katie's mom calls us into the restaurant. Our party room is ready.

Mrs. Foo sees our disappointment and smiles.

"Part two another time," she promises and holds her hand out to me. For the first time ever I take it.

After dinner, my two *meimei* come home with me. We make a cozy nest for ourselves on the porch so we can sleep in the moonlight under the stars. Foo A yi brings tea out to us, snuggled up in our sleeping bags. We are all quietly giddy, waiting for the rest of her story. The night is beautiful and the stars are just beginning to pop into view.

Foo A yi brings a candle. A tree trunk of wax, gnarled and twisted into three thick branches, each reaching out in a different direction with blackened wicks and drips of wax. It looks old and arthritic and reminds me of the oak tree from the restaurant earlier today, where we celebrate the Spring Festival.

Foo A yi takes a wooden match and strikes it. She holds the match out to Jessica who takes it and lights a candle, then blows out the match. Her eyelids flutter at a wisp of smoke that finds her eyes.

Katie lights the next match and then it is my turn.

Foo A yi puts the candle tree up on a shelf in the corner, then shuffles back to the kitchen.

Mommy and Daddy come in to say goodnight.

"Wow, fancy," Mommy says, noticing the candle.

"One branch for each of us," I point out.

"Make sure Foo A yi puts that out before you go to sleep," Daddy says.

"Okay, Daddy. Goodnight. Goodnight Mommy. I love you."

They kiss me and my *meimei* and turn to go up to bed just as Foo A yi returns.

"Not too late," Mommy whispers to her as they pass in the hall.

Still nodding, Foo A yi comes back holding our three dolls. She wears black pajamas and her feet are bare. She sits on her cot and picks at a toenail.

The three of us look at her expectantly.

"Part two?" she says as if she just noticed us.

"Yeah. Part two," we say. I feel like we are about to see the dancing lion again. I am excited, but very scared.

"Remember what happen before?" Foo A yi asks.

We all nod.

"Hearts," Katie says.

"Ah, yes. Heart," Foo A yi nods. "Emperor Wu Yi was very bad man. Bad king." She speaks quietly, barely above a whisper.

"Foo A yi, why was he so bad?" Jessica asks.

"Because, Yanyu, he have no gods. No belief in them. He make gods mad and tease them. Yes, but one day, the people get mad. They pray to gods. They make army and ride to palace to capture emperor."

Foo A yi stops. She looks at us and smiles. In the flickering light, her whole face changes. I am afraid. I can no longer tell if it is really Foo A yi sitting before us. That smile could mean anything.

Foo A yi takes a deep breath and continues the story.

"Now army come and search the palace. They take Wu Yi. Now they look for his wife. They check everyone. She will be dressed as a peasant woman, but there is only one real way to tell if it is her." She pauses again. "She has a birthmark behind her ear. It look like crescent moon." Slowly, looking directly at me, she says, "They never find her. Now her spirit walk in *du yi*, earth prison. She wait in hell for new body. Young body."

My skin prickles.

She leans in close to us.

"Boo!" Foo A yi shouts, grabbing our knees and making sure we all jump out of our bags. The four of us scream and laugh so hard, Jessica almost knocks over my tea.

Foo A yi hands our dolls to us, remembering who had which doll.

"Practice, yes?" She leans over to look up at the sky and points to the moon.

"It is not full yet, Foo A yi," Katie says.

"Only learn, not do. Practice now. Okay?"

We all nod and then Foo A yi teaches us each our sound and makes us practice until it is right. Jessica gets hers fast. For me and Katie it is harder, but finally Foo A yi says it is good. Then she holds her finger up to her lips to quiet us.

"We try, okay?" she asks in a whisper. We all nod. Then, using her finger, she conducts us to do our sounds together. She turns her ear as if it will help her hear the tiniest mistake.

I hear the way the sounds are supposed to come together, but it is hard to get it right. I get frustrated. Jessica pats me on the back, but I shrug it off. I get restless and lose patience. I start to get up, but Foo A yi makes me stay seated, coaxing the right sound out of me. Katie is almost there, but for me, it seems like I will never get it.

I start to feel dizzy. I look at my two *meimei* and, like mine, their foreheads are sweating. I shiver and some kind of energy starts to build inside of me. I feel like I will explode!

"Foo A yiiiii!" I scream at the top of my lungs, tears of impatience crawl down my cheeks.

It is over, though. Foo A yi puts my head in her lap and strokes my hair until I am calm again. She sits me up and asks us to try again.

Finally, we harmonize. It is one of the most beautiful sounds I have ever heard. Foo A yi was right, we each must do our part perfectly.

"Good. Again," and she quiets us with her hands, then conducts.

"Better. Again."

The third time she is pleased.

Through the porch's screen I watch Daddy's field. It is dark down there. A moving shadow catches my eye. A fox runs up the dirt road that lines the field. He sits for a moment and grooms himself, then glances back in our direction before he turns and darts into the barley, squiggling to get through, his bushy red tail waving like a flag. The fox disappears, pulling his tail in after him

"Did anyone see that? A fox!" I say, excitedly.

Foo A yi nods and winks at me. She saw him, too.

The wind blows through the screen and ruffles our hair. I can barely see Daddy's field in the dim moonlight, just enough to see the barley blowing all over the place, swirling first in one direction, then the other. It whips around in circles, making little cyclones of dust that drift to the sky.

"Good girls. Now sleep."

After putting the tea away, Foo A yi stands in the doorway, watching us. She has a look on her face, like it is a very happy moment for her. She brings down the tree and lets each of us blow our branch out. Then, she tucks us in.

"What happened to Wu Yi and his wife? Did they ever find her?"

"Another story, another time. Yes?"

We nod and then switch to our quiet language. It will be a while before any of us falls asleep.

It is the morning after my seventh New Year's party. The big party for the year of the tiger. Foo A yi comes from down the hall, leaning forward, holding something out to me that rests flat on the palm of her hand. She creeps toward me. Her black eyes widen and then settle as she watches me.

"I have seen this before," I tell her, taking it from Foo A yi's hand.

"This is a very old piece."

"What is it?"

"Oracle bone. *Gui*." Turtle. She gestures up and down her midsection. "Front shell. Look," she points at the characters that had been etched into the shell.

"What does it say," I urge her to tell me.

"Some day you will know. Then it will be yours."

She slips it into a little silk pouch, a flat square of dark blue satin. The front is embroidered with a monkey, the year I was born, and the silk rope strap is braided, ending in tassels. It is very small which makes it look fancy. At night, Foo A yi takes it with her back to her cottage.

It must be very important. I must learn it right.

I am anxious to put our sounds together. I want to wake the spirits. Foo A yi says it must be with my *meimei*. It takes all three of us and it must be when the moon is full.

"Next *chunjie* party, maybe. Year of the rabbit," she says.

I practice alone when the moon is not full to keep the spirits warm and ready.

"When they come, you feel earth tremble," Foo A yi says.

"What spirits will come?" I ask, not so sure of myself now.

"You see."

The clouds in the sky thicken. Grass in the fields sway and glisten when the waxing moon shines through. I hold the shell tight in both hands. Afraid I will break it, Foo A yi gently grabs my wrist and bounces it a little to loosen my grip. She taps the shell with her pointy forefinger.

"This, *gui*, mean nothing. Words. Together out loud, very powerful."

I ease my grip and read the first panel, careful with each word.

Foo A yi nods at me to go on.

I read the second panel still more carefully, then the third, the one most recently learned. I am extra careful with that one. I squeeze my eyes tight and whisper the words in Chinese, repeating them several times. The moon slides behind the clouds again. The porch and the stand of trees outside darken until it is so black it seems I am not even here.

On the road below, my soldier has come, kneeling on one knee, as if he has been there a while. He looks like my little barbarian, deep red uniform with black piping and an axe strapped across his back. He adjusts his boots and armor. I glance over at Foo A yi.

She nods. She sees him, too.

When I look back, the man barely escapes my eye before disappearing into Dad's barley.

He couldn't have been any bigger than me.

The Spring Festival is near. It is the year of the rabbit and plans are being made. Foo A yi went over the calendar with Mom. They picked a day with a full moon.

"It is brighter for the girls. They see more."

I am very excited. The coming party might be the night.

Foo A yi teaches me more.

"Why is it called oracle bone if this is a shell?"

"Because they were made of bone. Shoulder bone, hip bone. Only sometimes *gui* shell. Sometimes other things. King's scribe or shaman write his words. It is how king communicate with gods. Your *gui* shell was made for Wu Yi. These are questions he ask the gods."

"What does it mean?" I ask.

"I cannot tell you now. Only when it is time." Foo A yi draws her finger across the last two empty panels. "But, you see, story never finish."

I lie back on my sleeping bag trying to get a glimpse of the stars through the clouds. She sings me a song and rubs my feet.

. . . hmm hm-hmm hmm . . .
She walks the earth, a prisoner now,

a ghost ignored by all,
hungry to be living,
cursed to wander without a name.
Hmm hm-hmm hmm . . .

She brings out a black grease pencil and writes on my soles. I have a hard time staying still because I am so ticklish. She has taught me the breathing to calm me down, but it's never strong enough. Not for my feet. Somehow she always manages to get the characters written, no matter how much I squirm. When she is done, I turn my feet over and look at what she has written, tracing the rows and columns of characters with my finger.

It is our tenth *chunjie* party, year of the snake. Like every year before, my *meimei* and I gather to celebrate. Everything is the same, the restaurant, the big oak tree, except we are big girls now. We have met every year and Foo A yi has continued to teach us each year.

We have still not gotten it right, though. One year because Jessica was sick and could not sing. Another because Katie was so sick, she couldn't even go to the party. Foo A yi has convinced Mom that it is the best of luck to celebrate on the full moon, but I think Foo A yi is getting impatient with us. She promises something magical will happen if we get our notes right.

Foo A yi seems anxious this morning as she prepares for our celebration and slumber party. She walks from room to room, talking to herself. She feels it, too. The night we've all been waiting for, and she will finish the story when it's all over.

I am excited, too. Foo A yi is nervous like me.

After our party at the restaurant, my *meimei* come back to the house with me. Tonight, Mom and Dad go out to a movie for a night alone. Probably at Foo A yi's suggestion.

On the porch, there is a quiet buzz of excitement between Katie, Jessica, and me. We don't know what is going to happen. But we feel it out there.

Foo A yi brings the tea while me and my sisters get in our pajamas. She comes in with a tray just as we slide into our sleeping bags. She hands each of us a cup, "Two hand. Yes, both hand," then pours one for herself.

She brings down the tree candle. The wicks are lower and the drips of wax longer. The branches are clenched now, like an open claw.

We strike the matches on our own and light the candle ourselves. Foo A yi asks Katie and Jessica if they remember their tones and whether they have practiced. She already knows I have.

We practice until Foo A yi tells us we're ready. Ready to unlock the past. She hands me the oracle bone.

Jessica goes first and holds onto the note as long as she can. I feel sweat on my upper lip, but I begin my tone, wavering it in just enough to weave through Jessica's. Then, Katie comes right in, nailing her note without having to adjust her key at all and lets it drift, coiling around mine and Jessica's. The harmony is more beautiful than anything I have ever heard. Smokelike beings drift through it out into the night beyond.

The barley below thrashes about and the not quite solid smoke disguises itself into clouds, casting a heavy darkness across the fields.

Shapes form within the rows of the grass. They are small, like my soldier that one night not so long ago, no bigger than me. That's why I don't see them right away. But something shifts. Their buttons reflect the moonlight, giving away their presence. They stand in columns, carrying axes and swords, bows and arrows. They recede deeper into the fields, prepared to fight.

I pull my legs in tight.

A fox sits at the side of the road and grooms himself, waiting. Then, he looks up and, as if on cue, takes off down the road, as though drawing a firing line in the dirt.

I look over at Katie and Jessica. Their mouths hang open like mine, and our faces glow. We grip each other, even tighter now.

When the wind first reaches us, it is gentle. Then it builds up and blows the hair back off our faces.

A loud crack of a whip tears through the air.

The wind goes wild and sucks me toward the screen door. Foo A yi and Katie and Jessica grab on to me, trying to keep me there, but it pulls me right through, carrying me down the hill.

I hear my *meimei* scream and cry, as I am forcefully sucked through the air, spinning and landing into Dad's field.

I cry, too. I am confused and afraid. A bolt of lightning flashes across the sky and lights up the barley field bright white. I see the soldiers taking their places, preparing to fight.

Far across the field I see orange lights flickering. It must be Mr. Beyer's field. I stand up to see, and as I thought before, the soldiers are no bigger than I am and I can see over their heads. It is Mr. Beyer's scarecrow on fire. It shifts and settles, burning orange and smoky. It is alive as the wind blows its arms around.

As I cry, I hear Jessica start again, building her tone and cueing me. I am so frightened, but somehow I manage to reach my key immediately this time, then Katie comes in with hers, nice and steady. The harmony, again, is perfect.

We hold our notes and give them full power. I am shaking so hard, I think I will lose my key. The thickened clouds swirl in an angry mass over Dad's field and the soldiers stand at the ready beneath it.

As I tremble, the soldiers charge en masse toward Mr. Beyer's field where another army of soldiers awaits them.

My hands still hold the oracle bone and I read the questions just as Foo A yi had taught me.

The fire circles the post, then moves out away from the scarecrow, igniting the crops, burning as much of them as it can.

Someone screams my name, the very first name I ever had: 丽丝 .

My head spins. I am dizzy and fall to the ground. I hear men shouting, soldiers fighting, weapons upon weapons. My hearing fades and so does my vision until I completely black out.

In the morning, Foo A yi is ready with breakfast, special always when my *meimei* are here. We get up and go into the kitchen practically sleepwalking. I am so happy to see Foo A yi.

I am not sure if what happened to me was real. Then I look at myself covered in dirt and feel the grains in my mouth and I know.

Xiao-Qing and Yanyu fawn over me, looking at scrapes and scratches on my arms and legs. I run to the sink to rinse my mouth out, then go to the window to look at Mr. Beyer's field. Most of it is gone. The scarecrow is gone.

After my sisters leave, Foo A yi comes into my room where I stand looking at my turtles. I turn to her and hold out the shell.

She shakes her head, "It is yours."

"Look." I point to the shell. "There are etchings now across the third panels."

"Yes, there are." Foo A yi is excited.

"Can you read them?"

"Yes, but . . ."

"What is it?" I ask.

"The answer."

"What answer, Foo A yi?"

"My darling." She holds my chin in her hand. She looks withered, but her grip is strong. She smiles at me with affection, her teeth sharp.

I wait. Foo A yi is trying my patience now.

"The story is over. Wu Yi's wife. Her spirit no longer walk the earth prison. You finish it."

I let this settle in.

"Did you know this before you came to me?" I ask.

"I did not know the answer."

I try to hand it back to her.

"No. It is *gui*." She gestures across my turtles, pushing the shell back to me. "It is yours."

"I know you," I say.

"Who am I?" She looks fearful.

"From the orphanage. The one who fed me at her breast. But I wasn't your baby."

"But you were a good baby, smart. All three of you were. I held you up that day, and looked right at you. I would always know those eyes."

"Black eyes, like yours."

"Mmm. Do your mommy and daddy know I fed you?"

I shake my head no.

She pulls me to her and with her long tapered fingers presses my head against her chest. A big grin spreads across my face as she strokes my cheek, then twirls a strand of my hair in her finger.

My head tingles.

> *. . . hmm hm-hmm hmm . . .*
> *An open vessel, a count of three,*
> *someone to call her name,*
> *a young body for her soul to fill*

so she can rise again.
Hmm hm-hmm hmm . . .

SILVER NEEDLE

RICHARD GROVE

O pleasant is the fairy land
How happy there to dwell
But ay at every seven years end
We're a'dung down to hell

The morn is good Halloween
And our court a' will ride . . .

—1769 version of "The Ballad of Tam Lin"
from *The Ancient and Modern Scots Songs*

In the slowly darkening Halloween evening, Terry stopped for a minute directly underneath an old-fashioned yard lamp. He'd passed houses with carved pumpkins and homemade wreaths of witches and skeletons on their doors; some of the houses had colored lights shaped like skulls in their windows. But, all of the houses had free candy, and Terry's leather satchel bulged with it.

Looking about, he realized he had come to a dead-end street and would have to walk back up the block if he was going to continue trick or treating. Just over the tree line he saw Venus, the evening star. He loved how shiny and bright the star was. He could feel its silvery light on his face, and it made him feel powerful. He was thirteen and out on his own for the first time on Halloween night.

A cold autumn wind came up and whipped the branches of the trees lining both sides of the street. Terry's hand-made costume was mostly wool with a tartan kilt, a white blouse, and a black cape, but even so he shivered as the chill wind found gaps in his clothing. He had a slight build, with a high forehead and light brown hair that came down just over his eyebrows. Terry was usually a quiet, thoughtful boy, but tonight he was Tam Lin, the legendary Scotsman who had tricked the fairies when they'd tried to drag him into hell.

Hearing something behind him and thinking it might be another trick-or-treater, he turned toward the street, but all he saw were the leaves scudding across the pavement. Unconsciously, he reached into his leather bag and pulled out another one of the mini Snickers bars he loved so much. Pulling off the wrapper with a practiced hand he placed the entire bar into his mouth and chewed with satisfaction, savoring the taste.

There's that sound again. Is that a cat?

Peering into the darkness on the other side of the street, he could just barely hear a light mewling. He started across the street and got halfway there when, out of the darkness in front of him, a small black cat slowly padded to the edge of the light and sat on its haunches, staring at him. Terry saw it had only one eye, and the socket where the other eye had been was empty and had been stitched closed. Terry had never seen a one-eyed cat before.

He held out his hand and said, "Hi. Where did you come from?"

The cat ignored him and remained perfectly still, its eye slightly luminous in the yellow light of the streetlamp. The stitching on the empty socket looked crude. Its one good eye was a light green, and its coat was completely black with no other markings or colors.

Terry liked cats, but he knew that some of them could be difficult. After a few moments of holding out his hand, Terry thought that this might be a feral cat and could be aggressive. He decided to move on. The problem was that the cat was blocking his way. Grabbing another candy from his bag, he chewed and thought back to Grandma Toller's warning earlier that day.

"Be vigilant," she had said. "This is your first night alone on Halloween. Enjoy yourself, but be wary of things that seem out of place."

At the time he'd thought what she said was strange, but now her words echoed in his mind. This cat *did* seem out of place.

Trusting his intuition, Terry turned and walked quickly to the sidewalk at his right.

There were several homes in a row with glowing pumpkins on their porches. Moving too quickly, Terry nearly tripped on the curb, but willed himself not to look back. After a moment, the one-eyed cat suddenly bounded in front of Terry, startling him, and ran off into the darkness between the houses. Terry stood looking off after it.

I wonder what that was about?

He was now in front of a large house that had an especially nice jack-o'-lantern on the porch. Terry figured they'd probably have good candy there and started walking toward it, rubbing his arms a bit against the wind that had come up again. He heard the leaves crunch under his feet as he stepped on them and shivered in his costume. He was glad that Grandma Toller had knitted him an undergarment for his kilt.

As he walked along the cracked sidewalk, Terry hugged himself and rubbed his arms, trying to generate some warmth.

"Ow," he cried as he felt a sharp sting on one of the fingers of his left hand and quickly jerked it back from his shirt. Looking closely at his hand, he could just make out a spot of blood on his middle finger. Carefully examining his costume, he discovered a silver needle in the cuff of his puffy shirt.

A needle? What's it doing in my shirt? Did Grandma leave it there? He sucked on his wounded finger. *It isn't like Grandma Toller to forget something. I wonder if it means anything?*

As Terry stood on the sidewalk thinking, a set of very large, shaggy arms wrapped themselves around his body from behind and squeezed. Another figure stepped in front of him and put a masked face right into Terry's own and yelled, "Gotcha!"

Terry could hardly breathe. All at once the arms around him loosened and both figures started laughing and pointing at him. The laughter had a familiar ring to it. Terry recognized the two school bullies, Rocky and Louis, and his heart sank.

"*Stop it,*" Terry said as he violently shrugged off Louis's arms. Louis, in a *Star Wars* Wookiee costume, just laughed at him; and Rocky, who wore a *Scream* mask and a shapeless black coat, joined in. They both slapped their knees as they guffawed.

Saying nothing, Terry quickly walked past Rocky and down the sidewalk to the corner. But the two bullies were not going to be denied their fun and ran past Terry, standing in front of him and blocking his way. Terry stopped and glared at them, his hand clutching the strap of his bag, his heart racing.

Rocky, the larger of the two, said, "You think you're so smart, Mr. Brainiac, wearing some weird costume. All by your lonesome, huh? Well, listen up jerk-wad: We own this block and if you want to get any more candy we get a cut. Right, Louis?"

"Damn right," Louis said. "And if you don't like it we'll take your ass over to the old Cathcart house and dump you. That place is haunted as hell!"

Rocky grabbed the front of Terry's shirt and yelled, "You better pay attention, Braniac, or I'm gonna kick your ass." He shoved Terry back, letting go of his shirt at the same time.

Terry stumbled backward and fell on his rear. His hands reached out to his sides and caught his fall, but he skinned his palms. It hurt a lot, but Terry didn't make a sound. He wasn't going to let these creeps see him cry.

"You know, that's a good idea, Louis. Yeah, let's take him over to the Cathcart house. Perfect!"

Rocky and Louis grabbed Terry and, holding onto either arm, they started marching him across the street and down the block. As they turned the corner, Terry thought of trying to escape, but Rocky and Louis were much bigger than him. Their grip on his arms was so tight it hurt. He thought maybe he could talk them out of it when they got to the Cathcart house.

The trio traveled several blocks, turning this way and that, and they were all breathing hard when they came to a darkened corner with a broken streetlamp. Terry looked around him, but didn't recognize the street they were on.

The house to the left had a tall chain-link fence all the way around it. There were no lights on inside and all the windows were boarded up. A large dead weeping willow tree stood in the front yard and weeds were choking the lawn. The house looked abandoned to Terry.

He had heard the stories about the house: The twin Cathcart sisters had gone crazy and killed all of their cats before they took poison and died together in the kitchen.

He knew that they were going to force him to go inside this house.

The two bullies let go of Terry's arms and Rocky kicked open the front gate, saying, "You want to trick-or-treat, here's a house for you. Get your ass in there. And if you say anything we'll kick your ass every day for a week, got it?" Rocky flicked Terry's forehead with his finger on the last word to emphasize his point.

Terry rubbed his stinging forehead. Although it was cold, he was sweating in his costume. He tried to think of something to say that would stop them. Rocky stood to one side of the gate. Louis was behind him again, so he couldn't escape in that direction.

Terry saw that the front door was open just a bit. He wondered if the two boys were hoping he'd put up a fight. After a moment, he surprised both of them by simply saying, "Not a problem."

Louis slapped the side of Terry's head and Rocky laughed.

"Be my guest," Rocky said, and grabbing Terry's arm he pushed him hard through the gate toward the house.

"It couldn't happen to a more retarded guy!" Rocky said.

Louis closed the gate and quickly twisted some wire that was attached to the fence post. Terry figured that they must have placed the wire there earlier and had planned the whole thing.

The two boys stood on the other side of the fence, their fingers gripping the chain-link, smiling and jeering at Terry.

"Hey, go in and get your candy, dickweed. They've got plenty!" Louis said and they both pounded the fence with their hands. Terry stood with his back to the house.

Louis and Rocky froze.

"What the hell is that, Louis?"

"I didn't put nothing in there."

"Let's get the hell out of here. Leave the smartass to figure it out," Rocky said.

The two boys quickly turned and ran back the way they had come, leaving Terry alone but unable to leave the yard. He heard their footsteps fade away.

For a moment, Terry was glad to be out of the presence of the two bullies. He took a deep breath. *I don't know what scared them, but I should be all right if I just pay attention. Chances are there are no ghosts here . . . I hope.*

"And what do you think, Tam Lin?" a lilting female voice said behind him.

Terry turned and at first all he could see was a strong light coming from inside the house and shining out of the doorway. Peering between his fingers, he could just make out the dark shape of an oddly dressed woman swaying in the now fully open doorway. He heard music coming from inside the house behind her. The woman's movements were timed to the music.

Music? When did music start playing?

As Terry's eyes grew accustomed to the light, he saw that the woman had a bright red skirt with black hose underneath. Her blonde hair had dark roots and was tied off in two pigtails on either side of her head. She had green eyes ringed in thick, black mascara. Her body was covered with jewelry that tinkled as she danced. There were even tiny bells on some of her toes, which rang out in a high pitch when she moved.

"At last! The great Tam Lin has finally come. I hope you find everything acceptable. We've got candy and dancing and FUN!"

The green-eyed woman shouted out the last word and abruptly turned and ran back into the house, leaving Terry in the yard alone again.

Terry rubbed his eyes. He had never expected anyone to actually live inside the house.

She acts like she knows me.

Out of curiosity, Terry walked to the open door and peeked in. He saw a room completely lit up; candles on the floor, Halloween lights across the walls, and the light from many lamps made the room glow brightly. Although the room looked old, everything was clean, as if someone were keeping the place tidy.

As Terry stared in wonder, the music grew louder, but he couldn't see where it was coming from. Something about the music made him stop and listen. He suddenly remembered the name his father gave to this kind of music.

"Ragtime!" he said aloud.

It was his dad's favorite music. Grandma Toller used to play it on her old Victrola. Thinking of his dad, Terry sighed and pushed the memory away. He needed to pay attention now.

I wonder if someone has just moved into this house?

Touching the doorframe with his hand, Terry made his way slowly into the room.

They don't have any furniture. I wonder why?

The green-eyed woman reappeared in a doorway to his left. She waved at Terry, moving sinuously.

She never seems to stand still. Terry watched her. *Who is this lady? Is she alone here?*

As if in answer to his question she said, "Come on, silly. We've got other guests coming and I want you to get the best candy!"

Before Terry could respond the woman turned and ran away, her laughter trailing behind her.

Terry carefully walked to where the woman had stood and looked down a long hallway. It wasn't as brightly lit as the room he was in. At the end of the hallway was another room. On the walls of the hallway there were old pictures of castles or ruins of some sort. Each picture had a light shining on it, although Terry couldn't see the source of the light.

Terry stopped at the entrance to the hallway. He wasn't sure why he paused. He put his hand up to his cheek and it felt hot. But he wasn't afraid anymore. The woman seemed nice. And for some odd reason she seemed familiar. He thought he might have seen her before.

Looking down the hallway he saw queer letters and words etched into the walls. They were in patterns he couldn't understand; but, like the woman, he thought he had seen them before.

Maybe it was in one of Grandma Toller's old books.

"You recognize them, Tam? They are runes to protect you. Hello, lad. I'm Dun," said a male voice quite close and directly behind him.

Startled, Terry turned and faced the man who had spoken to him. He was even stranger looking than the woman. His face was very wide and he was quite short, almost as short as Terry. He wore no hat and the rich, red hair on his round head stuck out in patches. All in black, he wore tight pants and an open shirt where Terry could see bits of the same red hair poking out the front. He had a light beard trimmed close to his jawline and he grinned broadly. Terry had never seen someone with a smile as big as Dun's.

"All the candles and decorations are N'ony's work. She's a silly one, that. She likes to have fun at Hall'eve. Do you like to have fun, Tam? We've got candy like you have never seen. Come on back and dance with us," Dun said in a surprisingly high voice for such a strongly built man.

The woman Dun had called N'ony appeared right behind the strange man and put her arms around his neck. They both smiled at Terry, and then they started slowly dancing toward him, forcing him to move down the hallway backward. With both of their bodies almost on top of Terry, they abruptly separated and moved past on either side of him.

"Here we go!" shouted Dun and the two of them skipped down to the end of the hall and around the corner. Terry heard a shriek of laughter and a loud "*I won! I won!*" in N'ony's voice. He couldn't help but laugh himself—their sense of fun was infectious.

Without another thought he started down the hallway to join them. The hallway was longer than he expected and as he walked he noticed more picture frames on the wall, but this time they were of people. He noticed some of the faces smiled while others seemed to be screaming in pain as blood ran down their faces.

The last few picture frames were empty.

He reached the doorway to what looked like the kitchen. A simple white pine table stood in the middle of a medium-sized room painted a very bright white. On the table were bowls filled to overflowing with candies, nuts, and fruits. Behind the table, Dun and N'ony were dancing slowly with each other, their heads facing Terry. Beyond them was an enormous hole in the floor. Terry thought it might be the entrance to the cellar. The hole was perfectly round and he could see flickering light coming from below. There was the sound of water, but far away and distant.

The music started up again, loud in this room, and he could see that it was coming from an old Victrola phonograph on a side table against the wall to the right of him. There were more candles and lights along the window and a door to his left.

"Come, come, come . . . time to choose!" said Dun and he came around the table still swirling and dancing. "We've got all of your favorites! Take one, take them all, Tam!"

Dun danced away and swept his arm out toward the table, inviting Terry to sample the candy. Terry couldn't believe his eyes: It was the largest assortment of candies he had ever seen, all piled high in small black bowls laid out in rows. N'ony, standing behind the table, spread her arms wide and smiled as her lower body kept swaying to the music that was filling the room.

Terry rushed to the table, pulled his bag around in front of him and started to reach toward one of the bowls. More quickly than Terry thought humanly possible, Dun was behind him whispering, "Uh, uh, uh, you're forgetting something now, hmm, Tam?"

Terry thought for a moment, his hand motionless over one of the bowls. *Why do they keep calling me Tam Lin? And what did I forget?*

Then it came to him and he laughed aloud for the first time. "Oh, okay: Trick or treat!"

Both Dun and N'ony clapped their hands and laughed. "That's it, my lovely boy, take 'em all, take 'em all," Dun said.

Terry grabbed handful after handful of candies. Stuffing them into his mouth, he chewed quickly as he loaded more candy into his bag. When he finally swallowed one handful of candy, he grabbed another and started again. His strange benefactors stood watching him, still dancing to the music, which had once again started over from the beginning.

"Plenty more where that came from. There's a whole world full of candy and fun waiting for you. Come with us!"

Their dancing became more energetic as they pranced and skipped all about the kitchen, the music growing louder and faster. Terry found himself grabbing candies and eating to the beat of the music, which repeated over and over again.

"Come now, Tam Lin, dance with us. Dance with us, my child," Dun called out, his voice cutting through the music as he danced over to Terry's left.

N'ony came up on his right and said as loudly, "Dance and dance and dance and everything will be yours forever and ever. You'll have all the candy you could ever desire!"

Terry felt his body beginning to sway a bit. *What are they talking about? Come with them where? I don't really even like to dance.*

Dun's face loomed in Terry's vision to his left as N'ony's face came in on his right. The music had started again, but this time much slower than normal. Everything in the room was happening in slow motion now.

Terry looked at the two faces and realized that something was very, very wrong.

They're just pretending to be nice, he thought. He wished his Grandma Toller were there with him. He tried to think of a way to leave the house.

"Why not take off that vest, my boy? It's so warm here, you don't need it and you'll have plenty of room to dance with us."

Now all that Terry could see were two large faces on either side of him, their red mouths full of white teeth. They spoke to him with manic energy now.

"Will you? Will you?" the voices said in unison. Even the music seemed to take up the rhythm of their words.

Terry put his hands over his ears, trying to block out their voices.

"Now's the time. You'll eat candy every day. Just say 'yes' and come down with us to a land where you'll dance and dance all day," they chanted.

Both of them were before him now, backing him toward the large hole in the floor. Over his shoulder he could see a bright light coming out of the hole and the air above it seemed to ripple like the air over an open flame. And he could see some kind of steps leading down.

He looked back at them and the couple towered over him now. His heels were right at the edge of the hole.

They stood before him, their eyes wide, mouths open and red; both completely still. Terry wanted to move, but he couldn't. The room was completely silent now.

Slowly, both N'ony's and Dun's arms reached out to grab his arms. Terry knew he had to do something or they would take him down into the hole. All he could think of was Grandma Toller. Her face appeared in his mind and he could see her lips forming words, but he couldn't understand them.

Just as they were about to touch him, Terry brought his hand up in front of his face protectively. Right in front of his eyes he caught a glint of something stuck in the sleeve of his shirt.

The silver needle. He immediately pulled it from his sleeve.

"Stop bullying me! I'm not going anywhere with you!" he shouted and jabbed at one of the hands gripping his shoulder.

A piercing scream filled the room and Terry flinched. N'ony stood before him, staring at her hand which was now engulfed in flames. Everything had happened so quickly. Terry couldn't believe his eyes as both Dun and N'ony suddenly slid sideways to the hallway door, their bodies a blur. They both stood there for a moment, regarding Terry with unconcealed hostility.

Relieved, Terry understood that they would not come near or touch him again. The silver needle kept them away. He held it out in front of him threateningly.

"He's got the silver. She's given him a silver needle," hissed N'ony. Her hand had stopped flaming, but the skin was cracked and smoking as she cradled it to her chest. A foul smell filled the room. She held out her burned hand to Terry.

"See this? You're to blame, Terry. You could have come with us and had fun forever, but you tricked us. You and that old whore tricked us!" she said.

This last phrase was shrieked out so loudly and at such a high pitch that Terry flinched and closed his eyes. He began to take deep breaths to calm himself down.

After several moments had passed, Terry opened his eyes and N'ony was gone.

Everything had changed.

A very angry-looking Dun was standing next to the door that now opened to the backyard of the house. The table with all of its candy was gone. Where the hole had been there was now a flat, wooden floor. The Victrola had vanished and the room was bare.

A cold wind came through the open door and rustled Terry's hair. Everything was covered with a thin layer of dust. He looked up at Dun.

"Don't look at me like that, you little prick. You know what you did. You blew the chance of a lifetime. Now get the hell out," Dun barked at him.

Moving to the door, Terry was sure that Dun was going to hit him as he passed. Or worse. Terry could feel the fury in Dun's body.

But the blow never came.

He stepped through the door into a backyard filled with dead grass and moonlight. Terry let out the breath he was holding in and turned to look back. Dun's body was outlined in the doorway, the dim light from the kitchen framing him.

"Ask that witch of a grandma. She'll tell ya, all right. And we'll be waiting. Oh, yes, we'll be waiting! You'll see us again," Dun said.

With that he slammed the door so loudly and with such force that the entire building seemed to shake. Terry cringed and held his arms over his head, staying that way for several minutes.

After he was calm, he brought his arms down and turned toward the house. The back door now bore a large sign that read: **CONDEMNED**. Rotting bits of paper clung to the doorway and fluttered in the cold wind. The windows were boarded up.

Terry couldn't make sense of what had happened. Instinctively, he looked at his sleeve and felt for the silver needle that had saved him. He was careful not to stick himself this time. It was there, but was now very cold to the touch.

Why didn't Grandma tell me?

Looking behind him, he saw that the fence that was in front of the house continued around to the backyard. There was an overgrown path of broken stepping-stones leading to the back gate. He walked toward the gate, keeping his fingers crossed that it wouldn't be locked.

Although it was dark in the yard, there was just enough light from the moon, now directly overhead. He could see that the gate was broken and hanging off the fence. He moved quickly down the alley behind the house and out onto the sidewalk.

Glancing up at the moon, he knew it was very, very late. From its position overhead he guessed it was probably past midnight.

How long was I inside of that house?

Most of the lights in the houses around him were out. He continued walking, hugging himself for warmth. He could hear his boots clicking on the gray moonlit sidewalk.

He needed to see his grandmother.

"Terry? Answer my question: What did that dreadful thing say to you before he closed the door?" Grandma picked up the small cup of tea she had made and handed it to him.

" 'Ask that witch of a Grandma. She'll tell you.' "

At this, Grandma grunted and shook her head. "Those were his exact words?"

"Yes, Grandma Toller. That's what he said to me." Terry sipped the tea, trying to place the unfamiliar taste.

Grandma Toller sighed and looked away from Terry for a long time. He felt lightheaded and tingly.

Perhaps it's the tea. His sense of taste had sharpened. In fact all of his senses seemed to be just a bit sharper than usual.

"Do you remember this?" She held up the silver needle which had been in his sleeve. Terry started to speak, but his grandmother put her fingers on his mouth to silence him.

"You have been tested and you have passed, my child. It's time for you to know who you are."

Terry was confused. *What kind of test is she talking about?*

Seemingly in answer to the question he had formed in his mind, his grandmother said, "You've met those that want to control you and make you their slave. They want to take your power and use it for themselves. A bit of silver and they cannot touch. They cannot control. The needle in your sleeve? They didn't expect that. Nor did they think you would fight and refuse to come with them."

As she spoke she poured more of the shining hot tea into his cup.

"Why would they want to do that to me? And if you knew they were going to come for me, why didn't you warn me?"

"Because they are the *Sidhe*, the Fairy Folk, Terry, and you must never, never trust what the *Sidhe* tell you, my dear, especially on Hall'eve when they are the strongest." She leaned in toward him. "And I am sorry I could not warn you, but there are rules. You must find a way yourself, with no aid from anyone. Such is the way it has always been from generation to generation."

Whispering into Terry's ear she added, "But you've beaten them, my dear. I knew you would. Like Tam Lin. Why do you think you were dressed like him, Terry? You met your challenge and you've triumphed. And for that you must be rewarded."

As she finished, she placed a small box on Terry's lap. A gray, rectangular box with a small white lid. Terry looked down at the box, breathing hard. He handed his grandmother his teacup and as she smiled he removed the top of the box.

Terry took a short breath and reached in to remove the box's contents. It was a small bone wrapped on each end with sinew and covered with runes. The bone warmed to his touch as he held it up to examine in the light of the fire.

"It is your fetish, my child. You'll understand its use in time. There is much I have to teach you. Every warlock has his fetish. Keep it well and it will keep you well." Then, under her breath she muttered:

"Happy Halloween, my dear."

Terry looked toward the large picture window that dominated the study. The heavy window drapes were closed, but he could hear the wind outside. The bone grew still warmer in his grasp until it was hot. He took a deep breath and let it out slowly.

Grandma Toller watched him closely.

Near the floor under the window there was a small triangle of drapery that hadn't quite closed completely, and looking in through the window was the one-eyed cat. Light from the fire reflected in the cat's one good eye as he watched Terry for a moment, and then darted away into the black Halloween night.

THE MEASURE OF A MAN

GEORGE WILLIS

A vast body of fog stole northward along the coast, hugging the rugged terrain and chilling everything in its path. Discovering a small gap in the formidable wall of east South African mountains, it cautiously probed the opening. A hazy tendril of moisture unfurled from the main body of mist and wandered into a cove where it found a child keeping watch; if it were able to speak, it would have warned the boy of what was to come.

Lindani was on the long and difficult path to becoming a Zulu warrior, which he knew would be filled with many tasks and challenges. One task in particular was a growing point of resentment—spending long, exhausting nights fighting to keep awake at his assigned outpost overlooking the ocean.

I do not see the good in this. Zulu warriors fight their enemies face-to-face as men. They do not keep watch over the fish in the sea.

Seated atop a rocky outcropping high above the cove, his mind often strayed from his duty. He stared up into the spray of stars overhead, feeling he had been unfairly singled out for the unenviable post where he now stood guard. "I should not be the one to have the last watch of the night," the twelve-year-old grumbled aloud to the sea. "I am the son of the chief."

During the night the temperature dropped suddenly and the salty tang of sea water in the air became stronger than usual. Wondering what had brought on the abrupt change, he stood up from where he was huddled at the foot of an ancient baobab tree and strode to within inches of the cliff's edge. Looking out over the chasm before him, he strained to see in the dark. After a few moments he made out a low-lying bank of fog inching along the coast and slowly seeping into the cove. Satisfied he'd done his duty by investigating the change in his surroundings, he donned a meager coat of animal skins and settled back into his spot by the tree.

As the night wore on he was happy to see subtle hints of approaching daylight; the normally brilliant stars had dimmed and their numbers were diminishing. His boredom turned into restless anticipation while he waited for the sun to rise up from the sea, bringing with it much desired sleep and the arrival of his replacement.

Damp pre-dawn air coiled around him and caressed his exposed flesh. Lindani rubbed his arms vigorously, but it was not enough to stave off the cold. He desperately wanted to light a fire, but doing so would give away his position, so he decided instead to keep warm by practicing the fighting techniques he had learned in training. Not yet allowed a real spear, he executed the drills with a hand-carved lance he had fashioned over the course of many nights spent in quiet solitude. In the midst of shadow-fighting an imaginary foe, he suddenly stopped.

Something was moving through the fog.

Lindani thought he must be dreaming. He blinked several times to clear his vision but it did not erase the object from view; the tops of a ship's masts were just visible above the ridges which formed the horseshoe-shaped cove. The young Zulu had never seen anything like it and was only able to recognize its form by tales told round the campfire. The trio of dark objects moved slowly, appearing to float on the grey-white blanket of moisture.

Lindani froze to the spot, the blood from his rapidly pounding heart thundering in his ears. In his excitement he dropped his makeshift spear. The clattering sound it made on the rocky precipice jarred him into action. He ran to the base of the tree and snatched up a water buffalo horn and signaled the alarm. The skeletal rigging grew in size as it angled silently toward the mouth of the cove. Soon the dark profile of the ship's bow jutted out from behind the cove's exterior walls. As more of the massive vessel slid into view, Lindani willed his eyes to penetrate the thick swirls of fog cloaking its decks. Try as he might, he was unable to see anyone aboard the shadowy craft.

The ship came at the cove with no signs of slowing. "If they do not soon stop—"

It slammed into a reef separating the cove from the wide-open sea. A terrible crunching sound was unleashed as its timber beams ground into coral. Like some sort of monstrous sea creature trying to crawl onto land, the vessel's bow rose up out of the water and came to a sudden rest. Nesting gulls and terns abandoned their homes in the weathered cliffs near the craft. The air over the cove erupted in feathery chaos. The seabirds took startled flight and circled nervously overhead, emitting frantic cries. Lindani once again trumpeted the alarm.

Expecting to see men pouring over the sides of the vessel at any moment, his eyes darted nervously from the ship to the beach below in search of a runner from his tribe. To his frustration, his line of sight was interrupted by drifting clouds of moisture.

"Where is he? Where is he?"

Lindani felt like days had passed before Muzi, another young warrior-in-training, materialized from the fog and came running up the solitary footpath to the outpost.

"What have you seen?" Muzi demanded.

"Hurry!" Lindani beckoned wildly. "A ship has come in the mist!"

Muzi joined his friend at the edge of the cliff and peered out over the cove. Between ghostly wisps, he too was able to catch glimpses of the marooned vessel. Without a word he turned and flew back along the meager footpath. Once at the beach, Muzi hastened into a narrow canyon at the back of the cove. He raced toward a secondary outpost midway between the coast and their village. When he arrived, another runner would be sent to alert their clan.

Lindani continued scanning the ship for any movement. He anxiously paced back and forth at his outpost while waiting for warriors to arrive. He flinched at the sound of loud splashes coming from somewhere near the ship and nervously searched the water for the source. The haze around the sea vessel would not give up any secrets. "It must have been waves striking the ship," Lindani convinced himself as he stood alone in the mist.

Nearly one hundred Zulu warriors armed with spears and cowhide shields gathered on the beach by the time the sun, still hidden behind a blanket of clouds, began peering over the horizon. Lindani glanced down to where his fellow tribesmen set about readying themselves for any sort of invasion; the white, black, and gold feathers of their headdresses rustled and danced as they prepared for battle. Seeing everyone divided up into three *amabutho*, he was anxious to be relieved of his post so he might be allowed to join the *ibutho* of young warriors led by his good friend, Jabari.

Mindful he was still on sentry duty, Lindani quickly turned his gaze back to the hulking vessel, which was well beyond the range of their spears. Judging by the frequent competitions held in their tribe, he guessed the craft was maybe as many as five throws of a spear from the beach. Since his people were not seafaring in nature, they were left to wait for the enemy to come ashore and fight them at the water's edge.

Soon after the *amabutho* formed up on the beach, Themba, leader of the clan, made the long hike up the bluff to where Lindani stood. Close at his heel were Jabari and Muzi.

"How many men are there?" Themba asked, gazing out at the dark vessel.

"I have not seen anyone, Father. Maybe there is no one."

"They are there and will come soon enough. They have no choice. Their ship is damaged. The tide rises and it will be smashed by the waves." At that moment, Themba's voice became a low growl. "When these slave traders set foot on Zulu land, they will be made to pay for taking our people in times past."

"Father, I wish to fight with the others," Lindani blurted out.

No child, not even a chief's own son, was allowed to speak in such a familiar manner with their leader. The shift of Themba's expression spoke volumes. Too late, Lindani realized his transgression. While he awaited a sharp rebuke, his mind raced back to the day he turned six, and a private, shared moment with his father. The chief had confessed to Lindani that day how once, as a young boy, he himself was too eager to become a warrior and made a similar mistake. Looking into his father's eyes now, it seemed that Themba also remembered the moment; the elder

Zulu's face softened ever so slightly. "No," Themba replied. "You must remain here and alert us to any more ships."

Lindani was surprised not to have been sternly reprimanded, but more than that, he was crestfallen at his father's words. Pride told him not to let his disappointment show; he accepted the assignment with a set jaw and straight back. He was now more determined than ever to prove his worthiness to his father and his clan.

The chief turned to the young Zulus who accompanied him. "Muzi . . . you will stay just there," Themba pointed, indicating a spot halfway down the bluff. "You are to deliver any more reports."

Themba then put his hand on Lindani's shoulder and guided his son a short distance from the others. "Your life will be filled with many tasks you do not desire," he said in a low voice to prevent the others from hearing. "A true Zulu warrior accepts such burdens because it is best for his tribe."

"I understand, Father," Lindani replied solemnly.

Themba searched his son's eyes for a moment, then nodded before he turned and strode down the footpath. Jabari gave his friend a quick, sympathetic glance as he followed the chieftain back to the beach. Wearing his disappointment on his shoulders, Muzi trudged off to his newly assigned post, not wanting to remain behind and view the battle from afar.

Lindani watched the trio shrink into the distance, a fire burning within him. *I am ready to be a warrior.* He turned and marched back to his post at the end of the precipice. He cast his eyes down toward the assemblage of his fellow tribesmen. *I will show them. They will all see . . .*

Lindani was once again alone when a chorus of moans emanated from the grounded ship. The eerie sound echoed throughout the cove, amplified by its barren walls. Upon hearing it, Lindani took a nervous step back, then quickly looked to see Muzi had not witnessed his momentary display of cowardice; thankfully his friend was staring out to sea.

Fighting to overcome his fear, he recalled what he'd been taught. "Know your enemy. Know their strengths and weaknesses," he muttered to himself as he scanned the ship for people and weapons. Soon, shadowy, lumbering figures whose faces and forms were blurred by the moisture in the air began to emerge from below deck. Judging by their motions, these men were not at all what he expected; they were slow, unorganized, and wandered about in all directions, colliding with one another.

A longboat and two dinghies were haphazardly lowered down to the sea. The ropes supporting the longboat gave way, spilling its passengers. It dropped nose first into the water where it snapped in two; the rear portion sank beneath the surf while the front half stood upright, its bow lodged in the coral reef. Only a few jagged planks of wood remained, pointing skyward like rotting teeth. The dinghies also plummeted downward and struck the water with a sound like gunfire. Some of the men within them bounced out and landed on the partially submerged reef.

More men tumbled off the listing ship into the water, where they slammed onto the hard coral. *Do they not understand where their ship rests?!* Lindani's shock turned quickly to amazement as these same men stood up on the reef and staggered undaunted toward the beach, tearing their flesh on the razor sharp coral as they came.

While he counted their numbers, motion high above the ship's deck caught his eye; a man was climbing in the main mast's rigging. The lone man made a dangerous misstep and was suddenly tumbling seaward. Lindani gasped. He narrowed his eyes to slits, but he could not take them off the rapidly plunging figure. He felt his gorge rise when the man struck the upright remains of the longboat and was impaled; the mariner hung suspended for a moment before flesh and muscle gave out and he was sliced in two. In the short span of his life, Lindani had never been witness to such a horrific sight. He thought he was going to retch when the man's torso pin-wheeled down through the hollow of the partially submerged craft.

From his high perch, the normally emerald-colored water looked nearly black under the cover of cloudy skies. It was into the ominous waters of the cove that the sailors who cleared the reef quickly sank. Their sudden disappearance made it seem as though they had been swallowed up by some unseen creature hiding in the depths. With their numbers now dwindling, Lindani focused on the two dinghies moving slowly toward the beach, looking like a pair of insects skating on the surface of a pond.

Motion on the beach drew his attention away. Ten warriors, lead by Sipho, one of the most revered Zulus in the tribe, were moving down to the water line to meet the invaders. The first of the two small boats pulled to within a few meters of Sipho, who stood apart from his band of tribesmen. One of the men from the small craft half stepped, half tumbled out of the boat and splashed in the surf. Lindani focused on the newcomer. *That one must be their leader.* When Sipho addressed the sailors, Lindani could only make out some of his words. The rest raced past him and were lost forever, a jumble of sound borne on the wind.

The final boat arrived seconds later, within a spear's length of the first. A wave rose up, gently lifted the boats, and then quickly withdrew. Before anyone else could exit, the dinghies were carried back to sea. Their compatriot was marooned. He stood alone, face-to-face with Sipho. From his spot overlooking the scene, Lindani counted fifteen mariners in the two vessels, compared to the ten men in Sipho's unit. Even though the small party of Zulus was outnumbered, Lindani was confident they could make quick work of the invaders.

To his surprise the leader of the sailors lunged toward Sipho. In response, the battle-scarred warrior thrust his spear cleanly through the man's heart. Lindani let out a small cry of approval, but the sound quickly withered on his lips; the man continued toward Sipho in spite of the seven-foot-long spear protruding from his chest. Sipho quickly raised the end of the wooden handle and pushed hard while stepping forward, toppling the seaman. Another wave pushed the boats back to shore further down the beach and Sipho's men charged toward the two small craft, leaving him to finish off the lone mariner.

Without warning, a veritable platoon of invaders arose from the watery depths of the cove. Lindani stared in disbelief. "How can this be?" he exclaimed. "They all sank in the water. Not even the strongest Zulu can remain under the waves without breath . . ."

Sweeping into view, a full *ibutho* of warriors charged down to the water with a furious battle cry, hurtling themselves headlong at the men rising from the cove. The moment the tribesmen were in range they loosed their spears. The rain of deadly projectiles struck several targets, but this did not stop the invaders. Even those pierced through with spears pushed onward, wading through the shallow water toward dry land.

A low, hunger-filled moaning reached Lindani's ears from somewhere close by. He spun round to find the source, but he was alone on the rocky precipice. He turned back to face the sea and inched toward the cliff's edge to look down the rock face. There was nothing to be seen. He heard small rocks and pebbles tumbling downward and striking the ground behind him. Lindani turned, expecting to see a lost goat roaming on the steep slope above him. What he saw made his heart jump in his throat; a sailor had scaled the mountainous walls of the cove and worked its way to the cliff above Lindani.

The young Zulu suddenly recalled the splashes he'd heard earlier. The moment the thought crossed his mind he called out a warning to Muzi. The words barely left his lips when he spotted a second sailor on the cliff face above his friend. Too far to be heard by the others on the beach over the wind and waves, Lindani and Muzi were left alone to fight this new menace.

The man stepped forward and plummeted down to the ledge where Lindani stood. He landed awkwardly, snapping one of his legs on impact, driving bone through flesh, and toppled face-first onto the rocky surface. Lindani took a single step toward the sailor when the fallen man raised his head.

Lindani recoiled in horror at the sight of the man's face. A flap of skin and muscle dangled obscenely, exposing part of his skull; his right eye, dotted with sand and gravel, swung from its cord-like optic nerve, lolling back and forth across his cheek with the slightest motion. The nightmarish sailor inched toward Lindani, clawing at the hard earth with his bare hands. The jagged bone protruding from his leg raked across the rocks in search of traction to propel him onward.

Lindani's young mind resounded in terror. *This is no man! This is some sort of demon!*

Muzi was coming up the footpath to aide his friend when the second sailor launched himself from the cliff overhead and landed on the young Zulu, driving him to the ground. Muzi screamed in agony as the man bit into his neck and came away with a mouthful of flesh. With the advancing sailor between him and the footpath, Lindani was helpless to do anything for his friend. Blood gushed from the gaping wound in Muzi's neck. He struggled to break free from his attacker, but he was rapidly losing ground to the older, larger man. Their fighting brought the bloody combatants to the edge of the footpath.

"MUZI!"

Lindani could do nothing but watch when the two rolled over the edge; they dropped several meters before they caromed off an outcropping in the cliff-face. Their rapid descent ended suddenly on the boulder-strewn beach below.

Moaning ravenously at the sight of a warm meal, the fallen sailor continued to pull himself forward along the ledge toward Lindani. The young Zulu backed away and quickly found himself trapped, his bare heels resting on the edge of the cliff. Small clumps of dirt crumbled away from beneath his heels and scurried down the sheer drop to the beach. Just another slight step backward meant certain death.

Lindani stared at the creature crawling toward him, when he remembered what had been drilled into him from the day he was born—*We are Zulu. We are not afraid.* Adrenaline tore through his body, making his every nerve sing. Looking around for something to fight off the ghoulish thing, he spotted his practice spear lying on the ground halfway between him and the monstrous sailor.

Lindani raced forward. In one fluid motion he picked up the spear and ran headlong at his foe, covering the distance between them in a split second. The sailor had pulled himself up to his feet and was hobbling toward the young Zulu when Lindani threaded the tip of the javelin-like branch directly into the creature's eye socket.

The spear's finely honed point ruptured the sailor's eyeball and bore through his brain, erupting out the back of his head with a spray of blood, bone, and tissue. The speed with which Lindani struck forced his victim to stumble backward. Lindani kept at a run. He drove the spear protruding from the creature's skull into a crack in the rock wall, where it became lodged. The man's body slammed into the cliff face with a thud. Even though he was held firmly in place, the sailor did not cease his attempts to free himself and grab at his quarry.

With the mariner out of his way, Lindani ran down the path to the spot where Muzi had fallen. Below him he could see the demon-like man who had assaulted his friend; he was now feasting on Muzi's lifeless body. In a fit of rage Lindani picked up a large stone and hurled it at the creature. It missed his intended target, landing harmlessly in the sand near its feet. A loud snarling sound drew his attention back to the ledge; the impaled sailor was jerkily guiding his head along the length of the spear in an attempt at escape.

The sight gave the young Zulu pause. *Will nothing stop these things?!?*

Lindani darted back up to the ledge and frantically searched for some way to dispatch the undead sailor. When he drew near, he spied a hilted cutlass hanging from his enemy's side. In a flash he drew up a desperate plan. *If he will not die, I will cut off his limbs so he can no longer give chase.* He flew at the sailor, who was inches away from freedom. Ducking his flailing arms, Lindani slipped in between the creature and the cliff. His young face suddenly contorted into a grimace and his nostrils flared in disgust. At such close range, the putrid smell of the man's decaying flesh being driven in his face by the sea breeze was almost overwhelming. He hastily grabbed at the dangling weapon, but the sailor twisted his hips around; Lindani missed his target.

The man strained his every muscle in an attempt to catch hold of the young Zulu. Lindani knew he had mere seconds to seize the shining blade before the monster was loose. He lunged once more for the unguarded cutlass and snatched it from its hilt. The sailor came to the end of the spear and staggered forward, suddenly free from his bond. He turned around and faced his prey, hanging onto the wedged spear with his right hand for balance. Lindani wielded the bladed weapon with both hands and stepped forward, swinging it at the demonic thing before him. The blow severed the ghoul's right arm at the elbow. The newly dismembered limb dangled from the wooden lance like a grisly pendulum, held in place by its pale, pudgy hand.

The sailor toppled off balance and fell toward Lindani. The cutlass was brought around for a second blow. Once again it cleaved a path through flesh and bone. The sailor's head was held suspended in the air for a fraction of a second before it dropped to the ground and tumbled across the rocky surface; the headless body fell forward with a dull thump, kicking up small gusts of dust when it struck the dirt.

In that moment it ceased all motion.

Lindani stood over the creature, waiting to strike another blow, but it didn't move. There was no sign of life. He knew that this time, he had killed it.

Lindani returned to the cliff's edge to see what has happening on the beach. The fog had lifted and the sun was now shining down on the scene. The battle raged on. Nearly all his people had joined in the fight. They easily outnumbered the sailors, yet were still being driven back by the unarmed invaders, whom he could now see clearly for the first time. They, too, were just like the man he had killed; many were severely wounded and missing limbs, yet somehow they staggered and fought ceaselessly.

Lindani charged down the footpath to the beach. In one hand he held a bloodstained cutlass. In the other was the sailor's head, its matted brown hair bouncing with each jarring stride he took. He carried the heavy object with pride, as though bearing a prize. Lindani raced across the sand toward his father. The chieftain was giving orders to his lieutenants when Lindani dropped the sailor's head at his feet; everyone stared at the bloody, sand-encrusted object. "Taking their heads is the only way to stop these . . . *things*," Lindani said in disgust, offering the cutlass to his father.

"Our spears are not made to cut off a man's head," Themba said, turning the cutlass over in his hands, "and one man alone cannot take on all these demons."

"I will stay and fight them," Jabari offered.

"No. You are to lead your *ibutho* back to the village," he commanded. "Take the wounded with you, then gather up all the axes in the village and be prepared to fight these creatures." Themba turned to another young warrior. "Mulalo, go with Jabari. When you are halfway through the pass, take a small group and climb into the hills and remain there, out of sight. Wait for the creatures to pass and then fall in behind them. Then we will attack them from two sides."

"What of you, my chief?" another lieutenant asked.

"I will stay behind with more men and hold these creatures back. We will give the others time to prepare to fight them in the canyon."

Lindani stepped away from the small gathering and bent over to pick up an unused spear, when he felt a warm, leathery hand on his shoulder.

"I am proud of what you have done this day," Themba said, "but you are to return with the others."

"I am a Zulu and will gladly take this task," Lindani said with a weak smile, though the words felt hollow as he uttered them.

Three litters were made to carry the worst of the wounded. Once ready, Jabari led the small group of young Zulu warriors into the narrow canyon at a trot. They had not gone very far when two of the litter bearers abruptly stopped and set their charge down; Sibusiso, the boy they were carrying, moaned loudly and thrashed about, making the going difficult. "Don't worry, brother," Jabari said as he approached the wounded boy, "we will soon be at the village."

Chunks of flesh and muscle were missing from Sibusiso's calves, thighs, and stomach, leaving him unable to walk; a swarm of blood-drenched mariners was driven off him at the time of his rescue. When Jabari drew near his hastily bandaged friend, Sibusiso snarled at him. The young litter bearers who had been carrying him stepped back nervously.

"What is wrong, Jabari?" Lindani asked, coming up from the rear. "Why have we stopped? We must hurry." As though in answer, Sibusiso quickly rose to his feet and threw himself at Jabari, gnashing his teeth and attempting to bite him.

The other Zulus stared in shock at their fellow warrior, who was incapable of walking just a short time before. Lindani dove in shoulder first and rammed into Sibusiso, knocking him away from Jabari. The blow to his midsection sent Sibusiso reeling. He flew backward and tried to regain his balance, but stumbled to the ground. He quickly sat up, and it was then Lindani noticed a change in the other boy. His eyes, once dark as molasses, were now bulging, blood shot, milky-white orbs with barely discernable irises. His skin, too, had transformed and was now slightly ashen.

Sibusiso charged at Lindani, who raised his spear in warning, but the changeling never once slowed and ran full speed toward the chief's son. The others let out a cry as Lindani dropped to one knee and thrust his spear tip into the soft triangle of flesh between Sibusiso's chin and throat. Planting the end of the spear's handle firmly in the ground, Lindani launched Sibusiso over his head in a great arc.

A loud snap echoed off the canyon walls as the spear handle broke, sending its victim sprawling across the ground. Jabari, Mulalo, and the others watched in disbelief as Sibusiso continued to move against all reason. The broken remains of the spear-shaft protruded from his neck. The spear's metal tip, adorned with bits of brain and bone, jutted out the top of his skull. Yet he still scrambled to get on his feet. Lindani, squatting low to the ground, held on firmly to the broken spear handle, the only weapon he had to protect himself. Before Sibusiso could reach him, he felt a rustle in the air around him as three spears flew over his head; the weapons all struck Sibusiso and knocked him back, temporarily stunning him.

"His head!" Lindani shouted to the others. "We must cut off his head!"

"No!" Mulalo shouted. "He is one of us."

"You saw him," Jabari countered. "He is now like those other things on the beach."

The small band of Zulus made their way toward their fallen friend, who struggled to get up, straining against the weapons sticking out of him.

"Hold him still," Lindani ordered.

Everyone stopped where they stood, uncertain of what to do.

"Hold him!" he shouted.

Jabari grabbed onto one arm, while two other boys reluctantly joined him and held their friend down. Lindani stepped toward Mulalo and snatched away the knife his cousin kept sheathed at his waist. Kneeling down beside the thrashing changeling, he drew a deep breath. "I'm sorry, Sibu," he whispered, then commenced with the grisly task of sawing through his kinsman's neck.

"How did Sibu become like those things from the ship?" Jabari asked his friend.

"I do not know," Lindani sighed, as they trotted through the canyon.

"Will the other wounded become like Sibu?"

"I am not certain, but their eyes look nothing like his. And they do not attack. Still, you must watch them closely. If you see a change in them, you know what you must do," Lindani cautioned.

At the midway point between the beach and the village, Mulalo, Lindani, and a select group of young warriors broke off from the others. Once separated from their small regiment, they quickly climbed the steep canyon walls and secreted themselves amongst the rocks and trees. As the remainder of the *ibutho* departed, Lindani settled into his hiding spot and thought about the day's events and what had become of Sibusiso. A bird-call tugged at his attention and he looked for its source; a young Zulu was emphatically pointing down to the floor of the canyon. Lindani gave a start when he saw his friend Muzi staggering along, sniffing as he went, as though in search of food.

Mulalo, seated near Lindani, was about to call out, when Lindani held up his hand, signaling silence. Looking closely, he could see Muzi's eyes, like Sibusiso's, had changed. Keeping out of sight, Lindani quietly moved amongst the rocks and worked his way over to his cousin.

"It is their bite," he whispered.

"What do you speak of?" Mulalo asked.

"Like a sick dog, the bite of the creatures from the ship is what makes them change. Muzi was killed this very morning by one of those things. It was eating his flesh, and now look at him. He has changed, just like Sibu did."

"So how are we to stop them? We do not have the sort of weapons we need to cut off all their heads."

Lindani kept a watchful eye on Muzi who continued to work his way through the canyon, staggering from place to place and stopping to sniff the ground where Sibu had been killed. While mulling over their situation, Lindani absentmindedly tossed a small stone up and down in his hand. Realizing if he dropped it, the sound of it striking the ground could alert Muzi to their presence. As a precaution, he carefully set it down. In doing so, his focus came to rest on the stones at his feet. Soon his gaze changed to take in their surroundings and his eyes lit up.

"What is it?" Mulalo asked.

"I know how to stop these things," he whispered in reply.

"How do-"

Lindani abruptly cut off his cousin with a quick gesture of his hand; Muzi stopped and was peering into the shadows of the trees where the young warriors lay in wait. He was staring so intently, Lindani was certain they had been discovered. Muzi slowly turned his gaze back to the canyon floor, gave a few sniffs of the air and shuffled off in the direction of the village.

"Should we give chase?"

"No," Lindani said. "He is just one. Jabari and the others can stop him. Come, we have much work to do."

The sounds of battle echoed through the canyon. The first of the older Zulus came into sight, followed not far behind by an army made up of both mariners and changed-over Zulus. The warriors in Themba's *ibutho* struggled to hold off the swelling tide of changelings, before giving up ground and retreating deeper into the canyon. The mutated Zulus, like the seafaring invaders, no longer used weapons, but instead did everything in their power to devour their former friends.

Lindani peered out from behind a tree trunk and waited until the last of his father's warriors was directly in line with him. At that very moment he raised a water buffalo horn to his lips and sounded a retreat. The bugling tone filled the canyon and momentarily halted the invaders in their tracks.

Themba's men saw several young boys scattered about the canyon walls frantically waving them on toward the village, shouting at them to flee. The veterans took their cue and raced off in the direction of the village. An avalanche begun by young Zulus straining against large boulders crashed down both sides of the narrow canyon, demolishing everything in their path. A tremendous thundering sound filled the air as the giant stone monoliths, tugged by gravity, increased their speed toward the canyon floor. The ground trembled and vibrated beneath Lindani's feet. Trees cracked and exploded in a splintered frenzy, leaving only jagged stumps in their wake. Rocky shards issued forth when stone struck stone, ricocheting wildly in the air, slicing through everything in their path.

In a matter of moments a blanket of dust smothered the scene. When the last of the rocks came to rest, the only thing to be heard was the fading echo of destruction. A lazy breeze slowly snaking through the canyon cleared away the clouds of dust hanging in the air, revealing only a mountain of stone in what was once a narrow ravine.

The last surviving Zulus, bloodied and exhausted, returned to the village and delivered the news of their triumph. Before the entire assembled village, Themba praised Mulalo for his ingenuity, but the young Zulu would not take the credit for their success; he rightly pointed to Lindani as the one who defeated the invaders.

"Today is a proud and sorrowful day," Themba proclaimed. "We have lost many of our brothers and kinsmen to a terrible enemy, yet we have come out the victors."

"Also on this day, it is with great pride that I name our newest warrior, Lindani, for his bravery and his cunning in defeating our enemy."

Themba turned to one of his lieutenants, who handed him a spear of a full-fledged Zulu warrior.

"This spear is a symbol of our trust and faith in Lindani."

Lindani accepted the spear, which was adorned with feathers, and animal skins. He held it for a moment with both hands, admiring it. The heft of it in his hands felt good, much more than the simple handcrafted spear he had made for himself.

Pulling a solitary red feather from a pouch at his waist, Themba said, "This feather marks him as a warrior of bravery and honor."

Lindani turned and passed his new spear to Jabari, then stepped close to Themba, who placed the red quill in his headdress. Face-to-face with his father, Lindani noticed a fresh smattering of blood on the pelt covering Themba's shoulder. His eyes followed the trail to its source—a small piece of the chieftain's ear was missing. When Themba stepped back, Lindani locked eyes with his father.

They were pale gray.

Themba again addressed the village. "As the one who showed us how to kill this new enemy, I give him the weapon he used to stop them." Raising it aloft, he held it high for all to see, the very cutlass Lindani used to behead his nemesis; sunlight glinted off its long steel blade.

Themba handed the weapon to his son and whispered, "A true Zulu warrior will take on such burdens because it is best for his tribe."

Lindani took the shining blade from the chief's rapidly graying hands. He looked into Themba's eyes, searching for any last hint of humanity. He stepped back, drew a deep breath and raised the deadly instrument with both hands. At that very moment, he felt his heart split; the boy in him cried out in anguish at the loss of the father whom he deeply loved, but the warrior he had become knew his duty to family and tribe.

THE GRIEVING PROCESS

MIKE McCARTY

Richard Nance snapped his eyes open and stared at the ceiling. His head protested the first sign of light with a dull throbbing. He wanted a glass of water in the worst way. His tongue tasted like shit. He rubbed his tired eyes, digging his pinkies into the tear ducts while his index fingers massaged his temples. He felt the cuff of his shirt catch on his unshaven chin and glanced at the slightly soiled fabric. He kicked the cover off the bed. He was still wearing yesterday's clothes, shoes and all.

Must have passed out again. *Thank you, Johnnie Walker.*

To his left he caught sight of the nearly empty bottle, taken under the covers in a drunken stupor. A stain the color of old corn had soaked into the sheet. There was one swallow left, teasing him like a lover. It sloshed back and forth with every slight movement he made on the four-poster bed. *Maybe later.*

The clock read 7:15. He hadn't slept well since . . . well, he just hadn't been sleeping well.

Richard rolled over and found *her* pillow. He liked to sleep with it curled up in his arms, near his face. He inhaled deeply and found that her smell was just barely still there. One day, he knew, it would be gone. He wondered briefly if he was using up the scent particles with each selfish breath he took. Lately he had even switched to her shampoo so he could carry a scented reminder with him wherever he went. It smelled like night-blooming jasmine, her favorite. He carefully set the pillow aside to preserve it. He knew he could always spray it with her perfume, but that just wasn't the same. It smelled different straight from the bottle, before it had a chance to mix with the chemistry of her skin.

He rolled his legs out of bed and sat there considering whether today would be different from any of the others. Out of the corner of his sleep-blurred eye he spotted a half-empty glass of water on the nightstand. It looked anything but clean, having gathered the dust of at least two days of sitting there. In fact, he couldn't remember what night he had set it there. April had always kept a fresh glass of water by the bed. She was prone to coughing fits in the middle of the night, thanks to years of smoking. He picked up the uninviting glass and swallowed the contents hard, nearly choking himself. It was stale, all right. He slid it back onto the nightstand, distorting the red digital numbers of the clock radio he had gotten for her three Christmases ago. One of *many* cheap gifts he had gotten her over the years. He knew he should have spent more on her when he had the chance. Now it was too late. It was just one more in a long list of things he constantly ran through to feel guilty about.

He slowly made his way to the bathroom. The dim lighting reminded him that he needed a new bulb for the overhead. Maybe he could get to that later if he went anywhere near the hardware store. He gazed at his reflection. His image was mottled with the grayed streaks and speckles of old water splashes.

Who am I kidding?

He rubbed a spot clean with the cuff of his shirt and got a good look at his eyes. Sunken blood-red slits stared back at him, the skin around them puffy and gray. He pushed his index finger into the soft flesh of the lower lid and pulled down, revealing the wet raw inside. He thought briefly of pushing his finger deep into the socket until the eye itself shot out with a wet plop. Nobody would blame him; anyone who knew him would understand. It was just a phase he was going through, a part of the grieving process. It might even be considered normal. He chuckled at that. Life was *anything* but normal anymore.

He found his way to the kitchen and poured an ice-cold cup of three-day-old coffee. He didn't feel like making a new pot so it would have to do. He put the now-chipped cup—the one she had given him on his fortieth birthday—in the microwave and set it for two minutes. There was no more cream, so it would have to be black again. He reminded himself that he needed to get to the store and make his home life just a little more comfortable, even though comfort was the last thing on his mind. He went through the list quickly in his head: light bulbs, cream, bread, eggs, Johnnie Walker, and a new dead bolt for the basement door.

He shuffled his way into the living room and found himself staring at a photo taken on their honeymoon. Both of them were in their twenties, holding hands, kissing in the foyer of the Honolulu Airport in Hawaii. They were wearing leis they had received from some woman in a grass skirt the moment they had stepped off the plane. That same woman, he remembered, had also taken the photograph, the first of their honeymoon. Hanging next to the picture were the very same leis from the photo. They were covered in dust that he dared not blow away for fear of destroying the brittle mementos. A spider web had clawed its way across one of the desiccated flowers to the bottom of the picture frame. He wanted to clean it off. Hell, he wanted to do a lot of things.

The dinging of the microwave bell signified the end of the thought and the beginning of his meager breakfast.

He stared at the hot cup of black coffee for a moment, then drank its bitter overcooked taste down like a necessary medicine. It was time to say good morning.

Richard made his way down the hallway toward the basement door. His shoes clicked their way across the scarred dusty wood, creaking on every third or fourth board, reminding him of her many restless late nights while he had tried to sleep. Everything was better then, better before *it* happened.

She had been working late one fall night at Kranston's Department Store. She was the manager and had let her staff go home early before she locked up. When she arrived in the darkened parking garage, someone attacked and raped her.

She was left in tears and a torn dress, with a bruise on her eye, a split lip, and a few bite marks that were later swabbed for saliva at the hospital. Richard could have gone his entire life without ever needing to know the contents of a police rape kit. In the end, due to lack of semen evidence they called it an attempted rape. That rephrasing of the words didn't make him feel any better. It was still an attack, a violation of the love of his life. The hospital kept her overnight for observation and released her the next day. The police investigation, of course, turned up nothing. But Richard knew somewhere *he* was out there, roaming free.

Thinking about the sick bastard made Richard seethe with rage. His pulse quickened and his stomach twisted itself into little knots that flipped from top to bottom like an uncontrollable electrical charge of hate. He had wanted nothing more than to track that motherfucker down and end his life, slow and torturous. A thousand revenge scenarios filled his head with nightmarish images. He relished the thought of dragging it out. Cutting off his balls to start and ending it by shoving a .44 Magnum up his ass and playing Russian Roulette. His head swam with prison-rule shankings and shower rapes and how to bring as much pain as possible to another man with household products. Thinking about what he would do was the only way Richard could stop himself from going insane. He had wanted it so bad he could taste it.

For weeks after the incident, she wandered around the house in a sick depression, complaining of stomach cramps that got worse at night. She couldn't sleep, and he couldn't blame her. She drank bottles of red wine to lull her mind, but it didn't help. Things only got worse. He wanted to grab her and tell her it would be okay; that he would drive away the demons and make her happy again, but she would only scream "get away" or "leave me the hell alone." He just wanted to help, but she would have none of it. It was the most horrible feeling of helplessness he had ever encountered and his wife of seventeen years was never the same.

Richard made his way down the hall to the basement door. He unlocked two deadbolts and toed away the towel at the bottom with his loafer. The smell took no more than a second to reach his nose; he was going to have to do something about that. He swung the door slowly open. The wood around the deadbolts was stressed and cracked. He worried that anyone with a good foot would be able to kick it open if they really tried.

The stairs creaked out the morning song that he listened to everyday at this time. The stench was awful; he thanked his lucky stars that their house was a bit more off the beaten path and his nearest neighbor nosey Miss Henderson's house was a good football throw away. Miss Henderson, although nosey as hell, had been a good neighbor at times. She had offered her help in any way she could after the attack.

He made his way across the cold concrete floor, squinting his tired eyes in the dim light. Everyday it was the same. His stomach felt twisted and empty like it was gripped in an icy fist. His hands trembled in a weak fear, his mind tried to deny what his eyes saw. But everyday they saw the same thing. His beloved wife of seventeen years, the one he could not live without, the one he would do *anything* for, dead.

He approached her body, carefully laid out on a couch they had bought when they first got the house. He reached out toward her lifeless hand and took it tenderly into his own. She was ice cold and he involuntarily shivered. He wished that he would feel a pulse in her wrist just once.

He sat there holding her hand with tears in his eyes. His chest heaved in great sobs as he stroked her hair and spoke in kind soft tones, as if to speak louder would harm her in some way. "Come back to me, April, please come back. I'm a mess without you." He gripped her hand a little tighter. "The house is a wreck. There's nothing to eat. I miss you so much. I'm not even whole without you." He dropped her hand in anger. "Look at me I'm a fucking shallow husk. I'm nothing! I want it to be the way it was before. Why can't it just be like it was before?" He got down on his knees and leaned in close enough to kiss her pale lips and lovingly stroke her hair. "Just open your eyes and tell me that you'll love me forever." He stared at the lifeless lids and waited for a twitch or any sign at all, but there was nothing. In his rational mind he knew his words fell on deaf ears. They were never to be heard by her or God or anyone. If he had not heard them himself, they might not have even existed. He thought of the tree falling in the woods, and if no one is around to hear it does it make a sound? Yes, it did, and he knew it well—the sound of futility.

He sat there for hours, not sure of time anymore. The battery on his watch had died weeks ago, but he still wore it everyday; it had been a gift from April. He got up off of his knees and carefully laid her hand back to her chest. He kissed her lightly on the forehead and spoke again in a soft, loving tone, "Sweet dreams, princess. I have to go out now, but I'll be back in a while." He closed his eyes as a hot tear burned its way forward. He pushed it back down and tried instead to think of the good times. He thought about Hawaii and how happy she'd looked as she swam with the dolphins. He thought about the way she would smile wickedly when she was pulling a prank over on him. The way she arched her back and closed her eyes in passion when they made love, or how he missed her tender kisses and slow loving strokes, the way she ran her hands along his body. He missed everything except the end times. He tried not to think of how she looked the night he had to put her in the basement.

At the store, Richard picked up the few things he needed from his mental list. Seeing that other people actually existed outside his squalid life reminded him that he was starved for conversation. He would nod and smile as best he could, but he knew his appearance alone would have them talking in hushed tones over by the produce section the moment his back was to them. He smiled at the cashier and paid with credit. They hadn't denied the card yet, so he knew there must still be room on it. April had always done the bookkeeping.

On his way out, a disheveled man looking for handouts caught his attention. He had a dirty red flannel shirt that was torn at the bottom and jeans that hadn't seen a washer in forever. Perched on top of his greasy head was a John Deere baseball cap, its green not only sun-faded but also overrun with years of adjustments from filthy hands. Richard figured the man had probably found it on the street somewhere; perhaps it had blown off of a gardener's truck. The bum—for lack of a better term—stuck his hand out toward Richard. "Can ya spare some change?"

The old joke of "change comes from within" came quickly to mind first, but he figured the man wouldn't find it all that funny. Instead Richard reached into his pocket and came out with nothing more than a handful of lint and a crumpled receipt.

He stared at the receipt in the palm of his hand for a good moment. "I'll do ya one better," he said smiling. "When was the last time you had a home-cooked meal?"

The bum looked at him with a shock that sparked the tiniest of fires in the beaten man's eyes. "Are you puttin' me on, fella?"

"No," he replied.

"You mean to say you're invitin' me over?"

Richard glanced around. "Yes."

"Well . . . I don't know what to say." The bum raised his eyebrows in astonishment.

Richard knew it had probably been some time since someone had given him such a kind offer. "Say yes. I could use the conversation, and maybe you can even help me around the house."

The man stood up straight and proud, smiling. "Alright then, I appreciate it. Name's Mitch," he said as he stuck out his dirty hand in thanks.

Richard grabbed it enthusiastically while switching the bags to his other hand. "Nice to meet ya, Mitch."

Mitch offered to carry the bags, but Richard denied him as he led him to the car. He stuffed the three small bags of groceries into the backseat and leaned across, unlocking the passenger door. Mitch gingerly got into the car favoring one leg over the other. Richard hadn't noticed his slight limp before that.

The drive home had been informative; everyone has a story to tell and Mitch was no exception. A vet, turned drug addict, turned homeless man, forced to live on the streets and scraping for everything he could get his hands on. No family left, no friends, and no job. It was a sad story, but for Richard it was nice to hear someone else for a change talk about how their life had turned to shit. He thought for a moment about comparing stories one on one with the vet, but decided against it. He didn't really want to talk about his life. He was, after all, still living it.

They arrived at the house and Mitch carried the bags in. Richard prayed the old bum wouldn't notice the smell emanating from the basement door and ask any questions, or get nosey like old Miss Henderson. He just wanted to have a nice quiet dinner.

Mitch showered, shaved, and put on a borrowed pair of Richard's old sweatpants and a T-shirt. He walked into the kitchen a new man. Richard thought he looked a damn sight better than he himself did. "I really can't thank you enough," Mitch said.

Richard smiled and poured him a cup of hot coffee from a fresh brewed pot. "I think the world would be a better place if we just all took a moment and helped each other out. Cream?"

"No thanks."

Richard handed him the steaming cup. "Hell, by coming here you're helping me out."

"Really?" Mitch paused a moment and smiled. "I didn't want to say anything earlier, but . . . you do look a little rough around the edges."

"Believe me, I know, Mitch. It's been a real shit couple of months."

"I'll drink to that, brother," Mitch raised his cup and sipped. He looked deep into his coffee and pursed his lips together; he almost looked embarrassed. "Got a little something we could spice this up with?"

Richard grinned.

They always asked.

"I bet we could find something." He went to the cupboard above the coffee maker, rummaged around for a moment and pulled down an old bottle of Irish cream from the very top. He gave the bottle a little shake, topped off Mitch's coffee with it, and handed him a spoon.

Mitch gave the coffee a quick stir. "Am I drinkin' alone?" he asked.

"Never touch the stuff," Richard lied.

"Suit yourself." Mitch set down the spoon on the counter and took a long pull from the cup, smacking his lips in satisfaction. "Damn, that's good. It's been a while since I had a *real* coffee."

It took about fifteen minutes and a few more details about Mitch's life on the road before his cup was drained. He held it out to Richard and gave him the *fill-er-up* nod. Richard obliged and handed back the cup, again topped off with the dusty old bottle of Irish cream.

Mitch took it in his hands and paused with his face over it, inhaling its rich candied scent. "You see, everybody owns their problems, I *own* my problems, that's what makes them mine." He paused and hungrily slurped down some of the coffee. "My son, God rest his soul, meant *everything* to me. He was the most beautiful kid in the world. He could swim like a fish, took to the water more naturally than anyone I ever saw in my life. So my wife and I decided to get him involved in the swim team. He took first place in nearly everything he tried. The kid was a fuckin' genius."

Mitch took a long drink from the cup. He blinked and shook his head. "I was so proud . . . but not proud enough to put the bottle down. It's just me, it's how I'm wired. One night we were driving home from a swim meet. I musta swerved lanes or something. I didn't see the headlights dead on until it was too late." Mitch drunkenly slapped his hands together. "POW! Everything changed. I musta been out for a while." He put his head down and then lifted it slowly.

Richard saw the man's eyes fogging over and knew the Irish cream was taking its effect.

"I remember waking up. Glass shattered and I couldn't move my leg. Stephen was laying there clutching my hand . . ." Mitch lifted his hand and looked at it quizzically. "His little fingers were so cold . . . I can almost still feel 'em. He tried to say something to me, but I couldn't hear. The sirens drowned him out, those fuckin' cops and zose fuckin' sirens, fuckin' . . ." His hand dropped heavily to the table. "Can you understand what I'm sayin'? I couldn't fuckin' hear what my boy's dying words were 'cause of zose fuckin' sirens." He paused, his head slumped low on his shoulders. He took a deep breath and Richard could hear the man sobbing softly. "I'll never know what my boy tried . . . to tell me . . . the night I killed him."

Richard felt the man's pain and wanted to reach out to him. "He probably forgave you, Mitchell."

Mitch raised his head; tears had streaked softly down his cheek. "After he was gone, I just gave up . . . you know . . . you love someone so much that when that person is taken from you nothing else matters. You'd do *anything* to bring them back. *Anything* to hold on . . . *anything*."

Richard smiled and nodded his head. "Thank you, Mitch. Thank you for sharing that with me."

Mitch wiped the tears from his face and swallowed down the last bit of coffee. He glanced around the room and noticed the picture of April on the refrigerator. "Your . . . wife?" he asked.

"Yes," Richard said softly, folding his hands in front of him.

Mitch weaved slightly in his chair. "When do I . . . get . . . to . . . meet 'er?"

"Soon."

Mitch's eyes rolled back as he pitched face first into the table, shattering the empty cup.

On the last evening before everything in his life changed, he had come home from the store and found April sitting on the tile floor in the bathroom covered in blood. It was smeared everywhere—her nightgown, her neck, hands, even around her mouth. Her eyes were glazed and sated as if she were drunk, and her head lolled back and forth like it was held there by worn out springs. He asked her repeatedly what had happened, but she couldn't tell him. She just sat there grinning and bloody, staring blankly with innocent-looking eyes, dead to the world around her. Her skin was cold and clammy to the touch. He put her immediately in the shower and tried to warm her as he scrubbed her down. He searched all over for the telltale slash marks of a suicide attempt, but found none.

It was shortly thereafter that he found nosey Miss Henderson stuffed in the closet with her throat torn out. Later that night, when April viciously attacked and tried to bite him, he was forced to lock her in the basement and listen to her wail.

The thudding against the basement door was louder than usual. Richard turned up the stereo. "Mars, the Bringer of War" from Holst's *The Planets*—one of April's favorites—boomed out of the stereo she had gotten him for his thirty-eighth birthday. The basement door thudded heavily again, almost in tune with the bombastic timpani drums and overpowering strings. The third dead bolt he had added to the top of the door while Mitchell was unconscious was thankfully doing its job.

"Open this door you sick fuck!" Mitch screamed.

They always screamed when they woke up. He doubted it was the sight of his sweet wife that drove them insane with rage, or the fact that he had *kidnapped* them—such a strong term. It was probably the growing pile of corpses in the corner of the basement he had yet to deal with. No doubt it was the first thing they smelled when they woke up. It had taken him a while to perfect the amount of Rohypnol he used in the bottle, and the first two consequently never even woke up. He knew that had displeased her and he wanted his sweet April to be happy more than anything.

He knew Mitch understood deep down. He had talked about doing anything you could to bring back a loved one.

Anything to hold on. For the first time in a long time, Richard knew he was doing the right thing. It didn't matter what came out of Mitch's mouth now. It was how he had spoken when he was being honest that mattered. Richard glanced at the clock on the wall, dimly lit by the remains of the setting sun. Then he smiled as Mitch's rage-filled screams slowly turned into a terrified, high-pitched keening.

LATE CHECK-IN

VINCE CHURCHILL

God spit and rain streaked across my face shield. I concentrated on the curvy black ribbon of highway, the speed of my bike making the hypnotic flashes of the yellow dashes separating the two lanes run together as one endless strip. Somewhere behind the menacing bank of thunderclouds, the sun sagged toward the horizon. End of the day shadows draped across the road like spilled oil.

Raised in the Midwest but having made my home on the West Coast, I had forgotten summer's fickleness. One moment it would be sunny, with more mosquitoes than clouds in the sky. Suddenly a thunderstorm rolled in and had you running to close the windows on your car.

The wind had picked up and I could feel the bike fighting through every curve. My hands began to ache from gripping the handlebars.

I tried my best to ignore the dim glow from the cycle's gauges. Fucking no-name discount battery. I vowed that the next time I saw my buddy I'd kill him for talking me into buying this piece of shit. We both should have known better with me planning to cross the country in early spring. Damn.

As day edged into night, storm clouds continued to crowd up behind me like bullies, but I ignored them despite the threat of even worse weather. In a bad marriage people learned to ignore all kinds of shit.

As an experienced motorcycle rider, weather has never been a problem for me. A decade-plus survivor of Los Angeles traffic, I wasn't sweating it. A little rain, whatever. I'd ridden through fucking El Niño. Ain't nothing in Tennessee gonna match that. And no rain suit for me either. Uh-uh. The plastic pants always made me feel like I was going to slide right off the seat. And when you added in the humidity, the suit wrung sweat out of me like a one hundred and five degree fever. No, my only mistake was deciding to dip down into Tennessee to enjoy the scenic surroundings on my way to Miami. Should've just cut straight across the country, then followed the Atlantic coast down into Florida. My heavy sigh clouded the lower part of the shield.

In the deepening shadows of the breathtaking Smoky Mountains, the highway snaked through forest and hills. I had to admit the scenery sometimes bordered on spectacular and certainly made the ride worthwhile, despite the extra hours I was putting in the saddle. Thinking about my mileage, I nearly zoomed past the gas station that appeared like a ghost to my right. I hit both brakes and the bike skidded on the wet pavement, but I coaxed it enough to turn into the second driveway. The bike felt skittish in the station's gravel, but I managed to pull up to the pair of uncovered pumps. Thankfully the rain backed off to less than a drizzle.

I eased myself off my '81 Honda cruiser and cautiously allowed the bike to lean onto its kickstand. I looked up at the sign. **EFREM'S GAS**. Simple and eloquent, with just the right touch of backwoods flavor. The sign was pre-neon with just a hooded, big bulb shining down on it. By its shabby looks, I was surprised it worked. Probably weren't many customers to attract after dark anyway.

I swung my head toward the station as I tugged my chinstrap loose. The place had seen better days. What paint remained was sun bleached and peeling. A pair of garages was attached to the office, the windows so dirty they screamed the service department had long been abandoned. A rusty blue pick-up truck sat in front of one of the bay doors. The gas pumps had the look of original issue from the fifties and were covered in rust. A plump black spider was weaving a dew-covered web in the handle of the diesel pump. Oh yeah, the station was crawling with customers.

A frail, ancient looking man eased from his seat and wobbled down from the station's porch. His chair still rocked in his absence. A lightning flash made me flinch, and for a moment it looked like there were two men: One still rocked in his chair, chin to his chest, peacefully asleep; the second man, his twin, ambled toward me on wobbly uncertain legs. I blinked again and there was just the one approaching. Face half hidden under his cap, what I could see was creased and cut deep with wrinkles. His throat looked like it belonged on a turkey. I glanced beyond the man, looking over the building. Was gramps the only person here? Traffic had been non-existent for miles so this could very well be a one-man operation. Lord knows I wasn't looking for some *Deliverance*-type action. It suddenly seemed like a good idea to leave my helmet on.

The man's name patch might have been the only thing clean about his overalls. But it did confirm I was in the presence of the owner. Efrem offered a wave along with a friendly smile that was as much gap as it was teeth. He stepped past the pumps, eyeing the cycle with appreciation.

"Good evening. What can I do ya for?"

Behind the tinted face shield I returned his smile. "Hey, don't bother yourself there. I can pump my own gas, sir."

His hand beat mine to the pump. His head wagged on a pencil thin neck. "Day I can't pump gas is the day I lay down in my grave and make my wife a happy woman."

I quickly opened my tank cap and let Efrem do his thing. While the gas was pumping, he pulled a rag from his back pocket and cleaned the side view mirrors with a practiced swirl. He swiped the headlight too. He nodded up toward my head.

"Nice motorcycle you got here."

"Thanks. She's my baby."

"Know whatcha mean." He tilted his head back toward the truck in the drive. I acknowledged his ride with an approving nod. "Looks ain't everythin'. She gotta put out too." The old man's cackle was too infectious to ignore. I got caught up and chuckled right along. "I call my ol' girl Mabeline."

"Pretty name."

He glanced up at the sky behind me as if for the first time that day. He studied it for a few moments. "Got a real pisser comin' through. You might wanna consider gettin' off the road. Don't wanna mess 'round and get struck by lightning, such."

I glanced back at the dark clouds and shrugged. "Well, I'm not gonna worry about Mother Nature. I'll either outrun her or she'll chase me down and go on about her business."

He nodded again, resigned to let me make my own decision, but in a moment was squinting to try to look through my face shield.

"You want me to hit that visor for ya? You got plenty bugs on it."

"I'm okay, thanks. Makes the ride more challenging."

"Well, it ain't gonna be a good night to get left out on the road."

I frowned. "Left on the road?"

The old man nodded. "The headlight on your motorcycle weren't too bright when you swung in. I could put it on the trickle charger tonight while you got yourself a room down at the Harvest Moon."

I shook my head. "Thanks for the offer, but I need to be getting down the road a piece." I blinked at the wording of my own reply.

Efrem shrugged. "Suit yourself. But after the Harvest Moon, there ain't no services for quite a spell. Not a lot of traffic on this road neither. 'Specially at night. No need putting yourself in a bind, son."

I looked back at the dark sky, and then slowly took in my surroundings. Night was falling and the forest looked much more ominous standing still than it did at seventy-five miles per hour. Maybe the old guy had a point. I turned my head toward him and he was smiling. His mouth was a starving dentist's dream. The smell of tobacco wafted as he spoke.

"I can give you a ride to the Harvest Moon and swing by and getcha on my way to open up tomorrow morning. I eat half my meals there in trade for gasoline. They make a real tasty pecan pie."

I took a deep breath, thinking.

"Over the years I've dropped many a motorist off there while I worked on their cars. Wouldn't be no trouble for me, young man."

Getting some fresh juice in my battery wouldn't be a bad idea. I flipped open my visor so he could hear me better.

"You know, sir, I think I might just take you up on that offer. Ummm, is the Harvest Moon, you know, uh . . ."

"I think twenty will get you a soft bed and some of that room service, Mr. . . ." The service station owner looked up at me as he pulled the nozzle from the tank. I searched the man's face for any hint of surprise or animosity at me being black. If there was, he masked it well.

"Uh, it's Kyle, Kyle Mix."

He replaced the nozzle, and then swiped his hand down his pants before offering it to me.

"Efrem Johnson. Nice to meetcha." His clasp was firm, quick, and cool. A shiver coursed through me. "Pull the bike up over here, and then we'll take Mabeline on down to the motel." Then big drops fell from the sky, and the cackling pump jockey danced toward the garage and I sprang on the bike and followed.

Less than half an hour later, Efrem steered Mabeline into the parking lot of the Harvest Moon Motel. The place was dark, including its roadside sign. It looked closed on first glance, but a dim light bled through the office curtains. Despite its outward appearance, the truck ran surprisingly quiet and smooth. Mabeline pulled to a stop and I hopped out with my backpack and helmet. It was raining hard, so once I opened the door I was moving. I splashed toward the motel entrance and was happily surprised when the front door opened for me. I stopped a step inside, shaking the rain from my jacket. As the door closed behind me I looked up, a "thank you" at the tip of my tongue. But no one was there. My gaze carried across the shadowy lobby to the front desk.

There was a man behind the check-in counter, smiling as if he'd just told himself a joke. He was younger than me, maybe half my mid-forties. *How'd he get across the room so fast?* He straightened his nametag—"Jimmy"—and continued to beam his pearly whites. I couldn't tell if the smile was forced or practiced, like a kindergartner on class picture day. The clerk couldn't quite mask the slight twitch at the corner of his mouth. Some southern hospitality setting in.

"Welcome to the Harvest Moon. Do you have any luggage I can help you with?"

I shook my head. "Nope. I'm traveling light." Then I realized the minimal light was coming from a few candles. The corners of the lobby were dead dark. The front desk clerk noticed my concerned expression.

"Sorry for the inconvenience, sir. The storm is playing havoc with our power. I have been authorized to only charge you half rate for the room if you choose to stay with us."

I nodded, moving to the counter. The way he said "sir" didn't seem quite genuine. I tried to push it aside, but now the clerk's whole demeanor was suspect.

"Sounds like a deal to me." I heard Mabeline's tires grind through the gravel drive and pull away.

"Glad to hear it, Mr. . . ."

"Mix, Kyle Mix."

The clerk paused as if the name didn't fit me. "Excellent. Well, let's get you a room so you can get out of those wet things, shall we? And if we hurry, you might even be able to squeeze in a hot shower." We smiled at each other, and I know mine was forced. I almost succeeded in ignoring the shadows creeping in from every corner. Almost.

Minutes later I left the front desk clerk and followed my candle's light down the long corridor. For not being all that late, the place was eerily quiet. I shivered from a chill as I passed room number 9. A few steps further and I was at my room. I unlocked room number 11, pushed open the door, and tossed the key on the bed.

"Home sweet home," I sighed, glancing around the gloom. The room was nothing special, but appeared clean and well kept. The sight of the bathroom instantly stirred my bladder. I suddenly really needed to go. I set the candle on the nightstand and dropped my backpack on the bed.

I stepped into the bathroom and pushed the door closed. Before I undid my belt, I was swallowed up in darkness.

"Geez . . ." I spoke, fumbling for my zipper. I stood for a moment, letting my eyes adjust, but the darkness didn't seem to ease. Then I noticed the room's small window. The dusty frosted glass barely allowed any light. I took a step to my right and used the small crank to separate the glass slants. A little night shone in. It was just enough to see my porcelain target, and I was relieved in more ways than one when the initial splash meant I hit water and not tile floor.

I shook off and flushed, then stepped out into the room. I couldn't help but jump a little at the figure standing at the room's threshold. My lone flickering candle cast him as a human shadow. The desk clerk leaned just into the candle's light and I let out my breath. The name "Jimmy" gleamed from his silver nameplate.

"I'm sorry, Mr. Mix. I don't mean to disturb you. With the power out the diner is closed for the night. We're hoping it'll be open for breakfast in the morning. If you'd like to enjoy something from the vending machines, we'd be happy to reimburse you for any snacks when you check out. If you need anything, just pick up the phone and dial zero. I'll be on duty all night."

"Thank you. I really appreciate it . . ."

THUMP.

A single pound from the next room. I looked at the wall for a few moments, puzzled at the odd sound. I looked back up at the clerk. "What was . . . ?" The doorway was empty. The clerk was gone. I frowned, crossing the room to the open door. I peeked into the hall. Nothing. I glanced each way, but there was only gloomy darkness.

I stepped back into the room and pushed the door closed. After a moment's thought, I pushed the slide bolt into place.

I took no time stripping out of my damp clothing and headed for a hot shower. I carried the candle into the bathroom and sat it on the toilet tank. I closed the door behind me and rotated the knob so the door locked. I wanted no part of a *Psycho* shower murder moment. Fuck that.

I started the water and waited for it to get hot. I glanced at the candle, watching the flame flicker. A memory from my marriage crept into my mind, but I shoved it away angrily. I didn't want to think about her, and I didn't wanna get hard thinking about our old shit. She held enough power over me as it was.

I mixed some cold into the hot stream, and then stepped under the spray. God, it felt good. I slid the ocean-patterned curtain into place and went about getting clean. I wasn't under the water a minute when the phone rang. It rang and rang, finally stopping just as my irritation grew serious enough to consider getting out. I lathered up and rinsed, and then dipped my head under the spray to get the shampoo out. A faint knocking sounded. Probably the front desk clerk trying to call me, then stopping by with a power or diner update. He would have to wait. The knocking ceased and I enjoyed the water on my skin. As I closed my eyes to rinse out my second shampoo, I jolted to more knocking, but it sounded like it was on the bathroom door. I wiped my eyes and stared at the seashells and starfish on the shower curtain.

"Uh, I'm in the shower. I'll be out in a minute." Then I realized I didn't know who I was talking to, much less who would have entered my locked room and . . .

I blinked soap from the corner of my eye, and then I swear I heard the creak of the doorknob as if someone was testing to see if it was locked. I cursed under my breath, half mad and half freaked. I quickly washed the rest of the soap away from my face and turned off the water. I hesitated for a moment, and then pulled back the curtain enough to peek out. I froze at the sight.

The bathroom door was ajar.

I stared into the few inches of darkness between the door and the frame. Dormant boogeyman fears raised every hair on my body.

I stood like a statue until I got goose bumps. Finally my mind and body thawed enough for me to reach out for my towel, my eyes never leaving the frightening gap. I drew the towel into the shower like a rattlesnake handler.

I dabbed at my face, then hurriedly slung the towel around my waist. I stepped out of the tub and reached for the doorknob but found myself hesitating, my fingers just inches away. I couldn't see a thing on the other side of the door. I swallowed hard, and then took a deep breath.

"Oh fuck it," I growled, jerking open the door. I stepped into the room, the candle held out for light.

The room was empty. I moved straight toward the door. The slide bolt was still engaged. I stood staring at it, mind working over the possibilities. And then slowly I turned toward the closed accordion closet door. For a moment my blood ran cold. Casually, I walked back toward the bathroom. As I passed the closet I suddenly grabbed the handle and jerked the separator out of the way.

Empty closet.

"Fuck me," I whispered, glancing around the room. I considered looking under the bed, but decided I felt silly enough, though the truth was I was still more than a little creeped out.

I slipped under the sheets, cool and clean and slightly stiff. My nerves were now worse than before I took a shower, but at least I'd gotten the road dust off. And the hot spray reminded me just how tired I really was. As my head hit the flat pillow, I glanced at the phone. I should probably call Jessica, let her know where I was. My arm flinched as if it might reach out, but it stayed draped across my middle. Fuck her. She wanted the divorce, so why the fuck should she care if I was okay and where I was at? Pain sliced my heart and I sniffled, wounds bursting back open. I rose enough to blow out the candle.

THUMP.

I froze, the smoke from the extinguished wick wafting back across my face. I held my breath, staring into the darkness, waiting for another sound. Moments passed before I let out my breath. What the fuck was that? My nerves were jangling and I was exhausted. The day's ride obviously took more out of me than I thought. That was it. With another couple of long riding days ahead, I needed to get some rest. I forced myself to close my eyes and think about Miami. The L.A. of the east. Ocean, beaches, hot women. The perfect place to be while my lawyer tied up the divorce and my soon-to-be ex moved out.

RING! RING!

The phone startled me so badly one of my calves cramped. I rolled around as if gunshot.

"Shit! Shit! Shit! Shit!" The phone's double ring blared again and I rolled toward it, reaching as my other hand grabbed at my lower leg. "Hello?" I asked.

There was quiet whispering. Loud enough to be distinguished as voices but too soft to make out what they were saying. "Hello?" I asked again, and the whispering changed to quiet, child-like giggling. I frowned, suddenly sure it was a stupid prank. Maybe bored kids in another room calling up other guests.

"Whatever," I spoke and moved the phone from my ear to hang up. In that moment the giggling became loud, full-out laughter. A shiver rolled up my spine and I jerked the phone back to my ear. The laughter was no longer child-like and the tone was not humorous. It was malignant like a mad clown. I slammed the phone down in an instant of panic, and then grabbed it up again. There was no laughter, but there was also no dial tone. It was just dead air. Hesitantly, I spoke into the mouthpiece.

"Hello?" There was no answer. Nothing.

THUMP!

I jolted, twisting to look at the wall. Jesus . . .

THUMP! There it was again. I pushed myself upright, almost forgetting the phone was still in my hand.

THUMP!

What in God's name . . . ? And then it happened again. And again. And again.

THUMP! THUMP! THUMP! THUMP! THUMP!

I stared at the wall, my breathing getting louder, faster. I could feel my heart pounding in my chest and my imagination began to search the darkness . . . the darkness surrounding the bed and the darkness in my head where nightmares took root. And suddenly it hit me. What the pounding was.

A monster's heartbeat.

I rolled over and slammed the phone down, then grabbed it back up. No dial tone. Suddenly the mad laughter started again.

"STOP IT!" I shouted. And the laughter stopped. The line was quiet. Then suddenly there was a garbled voice. Voices, actually. I couldn't tell if they were male or female, young or old. But there was something wrong about the collection of them. Hearing them made my nerves continue to feel like plucked guitar strings.

"Aren't you glad you got out of the rain?"

I stared at the dark lump of the phone, fear slipping into my veins like ice water.

"Who are you?" My voice was quiet and small.

"You shouldn't have come here. Now it's too late . . ." The line cut off and the dial tone returned before I could respond. I set the receiver into its cradle, my attention drawn back to the wall. The heartbeat continued slow and steady.

"Fuck this," I mumbled, flinging the covers away. I didn't even bother to re-light the candle. I quickly got dressed, ignoring the cool damp of my clothes. I skipped the socks and just pulled on my boots. I grabbed up my backpack and stepped out into the dark hall. Even in the deep gloom it looked a mile long, telescoping in length. "What the hell's going on?" I whispered. I took a cautious step, and then decided to jog. But it was forever before I drew even with neighboring room number 9. Why wasn't I down the hall and out of the motel? The pounding was deafening and I tried to run harder, but for whatever reason I wasn't covering any ground. It was like I was under water, and I strained to move forward. And when I heard the click of the door opening to room number 9, I was torn like the passerby of a major car wreck. Despite my mind's urging me not to look, I couldn't stop my head from turning, drawn by the source of the noise hidden in the darkness beyond.

I stared as the door creaked open and fear prickled my skin. I suddenly didn't want to see what lurked in the room, what was causing that noise. But my head wouldn't turn away and a little-used part of my subconscious prepared me for something far beyond the realm of normal star-filled, good sleeping nights.

Room number 9 was darker than the hallway. There were no shadows or any traces of gloom. It was nothing less than hell-pit black. When the door was half open the darkness inside began to force its way into the hall. Shapeless at first, the black entity molded itself into a hand. And then it made another. And another. And another. A mob of hands, some as small as a child's and some as large as an ape's, reached and clutched, stretching from beneath shadows that might have been tar. All reaching, reaching out to me.

For me.

A foul stench forced itself into my nose and lungs. Death's fragrance was unmistakable.

I heard a scream and jumped before I realized it was my own. Then I was running fast, too fast. The hallway blurred as I flew down the corridor. The mad laughter snapped at my heels, echoing in the darkness.

Suddenly, I was in the lobby, the flames from the candles causing shadows to dance on the walls like a tribal celebration. I caught a glimpse of the desk clerk, standing behind the counter and grinning exactly as he had been when I first arrived. But then he was eclipsed by the hulking form of a man on the customer side of the reception desk. The desk clerk's painted-on grin slipped, and his whole expression wavered with worry. There was something in the hulk's hand, but in the instant I couldn't make it out. Suddenly, the big man with "Morris Trucking" stitched across the back of his jacket whipped a crowbar flat-edge head high. The rough tip caught the desk clerk across the throat, tearing deep into the flesh. His head flipped back like a loose toupee and blood sprayed the air, splashing the nearest wall. The red was so vivid I flinched from the sight as much as the disgust of the blood somehow getting on me. Even as the desk clerk's body sagged out of sight, the hulk was moving around the counter, the crowbar raised for another swing. The sight was paralyzing, and my heart seized as if in the crushing grip of someone's fist. My legs suddenly lost their strength and buckled. Out of control, I pitched forward, my arms flailing for balance. My last staggering steps had carried me out of control across the lobby and I watched as the edge of the front desk rushed toward my face.

A blink before I heard the snapping of my neck, I swear the candles blew out and the Harvest Moon Motel became a tomb.

I never felt my body hit the floor, but my last sight was death's darkness settling over me, smothering me like a cold wet pillow.

I stand in the lobby's picture window, peering through the grimy glass at all the police activity. I've stopped trying to speak with the cops. It's obvious no one can hear me, and I turn my back on my lifeless body as soon as someone shakes open a body bag. From behind the counter, the clerk grins silently at no one in particular, his head firmly back in place. The murderous hulk is nowhere to be seen; perhaps he's returned to room number 9. Strangely, I no longer feel afraid.

A highway patrol car enters the parking lot from the highway and brakes hard in the gravel. A trooper steps from his vehicle, glancing at the rising sun. There is already a pair of county patrol cars and an ambulance in the parking lot. A county deputy looking like he should be shopping for a prom tux nervously approaches the late arrival. I lean closer to the glass hoping to hear their conversation. I've already tried to walk outside, but I can't seem to cross the threshold.

The trooper nods toward the motel. "Whatcha got?"

The Adam's apple of the young officer bobs as he gathers himself.

"It's all pretty weird stuff, sir. A deputy stopped for gas about an hour ago and found Efrem Johnson dead out front in his rocking chair. We're not sure for how long, but I drove by to check on him late yesterday afternoon and he was fine. It doesn't appear like it was a murder or robbery or anything. Old as he was, probably just gave out. But there was a motorcycle with a California plate registered to an Aaron Kyle Mix of Los Angeles parked at the station."

The trooper glances past the other officer at the motel. "What's that got to do with this?"

"Well, I was on my way to Efrem's station when I passed the Harvest Moon here and something seemed funny. I wheeled around for a look-see and found the front door swinging wide open." The kid cop glances at the dark entrance. He looks apprehensive at best. "This place been closed a couple years, right?"

The trooper nods and looks like bad memories are tumbling into his mind like a spilled trunk of broken toys. "Yeah, ever since the trucker . . ."

The young officer steps closer and his voice drops low. "Is it true about that fella sitting in room number 9 bouncing the head of Jimmy Stark off the wall like a damn basketball?"

I fall back a step, the words buzzing in my mind. I can't help but glance at Jimmy behind the counter. The clerk's head swivels like a puppet to face me, but I jerk my head back around to face out the window. I ignore his reflection. I can't look at that grotesque grin any more.

The trooper stares at the deputy, his eyes shielded by his sunglasses. I can tell he's imagining that damned thumping sound in his head right then and there. The youthful officer continues.

"I mean, it ain't every day in Seviar County we get a nut job butchering umpteen folks . . . How many people were in the motel then?"

"There were fourteen victims," the trooper's voice is monotone.

The deputy shakes his head and then spits, but a little hangs to his bottom lip. "Jesus H. . . . My cousin Juney went to school with Jimmy Stark. They were on the baseball team together. Shit."

The trooper doesn't speak as he moves toward the motel. The deputy falls in at his side and continues.

"Anyway, I could see Mix dead in the lobby from the entrance. His head was twisted around like a bottle top. Looks like he might have fallen, caught the edge of the front desk. Crunch . . ." The deputy looks down, kicks at the gravel as he walks. "The guy's eyes were open, staring . . . his expression was fucked up, like he died seeing the devil or something."

The trooper stops walking as the paramedics suddenly appear from inside. They roll a dark plastic shrouded body on their transport cart. The trooper frowns and begins to think out loud.

"But the place has been closed . . . chained up . . . to keep the kids out . . ."

The baby-faced deputy shrugs and sighs. "No idea how he got in or what he was doing. Can you imagine going in there after dark? With no power? Hell, no. I'd rather live with my retard mother-in-law and rub her smelly feet every night."

The trooper glances at the deputy, and then stares long and hard at the abandoned motel. He takes a tentative step across the motel's entrance, then suddenly turns and starts back to his patrol car. He speaks under his breath.

"I wouldn't be caught dead in that place."

But, watching the highway patrol car, then the ambulance leave the parking lot, I know I have.

INSIDE OUT

LISA MAJEWSKI

Red chiffon drapes floated away from the window, nudged forward by a persistent breeze. A full moon peered through the opening, bearing silent witness to the attractive couple lying on the bed. Dozens of black candles in varying shapes and sizes illuminated the room; the largest two, more than five feet in height, stood sentinel.

Connor placed his hand tenderly on Sophia's neck and she responded by laying her palm against his cheek. He leaned in, bringing his lips to her delicate ear.

"Sweetheart," he whispered, "if you put your hand between my face and the camera one more time, I will *break* it off." Sophia's eyes widened and she jerked her hand away as if burned by his blistering words.

"Soph, put your left hand on his right bicep," the photographer called from behind the camera.

Sophia placed her fingers lightly on his arm.

"What the hell is that?" Angela asked, lowering the Nikon to her hip. "The heat just nose-dived in here. Grab his arm with some passion, girl."

This time she clutched Connor's arm with more force than necessary. He didn't care. Anger was a passable substitute for lust—at least in a photo shoot.

"That's it. Great. Now if you could just smile," Angela chastised. "Look who you're in bed with, for Christ's sake."

Sophia smiled. She was paid to.

Angela took a few more shots before declaring it a wrap.

"Good work, Sophia. Connor, as always, perfection," she said. To the crew, Angela yelled, "Kill the wind, kill the moon." Nature's stand-ins were quietly snuffed out and several large Tungsten lights took their place.

Connor sprang out of the bed. Naked except for a pair of beige briefs, he stretched, allowing everyone a look at his chiseled frame. He knew they were fondling him with their eyes and welcomed the visual foreplay.

Connor sauntered over to a small group of models getting their hair styled. Even when surrounded by others, who by the luck of genetics or the precision of a scalpel were drop-dead gorgeous, Connor knew he stood out as an Adonis. He spoke to them for a few minutes and then grabbed a robe from the stack on the table. Before he even finished tying the belt Angela was at his side.

Connor planted a quick kiss on her cheek. She playfully slapped his ass, allowing her hand to linger a few seconds. He rewarded her with a perfunctory laugh.

"So? You never said anything about the set. What do you think?" Angela asked.

He took a deep breath and pretended to study his surroundings. "I'd say it's pretty spectacular," Connor replied, thinking spectacularly awful was more like it. "Very hip."

Angela nodded in agreement. "I knew you'd get it."

"You're the best," he said. "Can't wait till next time."

"About next time."

Here it comes. Everyone knew Connor was about to become the biggest thing in the modeling world and they all wanted a piece of the action; a piece of him.

"I hope you'll put in a rec for me at Genesis. We could really do some insane spreads for the campaign," she said.

Angela's desperation wafted from her like cheap perfume applied with a heavy hand. She disgusted Connor on every level.

"Hey, I don't have the gig yet," he replied. Connor was vying with two other models for the largest endorsement deal in history. The chosen man would be the face for every product put out by Genesis: clothes, watches, cologne. *Of course I'm going to get it. But I'll be damned before I work with any of these hacks again.*

"Oh please. It's a done deal," Angela said.

Connor looked at the annoying woman.

"So, you and me?" she asked.

"Absolutely," he replied

Angela clapped her hands together. "I'm tellin' you, it's gonna be *insane*."

Connor left her to daydream about a future photo shoot that would never happen and made his way back to the make-up table. He settled into the director's chair and sighed. It had been a long day and he was exhausted. Connor grabbed his satchel and rummaged around for some liquid lady. After a few seconds he found the small white bottle whose well-worn label promised relief from nasal congestion. It was false advertising, as Connor had altered the contents.

He twisted off the cap and sprayed a stream into each nostril, welcoming the familiar sting. He pinched his nose to keep the solution of cocaine and water from dripping out. Connor dropped the bottle back into the bag and pulled out his cell phone. He had fifteen missed messages. All were from his former manager, Neil.

The two had worked together almost nine years when Connor suddenly dumped the man last week. Neil wasn't incompetent; he just didn't have the right image. This business was all about impressions and perception, therefore Connor couldn't have a balding, overweight mid-level representative. He had already signed with the biggest agency in town when he broke the news to Neil. The man actually cried, a sign of weakness that only reinforced Connor's belief that he'd made the right decision.

He tossed his bag onto the floor and leaned back in his chair. Connor could see the set reflected in the mirror. Every bit of it was disgusting, but the worst part was the candles, all gnarled and misshapen. *Angie has really lost her mind.*

Connor grabbed the open beer perched next to a box of tissues. He tipped the bottle back, swallowing what tasted like backwash with a few hops. He grimaced and twisted around in his seat to look for the gopher who was supposed to take care of the models. He spied the rotund man ogling a voluptuous blonde whose strapless dress was losing its insincere battle with gravity.

"Hey. Matt. Can I get a beer?" Connor shouted.

Matt shuffled off to the craft service table where he grabbed two bottles and held them up for approval. Connor pointed at the dark beer. Matt nodded and put the other one back on ice. He shuffled on the return trip as well.

"Thanks, man," Connor said, grabbing the bottle and taking a sip.

"No problem. Hey, some of the guys were just wondering which of the girls you'll be taking home," Matt said.

"Is my reputation that bad?"

"Hell no. It's that good," Matt replied.

Connor laughed. "My agent's got me so tied up it'll be all business and no pleasure the next few weeks."

"Yeah, I heard you signed with Jeffrey Reynolds. That guy's badass. One of the best."

Connor nodded. *The best for the best.*

"So you don't even have time for one of these babes?" Matt asked, swinging his arm out to indicate all the choices.

"Sadly, no. But hey, you should definitely go for it." Connor loved to tease.

"I think I will. Catch ya later," Matt replied.

Connor watched as the pathetic troll waddled off to be humiliated. Actually, he did plan on taking someone to bed, but it wasn't going to be one of the models. To Connor, good-looking women were strictly arm candy; hot pieces you took to red carpet events and nightclubs. He just wasn't interested in having sex with them. The better looking the woman, the less she thought she needed to do in bed. At the end of the day he wanted to lay back and let the woman do all the work. The homely girls were grateful for his attention and were willing to do almost anything, no matter how degrading.

Connor spied his future conquest the moment he arrived on set. She quietly did her job and spoke only when someone asked her a question. Her pale complexion was not enhanced by the shapeless oatmeal-colored dress she wore. He could barely tell where skin ended and fabric began. She did not possess a single physical trait that made her stand out.

She was unremarkable. And she was perfect.

"So, you're the candle wrangler," Connor said.

She spun around at the sound of his voice, the large candle she held slipping from her grasp. He caught it effortlessly in one hand.

"I'm sorry. I didn't mean to startle you." Connor gestured to the cardboard box at her side. "You want this in there?"

She nodded. He gently placed it inside.

"Thank you," she said without making eye contact.

"I'm Connor, by the way."

"I'm—"

"Mindy," he answered for her. "I asked about you."

Her eyes widened. "Oh. Did I do something wrong?"

"No, not at all. I just wanted to know the name of the lovely lady who brought all the spectacular candles."

Connor watched as she tried to process his compliments. When she didn't respond he picked up a smaller candle and stroked the outside, knowing the provocative gesture would make her uncomfortable. Connor wasn't disappointed as her cheeks quickly turned crimson.

"Where'd you buy 'em?"

"I made them," Mindy replied, her eyes focused on the boxes.

"Impressive. Beautiful candles. Beautiful artist."

Mindy shook her head, loosening several damp strands of hair from behind a chipped bobby pin. The errant wisps stuck to her sweating forehead. She wiped the offending hairs into an upright and comical position. Connor reached out and slowly removed the clip. He smoothed her hair back and replaced the bobby pin.

"Thank you," she said.

"You are most welcome."

Connor pointed at the label on one of the boxes. "Candles and More. Is that your place?"

"No. Yes. It's my family's," she said.

"A family business? That's nice. What's the 'more' part?"

"Oh, we also make—"

A loud crash made Mindy jump and she whipped her head around, looking for the source of the noise.

"It's okay. Probably just a light stand falling over," Connor said.

She turned her attention back to Connor.

"Do you take custom orders, by any chance?" he asked.

Mindy nodded. "I have a book of designs at the store." She reached into her pocket, pulled out a business card, and with a shaking hand gave it to him. "You can come by anytime and look at it."

"That'd be great, but I'm really awful at the whole visualizing thing. I once picked out a comforter and curtains on my own." Connor covered his eyes for dramatic effect. "Talk about clashing. I had to sleep in the living room till I got rid of them."

"Oh."

"I don't suppose there's any way you could come by my place and maybe make some suggestions?" he asked. "Of course I'd pay you for your time," he added.

"It's not the money. It's just that I've never done anything like that before," she replied.

"Great. I'll be your first." Connor held her gaze as he said this and she ripened even further. The deepening color told him it might be cherry-picking season.

Mindy placed the last candle on the fireplace mantel. "What do you think?" she asked.

Connor frowned.

"You don't like it?" Mindy removed the candle and inspected it.

Connor took the piece from Mindy and returned it to the mantle.

"I *love* it. I love all of them. I just hate the thought of not seeing you again."

"Really?" she asked.

Connor took Mindy's hand and led her to the couch. He pulled her down next to him.

"I haven't been able to stop thinking of you since the day we met." Connor paused to gauge her reaction. He didn't want to pile it on too high out of the gate.

"I've been thinking about you, too," she replied.

"Wow. I'm *so* happy to hear you say that."

Connor could see the tears of joy beginning to form. *She's really buying the bullshit.*

"I hope you won't think I'm out of line, but I've been dying to do this since you walked in the door." Connor leaned forward and took her face between his hands. He brought his mouth to Mindy's lips and gently kissed her. After a few seconds he broke the embrace. Connor took her hand and placed it on his chest.

"Feel how fast it's beating?"

Mindy nodded.

"You do that to me," he said.

She smiled.

And it was dazzling.

Connor thought how unfortunate such a smile was wasted in the middle of all that nothingness.

"May I be so bold as to ask for another?"

"You may," she replied.

Connor rolled over and set his alarm. Mindy was already up and dressing. This girl turned out to be quite a find as she still lived with her parents and didn't feel comfortable spending the night at a man's house. It saved him from having to kick her out each night. Connor had to cajole Mindy a bit more than the others to get her in bed that first evening. But after a few hours reciting shallow terms of endearment and disingenuous promises he had gotten her there.

Mindy came around to his side of the bed and planted a quick kiss on his cheek. She picked up her purse and headed for the door.

"Hey, why don't you come over early tomorrow. Around two," Connor said. Normally he only let Mindy visit late at night, but tomorrow evening was the big party for the final three Genesis candidates and he wanted a little release before then.

Mindy smiled. "That sounds great. See you then." She closed the door behind her.

As he lay there a familiar feeling washed over him—boredom. Mindy and her hideous candles were on borrowed time.

Connor stepped out of the bathroom, a thick green towel wrapped around his waist. He walked to the dresser and grabbed socks and underwear from the top drawer. He tossed the garments on the bed as he passed Mindy on his way to the closet.

"Time to get my show on the road," Connor said. He clapped his hands while repeating, "Come on, come on."

Mindy slid out of bed, gathering the top sheet around her. "I have a surprise," she said.

"Oh yeah?" Connor continued to get dressed as Mindy spoke.

"My parents have left for the holiday weekend and won't be back until Monday night. I have to go in and do some bookkeeping, but I can easily finish that in the afternoon." She laughed. "I'm rambling. What it means is, I can finally spend the night."

Connor barely paid attention. He heard something about being alone and a closed store. Mindy was clearly waiting for a response, so he said, "Great," in the hopes she would hurry up and leave.

She lifted her garment bag from the chair and squeezed past Connor into the bathroom. He splashed some cologne on his neck and then pulled his Hugo Boss suit out of its dry cleaning bag. He'd just finished buttoning his shirt when Mindy emerged from the bathroom.

Connor looked her up and down. She was wearing a designer dress. It wasn't couture, but definitely designer.

"Why are you all dressed up?" Before waiting for an answer he turned back to the dresser and reached into a small carved box, withdrawing an amber vial and a tightly rolled hundred-dollar bill. Although any denomination would work, he never snorted with anything less than a C-note. To Connor, this set him apart from the junkies. He tapped out a small pile of powder and snorted.

"I couldn't go to the party in one of my old dresses. The sales lady said the lavender brought out the color of my eyes."

Connor snorted another line. He lifted the vial up to the light and saw it was empty. *Just great.* He dropped it back into the box and turned to face Mindy.

"What did you say?"

"My eyes. The fabric. It matches," she said in a halting voice. Mindy's hand fluttered from the fabric up to her face.

"No. The other part," Connor said.

Mindy smoothed the front of her dress. "I bought it for the party."

Connor threw his head back and howled. "You have *got* to be kidding me. What makes you think you're going?"

Her smile, which moments earlier had been in full bloom, now wilted from his words.

"I just thought . . ." Mindy paused for a second. "Oh, is it just an industry party? Are girlfriends not invited?"

"*Girlfriend?*" Connor spit out the word. "Is that what you think you are?"

"I'm . . . you're right. We haven't really been dating that long. I shouldn't—"

Connor cut her off. "Dating? You *are* getting funnier by the minute."

"But . . . but . . . you've asked me out almost every night since we met."

"No. I never asked you *out*. I asked you *in*."

"I don't understand."

"Did you really think I was so busy I couldn't take you to a club? A movie? *One* dinner?"

Mindy did not respond, but instead shifted her weight from one foot to the other. The new lipstick she held slipped out of her hand and rolled under his bed, unopened.

"We've been fucking," Connor said, dragging out the last word. "Not dating. I don't date ugly chicks." He removed his jacket from the hanger and laid it gently on the bed. He turned back to face Mindy, crossing his arms in front of his chest. *Ugly might have been a bit harsh.* "You're not so much ugly as you are plain." He nodded, proud of his revised and accurate assessment.

Mindy stared at him, a confused expression etched on her face.

Connor let out an exasperated sigh. He looked over at the stack of fashion magazines on the table and grabbed the top one. "This," he smacked the cover with the back of his hand, "is the type of girl I date." He tossed the publication toward Mindy, who made a feeble attempt to catch it. She missed and the magazine hit her stomach before sliding down to the floor. She looked at the glossy cover. A stunning brunette with sea-green eyes and a ripe mouth looked up at Mindy.

"You, on the other hand," Connor pointed at Mindy, "are the type of girl I fuck."

Mindy flinched but kept quiet.

"Ah, come on. What's the big deal? You got to be with a guy like me and I got what I needed. A win-win situation."

"No. That's not true. We have so much in common," she replied.

"We have *nothing* in common."

"But you said I was special, that I was—"

Connor held up his hand. He didn't need to hear a rundown of the lies he told her. "All that stuff I said to you? Made it up. Probably couldn't remember half of it if you quizzed me."

"I don't understand," Mindy said.

"*Jesus.* How many times are you going to say that? Come here."

Mindy walked slowly to Connor. He grabbed her by the shoulders and spun her around so they both faced the mirror.

"Look at you. You are a mouse in human form. Now, look at me. In what twisted part of your brain do *we* make sense?"

"My mother always said it's what's on the inside that counts," she whispered.

"Well, she was wrong," Connor said. He pointed at their reflections. "What you see there—it's the *only* thing that matters."

He pushed her away.

Mindy made a small squeaking noise as she stumbled on her new high heels.

"Christ, you even *sound* like a mouse." He shook his head. "Mindy Mouse. That's what you are." Connor laughed, amused by what he considered an incredibly witty remark. He glanced at his watch. "Shit. I gotta get out of here."

Mindy stood frozen, the only movement coming from the mascara-colored tears streaming down her face. Connor grabbed her bag and coat. He shoved them into her hands and pushed her through the door. "That means *you've* got to go." She left his place without looking back.

Connor reached into his wallet and pulled out her card, tearing it in half before depositing the pieces in the trash.

"Connor."

"Over here."

"Come on, Connor, one more this way."

The photographers shouted his name and pleaded for his attention. They couldn't get enough of him. Bony fingers grabbed his wrist and he smiled at his date for the evening. Lyrica was the new Dior model. She was Brazilian, eighteen, and cadaverish. Perfect for this evening.

Lyrica pulled Connor close as they walked through the door. Once the pictures were taken, he wasn't interested in spending the rest of the evening with her. He pointed out a film producer and encouraged her to chat him up. She teetered off on spindly legs and Christian Louboutin heels.

Connor signaled a waiter and asked for a glass of champagne. Someone tapped his shoulder and he turned to face his new agent. The two men shook hands.

"How's it going?" Jeffrey asked.

"Fine. Just got here a few minutes ago."

"Saw you brought Lyrica. Excellent choice."

Before Connor could respond the agent slapped him on the back. "I see some people, so I'll catch up with you later." Jeffrey disappeared into the crowd.

Connor spent the rest of the night fielding congratulations and propositions. He scanned the room hoping to find a replacement for Mindy, but even the waitresses were gorgeous. He spied his rickety date heading to the buffet for some more window-shopping. Even at this distance he could count her ribs. She waved at him, but he pretended not to see her.

Connor was feeling around in his pocket for the vial of coke when he remembered it was at home. And empty. *Damn it.* He looked around to see if there was anyone good for a score when he was called to the stage. Connor and the other two models were greeted with applause. After each one took his turn feigning modesty at the microphone they were sent home, where they were to remain until the announcement tomorrow night.

A drunken Lyrica let him know she was available for an after-hours party. In a hurry to get away from her skeletal embrace, he had the driver drop him off first.

Connor sauntered up to his gate and punched in his code. It swung open, revealing Mindy standing in the driveway. *What the hell? Now the skank is turning into a stalker. Playtime's over.* "Look—"

Mindy raised her hand. Dangling between her finger and thumb was a baggie holding what looked like a few ounces of coke.

"What's that?" Connor asked.

"An apology. You were right. I should be thankful for the time we had."

Ignoring her yammering, Connor demanded, "Where the hell did you get it?"

"I asked around. You've mentioned the type you like so many times, I knew what kind to buy."

Connor couldn't take his eyes off the bag. "That's some mighty pricey Perico you got there. How'd you pay for it?"

"I returned the dress. You were right about that, too. What's the saying? You can't make a purse out of a sow's ear?"

Connor approached Mindy. "I have no idea *what* the hell you're talking about, but I *will* take that blow." He snatched the plastic from her hand and continued up the walkway. Over his shoulder he shouted, "I won't be seeing you around, understand?"

"I understand." Mindy walked down the driveway toward the gate.

Connor threw his arms out to his side and let out a yell. "*Hallelujah*. She finally understands something. Hey, you deserve a reward for that."

Mindy stopped and slowly turned to face him.

"Why don't you come on up for one last ride."

Mindy smiled. "I don't think that's a good idea. We are who we are. No more pretending."

"Yeah, well, I was just yankin' your chain." He pushed the button near the staircase, closing the gate on Mindy. Connor tossed the baggie in the air and caught it behind his back.

Looks like I'm goin' on a sleigh ride after all.

A shrieking car alarm cried wolf, piercing the drug-induced caul wrapped protectively around Connor's brain. He groaned and pulled a pillow to his face. The noise, while muffled, still assaulted his ears, ending any chance of sleep. He tossed the pillow aside. Shards of morning crust poked the corners of his eyes and it took several attempts to remove the painful remnants of sleep. Connor flicked the debris out and turned his head to the clock on his nightstand. The illuminated dial screamed the time in blood-red digits.

2:43 p.m.

He blinked, certain he had read the numbers wrong.

2:43 p.m.

He'd slept for fourteen hours straight.

Christ.

Connor sat up and stretched his arms over his head, a medley of pops accompanying the movement. He threw his legs over the side of the bed, his toes curling around something cold and sticky. Connor bent over and peeled the empty plastic bag off the bottom of his left foot. *That stuff was a major mind blow.* He scratched his head, trying to loosen any memories from the previous night. He remembered the party, coming home and getting the coke from Mindy. After that, nothing. *Need to cut down on that shit.* He tossed the bag into the trashcan.

Connor patted his stomach; all packs still there. He grabbed a pair of sweats from his dresser, pulled them on and padded into the kitchen.

He grabbed a bowl, spoon, and box of cereal from the cabinet and set them on the black granite island. Just as he was getting milk from the refrigerator, the phone rang. He placed the carton on the counter and grabbed the receiver.

"Hello."

"Connor, Jeffrey here."

"Hey, Jeffrey."

Connor knew why his agent was calling and he wasn't disappointed. Genesis had chosen him as the new face.

"Here's the drill. A car's coming to pick you up at six sharp. I'll meet you at the hotel. You are to tell no one, and I mean no one about this. Any leaks and they'll have my head."

"Got it," Connor replied.

Jeffrey went over a few things he wanted Connor to say at the announcement before congratulating him once more.

"See you soon." Connor put the phone back. He was it. Smiling, he gave himself a mental high-five. The grin remained all through breakfast.

Connor sauntered into the bathroom. He turned the faucet on, letting the cold water fill the sink. He poured soap into his hands and massaged his face with the cleanser. Two of his fingers brushed over a small bump.

"What the hell?"

Connor tried to push the suds out of the way, but his wet fingers only generated more lather, further obscuring the offensive mark. He splashed water on his face until it was clear.

Dead center of his right cheek was a red splotch.

Smaller than a baby aspirin and only slightly raised, it resembled the tiniest of insect bites. The blemish would not warrant a second glance on most faces, but camped out in the middle of perfection it had the drawing power of a neon sign on a deserted night's highway.

"Motherfucker," he mumbled. Never. Not once in his life did he ever have a pimple. He flipped on the light switch.

Connor leaned closer, causing the edge of the sink to cut into his abdomen. His eyes drifted from his cheek to his forehead. *Fuck. Another one.*

It peeked out from behind his perfectly groomed right eyebrow. Again, nothing major. Not even big enough to cause the most sensitive of teenagers to stay home crying on prom night. His hands went on a reconnaissance mission, sliding over his face searching for more invaders.

A slight tingling sensation alerted him to a new intruder. Connor pushed his nose to the left, exposing the area for better inspection. A small pea-sized bump was nestled in the space. With his index finger he pressed the cyst. It popped, spraying the mirror with a brownish streak not unlike insect residue left behind on a speeding car's windshield. A foul smell made its way to his nose.

He squeezed his eyes shut. *Shit. Wrinkles.* He quickly relaxed his muscles and ran into the kitchen where he grabbed some ice out of the freezer. Connor pressed a cube against the lumps, hoping it might help the swelling go down. He closed the refrigerator door and caught his reflection in the stainless steel Thermador.

A cluster of grape-like growths snaked across his cheek, disappearing into the hairline. He checked the time on the kitchen clock. The car would be arriving in a few hours. Connor took a deep breath. *Gotta keep it together.* He grabbed the phone and dialed. *If they want me so badly they can postpone the launch.*

Jeffrey greeted him warmly. Connor explained he was developing a rash and thought they should try to push the announcement forward a few days.

"Where's the rash?" Jeffrey demanded.

Connor knew better than to tell the truth.

"On my chest."

His agent exhaled loudly. "Jesus, Connor, you almost gave me a heart attack. We have at least three weeks before the first shoot.

I'll bring you a tube of cortisone cream tonight and on Tuesday I'll get you an appointment with a top derm."

Connor argued that a postponement was a better option.

Jeffrey cleared his throat. "There are no options here. I was willing to look the other way when you showed up tweaked last night, but whatever other bullshit you've got going on ends right now. They will *not* wait for you."

"I'm thinking—"

"Save it," Jeffrey interrupted. "This announcement is going live. If you're not there, Genesis will give your contract to one of the other two guys."

"But they—"

"This isn't some goddamn idle threat. Their second choice may not be as perfect as you, but I can guarantee you one thing. He'll have his ass spit-shined and down at the hotel *on time*."

Connor started to protest, but was cut off for the third time.

"I don't know what kind of relationship you had with your old agent and frankly don't care. Here's how I do things. You show up, do your thing, everyone's happy. You fuck around in any way and not only will Genesis dump you, but I'll kick your ass to the curb as well. Embarrass me and I'll make sure no one picks you up. Are we clear?"

"Yes," Connor replied.

"See you at six-thirty."

The sound of Jeffrey hanging up reverberated in his ear. Connor dropped the phone on the counter.

Goddamn it! Goddamn her! He should have known Mindy couldn't afford high-end blow. She probably bought some cheap beam off a dealer who cut his stash within an inch of its life. He had to be having a reaction to the filler.

Just as Connor was trying to figure out what to do next, a searing pain shot through his jaw. He let out a low moan as the pain hopscotched across his face. It felt like a sadist was doing acupuncture on him with knitting needles. He raced to the medicine cabinet to search for some relief and found it in a couple of extra strength Vicodin left over from an old prescription. He dry swallowed the tablets. The pills went down fine. Closing his mouth was the problem. Connor slowly shut the cabinet door and for the first time in his life recoiled from the image in the mirror.

One of the boils, now the size of a twenty-five cent gumball, protruded into his mouth. Connor grimaced. The slight pressure from his lips caused the rubbery sphere to burst. The glutinous discharge, both brackish and sour, coated his tongue. The disparate tastes dueled for supremacy. He gagged on their battle and spat out the carnage. He felt light-headed and worried his breakfast would soon find its way north.

Connor grabbed a bottle of mouthwash and tossed back several capfuls. The previous taste did not disappear completely, but at least now it was tolerable.

The empty boil looked like a small deflated balloon hanging from the corner of his mouth. He gently pulled at the membrane, but like a stubborn hangnail it refused to separate from his skin. Connor searched through his grooming kit and removed a small pair of scissors. Slowly he closed the blades, bracing himself for the pain. None came. He snipped off the dead skin and dropped it into the sink.

Connor knew he had to get to the hospital. Once there he would make them call in the best plastic surgeon. He was sure things would return to status quo, which in Connor's world meant he would be in the number one spot. *Fuck what Jeffrey said. There's no one like me.*

The pain receded enough to allow him to think. He couldn't tell the doctors he was doing cocaine. Everyone was on the take and it would only be a matter of time before the tabloids regurgitated that story. Connor needed to find out what was mixed with the coke and then somehow convince the hospital he had accidentally ingested whatever it turned out to be. He felt panic teasing the edges of his mind, but refused to let it in. At least for now.

Connor hadn't bothered programming Mindy's number into his phone as she wasn't worth the effort. He raced into the bedroom and lunged at the small wooden basket by his bed. He dumped the contents onto the floor and picked up the two pieces of her card, fitting them back together. Connor dialed.

A recorded announcement informed callers the store was closed for the holiday. *What did she say yesterday?* He couldn't remember all the details, but two important bits of information did stand out.

She would be at the store. And she would be alone.

Connor attempted to hang up, but the receiver wouldn't budge. He pushed a finger between the device and his ear. Something sticky connected the two, but with some gentle manipulation he was able to separate soft skin from hard plastic. Connor reluctantly made his way to the dresser mirror, afraid of what new abomination would meet his gaze.

"Oh my God."

Two small boils co-mingled in one sack, creating an obscene scrotum-like appendage. It hung heavily from his earlobe, swaying back and forth.

The rage circulating through his body was the only thing that kept Connor from passing out. He stormed to the closet and pulled down a large mahogany box from the top shelf. The collection was a gift from a weapons distributor he had done a catalogue shoot for early in his career. Connor's favorite was the BlackHawk Nightedge. He removed the knife, careful not to touch the reinforced tip. He planned on re-gifting them this evening. If Mindy couldn't or wouldn't tell him what was in the powder he snorted, Connor was going to leave the bitch with some memorable souvenirs on her face.

Connor surveyed the supplies on his bed. First, he wrapped a scarf around his lower face. He then slid on a cashmere sweater and pulled the hood up over his head. A pair of Christian Dior oversized aviators completed his look. His face was almost entirely camouflaged. He snatched up the BlackHawk and dropped it into his duffle bag. He grabbed his car keys from the small dish on his dresser.

For the second time since they met, Connor thought about all the things he would do to Mindy.

Except for a few people out on an early evening stroll, the street was deserted as the shops in the area closed early on Sundays. Connor parked a block away from Candles and More. With his face turned downward, he walked over to Mindy's store. He twisted the knob on the front door, but, as he expected, it was locked. He looked through the window and noticed the interior was dark except for a light coming from a back room. His gaze drifted to the front display.

Mindy's candles were featured prominently along with several large skulls. Jars of different colored powders lined shelves just inside the window. Connor squinted but couldn't make out the small writing on their labels. Necklaces with unfamiliar symbols hung from branches spray-painted black. He thought the stuff looked like voodoo or witchcraft paraphernalia.

That goddamn bitch.

A street hustler hadn't sold Mindy some tainted blow. *She* had doctored the drug herself. *She* had deliberately poisoned him.

On the side of the store, he noticed an alley closed off by a narrow gate about eight feet high. A door stood open and Connor could hear music coming from within. He looked down and saw a lock on the gate. He pulled, but found it wouldn't budge. Connor hefted his bag up on his shoulder and tossed it over. He stood still, waiting to see if Mindy heard the noise. When she didn't appear, he grabbed the gate with both hands and placed his right foot on the bottom ledge.

Before Connor could pull himself up, a flurry of giggles stopped him. He let go and moved several stores down. He faced the window, pretending to look at a display of shirts and sweaters. A trio of teenage girls came barreling around the corner, an older woman trailing behind them.

Connor breathed heavily as he waited for them to pass. He lifted his eyes from the ground and looked into the store.

And there he was.

Connor removed his sunglasses and stared at the large poster. His two-dimensional twin stood between the other models, and beneath them the caption read, "Who will be the Face?"

His breath came out in short hot bursts, boomeranging off the wool back into his mouth. He gasped. Connor yanked the fabric from around his face and gulped in some air. He tried to take a deep breath through his nose, but was unsuccessful. His right nostril was blocked by a congealed dark ball that resembled the useless tapioca beads at the bottom of trendy Taiwanese drinks.

The streetlights flickered to life, their intensity brighter than the fluorescent store bulbs, causing Connor's reflection to suddenly appear on the window's surface.

A monster stared back at him.

His dimple, once cooed over by fawning women, was gone. The divot was now filled with a cauliflower-like mass of pulsating nodules. In some places his skin was stretched so tightly it appeared on the verge of ripping. He could no longer discern individual cysts as they had congealed into one fleshy volcano. Amber colored liquid dripped down its side, pooling at the base.

Connor's eyes bounced back and forth between his reflection and the picture. All hope drained from his body. Even if a doctor was somehow able to get rid of these grotesque ulcers and growths, Connor would be scarred.

He was finished.

Connor took a step forward, his shoe hitting a soda bottle left on the ground. As it rolled harmlessly away he bent down and grabbed the bottle by its neck. Connor knew it wasn't strong enough to break the window, but the urge to hurl it at his reflection was intense.

At that moment he felt a slight twinge on his cheek. For a moment he feared the pain was returning.

He wished it had.

The itching began, not in one spot, but all over his entire face.

"Excuse me."

The voice startled Connor and he spun around without thinking.

The young girl screamed.

He groped for the scarf, but it slipped from his hand to the ground. It was too late to cover his face.

Another girl screamed.

This time Connor joined in.

The itching was worse than any pain he had ever experienced. He clawed at his face. A few of the smaller, superficial pustules burst open, offering a brief respite from the mind-numbing irritation. His nails weren't strong enough to penetrate the harder ones.

Connor swung the bottle at a lamppost. Its bottom shattered, leaving a jagged neck in his hand. He raised the glass and brought it down at an angle into his face, ripping the largest boil open.

Connor didn't feel any pain, just blessed relief. His cheek split open like a bloated corpse, spilling its contents onto his jacket. He gripped the remnant tighter and plunged it into his chin with such force the glass embedded in his flesh. He struggled to remove it but quickly gave up.

Connor dropped to the ground, picked up a long shard of broken glass and slashed at his face. With the second swipe he sliced open his forehead.

On the third pass the tip of his nose came off.

A body slammed into Connor and he fell to his side. He screamed for a final time when the viscous-coated glass was wrested from his hand.

Connor fought the two EMTs as they struggled to strap him to the gurney. The larger of the two grabbed his left arm as the other injected him with a syringe.

The woman stared in horror.

"Ma'am, I need you to answer my question," the police officer said in a slightly exasperated voice.

She shifted her focus back to the officer. "My girls . . . ," she said. Taking a deep breath she started again. "They wanted to take a picture standing in front of that poster." The cop glanced in the direction indicated.

"Why?" he asked.

"They're both crazy about the one in the middle. Connor Madison. A man was blocking their view so my eldest called out to him." Connor's moans drew her attention back to him. He twisted his head to look at her. She quickly turned to the officer. "My girls screamed."

"Why would they do that?" he asked.

She exhaled and the words came out as quickly as her breath. "The man turned around and it was him. Connor Madison. Before they could ask for a picture he started . . . he started hacking away at his . . . that perfect face, how could he?" She stole another glance at Connor. His head lolled weakly from side to side, the sedative taking effect.

She said I was perfect.

I was perfect.

Perfect.

Connor was wheeled to the waiting ambulance. A small crowd gathered on the sidewalk, eager for a front-row seat to the unfolding tragedy. He scanned their faces as he went past. Some of the people turned away in horror while others stared and whispered.

But only one smiled.

And it was dazzling.

DIANA AND THE GOONG-SI

LISA MORTON

Diana stood on the deck of the *Althea* as the ship steamed past the island of Hong Kong and wondered (as she had throughout the long trip from England) what she'd find in this strange and ancient land.

It was 1880 A.D. in her world, but she'd been told the Chinese reckoned the year as 4576. Language, food, clothing, religion, even time itself . . . everything would be different here. She'd tried to study the Oriental culture during the forty-one days since they'd left London, but the books she'd brought were so filtered through western perceptions that she felt no wiser after reading them. She'd befriended the *Althea*'s lone Chinese crewman, a wiry seventeen-year-old with long, glossy black hair named Leung Yi-kin, who spoke good English and had begun teaching her the intricacies of his Cantonese dialect; with its inflections and tonalities, the language sounded to Diana's ears like a cross between music and a bawdy joke.

One cloudless, moonlit night as they'd been crossing the glittering Mediterranean, she'd asked him to explain the word *goong-si*. His youthful features had clouded. "*Goong-si* . . . *ho geng*," he'd said, shaking his head.

She thought "*ho geng*" meant "very frightening."

Now, as the ship entered the mouth of the Canton River at an area known as "the Bogue" (a place that, according to Captain Hughes, had experienced heavy fighting in the Opium Wars four decades earlier), Diana found herself thinking back to that first time she'd heard the word *goong-si*.

It was the day before she left for Canton. It was *why* she left for Canton.

She'd been enjoying a comfortable morning in her London apartment, sipping tea and responding to letters, when her servant entered with Sir Edward Hinton. Her heart had instantly begun to jitter—Sir Edward was both her husband's uncle and his employer. The only possible reason Sir Edward could have for paying her a mid-morning visit was to convey bad news.

About William. Her William.

Her husband had been sent to the Hinton Trading Company's outpost in Canton two months ago; they'd been having some difficulty with the locals, and William had been dispatched to oversee the situation until it returned to normal. A simple job. He was expected home in another month.

Or had been. The instant Diana saw Sir Edward's grave expression, she'd taken his hands in concern.

"Oh my dear," he'd told her, "I've just received some very unfortunate news from our Canton branch. William's gone missing."

"Missing," Diana asked, breathlessly, "or dead?"

"Missing," Sir Edward confirmed, and Diana felt a tremor of relief. Her eyes had been drawn for a second to the framed daguerreotype on her desk: William, his dark hair slicked back, a hint of smile on his handsome features, and Diana next to him, her auburn hair turned slate gray by the photo, her own expression one of impatience with the amount of time required to expose the photographic plate.

Diana forced her gaze away from the photo and back to Sir Edward. They'd both taken seats then (Sir Edward easing his considerable bulk down onto a velvet couch), and Diana had waited for the story.

"I don't know how much you know about the Hinton Company's business dealings," Sir Edward began.

Diana shrugged. "I know that you trade for tea at the Cantonese port."

"Quite so," Sir Edward answered, nodding in a way that shook his jowls. "The recent trouble there started with our comprador."

"I'm sorry, I'm not familiar with that term, Sir Edward."

"Ah, of course. The comprador is an English-speaking Oriental chap who ensures that our trading functions smoothly. Our comprador is a fellow named Mr. Wong.

"Now recently this Wong informed the captains of several Hinton ships that they might wish to consider postponing trade in Canton for some time. When they questioned this Chinaman, he told them that there had been a series of murders and disappearances among the men who worked at the docks and that there was some difficulty in acquiring new workers."

"And that's why you needed William there, I take it?"

Sir Edward offered her a wan smile. "Yes. Always a pleasure to deal with a rational female."

Diana tried not to be insulted, instead waiting for him to continue. He finally cleared his throat and went on.

"Yes, well . . . apparently when William arrived, he suggested assembling an armed force of English soldiers to restore order—a capital suggestion, in my opinion—but Mr. Wong told him it would be useless. He informed your husband that the culprit was something that sounded like a *goong-si*; he would provide no further translation."

" '*Goong-si*,' " Diana repeated, trying out the strange syllables on her own tongue.

"Yes. It's a damnably idiotic language these Chinamen speak, if you've never heard it before; it really is like baby-talk. Anyway: Your William, bless him, didn't take Mr. Wong's words at face value, but went ashore and met with the British vice-consul and several merchants. Eventually they got together an armed squadron and William led them to our docks and warehouses, which they found deserted; they were also unable to unearth any clues as to the whereabouts of the missing workers. They questioned a beggar they spotted in the streets near the docks, but he just kept repeating that ridiculous word over and over: '*Goong-si . . . goong-si . . .*' Finally he scuttled off, and William returned with the squad, baffled and empty-handed.

"William once again met with the comprador and asserted that he must hire new workers. This time Mr. Wong was somewhat more forthcoming in his explanations. He told the seamen that workers could not be found, because the Oriental residents of Canton knew what the Englishmen did not: That a *kap-huet goong-si* was a member of the living dead, a creature that takes the blood of men to survive. What the Chinese feared was an evil spirit in human form, a creature of the supernatural that brings certain doom to those foolhardy enough to approach it."

"That sounds like the European legend of the vampire," Diana noted. She'd always had an interest in folklore, and had read several accounts (mainly Eastern European) of undead monsters that rose from their graves at night to feast on the blood of the living.

"Oh, yes, vampire, well . . ." blustered Sir Edward. "Yes, I suppose it could be somewhat akin to that . . . sort of thing."

"Please continue with your story, Sir Edward. What happened to William?"

"I'm coming to that. Well, William was, naturally, skeptical. He scoffed, and wondered how even a superstitious heathen like Wong could accept the existence of such a myth. Mr. Wong insisted it was no myth, and that he could see the thing for himself, if he dared venture into the warehouse at night. William, thinking that perhaps a night spent successfully at the docks would convince the locals that the *goong-si* was just a fairy tale monster, agreed.

"That very night the five hardened seamen and William returned to the docks. Only one man reappeared the following morning, his senses apparently so badly rattled that he could only utter a high-pitched, hysterical laugh and talk about 'the monster . . . the hopping thing with claws and burning eyes.' The English port authorities sent a delegation into the docks, and a single body was found. It was that of one of the sailors, Joseph McKay, a burly, strong fellow of thirty years experience. McKay's body was—" Sir Edward broke off, peering at Diana. "Are you quite sure you should hear all of this?"

"Quite sure," Diana told him, even while she gripped the arms of her chair with such ferocity that her knuckles were completely white.

Sir Edward continued, somewhat reluctantly, "Very well. Captain McKay's body was found with the eyes open, staring wide in terror, his skin strangely wrinkled and pale, and the poor fellow's corpse was quite bloodless. There was no trace of William or the remaining three men. And that's as much as I know."

Diana abruptly rose and walked to the nearest window. She needed to have a moment to think, to not let Sir Edward see weakness on her face lest he think her "another silly woman", as he'd frequently exclaimed.

After a moment, Sir Edward continued. "I'd rule it as just more fancies of the Chinese mind—they're rather simple, you know—but for the fact that at least one man is dead, and my nephew is missing."

Diana finally composed herself and turned to face him. "I must proceed to Canton immediately."

Sir Edward's jaw dropped, then snapped shut. "It's a primitive and savage place, Diana, unlike anything you've ever experienced. Now, I've sent Antonia to deal with the situation, and I'm sure she's more than capable of resolving the mystery."

"Sir Edward," Diana responded, with steel in her voice, "I have every confidence in your daughter, but if she is unable to locate William . . . well, I won't go through life not knowing whether my husband is dead or alive in some foreign land."

Sir Edward furrowed his overgrown brows. "You don't know what it's like there, Diana. We English have managed to transform a few small areas into something comfortable, but the Chinese themselves are a degenerate race. For goodness sake, their current dynasty is governed by a *child!* No, I must forbid it."

"That's unfortunate," Diana said, fixing him with a glare. "Then I'll have to find passage on a ship of some other line, I suppose."

A groan escaped Sir Edward, and he tried a different tack. "Antonia left on our last cruise vessel yesterday. The only ship we have in port now is a tramp steamer, and you certainly don't—"

"That will be acceptable."

Sir Edward sighed deeply, then rose. "I'll make the arrangements for your passage. But I want you to know I'm not very happy with this, Diana."

Diana walked over to plant a small kiss on Sir Edward's red cheek. "I know you're not, but you surely knew I would ask this."

Sir Edward, his cheeks flushed, didn't look up as he grumbled, "There is something to be said for weaker women after all, I suppose."

"Yes," Diana agreed, "perhaps there is, but I wouldn't know."

That had been six weeks ago.

The voyage on the *Althea* might have been enjoyable for Diana under other circumstances. The ship was one of the newer steamers, with a steel hull. The crew was experienced, efficient and amiable, even if they did have a tendency to curtsy and nod to Diana (who, as the wife of Lord William Furnaval, was a Lady of the Empire). The ship carried a cargo of English woolens, which Sir Edward had informed Diana was much desired by both the Chinese and the Indians. He also told her they would pick up more cargo at a stop en route to Canton.

That stop had been Calcutta, where Diana had been dismayed to learn that "more cargo" was opium.

She cursed her own naïveté. She'd certainly known that a few woolen goods weren't enough to buy the quantity of tea the British demanded. But she'd still been unhappy to learn that Sir Edward's prejudice toward the Orientals was accompanied by vigorous participation in a ruthless and lethal drug enterprise.

Of course her beloved William had been part of the same unconscionable enterprise.

No.

She shook her head, as if to fling such thoughts into the cool morning water. The weather was fine and the land on either side of the river was really quite picturesque, with rugged cliffs on one side and a broad estuary on the other. Fishing boats and Chinese junks lined the shores, and the blue expanse was dotted with smaller islands.

The shore was also lined with military forts.

Most were built on high peninsulas that thrust into the river like tall fingers, and they seemed to be largely in ruins, with tumbledown stone walls and no evidence of habitation.

"Why are all these forts deserted, Yi-kin?" she asked the young man, who was working the deck nearby.

He squinted up, saw the one they were just passing, and answered, "Oh, old forts. There are many on river. Many year before, Chinese use them against British opium ship. Then Chinese say opium is legal, so fort no more need."

"Yes, when the Chinese lost the Opium Wars," Diana said.

Diana hadn't realized they'd been joined by Captain Hughes, who was watching the conversation keenly. "The forts served another purpose, too, after the Opium Wars: They guarded river traffic from pirates."

"Pirates?" Diana asked.

"Oh yes. I have an aunt who was once sailing from Canton to Macau when her ship was attacked and she was taken hostage by pirates. They held her for a week in a small space below deck no bigger than a coffin. She received a bowl of rice each day, and was beset at night by all manner of vermin—insects, spiders, rats. She thought surely she would die in that horrible, cramped little cell when suddenly one day the hatch was thrown back. After a time she managed to lift herself up, and discovered she was quite alone on the ship. It seemed that the pirates had spotted a British gunship approaching and had all fled in terror. My aunt swore she would never return to China after that."

When Diana didn't answer, Hughes nodded. "That was barely twenty years ago, Lady Furnaval. You see, the Chinese really are barbarians."

Diana found her eyes seeking Yi-kin's, but he had turned to busy himself elsewhere.

They arrived in Canton that evening.

After steaming up the river past the great island of Macau and the shipyards at Whampoa, they docked at the large island of Honam, which served to house the docks and *go-downs*, or warehouses, of many of the British companies. Although Diana was anxious to feel solid land beneath her feet again, Hughes told her no one would be allowed to disembark until they'd checked out the situation. A messenger was sent to the Hinton Company offices, and returned near midnight with dire news: The comprador, Mr. Wong, had now joined the missing.

By morning, Hughes had gathered all the Hinton representatives and ship captains in the area, and made arrangements for a meeting in the company's offices. Without the Hintons' chief Chinese contact, it would be necessary to deal with other local officials, and so Hughes put together a packet of something he euphemistically referred to as "tea money," then he set off down the docks toward shore while Diana and Yi-kin remained behind with the rest of the ship's crew.

Poor Yi-Kin was positively champing at the bit; he did miss his native soil more than he admitted to, and he peered wistfully toward the mainland, pointing out local landmarks, such as the huge, red, Five-Storied Pagoda, and regaling Diana with tales of Chinese food and festivals. He was particularly sorry to have missed *Ch'ing Ming*, a celebration of ancestors that included visiting cemeteries and cleaning graves (and which Diana reckoned to be similar to the European November 2nd celebration of All Souls Day). They watched the boats negotiating the Canton River, many ferried by women, and Yi-kin pointed out the "house-boats", opulent sampans that served only particular British companies or families.

It was near sunset when Captain Hughes finally returned to the *Althea*, with the happy news that arrangements had been made for Diana to immediately occupy the Hinton family residence in the Shameen district. Diana quickly bundled up her things, and half-an-hour later she was stepping into one of the "house-boats". She was mildly distressed that Yi-kin would not be joining them (no Chinese were allowed in Shameen, unless employed there as servants), but he assured her he had his own place to stay in Canton. The sun was setting as the little boat finally crossed the Canton River, tied up to wooden moorings behind one of the mansions in the Shameen district, and Diana first set foot onto Chinese soil.

She was surprised (and perhaps slightly disappointed) to discover that the British section of Shameen looked much like parts of London. The Hinton family house was decorated largely in Western style, with only a few touches of local elegance: an exquisite jade carving, an antique porcelain vase, a lacquered end table. The only Chinese she saw in Shameen were all servants, who were treated with a disdain that made Diana acutely uncomfortable. However, she was pleased to renew her acquaintance with Antonia Hinton, Sir Edward's only child and a bright young woman whom she hadn't seen in three years and had always liked. Diana wasn't surprised to discover that Antonia was heavily involved with the local operations of her family's firm, and that this was her third trip to China in the last five years. Antonia had only arrived two days earlier, and told Diana that although she was quite intent on locating William, she hadn't gotten far in the search yet.

After a superb dinner of turtle soup and curry roast beef, Antonia excused herself, saying she had Hinton Company business to attend to. Left to her own devices, Diana took a quick stroll of the small Shameen area (which she was told had been reclaimed by the British from river silt at great expense), and was dismayed by one scene in particular: An Englishman in a neighboring house was beating a cowering young female servant with a bamboo switch. As Diana gaped in horror, the British man was joined by a woman— undoubtedly his wife—and Diana breathed a silent sigh of relief, assuming the woman would stop the beating.

Instead she laughed, and Diana caught the phrase "yellow imbecile" before the beating continued.

Diana nearly stepped forward to stop the scene, but the man finally seemed to grow tired of the activity and allowed his wife to lead him back inside. The young Chinese girl was shaking badly as she pulled herself to her feet, her dress was torn and bloodied . . . but she returned to the house as if it were all just part of her regular routine.

Diana stayed up late into the night, hoping to discuss what she'd seen with Antonia, but it was well after midnight when Diana adjourned to her quarters, distressed by Antonia's absence.

The following morning, Diana awoke to find Antonia still missing. Although Diana was anxious to proceed into Canton and begin her own hunt for William, she had no idea where to begin and was forced to wait for Antonia's return. She tried to relax with an excellent local "gunpowder" tea, but found herself pacing before a window overlooking the river.

It was nearly noon when Diana looked up to find herself staring at an ashen and shaking Antonia. She rushed to the young woman's side, helped her to a seat, poured a second cup of tea, then waited while Antonia collected herself. Diana noticed that Antonia's lovely silk dress was torn and stained.

"I did a foolish thing, Diana," Antonia began, gazing down into her teacup as if searching the unfurled leaves for omens. "I went to the docks last night."

"Oh, Antonia," Diana cried out, "why didn't you tell me? I should have been with you."

Antonia ran a hand through her disheveled hair. "I hoped to offer you some good word about your husband . . ."

Diana felt a surge of affection for Antonia, and reached across the small table between them to take her hand.

Antonia returned the grip, as if hanging on to Diana for her life. "Plus, truthfully . . . I heard the stories, but I didn't believe them. I thought they were surely naught but the imaginings of superstitious men, some Oriental fantasy . . ."

"And what did you find?" Diana asked, feeling her own distress mount.

Antonia shook her head. "What I saw . . . I shall never speak of. *Never*." Suddenly she uttered one choked cry. "I took six crewmen with me, and only I returned. Dead, they're all dead—or worse."

The last of Antonia's reserve gave way, and she broke down into shuddering sobs. Diana quickly moved to comfort her, and Antonia unabashedly sank her face into Diana's shoulder, drenching the fabric of Diana's dress in tears.

"I killed them, Diana—it's my fault—"

Diana made soft *shushing* noises and held onto her friend—and then felt her own stomach clench as she finally asked the question she most dreaded: "Antonia—did you see William anywhere?"

Antonia shook her head. "He wasn't there. At least I didn't see him."

Diana exhaled a long-held breath, although she felt little hope; she knew that trying to extract the full story from Antonia would be useless. Then another terrible thought occurred to her: Antonia had taken crewmen from the *Althea*. "What about Yi-kin," she asked, dreading the answer, "did you take him with you?"

Antonia shook her head. "No. He was on leave, visiting friends in the city."

That answer at least provoked some small measure of relief in Diana, as she renewed her hold on Antonia. "What's important is that you got out alive."

"Alive, yes," Antonia said between sobs, "but I don't know how I'll ever sleep again. What I saw today . . . dear God . . ."

"It's all right," Diana said softly, "at least one of them wasn't William."

Diana wrapped a throw around the shoulders of her friend, even as she realized that solving the mystery of William's disappearance was now entirely up to her.

Had Diana needed any confirmation of Antonia's story, she received it the next day, when the dead body of the one of the vanished sailors was found floating in the Canton River near the docks. He was hauled aboard a Chinese fishing junk, identified by his western garb, and turned over to the British authorities. The Hinton Company was notified shortly thereafter.

Diana had arranged for a local practitioner of western medicine to give Antonia something to calm her nerves, and had then stayed with her through the following day and night. Antonia actually slept, although it was not a peaceful rest—several times she cried out something about "burning eyes" and writhed in her sleep. Still, when she awakened the following morning she seemed much improved; she was pale and drawn, but anxious to proceed with company business.

Diana accompanied her to the offices of the British consul, where they viewed the body. The knot of tension in Diana dissolved when she realized the man wasn't William, but was instantly replaced by a small thrill of revulsion upon seeing that the man had plainly been drained of all blood. His skin was so white it nearly shone, and seemed to have lost some of its elasticity. While Antonia went over paperwork with the officials, Diana examined the dead man's neck, then wrists, idly wondering if the telltale signs of the traditional western vampire were present, but the corpse was curiously free of any puncture or bite wounds. The Chinese fisherman who had brought the body was still present, murmuring the same phrase (*kap-huet goong-si*) which Yi-kin had told Diana translated to something like "blood-breathing corpse".

Diana was quiet after they left the consul, mulling over the meaning of the bite-less body. She'd always prided herself on her skepticism; although she did believe in God, she wasn't sure she believed in the same God that the Church would have her believe in. She'd always enjoyed ghost stories as fiction, but she'd never given any credence to the idea that such things might actually exist; she was no likelier to believe in ghosts and vampires than fairies, hellhounds, or horned Celtic deities. However, she couldn't argue that something beyond her reckoning was happening here. First, William was missing; second, she'd known Althea since the young woman had been barely out of the crib, and she knew the Hinton daughter had never been given to wild flights of fancy; and third, she'd seen the bloodless corpse with her own eyes.

At what point did it become more foolish to deny that the supernatural might exist?

If she were to accept the existence of such a monster as a vampire . . . how could she fight it? She thought back over the mentions she'd read of revenants.

Crucifixes . . . holy water . . . something about a stake through the heart . . .

Of course all those protections had been applied to *European* vampires. Would a crucifix or holy water affect a thing that had probably never even heard of Christianity?

It was lunchtime as they returned to the Hinton Company offices. Diana was still pondering these questions when a clerk entered Antonia's office to announce that a Chinese priest of some kind had requested a word. Curious, Diana asked Antonia if she might stay for this audience, and Antonia assured Diana that she would very much like her present.

The clerk exited, returning shortly with a most curious personage: The man admitted into the office was Chinese, middle-aged, wearing a somewhat garish yellow robe, emblazoned with exotic signs and symbols, and a tall black hat likewise ornamented. He bowed to the two women and began to speak in Cantonese. Antonia motioned for him to pause, then sent for an interpreter. A few moments later Yi-kin entered and gaped briefly at the sight of the yellow-robed man before bowing to him and exchanging a few words.

Diana and Antonia soon found they were in the presence of one "Master Li", a highly skilled practitioner (actually Yi-kin used the word "sage") of the local religion known as Taoism. He said he'd come from "the mountains," and had been sent for by the terrified Cantonese. Master Li (through Yi-kin) claimed to be skilled at dealing with monsters, including that known locally as the "*kap-huet goong-si*," or vampire. He stated that only a Taoist master such as himself could seize this kind of monster and return it safely to hell.

Antonia listened politely and then said, "There's more than one monster at work here."

Yi-kin translated, listened to the Taoist's reply, and then said to Antonia, "He say he know what you see, that you see many monster, but these are only *goong-si* servant. The *kap-huet goong-si* make people into *goong-si*—"

Diana turned to Antonia with raised brows. "*Many* monsters?"

Antonia blanched, but otherwise ignored Diana.

Master Li said something else, and after a moment Yi-kin relayed the message: "Master Li say *goong-si* are hard to control, but he can do. He say he can stop them and bury them with proper . . . uh . . . *feng shui.*"

"What is *feng shui?*" Diana asked.

"*Feng shui* is . . . very hard . . . like . . . correct way to place thing . . ."

Yi-kin finally shrugged and threw up his hands helplessly.

Master Li added something else, then waited impassively. Yi-kin's jaw dropped at whatever had just been said, then he turned back to Antonia. "He say he want five hundred pound to kill *goong-si.*"

Antonia burst out laughing.

"Are you sure you translated that correctly, Mr. Leung? Because otherwise the man is surely mad. Five hundred pounds is a small fortune!"

Yi-kin reddened and addressed a question to the Taoist. To Diana, it sounded something like, "*Nei jaan yiu pounds ng baak ma?*"

The Taoist merely nodded, stoic as ever.

Antonia smirked. "I'm sorry, but I know when I'm being hoodwinked. Please show him out, Mr. Leung."

Diana started to object, but Master Li had clearly understood both Antonia's tone and expression; he bowed and turned to go.

"Wait, please," Diana blurted out, before turning to Antonia. "He might be useful to us—"

"Please, Diana. He is clearly a charlatan. Have you ever heard of a genuinely religious man demanding such a sum?"

Diana thought she had, but didn't bother to mention that to Antonia.

Yi-kin was looking guilt-stricken and fortunately Antonia noticed. "Mr. Leung, no need to translate any of that. Just show him out, please."

Yi-kin bowed and gestured toward the door, but the movement was unnecessary, since Master Li was already halfway out.

Diana considered for a moment, then jogged out after the Taoist. She caught up to him in the hallway outside and threw out a Cantonese plea Yi-kin had taught her, hoping she didn't mangle the words too badly. "*M goi, cheng dang.*"

Master Li turned to her with one eyebrow raised in amusement. She'd made *some* kind of point, at least.

Diana turned urgently to Yi-kin. "Yi-kin, please tell Master Li that I'll gladly pay him the sum he asks."

Yi-kin blinked in surprise, then he relayed the information. After a moment, Master Li uttered a few words, offered a bow to Diana, and then turned and walked away.

"Yi-kin," Diana said, disappointed, "what happened? Why did he walk out?"

"He say good. He say at two p.m. today go to dock."

"Oh."

After a few moments, Diana returned to Antonia's office. Antonia seemed to have already forgotten the matter, as she was busily poring over a sheaf of documents. "Well?" she asked without looking up.

Diana answered, "I've hired Master Li instead."

"It's your money, I suppose, but I think you've just spent it foolishly. He's nothing but an Oriental hoaxer—what can he really do?"

Save my William, thought Diana.

A few moments later, Diana found Yi-kin in conversation with several other Chinese workers in a storage room behind Antonia's office. As soon as he spotted her, Yi-kin excused himself from the other men and joined her.

"Yi-kin, I need to talk to you very seriously," Diana began.

They moved off to a quiet corner, standing near a dusty window that let in some of the hazy midmorning sunshine. "You know why I made this trip," Diana said to the young man.

He nodded. "To find husband."

"Yes," Diana said. "And . . . well, Antonia can't know this, but—I intend to be at those docks today with Master Li to do just that."

"I go, too," Yi-kin said.

"There's something you don't know, though, Yi-kin: Miss Hinton went to the docks last night with six crewmen—"

"—and they all die there. I do know," Yi-kin finished.

Diana gaped for a moment, then asked him, "How?"

"Everybody here know that. Yesterday sailor leave with Miss Hinton; today they are not here. They find one dead in water."

"Yes."

"Miss Hinton see *goong-si?*" Yi-kin asked.

"Yes. At least I think so . . . she wouldn't really talk about it."

Yi-kin nodded soberly.

"Yi-kin," Diana said, "do you believe in the *goong-si?*"

Diana was pleased to see the young man take his time before answering, "I believe."

Diana nodded, then added, "And did you think Master Li was genuine? Could he stop the *goong-si?*"

Yi-kin looked away, then answered softly, "Maybe. Taoist are very strange. They know many strange thing."

Diana realized she had very little familiarity with the religions of China, virtually none with Taoism. "Do you know much about what Taoists believe?"

"I know little. They believe in many, many god. They believe in Eight Immortal. They believe Heaven and Hell have General and they pray to them. They believe they can live always."

"Yes, immortality," Diana nodded. "I think all religions believe in that—"

"But Taoist are different. They believe *body* can live always, not just . . ."

"Spirit," Diana filled in.

"Yes," Yi-kin affirmed.

Physical immortality, Diana thought. *You'd think that would be easy to prove, wouldn't you? Perhaps the man is just a charlatan, after all.*

Diana said, "Well, I haven't paid him yet. If he is lying and can't stop them—"

Diana broke off, realizing the next part of the sentence would have run,—*then I probably won't be alive to pay him.*

"You should not go to dock," Yi-kin said, having evidently surmised her thought.

"I have to. I have to find William. But you don't need to accompany me."

"I will come," Yi-kin affirmed, then added with a grin, "I can help. I am very good at *gong fu*."

Yi-kin shifted his weight suddenly so that his front leg extended, the back bent to take his weight, his arms held stiffly before him. Diana found the stance both somewhat comical and curiously intimidating. "What is that?"

"*Gong fu*. I know many style. I can help protect Diana *siu jeh*."

Diana felt an immense surge of affection for this young man, even while she realized she would never forgive herself if anything happened to him.

Diana didn't bid farewell to Antonia. They took only enough time for Yi-kin to jot a quick letter before leaving the Hinton Company. He told Diana the letter was for his sister, Leung Mei-yi, who lived in Shanghai with his parents. The letter was to be mailed to her in the event of his death or disappearance. Yi-kin also changed out of his uniform into local clothing, reasoning that it would be easier for them to move through Canton if he were perceived as a local.

Diana returned to the Hinton house, where she changed clothing into a Hinton Company officer's uniform she'd borrowed from the offices. With her hair tucked up and the cap pulled down low over her face, she thought she could pass for a man. When hunting in the countryside back home in England, she'd occasionally aroused both disdain from neighbors and laughter from William by donning men's garb, and if truth be told, she found it infinitely more comfortable. Here in China, she hoped the uniform would both arouse less suspicion than her western-style skirts and petticoats, and ease any strenuous activities that she might be forced to engage in.

Next, she gathered up supplies: A loaded pistol. A crucifix she found in a desk drawer in her bedroom. A knife with a silver blade. She tucked the small arsenal into the various pockets of the uniform, even as she doubted that any of them would prove useful.

At slightly past noon she met Yi-kin at the Shameen bridge, and they proceeded toward the river. Canton was famous for its temples (Diana had read that it contained over 800 in its mere six-mile circumference), and their route took them past one. Yi-kin paused, gazing at the entrance, and Diana joined him. Like almost everything else in Canton, the temple—which had once been glorious and ornate, with its curving roof and heavy blocks of stone and gilt trim—now seemed somewhat rundown.

"What is it?" Diana asked.

"Temple of Five Genii. These were five men who start Canton. They ride here on five ram, say they will always protect us. I want to go in."

"Then do, please," Diana told him, curious.

They passed through an outer courtyard, full of lovely blossoming jasmine and cherry trees, and the sweet aroma of petals and incense wafted about them. Diana was suddenly glad they'd made this detour; she felt her spirits both soothed and emboldened by the luscious scents.

They walked up a short run of wide steps and in through the entrance to the temple. Immediately ahead were five colossal statues, each seated, each with an upraised right hand offering benediction. The temple was quiet at the moment, although there were a few other supplicants bowed near the altar before the statues, and Diana caught a glimpse of a priest off in the shadows to the side.

She waited near the entrance, watching as Yi-kin stepped forward, took three joss sticks from a large container, lit them and then bowed three times to the five figures. After a brief moment of silent prayer, he placed the smoking sticks in a large sand-filled pot, bowed again, and then reached for a long bamboo cylinder in front of him. He shook the cylinder vigorously, then tilted it down, and Diana saw that it contained long thin strips of wood. Yi-kin grasped the one that had slid out the farthest, then returned the cylinder to its place.

He took the strip of wood to a man seated near the entrance. The man examined the strip for quite some time, then turned to Yi-kin and spoke to him in low tones. Yi-kin listened, dropped some coins in a plate near the man, and rejoined Diana.

"What was that you just did?" Diana asked, as they walked from the temple.

"First, I pray to Five Genii for protection, then I use stick to tell fortune."

Diana had read that the Chinese had a penchant for fortune-telling. It was a significant part of their religion, of their festivals, and even of their language; with its many different tones and inflections, Cantonese was rich with homonyms and provided the basis for considerable belief in numerology. Back on the *Althea*, Yi-kin, for example, had told Diana that his people believed the number four to be bad luck because the word, *sei*, was a homonym for the word for death.

Although Diana personally found the notion of fortune-telling quite absurd, she supposed it was still easier to believe in than the existence of *goong-si*.

"And what did your fortune reveal?" she asked.

"*Ha ha.*"

Diana glanced over at Yi-kin, uncertain whether he was joking or saying something in Cantonese. "What is *ha ha?*"

"Very bad luck. We probably die."

Not very funny at all, Diana thought.

They were almost to the docks and about to hire a sampan to cross the river when they heard the sounds of commotion behind them—shouts, tramping feet—and suddenly Yi-kin tugged Diana urgently into a small shop.

"Yi-kin, what—?" she barely got out, before Yi-kin held a finger to his lips and guided her to the back of the lacquerware store.

Looking anxious, he took her as far to the back of the shop as it went, where he feigned interest in a low chest of drawers. The merchant approached, smiling, and bowed. "Welcome!" he offered in English.

"Do not move," Yi-kin whispered in Diana's ear, then moved to place himself between her and the entrance to the shop.

"Yi-kin, what—"

"*Ai Ho Chuan*. Righteous Harmony Fist."

Diana started to laugh at the absurdity of the name ... then she remembered something she'd read once, an article buried on the back page of a London newspaper:

The Righteous Harmony Fists were a secret society—a triad—that was vehemently opposed to foreign intervention in China. So vehemently opposed, in fact, that they had supposedly murdered a number of British missionaries in rural parts of China, and had recently stirred up trouble with demonstrations in several major Chinese cities.

Including Canton.

Diana risked a look past Yi-kin out into the street, where she saw a large parade of people passing. Many were dressed as coolies, some as farmers, but they all wore red bandannas, red sashes, and, about their necks, lengths of red cloth inscribed with characters. They were handing out small booklets to onlookers, who were handing them coins in exchange, and they chanted a slogan over and over.

"What are they doing?" Diana whispered to Yi-kin.

"They sell anti-European literature. Anyone not pay them get beaten."

Nice chaps, thought Diana.

"They say 'force out all foreigner,' " Yi-kin added.

"Oh dear," Diana said, attempting to make herself as small as possible.

Then several members of the group entered the shop.

Yi-kin saw them, and immediately began calling out, "*Ni jeung toi gei chin a?*"

The merchant, startled, turned to Yi-kin, but he was plainly also keeping one eye on the Righteous Harmony Fist men—and on Diana.

Yi-kin spoke in an abnormally loud voice, and Diana realized he was trying to let the sect members know they were natives. "*M goi, ngoh seung maai ni jeung toi.*"

Diana dropped to the floor, pretending to examine the legs of a dresser.

Yi-kin leaned down over her and whispered urgently, "Do you have money?"

She nodded, dug briefly into a pocket, and produced a handful of local *taels* she'd gotten from Antonia.

Yi-kin took them and shoved them at the merchant, whose attention was instantly diverted from the Righteous Harmony Fist men.

"Ahhh, *do jeh!*" the merchant responded, bowing.

At the front of the shop, another customer was buying some of the booklets. As the Fists completed the transaction and were turning to look back toward them, Diana's heart beat a tarantella.

After what seemed an eternity, she heard two loud thumps on the table above her. *This is it,* she thought. *Not a very heroic way to end.*

And then Yi-kin's smiling face appeared beneath the table as well, as he said to her, "You just buy this table."

Diana straightened up and saw instantly that the Fists had left the shop and moved on down the street. The merchant stood nearby, making notes on a paper.

"I ask him to deliver table to Hinton house," Yi-kin informed her.Diana felt a rush of relief that left her weakened, and she actually had to grasp her new table to remain steady. She glanced down, saw that it was a very beautiful thing indeed, and made an instantaneous decision.

"No, I'll give him my address in London."

She managed to leave both the merchant and Yi-kin quite astonished, but she thought the table would serve as an attractive reminder of the fact that the most dangerous enemies could still be quite human.

After they completed the shipping instructions and left the shop, they reached the river's edge and hired a sampan, rowed only by a silent, sturdy woman with a baby strapped to her back.

"Yi-kin," she asked, as they were ferried across the expanse of water, "is it possible William was ... hurt ... by the Righteous Harmony Fists?"

Yi-kin shrugged. "Possible. Maybe Master Li work with them ... ?"

Diana was suddenly glad she'd brought the pistol.

The sampan deposited them on the island of Ho-nam, where a short walk brought them to the Hinton Company's *go-down*. It was a dank, foul place, with weathered, dark wood and the smells of fungus and decaying fish. Diana detected another scent in the air as well: It was the tang of death.

Yi-kin was clearly unnerved by the odor and halted his pace, grimacing.

"Yi-kin," Diana told him, "you don't need to do this."

Yi-kin glanced at her, then held one of his sleeves up over his nose. His voice was muffled when he said, "I will not leave."

"*Doh jeh*," Diana told him, and she was genuinely grateful to have him with her.

"*M sai.*"

They entered the warehouse wherein Antonia had suffered her unspoken, terrible experiences yesterday. It was easily identified by the flags of the British Empire and the Hinton Trading Company flying above its doorways. Even though it was still afternoon, it was gloomy inside the large building, and their eyes took some few seconds to adjust.

"Master Li?" Diana cried out, her voice echoing in the cavernous space. The interior of the *go-down* looked like any other coastal storage space, a maze of stacked wooden crates and moldering ship's rigging. Light entered through a few filthy windows set high overhead.

There was no immediate sign of either the Taoist or *goong-si*. Diana was about to start a search of the building when she heard Yi-kin gasp, then cry out, "Diana *siu jeh* . . ." She rushed to join him, and then likewise inhaled sharply at what she saw:

He'd found streaks of blood and a knife on the floor. The blood had also spattered nearby boxes and the rough walls, and left its own acrid, coppery smell hanging in the air. A crimson trail led to the closed door of a side room.

She instinctively removed the pistol from a pocket, but didn't immediately move. Her ears strained for any sound, from either Master Li or something else, but there were only the small creaks of the old wood and the distant urban drone from Canton. She checked a pocket watch, saw it was now after 2 p.m., and turned to Yi-kin.

"I'm going to check that room."

"We not wait for Master Li?"

"I don't think he's coming. We'll be careful."

Diana guessed the smaller room might be windowless and dark, so first she found and lit a lantern, which she passed to Yi-kin. No words passed between them as she gestured at the door; he offered her only one small nod. She crept forward, then, as quietly as possible, opened the door to the side storeroom.

Diana and Yi-kin were immediately staggered by a redoubling of that nauseating scent of death. Even as she fought down her gorge, Diana knew that hideous reek meant that there were corpses—reanimated or not—present somewhere in this place.

The room was small, and as Yi-kin raised the lantern they spied only more crates of varying sizes. Moving carefully, they peered around the stacks of boxes, but found nothing. In one corner stood a large shrouded object; as Diana tensed, Yi-kin pulled the tarpaulin aside, but what was revealed underneath was nothing more than a heap of rice bags. Some of the canvas bags had split open and Diana saw squirming maggots mixed in with the white grains.

They were about to examine the roof overhead when Diana heard a hollow sound underfoot. She looked down at her feet and saw the plain outline of a trapdoor and handhold. She motioned Yi-kin over with the lantern, then knelt by the trapdoor and experimentally fit her hand into the handhold. The trapdoor gave an inch; it wasn't bolted from the other side.

She hesitated long enough to exchange a look with Yi-kin, who nodded back to her again, his shoulders suddenly hunched with tension. Holding the gun carefully in one hand, with the other she wrenched the trapdoor up and back.

If the noxious odors had been bad before, now they were nearly intolerable, striking Yi-kin and Diana with an almost physical force. Yi-kin struggled briefly, then turned aside to retch.

Diana swallowed down her own revulsion, waiting, every nerve vibrating . . . but nothing followed the vile smell out. As Yi-kin struggled to recover, Diana gently took the lantern from him and tentatively bent forward over that hole in the floor, trying to peer down.

At first she saw nothing but a ladder descending. Diana figured this space had probably once been part of the warehouse's system of handling contraband, although now it had been put to an even more malevolent use. The lantern's yellow glow seemed to barely penetrate the miasma of rot, and Diana could make out nothing past a few feet down. She looked around and spotted a rusted pulley that had fallen to the floor; she picked up the heavy device and tossed it into the hole. It hit after falling no more than twenty feet, but Diana couldn't tell what it landed on—the noise had been muffled, without the splashing sound of water. She considered a moment further, then made her decision and began to lower herself into the hole.

"No, *siu jeh*, no!" Yi-kin cried out, when he saw that she intended to climb down the rickety algae-covered ladder under the trapdoor. "Not careful!"

She hesitated, her feet already on the ladder's top rung. "William may still be here."

"And *goong-si* may be here. Or Righteous Harmony Fists. If either find us, we die; if *goong-si* find us, we die and become *goong-si*," Yi-kin whispered to her.

Diana considered Yi-kin's words. Even if the *goong-si* turned out to be nothing more monstrous than disguised thugs with a penchant for bloodletting, her pistol carried only six shots. But then she reminded herself why she'd traveled around the globe to come here, and she could only grip the pistol tighter as she prepared to lower herself.

"That won't happen," she told Yi-kin, then started down.

Diana moved the gun to the belt of her Hinton uniform, then reached up and took the lantern Yi-kin held down to her. She lowered herself about two yards before her feet made contact with sodden bare ground. She made sure her footing was solid, then she moved the lantern around—

—and her heart nearly stopped at what she saw.

Around her lay at least a dozen bodies. She saw the *Althea* crewmen; she saw several men she didn't know, dressed as officers; she saw local workers in tattered Chinese clothing; she saw one Oriental in fancy robes who she guessed to be the missing comprador, Mr. Wong. That they were all clearly dead, there could be no question; for one thing, no living man could repose on this fetid swamp.

Was William here . . . ?

She began to bend closer, examining each face frantically. Some of these men had clearly suffered grievous wounds, wounds now long since dried and caked over. The skin of the cadavers was ashen and shriveled, and there was even one figure partly covered with the same awful moss that grew on the slick stone sides of the room.

None of them were him.

Diana was turning to Yi-kin to tell him of her discovery when some movement caught her eye. She turned, holding the lantern out, but saw nothing. An obvious scraping noise sounded from behind her, and she turned just in time to see one of the abominations rise to its feet. Impossibly, it tilted upward in a diagonal arc, never bending its knees or hips. It was one of the sailors, a particularly fearsome-looking brute in life whose long beard was now matted with clots of gore.

Then its arms swiveled up and it *hopped* toward her. It was a ridiculous, straight-legged leap, slow and heavy, like something from a dream, and under any other circumstances Diana would have laughed.

But there was no mistaking the thing's intention: It meant to kill her.

For a moment Diana could only gape, paralyzed. Then she raised the gun and fired directly into the thing's chest.

"Diana *siu jeh*—!" Yi-kin cried out above her.

The *goong-si* (which Diana knew it to be) took another of those terrible jumps toward her, its claw-like fingers grasping at the neck of her uniform.

Diana fired again, this time into the monster's head. It staggered back briefly, and she dared hope she'd stopped it. But then it came forward again, hopping, and Diana uttered a small cry of disbelief as she saw the slow-oozing hole in the center of the thing's forehead.

She dropped the gun and dug in her pocket for another weapon. Her fingers found the crucifix and she drew it forth, extending it toward the approaching *goong-si*.

The nightmare hopped forward, and suddenly its jaws opened and then clamped shut around the crucifix. Diana released her hold on the cross and stumbled back, watching as the *goong-si* bit down and snapped the holy object in half. It opened its mouth again, and the broken parts of the cross tumbled out.

Diana could think only of escape. The lantern fell from her hand as she turned, ready to make a desperate attempt to reach the ladder—

—and William was there.

She started to cry out his name in joy, but only got out the first syllable before she saw his face more clearly, lit from below by the rays of the lantern she'd dropped. His eyes were glassy and sunken, his skin the color of cobwebs, his arms outstretched before him.

William was a *goong-si*.

"William!" Diana cried his name, but there was no flicker of recognition, no reaction whatsoever. He hopped forward and

Diana staggered away from him until her back hit the ladder. "William, it's me, Diana—"

He leapt forward again, then his icy hands wrapped about her throat, with a grip like a steel band. Diana struggled to cry out, to tear at the William-thing's arms, to do anything, but somehow all she could manage was a choked gasp, as her vision began to darken.

I'm so sorry, William, she thought.

And then the pressure was gone and she fell to her knees, her strength done but not her life. She looked up to see someone between her and William—a man in yellow Chinese dress. Her brain still reeling from the attack, it took her a moment to place the distinctive canary colored robes:

Master Li, the Taoist monk. He really had come.

Li turned away from the *goong-si* to Diana, and she looked up to see that the monster she'd once called husband had completely frozen. Blinking in surprise, she saw a strip of yellow paper inscribed with Chinese pictograph characters fluttering from the *goong-si*'s forehead. It was completely motionless, its arms still stiffly extended, arms that had held her in their death grip until the priest had intervened.

He quickly motioned up the ladder, and Diana, still weak, started to climb; she was grateful when she felt Yi-kin's arms pull her up and out. Once she was safely out of the hole, she collapsed onto a nearby crate. She looked toward the hole, expecting to see Master Li follow her up, but he didn't. For several minutes she and Yi-kin waited breathlessly, half expecting one of the monsters to come vaulting up out of the trapdoor opening. They heard nothing from below, neither screams nor moans nor sounds of fighting.

Then Master Li did reappear, climbing slowly up the ladder, completely calm.

As he stepped out onto the floor the Taoist spoke rapidly in Chinese, which Yi-kin translated for Diana. He said he had secured all the *goong-si* below by placing a sacred *sutra* on them; once he finished with the *kap-huet goong-si* that had created and controlled these innocent victims, it would be safe to move the bodies to their final resting places.

"So they can't be brought back?" Diana asked, clinging to a last shred of hope.

Yi-kin translated the question, and Diana received all the answer she needed when she saw the priest shake his head in the universal gesture of *no*.

Diana rose and started toward Master Li. "I'll pay you more," she said, forgetting in her grief that the Taoist understood no English. "Whatever you want, if you can bring him back . . ."

The priest muttered a few words to Yi-kin, then turned to Diana and bowed, with both hands held out before him, the left hand cupped over the right fist.

Yi-kin turned to Diana, his eyes downcast. "Master Li offer you sign of great respect, say you are very brave today, but husband is dead."

Diana stood and attempted to repeat the bow, offering it to Master Li, but collapsed before she could finish the gesture.

When Diana came to a short time later, Master Li had gone, but Yi-kin said he would return tonight to deal with the *kap-huet goong-si*.

Diana felt drained and numb (some part of her mind told her she was in shock), but with Yi-kin's assistance she was able to leave the warehouse and return to the English Consul in Canton, where arrangements were made to cash a large check. It took some time, but eventually she left the Consulate with an envelope full of five hundred-pound notes. After that, she and Yi-kin found a quiet corner in a tea shop, where they sat beneath cages of singing birds while around them merchants conducted business over tea and *dim sum*.

After a long silence, Yi-kin offered, "I am very sorry, *siu jeh*."

Diana nodded and sipped more of the fine tea, which seemed to be restoring some of her energy. "I know now that I never really expected to find him alive, but that thing . . ." The way she fingered the bruises on her throat spoke more eloquently than words could have. Yi-kin only nodded.

"You should not go back tonight," he told her earnestly. "I can pay Master Li."

"No," she said, without looking at him.

Yi-kin blinked, confused. "We not pay him?"

"No. *I* will pay him."

Slightly hurt, Yi-kin said, "Oh. You not trust me?"

Diana surprised him by reaching across the table and grasping his hand, an expression of camaraderie that left the young man both pleased and slightly embarrassed. "Oh, Yi-kin—I'd trust you with my life. No, I want to be the one to pay Master Li because I want to be there to watch when he destroys the monster that murdered my husband."

For a second, Yi-kin thought the fierce expression on his friend's face was nearly as frightening as anything else he'd seen today.

Four hours later they returned to the warehouse and were surprised to see what Diana could only think of as an altar, now erected in the middle of the space. Long tables, draped with vivid red cloth, had been placed on an elevated platform. Incense burned, slightly masking the odor of decomposition with a musky aroma. There were bowls, strips of paper, calligraphy brushes, idols, and, strangest of all, a live chicken tied by its feet and squawking noisily. Master Li appeared nearby, standing over the table, muttering a chant and making exotic gestures with his fingers.

As Diana watched, grimly intrigued, Yi-kin leaned close to her and whispered, "Master Li call on General of Heaven to seize *kap-huet goong-si*."

Master Li, while still chanting, lifted the poor fowl, picked up a blade and quickly slit the bird's throat, making certain its lifeblood drained into the bowl. He flung the twitching corpse of the chicken aside, added some sort of powders to the bowl, and mixed it swiftly with one of the brushes, which he then used to inscribe yellow paper talismans similar to the one that Diana had seen him apply earlier to stop the *goong-si*.

Diana found herself mulling over the ramifications of what she was watching. Although she'd lost much of the Christian belief she'd been reared with, she was still a nineteenth-century European, so at first she thought this ritual rather primitive. Animal sacrifice had been extinct in western religions for hundreds of years, and surely if she found belief in one god difficult, then how was she to accept an entire pantheon? And yet the Taoist's magic had prevailed where her gun and crucifix had failed, so who was really the primitive here? Wasn't it possible that each culture had its own good and evil, and that the western crucifix was no better than the eastern *sutra*? Or was there a universal force for good that operated through the symbols of different beliefs?

Diana's thoughts finally circled back to the one fact she accepted wholeheartedly: This evil that had taken William must be stopped by whatever means were necessary.

Her reverie was interrupted just then by a clap of thunder. Next to her, Yi-kin grinned.

"I think Thunder General come," he whispered to her.

Suddenly the doors of the warehouse erupted inward from a mighty gust of wind, and there, framed by an intensifying night storm, stood the vampire. The *kap-huet goong-si*.

The creature was the size and shape of a man, dressed in tattered robes that indicated a Chinese who had once owned considerable wealth, perhaps a warlord or land baron. What had been a human face was now little more than patches of yellowing bone showing through strips of browned flesh; the most arresting feature of the thing was the eyes, glowing red with tangible malevolence.

Burning eyes . . .

Diana shivered, not from the storm but from the presence of an evil so old and all-consuming that no heat could exist in its presence. The thing began to glide forward, not walk, not hop like its ghoulish minions, but simply glide along the floor toward them. Diana and Yi-kin were completely stunned, and could only tremble in the frigid night and stare.

Master Li, however, suddenly hefted a long, ornately carved sword and advanced, still chanting, moving in a very curious way. At first Diana wondered if the man was drunk, but then she watched his feet carefully, saw the look of concentration on his face, and realized that he was dancing, moving around the vampire in a very specific pattern, thrusting his sword at it while not actually making contact with it.

Her paralysis broken, she leaned over to Yi-kin and whispered, "Do you know what he's doing?"

"He dance star," Yi-kin answered, without explanation.

Diana continued to watch Master Li's feet (while Master Li reiterated his chant), and she abruptly understood:

He was outlining the shape of the constellation known as Ursa Major—the Big Dipper.

The vampire stopped before Master Li and opened its skull-like jaws, as if trying to inhale. Master Li stumbled, and it swiftly became apparent that he was involved in a titanic struggle with the monster. His chanting became louder, more forceful, his thrusts at his opponent more violent. The very air between them began to fill with a reddish mist, which Diana saw with considerable astonishment was actually emerging from Master Li; the vampire was sucking his blood simply by inhaling, pulling it out through the man's very pores. Now she knew why she'd seen no bite marks on the victim she'd examined.

This abomination is so powerful it need not even touch its victims, she thought with a shudder.

Master Li redoubled his efforts, screaming his chant, but the monster was not deterred. His arms trembling, face turning pale, the priest reached behind him with the sword and stabbed the talisman he had created earlier, then turned to the vampire as it continued to suck the life from him. With a final, shaky invocation Master Li drew back his arm, preparing to thrust both sword and talisman at the vampire's chest—

—and his strength suddenly failed him. He dropped the sword and fell to his knees.

There was no hesitation in Diana as she leapt forward, seizing the sword where it lay. She barely heard Yi-kin call out her name in alarm, but it didn't matter; her world was about the fury that threatened to explode her, that would be extinguished only by the death of the abomination before her. Screaming over the roaring of the *kap-huet goong-si*, she drove the sword and talisman deep into the chest of the demon. Outside there was a clap of thunder like a hundred cannon-shot, and suddenly the *kap-huet goong-si* was simply gone. No final hellish screech, no fountain of stolen blood; it had just winked out of existence.

Diana was panting, and she was very glad when Yi-kin was suddenly there beside her, holding her up.

"Diana *siu jeh*, you are hurt—!"

Puzzled, Diana looked down at herself and realized she was covered in a fine misting of blood, but not hers. "I'm fine, Yi-kin. But Master Li . . . ?"

She turned and saw the Taoist rising slowly to his feet. His skin was too white, his features sunken, but she knew he would live. After a moment to regain his breath, the priest turned to Yi-kin and spoke a few words in a soft, weakened voice. Yi-kin turned to Diana to translate.

"He say heavenly general have seize *kap-huet goong-si* and take it to hell," said Yi-kin. "He say dock again safe."

Diana found her satchel and withdrew the envelope of pound notes, which she offered to Master Li with a bow and the respect gesture. Master Li accepted the envelope, returned the bow, gathered a few of his things (brushes, bowls, red cloth), and turned to go. Just before he stepped out into the eastern night, he looked back a final time and said something to Yi-kin. Then he was gone.

"What did he say?" Diana asked.

Yi-kin smiled. "He say you would make good Taoist."

On the day following the exorcism of the *kap-huet goong-si*, Diana reported to Antonia that the docks were quite safe again, and she made arrangements for William's remains to be recovered and returned to England. The Furnavals maintained a family crypt on their ancestral estate at Derby (she hoped the crypt had good *feng shui*), and William would be interred there—as would she, one day.

But, to her own surprise, she hoped that day wouldn't arrive soon.

Later, Diana found out that British troops outside a small portside Chinese town had just killed several peasants who had protested opium importation. The British had thus far refused to hand over any of the soldiers involved in the incident, and Diana knew they never would.

It was of course news throughout Canton, although Diana was quite sure it would never reach England. Even if it did, it would be dismissed as a simple "disciplinary action", something designed to keep "John Chinaman" in line.

Diana began to hate her own people.

Although she'd become very fond of Yi-kin, she felt increasingly that she didn't belong in China; in fact, she felt that *none* of the Englishmen belonged there.

She also began to realize that she was specifically angry with Sir Edward. The Hintons had made their fortune off the opium trade, and had convinced themselves that the Chinese were simpletons, to be exploited in the name of greed. Diana's outrage, in fact, became so great that she finally marched into Antonia's office, gave her a letter to deliver to Sir Edward, and informed Antonia that she would not be returning to England aboard a Hinton Company vessel. Antonia reacted coolly, and Diana suspected that Antonia both regretted breaking down before Diana in the wake of her experience with the *goong-si*, and the triumph of the Taoist after Antonia's refusal to meet his price. In fact, Diana thought—sadly—that Antonia would probably be happy to see her go.

After she left Antonia's office, Diana sought out Yi-kin. She found him in an office, checking over a number of documents. He looked up as she entered, smiling, and Diana had a pang at the thought of leaving this young man behind.

"Yi-kin, I just wanted to tell you that I'll be leaving Canton soon, to take my husband's body back to England."

Yi-kin stared down at the floor, his voice low. "I am also leaving."

"Yes, you'll be shipping out on another Hinton ship quite soon, I expect—"

"No," Yi-kin blurted out, cutting Diana off. "I am leaving Hinton Company."

"To go where?"

"I do not yet know." Finally he looked up at her, and his handsome young face was creased in pain. "You ask me about opium and I say it is legal, so I do not think about it. But now . . . I do think. You are right, *siu jeh*. Opium is very bad. I cannot do this work. I will find another job."

And with that Diana had a sudden inspiration. She didn't stop to think about the ramifications, or the difficulties built into the idea. She simply blurted it out:

"Yi-kin, would you like to work for me? I'll pay you more than whatever you've made here. I promise you'll never have to transport opium."

Yi-kin's face nearly split apart from the resulting grin, and he literally leaped over a desk to bow to Diana, who waved at him to stop. "Yi-kin, really, that's not necessary—*m sai* . . ."

Diana was astonished to realize she was smiling. She knew her grief would be long, and that life without William in a country she no longer loved would be difficult and lonely, but she thought that just maybe—with this remarkable young assistant by her side—she could face whatever fate still had in store for her.

ALLEY OOPS

DEL HOWISON

Darkness had been arriving earlier ever since the time change had gone into effect. The gray of the evening had been pushed from the sky by the heavy curtain of night, and the autumn wind's piercing damp chill easily cut through thick layers of clothing as people on the street bowed and braced themselves against its breath. With their hats pulled down and collars turned up they appeared to be a race of faceless alien creatures that leaned forward when they walked. Shafts of light from the department store windows created square yellow pools on the sidewalks, beckoning those outside to come in out of the cold.

Inside, the customers still shuffled from counter to counter in search of some final closing time bargain. The anxious clerks alternated between looking at their watches and straightening counters so they'd be able to leave as soon as the store door hit the last customer in the backside on their way out. In different areas, sections of the overhead fluorescents were shut down as a "last call" to spendaholic patrons. A general cattle-like movement toward the doors began with the occasional heifer housewife clutching her purse and looking up uneasily at the areas of darkened lights. The old timers smiled to themselves with the knowledge of another fifteen minutes of shopping time still available. It was to this latter group of regulars that Lupita belonged.

Actually, Lupita was part of an even smaller subspecies of consumer. Lupita was a counter-window shopper. The difference between regular window-shopping and what Lupita did was that she did it from inside the store. She was in her seventies. She needed more calcium than she would ever see again (as her teeth offered testament to) and she was having a harder time seeing since the onslaught of her cataracts. In reality, these daily shopping sprees were the highlight of her life—these and the *700 Club* on television. She would just listen to it, with her eyes closed so as not to cause herself undo pain and strain, and feel the spirit of the Dove filling her entire two-room apartment with love and understanding and a hand held out for a minimum ten percent tithe.

She rationalized that ten percent of what little she received was a very small price to pay for eternal life and the answers to all of her prayers. The eternal life was yet to come and she was positive that before she died she would manage to get all of her prayers answered. God couldn't do it all at once. There were other people in the world to consider. A good, God-fearing woman like herself couldn't be a pig about blessings and still plan to receive her reward in heaven.

She didn't mind not being able to buy the things she pawed at and picked through in the department store. No coveting here, even though she did imagine herself wearing and owning the prized goods that were on the tables and hanging from the racks. It was enough for her just to be able to touch them. But she had used her current prayer to ask God to let her see things a little better. Since her cataracts took deed to her sight, the colors had faded, even in the store's bright neon lights. The materials she ran through her fingers still felt lovely. There was no change in her sense of touch. But the fashions just weren't the same without color. Despite her age she'd always felt knowledgeable on fashions. After all, she saw the latest ones every day in the department store. But if God could only help her with a little more color sense . . .

Fifteen minutes, and the time to leave this wonderland for the day had come at last. There was always a strange feeling when she left each day at closing time. It was like leaving a bar at two a.m., except here she became her real self at closing time, instead of better looking, like through the eyes of drunken men. That's what they say, isn't it? Everybody looks good at closing? She paused for a moment. Yep, it was just the opposite here. She felt like she looked good until closing and then went out into the real world her old self.

"Lupita."

She raised her hand *goodnight* to the sound of the guard's voice and started shuffling out of the door. Tomorrow was another day and her daily store routine would begin again.

He always felt he was running faster when he was running into the wind. The rush of air against his face as it blew his hair back, the extra roar in his ears, all combined to make him feel like the comic book character The Flash. He could only imagine what it might feel like to ride a motorcycle. Right now he was just a wannabe. But someday he would have enough money to buy that motorcycle or just about anything else he wanted.

He still had the purse clutched tight to his side as he ran into the wind, a blur moving swiftly across the comic book page. He wanted to be sure he'd put enough distance between himself and the origin of the purse before he stopped. The woman had been in such a tizzy when he'd snatched it that he knew it would take her a few moments to recover from the shock. Then she'd probably act like a typical female and run in circles yelling and flailing her arms. He had to laugh at the imagery. Like a chicken with its head cut off. Ha! They were all so damn pathetic, so damn useless. His father had been right.

With a little distance between him and the woman he felt safer and finally slowed down. The alley before him offered a large, dark refuge from prying eyes and he headed into it to find a place to check out his prize. Except for the streetlights at each end of the alley, it remained shadow-filled and secretive. Halfway down the tarred strip he stopped and crouched down on the ground. The purse was already unzipped (another smart move by a stupid woman), so he dumped the contents out onto the ground. Quickly, he spread everything out in front of him so that he could easily see it all. Outside of the wallet and some loose change there didn't appear to be anything of value to him. He scooped up the silver change from the ground and stuffed it into his pockets. The wallet contained a twenty and two tens, which he also took.

Swearing silently to himself for such a small take, he hurled the wallet over the fence into an adjoining backyard. He kicked and scattered everything on the ground in different directions. Then he began to walk toward the end of the alley carrying the empty purse with him. After he'd gone a couple of blocks he'd drop the purse in a trashcan or shrub. Nothing would be left together, no arrows to point toward him. He had to cover his tracks every time. He'd have to do it again. No one who really knew how to party could live on forty bucks a night.

The wind caught Lupita on the side of the face and shoved her sideways against the storefront. She sidle-hopped on one leg a moment trying to balance herself and turned in toward the side of the building.

"The Devil's wind," she muttered through a mouthful of stalactites.

She stuck her hand inside of her coat pocket and pulled out her babushka. The wind pulled and grabbed at the material, turning it into a windsock. She held the corners tightly and yanked it down across her hair. The wind continued to tear at it, this way and that, until she finally had wrapped it on to her satisfaction. She pulled it down close against her head and tied it storm-tight under her chin. Her head almost felt hermetically sealed against Satan. She couldn't see very well anyway, so having it pulled so far down over her face was no additional problem. Once she managed to arrive home she would have to brush her hair for hours before she could sleep on it. Such were the idiosyncrasies of old-timer's disease.

Now that she had battened down the hatches, she was ready to forge ahead and find her way home. It wasn't far, only a couple of blocks. The wind was cutting through her thin summer coat. It pierced every threadbare inch of the cheap ancient material and she was feeling naked against nature's onslaught. It was, however, the warmest coat she owned. It was the only coat she owned. There would come a time when she would be able to get one of those quilted thick coats she'd seen in the store tonight. She would be so toasty and warm in a number like that. All of her friends would stop her on the street and want to touch her lovely coat. Someday. In the meantime, she layered underneath it for insulation.

She looked ahead at the two windy blocks before her. The traffic signals bounced and swayed in the air and newspapers scrambled past her like they were trying to shake their printing loose. She sighed. Just because you are old does not mean you have to fall into a routine, she thought. If she took the alley just tonight she'd not only cut off some distance but maybe some of the breeze too. She slid the strap of her battered purse up her arm and headed for the entrance of the alley.

He moved quick and light, like something being buffeted about by the wind. Almost invisibly, he breezed down the alley, keeping his eyes and ears open to any opportunity that might blow past. The wind was both a curse and a blessing. While it covered up any sounds he might make, it also caused him to jump at each and every scuttle of paper or clang of metal. He didn't like it. He was nervous enough without help from Mother Nature. He would have been a lot happier sitting in some still corner with a joint and a full paper of cocaine. But he'd need much more than forty dollars to come up with a good bindle and something to drink too. One more really good snatch could make his evening and he was anxious to get it over with as soon as possible.

He came to the mouth of the alley and stood with his back against the gritty side of the building. He needed to plan his next move. While he stood there sniffing the wind, it brought the sound to him. The noise was human in origin, no doubt, and it was talking. But it was only one voice, like a radio. There was no response from a second party.

He peeked around the corner of the building trying to focus in on the sound. What he could make out was a lump of clothing, a shapeless, formless, indefinite mass of clothing. He knew it was human from the sound and he could tell it was female by the pitch. But the way it huddled inside of its clothes left its configuration up for question. But there! Right there! High up on the part of the lump he took for an arm and a shoulder was a purse. His ticket for fun and games had just been punched.

Lupita reached the mouth of the alley and turned toward home. The changing of direction as she rounded the corner stopped the wind from slamming her sideways and it became a head-on battering as she was shoved forward and back. She wrapped her clothes about herself a bit tighter, gritted her teeth, and thrust her body forward with determination. She wasn't thrilled with traversing the alley but anything that cut down on the travel time home tonight was a plus in her book. She wasn't able to shrug off colds and flu like she used to and her old bones would ache for days after a bout with illness. If she could get home relatively quickly maybe she could avoid getting sick.

The clanging of a metal trashcan lid blowing off and smacking down onto the asphalt made her jump to the side. A newspaper dancing down the alley wrapped itself around one of her legs, causing her to jump and kick it with vigor before she realized what it was that had latched onto her. She felt like a complete fool to be so nervous. After all, it was her neighborhood, her old familiar neighborhood where she'd grown up. There was no need to be frightened. But for some reason she couldn't shake her feeling of encroaching fear.

She'd finished walking the length of one alley and only had one more to go. Then she would round the corner and be home. Then she'd be warm and safe. Then she would have something warm to drink and put her feet up. It was so silly to worry. She'd truly get a chuckle about this. So silly. She tried the mind trick of thinking warm toasty thoughts and felt a little better.

He watched and then followed behind her across the side street and into the mouth of the next alley. He'd been watching her ever since he'd heard her approach. He'd backed into the darkness, and she had passed within no more then ten or twelve feet of him in the alley. She didn't see him because she had her rags wrapped down so tight about her face it must have been like looking through a periscope for her. Lost in her own world of muttering, she plowed as straight and narrow a course as she could. He knew she couldn't hear him. Occasionally, the sound of her one-sided conversation would carry down to him on the wind. He could tell by the way she jumped when some papers blew against her leg that she was pretty skittish and he'd have to be quick. He laughed. Maybe she thought it was a rat or something.

"No rats out tonight, lady," he whispered. "Only one mean old junkyard dog come to get his bone."

He moved faster now to catch up to her, skirting the shadows in case she happened to look back. He wanted to grab her before she reached the end of the alley. He wanted to keep his face in the alley's darkness when he caught her. There would be no chance for identification on this snatch and grab. The way she was bent into the wind, she'd never be able to stop him. Hit it and run. His heart thumped in anticipation. The preparation was always the fun part. Cleaning the weed was almost as fun as smoking it. Chopping the rocks was the mental preparation for snorting the coke. Lining up the attack was as fun as the grab. Anyway you looked at it, it was all about the rush.

Lupita stuck out her chin and allowed herself one deep cold breath of relief and a small smile of satisfaction. She could see the streetlight at the end of the alley; shadows from tree branches danced across the face of it, waving to her to hurry and come home. It wouldn't be long now. Home was just around the corner. She pulled the babushka down tighter about her face. So close and yet . . .

She was knocked sideways by his assault, like being blindsided by a car. It was a move he had perfected long before tonight. The idea was to knock the victim one way while grabbing the purse and moving in the opposite direction. It almost always snapped the woman and her purse apart like a wishbone. Almost always. This time the strap sat up so high onto her shoulder that it actually helped to right her stance when he pulled on it. He was running to beat the band in the opposite direction when he realized he wasn't going anywhere. He turned and saw the woman with the scarf-covered face holding on to her purse strap like it was a lifeline to a rowboat. He couldn't believe it. It just wasn't his night.

Holding firm onto the strap he quickly glanced around the alley for some help. There it was. The gods were surely joking with him now. A stick the size of a thick cane lay not eight feet away from where they struggled. Although he couldn't get her to release the prize, he could begin pulling her in the general direction of the wood. She might not let loose right away but she wasn't strong enough to stop him from pulling her in that direction.

Keeping one hand grasped firmly around the purse strap, he reached out with the other for the stick. A bit more, just a step. His fingers scraped at it, bumping against it and pushing it further from his grasp. More, dammit, just a little more. It felt like a scene from an old film where the prisoner is reaching through the bars, attempting to gather up the keys to his jail cell. The only audible sound was the wind, its rushing past their ears with a locomotive moan and covering up the grunts and groans made by the two of them. Nobody spoke a real word. Until finally, just barely, his fingers were on top of the shaft, and now over the top, grabbing it firmly. It felt good in his hand, weighty enough. He turned back and took one last look at the living clothes hamper still holding the purse strap. He swung his club for all he was worth.

The blow caught her on the upper left side of the face, snapping her head back with a loud crack, stunning her. But her grip on her purse never weakened. She was probably holding on more by reflex, using the strap as a lifeline. He turned, facing her straight on, and swung again. This time the blow came down from above, hitting her on the top of the head and slamming her to her knees. Still she held on as he jerked and wiggled the purse in her hands. He was getting angry. From his hip he swung his bat one-handed, putting his body behind it, and embedded the scarf in the side of her face, opening up and fusing skin, meat, and material.

She fell to the pavement, finally, the cheap faux leather strap snapped under her weight and the purse was freed. The bloody side of her face thumped onto the asphalt with a sickening thud. A dark stain soaked its way quickly through the material, spreading out and forming a small stream that ran from her head. The ends of the kerchief fluttered in the wind, which unsuccessfully tried to pull it out from under her wet face. Breathing hard, he held up the purse like a trophy. He had his prize, but it had been too much work. It had taken too large of a toll, too much time, too much effort. He dumped the contents carelessly on the ground and scattered them quickly. There was no wallet, no money.

He was angry about the effort involved. He was angry with her resistance. He was angry about her strength and sheer determination. He was angry it had all been for naught. He swore and kicked the purse into the darkness of the alley walls. Raising the stick, he rained a series of blows to her body. The thuds sounded like he was beating a mattress.

"Bitch! You bitch," he screamed, working the frustration out of his system.

Smacking her a final blow on the top of the head he saw her split brains glisten and reflect the streetlight from the end of the alley. The blood from the battered side of her head oozed out from under her mouth, in a puddle. Finally he tossed the stick aside, breathing heavily but strong again with the emotional recharging of the beating. He spat at the form on the ground and wiped his mouth with the length of his sleeve.

Another sudden blast of frigid air raced down the alley, scooping up under her kerchief and finally peeling it away from her bloody face. He stood there and stared down into the face of his grandmother.

THE MYSTERIOUS NAME

KELLY DUNN

Dina Tempris awakened hours before dawn, drenched in sweat that cooled to icy wetness on her skin. In her dream she had been naked, surrounded by blackness that pressed in on her. Nothing to see. Nothing to touch. There had been voices in the void, chanting a word she could not understand. In her night-shrouded room, Dina knew she had to get up, had to reassure herself with tangible reality. She needed to look at *it*, to see its strange eyes and its arm extended as if wanting to take her hand.

She stepped out of bed, put on her cashmere robe, and grabbed the emergency flashlight she kept on her nightstand. The light's narrow halogen beam guided her through the hall and down the old servants' stairway to the huge kitchen, built like the rest of the house for a prosperous nineteenth-century family. Closing the stairway door behind her, she crept as quietly as she could past the door at the back of the kitchen, which led to the spare rooms where Gabi lived.

Gabi would be asleep. Dina kept early hours and expected her employees to do the same. Still, Dina wanted to make sure she would have this time all to herself. She turned right and went through the third door, which led to the three downstairs parlors.

She kept the idol at the front of the house, in the day parlor. It stood about three feet tall, elevated on a low marble-topped table in the bay window, which was shrouded by lace curtains. During the day, filtered sunlight brought out the transparency of its surface. At night, the orange light of the streetlamps bathed it in an otherworldly glow.

The strange dreams had troubled Dina for the last two weeks, but staring at her new possession calmed her, helped her clarify her thinking. The figure looked different to her each time she saw it. Sometimes it looked like a benevolent god, or then again, like a malevolent angel.

Though she did not know its exact identity, Dina did recognize its rarity: one of a kind. In all her years as an estate specialist, she had never seen another statue of its type or size that so artfully incorporated this many minerals and gemstones.

As she turned a corner she saw the table lamp in the parlor already shining. In its light a shadow moved: a human figure. Dina froze. In almost the same instant she recognized Gabi's skinny frame, the long chestnut braid she always wore. Gabi, not moving about in a whirlwind of activity, not consulting Dina about the priority of household chores or the day's appointments, the way Dina had become accustomed to seeing her. Gabi never held still, never expressed interest in objets d'art. But there she stood, simply staring in awe at the idol, which the table raised to her eye level. Its figure was slim and finely muscled, its surface pearly and translucent enough for the light to penetrate it partway, illuminating it the way blood limns the skin.

Dina stepped behind the doorway, watching as Gabi tentatively reached out and touched the statue, running her fingers over its chiseled musculature. Dina herself had done this many times, so she knew exactly what Gabi was seeing and feeling. The cool stone of its body warmed to the touch. But though the figure's torso resembled that of a perfectly proportioned athlete, it had strange features. Gabi tilted the lamp a little so the light shone more directly on it. The sculptor had given the idol two extra nipples, one in the center of the chest, and one on the right side just under its rib cage. From there Gabi traced the length of the idol's right arm, which extended outward, ending in a hand with only four fingers, which Gabi tapped with her own. Dina felt the familiar longing to place her hand in the statue's outstretched palm. The left hand's six fingers curled around a scimitar at the figure's waist, its curved sheath inlaid with glittering precious stones.

Gabi moved the lamp back a little and leaned over the table to marvel at the wings branching out of the idol's back, three pair pointing upward. The idol also had a pair of horns jutting from its back, curving downward like tusks. The horns, bizarre and macabre, provided a counterpoint to the abundance of wings, as if they would keep the idol from getting too close to heaven should it choose to fly.

Dina felt almost as if she were watching herself as Gabi stood back so that she could stare into the figure's face. Its eyes captivated Dina the most, and she could see Gabi's fascination as she stared at them, the right eye of faceted sparkling sapphire, and the left of opaque green jade. Though the figure's facial features had been perfectly rendered, the strange jade eye, a little too big for its socket, gave the left side of the face a somewhat deformed appearance.

Gabi reached out to touch that face, and Dina found herself calling out, in a harsher voice than she intended, "Is that you, Gabi?"

"Oh!" Gabi spun around, gasping a deep breath. "You scared me."

"Well, I thought *you* were a burglar, at first."

"Sorry."

Dina fought down the irritation that, for her, always followed fear. *What's wrong with a little curiosity?* she thought. *Gabi didn't mean any harm.* She approached the table and gestured toward the statue. "It's beautiful, isn't it?"

Gabi nodded. In her voice, only the faintest trace of a Colombian accent remained. "Yes. I couldn' sleep. I didn' mean to come out here, but . . ."

"Do you like it?" Dina interrupted.

Gabi nodded. "It's so pretty. What's it s'posed to be?"

"It's something very precious. That's really all I know."

"Must be old, huh?" Gabi started reaching for the statue again.

Dina surprised herself by putting her own hand over Gabi's, stopping her. "I'd really prefer you not touch this statue. Old things are sometimes quite fragile."

For the first time, Dina saw a spark of irony, or perhaps resentment, in Gabi's huge obsidian eyes as she obediently dropped her arm.

"Yes." She gave Dina the subtlest of once-overs. "I can see that." And she walked out of the parlor toward her own rooms.

Dina remained in the parlor for another hour, gazing at the idol. It really was the most beautiful thing she had ever acquired, and the only one she had come across that she had to have at any price. It had definitely been worth haggling with Mrs. Lyon over the value of her late husband's estate.

The widow was a wreck when Dina arrived at the house.

"It's been so hard for us." Mrs. Lyon looked ready to cry again. Her grief made her appear older than her sixty-two years, as did the incongruous, rhinestone-emblazoned sweatsuit she wore. The much-used tissue in her hands started to shred. Her outfit had no pockets, so she kept crumpling the tissue, transferring it from one manicured hand to the other.

Dina nodded. "I understand." And she did. As an estate specialist, she'd dealt with the same situation, more or less, in endless variation during her twenty-year career.

The Lyon house was filled with a mix of exquisite antiques and costly modern items. Dina walked in Mrs. Lyon's wake, silently appraising each table, each display case with its precious collectibles, the limited edition lithographs on nearly every wall, the grand piano in the great room, the ostentatious furniture suite in the master bedroom.

Finally, they entered the guest bedroom. Unlike the rest of the house, this room contained only the essentials. A simple twin bed took up one corner, a cheap chest of drawers another. The bureau had a piece of red satin draped over it, upon which a statue towered toward the ceiling, apparently a mythological figure, a god or an angel.

Dina knew she had to have it.

"We slept in separate rooms, there at the end," Mrs. Lyon said, heedless of the fact that Dina was no longer paying attention.

"Larry always worked so hard. It was a real sacrifice for him—for all of us—but he was finally getting all the lovely things he wanted. But there at the end, nothing seemed to satisfy him. And after he went blind, it was like nobody else existed. Not me, not the kids... nothing but that—that statue there..." Mrs. Lyon smothered a sob. "I've got to downsize. I just can't bear to look at all the things he loved so much!"

"Don't worry," Dina assured her. "I'll take care of everything."

She slyly suggested that Mrs. Lyon sell the entire contents of the house for one price. "It's the easiest option. And that way, I can write you a check right now." The woman's eyes lit up, the prospect of immediate payment soothing her distress.

When they finally agreed on a sum, Dina had her employees pack up the contents of the house, sweep the floor, clean the windows, and deliver the goods of the Lyon estate to her warehouse. She was there to receive them, and to take the idol home herself.

She had sensed something special about the figure. The more she looked at it on that first day she had it set up in her house, the more she marveled. Mrs. Lyon really hadn't known what she'd given up.

Alice Abernathy thought the same when she came to the house to see it. "This is an amazing find!"

"Can you tell me anything about it?" Dina asked. "You know more about these things than I do."

Her old mentor squinted behind her bifocals as she examined the figure's skin. "Beautiful workmanship. Almost certainly meant for sacred purposes. Materials include alabaster, coral, quartz, amethyst . . . It *is* ancient, that much I know."

"I would love to know if it has a name or what its significance is."

Alice considered. "It reminds me a little of a story I once heard. In the book of Exodus, you know, there is the tale of how the wandering Israelites made themselves an idol in the shape of a golden calf to worship. According to that story, God became angry at such sacrilege. As a punishment, the calf was ground into powder, and the Israelites were forced to drink the gold dust with their water.

"But the verbal legend I heard said that afterward the disappointed people decided to secretly fashion their own idol to guide them through the wilderness. This time, instead of gold, they used the discontented cravings of their souls and the gold-dusted desires of their hearts to create something indestructible. Something small enough to carry with them, but in some way large enough to carry the sum of their ambitions."

Alice laughed, balancing her bifocals on the bridge of her nose. "Fortunately, we can see that this statue is made of recognizable materials."

"Did that idol have a name?"

Alice's eyes twinkled, but she only said, "That particular story didn't mention it."

"So what happened to it—the idol?"

"I don't know. Some people say it was destroyed, just like the golden calf. But others . . ."

Clearing her throat, Alice studied the idol once again. "Of course, something like that could never belong to just one person. It would be a public treasure. And I'm afraid you'll find that this statue belongs in the same category, my dear. It's really exquisite." She paused, tapping her wrinkled cheek with an emaciated finger the way she always did when something troubled her. "Dina, you may have stumbled onto something that you cannot keep. Are you prepared for that?"

"Yes. But of course I wouldn't want to let it go."

She winked, but Alice still wore an anxious frown. "Dinara, you've always done very well, and I'm very proud of you. Do you really need anything more? With your acquisitions and investments, I'm sure you could retire and start enjoying your things any time you wanted to."

Alice Abernathy only called Dina by her full name when she was worried about something. Dina just shrugged. "And leave the Ortegas with no competition?"

They both laughed. In the last few years, the innumerable Ortega family had moved up from swap-meet royalty to dealers in handmade furniture and bizarre knickknacks from all over the world. They had finally bought a large shop on Center Street. The only other shop in town that could boast more square footage belonged to Dina.

Yes, Alice was right: Dina knew she had done well. Not only could she give the Ortegas a run for their money, she could also afford to keep her mother in a fine assisted-living facility, with personalized care. She herself had everything she needed and more. And yet, when she allowed her mind to wander, there were so many other things she wanted for herself, so many more rungs to climb on the ladder to wealth. Retirement would have to wait. And the idol would, too. For now, at least, it belonged to *her*.

She cowered alone in the dark. Something had stripped her of everything she possessed—everything she loved—and dropped her into blackness. All around her, echoing in the emptiness, sounded a word she strained to understand, even as she plummeted onto a hard, cold surface with a stinging thump . . .

Dina's eyes snapped open as John Whitehead's hand slapped the table. "That's true, but this proposal simply isn't in line with this city's core values." Whitehead steepled his gold-ringed fingers and cast a smug look around the table.

Dina tried to focus on the city council meeting, but she could still hear the ominous echoes of her dream.

"Exactly what values are you talking about, John?" Carlos Muratalla loosened his silk tie as his face turned an angry shade of maroon.

"Look, the bottom line is, this proposal for 369 Central doesn't technically violate the ordinance," young Travis Lee pointed out. "I looked it up." And he held up the screen shot on his new iPhone as proof.

"He's right," agreed mayor Bleeker, dabbing at her face with a monogrammed handkerchief. "The Ortegas may make the changes they see fit, as long as they keep the letter of the law."

"But . . ." John Whitehead began.

Mayor Bleeker put on her most benevolent face. "John, the soup kitchen at 369 Central had its day, but what this city needs is revitalization. Since the Ortegas set up shop last year, business has really picked up. And when they get that kitchen gutted, they'll have room to expand. That means even more business for the city of Logro. Now I think that a store—any store—that can generate as much income as they have deserves a break. It's a sacrifice in terms of service, I know, but look at their numbers. It seems to me that the payoff in revenue will be well worth it. Don't you agree?"

Whitehead nodded, mulling it over.

"Dina? Your shop isn't too far from theirs. Do you have anything to add?"

Dina took another sip of coffee to combat the overwhelming urge to fall asleep again. She hadn't really followed the mayor's argument, so she just smiled at her. "I'm with you."

"Good. All in favor?"

After the vote, the mayor concluded with a little speech in which she not too successfully combined the concepts of civic pride, a high standard of living, and what she called "progress."

By the time the city council meeting finally adjourned, Dina was more than ready to head for home. She told herself this was because she felt so fatigued from sleeping badly over the last few weeks, but deep within her she knew she could not wait to admire her idol again.

With the meaningless monotony of the meeting still droning in her mind, Dina drove through the center of town on her way home, passing the Ortegas' store. Within the brightly lit interior, customers browsed and debated. The space next door, the ill-fated number 369, stood empty and dark like a sightless eye.

Two or three people whom Dina recognized as local homeless residents hung around outside—people who called the city home, even without an actual place to live. Dina wondered when they would find out that the suspended soup kitchen would never re-open.

The Morning Star Assisted Living facility was only a few miles from downtown. Dina knew she should take the opportunity to visit her mother. Dina was the only family, and probably the only friend, that her mother had left. Today, though, Dina felt reluctant to go. She wanted to spend some time with the idol, reflect on her life and goals.

Instead, Dina dutifully drove to the facility, which resembled an upscale condominium complex. On the inside, well-dressed elderly people sat in the designer lobby or hobbled out to waiting transportation, and two concierges and a receptionist manned the front desk.

Dina's mother had her own small apartment on the second floor. A uniformed aide opened the door, then discreetly left them alone.

"Oh, Dinara, I've missed you!" Dina's mother exclaimed from her wheelchair, her Eastern European accent still thick after nearly forty years in the U.S. "Oh, this makes me so happy!" She proudly pointed to the fresh flowers on the table and the neatly made bed. "See? Just like a hotel."

"I'm glad you like it, Mom. Are they taking good care of you?" *They had better be—I pay them enough*, thought Dina, and then felt ashamed for her selfishness. *It's the least I can do for her.*

Her mother beamed. "Yes, yes. Food is good, help is good, everything good." She put her arthritic hand on Dina's, her red-veined eyes moist with emotion. "But I would like to see you more."

"I'll try, Mom." But already Dina's thoughts were struggling with the competing demands of business versus family. *How can I visit her more often and still make enough money to pay for this?*

Dina's mother said, "I have something for you over there."

On the table lay a jewelry box. "Take out the black-and-white bracelet," Mother instructed.

Dina knew which bracelet her mother meant, a delicately threaded chain of tiny black-and-white glass beads in an intricate design. Mother's grandmother had made it. As a child Dina had always admired it. She brought it over to her mother. It was still in perfect condition, a testament to family legacy.

"You want me to have this?"

Her mother nodded, a tear falling down her wrinkled face. "I love you, Dinara."

"I love you, Mom." Smiling, she carefully wrapped the bracelet around her wrist, admiring the way the miniature facets of the beads caught the light.

It was dark when Dina finally pulled into her garage, and she worried whether Gabi had obeyed orders and left the idol alone. The girl's interest in the statue mystified and vexed Dina: Before, Gabi had simply treated the contents of Dina's house as things to clean and reposition, nothing more.

But the girl had been changing—especially in the last year. Certainly her habits now did not even resemble those of the frightened, barely literate girl of eighteen that Dina had hired six years ago. Back then, little Gabrielle had spoken virtually no English and had jumped every time someone knocked on the door. Now, she answered the door with hauteur, and could read and speak English as well as any American kid. Slowly, Dina's dependence on Gabi had grown, and now she knew as much about Dina's house, and almost as much about her business, as she did.

Dina found Gabi in the day parlor, wearing her crisp uniform apron and cleaning with an ostrich-feather duster, conspicuously ignoring the idol. A glint of silver on Gabi's wrist caught Dina's attention: a Tiffany ID bracelet, sparkling in the light.

Curiosity got the better of Dina. She indicated the bracelet. "That's new, isn't it?"

"Uh-huh." Gabi played with the bracelet's large silver tag. "From my boyfriend."

"What's his name again? Eric?"

"Nah—we broke up." Gabi laughed at the thought. "He was a loser. This new one, he treats me better." She held her head high.

Dina knew she should be happy at this flowering of Gabi's womanhood, at her newfound appreciation of the finer things. Yet fear crawled in Dina's stomach; jealousy stabbed just below her heart. An overwhelming urge to find out more about this new creature, this stranger who scared her and yet whom she could not live without, overtook her.

"Gabi, I'll be eating at D'Argent et D'Or tonight. Would you like to join me?"

Gabi's eyes became secretive. "Can't. I'm goin' out with my boyfriend tonight."

But Dina returned from dinner to find that Gabi and her boyfriend had stayed in, sitting at the base of the idol as if supplicating a saint. The boy looked about Gabi's age, with spiky black hair and broad shoulders. His cologne wafted through the room like incense. He wore a Lacoste sportshirt and athletic shoes, brand new. Dina had met him once before, at the Ortegas' grand opening party. His name was George, the third son in the Ortega dynasty.

"Hey," he greeted her. "It's nice." From his sitting position, he craned his neck up at the idol in covetous admiration. "My dad would love this. What do you call it?"

Dina tried to smile. "I'm not sure yet. Please make yourself at home."

Then George put his arm around Gabi's waist, and an irrational burst of anger propelled Dina upstairs.

In her own room, in front of her full-length mirror, Dina examined her face. Could it be that age brought with it a certain bigotry? Dina did not feel decrepit, but Gabi's one ironic reference to her age had hit home. When Dina looked at her reflection she still recognized the face of the twenty-year-old blonde who had begged Alice Abernathy to take her on as a junior appraiser, but she also detected little flaws that had not been there before, the harbingers of middle age. She did have a certain fear of getting older. Not of age itself, but of being squeezed out somehow before she had finished getting what she wanted. Her business made a tidy profit, but so far Dina had disdained the unethical business practices, the corner-cutting, that had made some of her colleagues not merely well-off, but rich. Someday she would double her savings and investments, become a landlord, buy a cute beach cottage for herself. For now, those things had to wait.

No, it had not been the sight of young love that had disturbed her, she decided. It was just the feeling of others moving in on her dreams. The idol, her idol, represented what belonged to her—the things her astuteness and hard work had bought. More importantly, it represented the things yet to come.

For the rest of the week, Gabi remained distant during the day. She worked as hard as she ever had. The house stayed well maintained. Dina's schedule ran as smoothly as before. But in the evening, Gabi's off hours, George Ortega would appear. The two of them would sit as close as they could to the idol, whispering in Spanish together.

Dina could not sleep at all. She would stay awake, anxious yet somehow ashamed to go downstairs in her own house. Something about the combination—Gabi and George in the presence of the idol—forbade her to get too close. On Wednesday night, Gabi's jilted boyfriend Eric showed up at the house.

Dina had already gone to bed, leaving Gabi and George downstairs in what had become their routine. She was just going into her room when she heard a cacophony of raised voices: Gabi and two young men. It sounded like an argument. Then, an awful bellowing and blubbering. It didn't last long, but after only a few seconds of it Dina wanted to cry, to comfort whoever was making all that heartrending noise.

Halfway down the stairs Dina saw the young man standing in the foyer. He held his head so low it almost touched his chest. His hands were pressed against his face, but they did not muffle the sounds of his sobbing. Dina recognized Eric's dark brown hair and gangly build before he turned around and left, leaving the front door open.

Dina went down and closed the door, locking it behind him. She found Gabi and George in the parlor sitting near the idol, in the same serene attitude as before Dina had gone to bed.

"What happened here?"

Gabi gave her most insouciant smile. "Just Eric. He didn't do nothing—just cried." She said it as if reporting the time of day, with no trace of emotion.

George obligingly added, "I kicked him out. Sorry if we disturbed you."

"Then you're all right, Gabi?"

"Of course."

"Will…Eric…be all right?"

Gabi shrugged. "Doesn't matter. We want different things. I told him that. Anyway, we gotta think of the future." She squeezed George's hand.

"Yeah," George grinned. "We're gonna have a real good life." As if on cue, both Gabi and George raised their heads to regard the statue.

Their callousness troubled Dina as she struggled to sleep that night. But as she sank into twilight consciousness she decided that perhaps she had made too much of the situation. An unpleasant aftermath almost always followed a bad breakup.

She didn't think of the confrontation again until the next day when Gabi, looking the same as usual, brought in the morning paper. The *Police Reports* section carried a small item, one of many such articles, on an evident suicide: A young man who had been upset over a breakup had been found with his wrists slashed down to the bone. Dina knew the name before she read it. Eric. Gabi's Eric.

If Gabi had seen the news, it didn't seem to upset her. On Friday night, her eyes glowed dark fire as she and George sat in their usual place at the idol's feet, and she wore a new Tiffany necklace to go with her bracelet.

On Saturday night Dina decided to go to bed early. She would take half a sleeping pill, get the rest she needed, and then wait out Gabi's day off on Sunday. On Monday morning, she would have a little chat with the girl about having George over to the house all the time…and about the idol. *Dina's* idol. Instead of real sleep, though, Dina half-dozed in her room, the darkness chasing her, until the idol looked at her with its mismatched eyes and closed its strong hand around hers, crushing it until she could hear her bones crunch and shatter.

Once more Dina found herself sweating in the blind dark with that gut-twisting sense of loss. And again, her steps guided her to the day parlor, which for the first time all week lay dark. Even before Dina found the lamp smashed on the floor, she sensed the emptiness where the figure had stood. No alabaster-and-coral silhouette, no strong hand reaching for hers, no protection of the many-jeweled sword.

She rushed to the front door, flinging it open just in time to see two people hop-running at the far end of the street, an inert figure, dead weight, slung between them. The one on the left was small and thin, a long braid bobbing behind her. Gabi. The person on the right was quite a bit taller, with spiky hair and broad shoulders . . . George Ortega. As they reached the end of the street two more tall male-shaped figures came out to greet them, taking their part of the idol's weight. No doubt George's brothers. Of course they were all in it together. All wanting to take what belonged to her.

Outrage overshadowed Dina's mind. She ran after them, not even caring that she only wore her nightgown, her soft bare feet suffering on the rough asphalt. She could barely see the thieves as they reached the end of the street, made a sharp left turn, and disappeared. Where did they think they were taking her idol? It was not as if she didn't know, couldn't have Gabi and the entire Ortega tribe prosecuted, made to pay for what they'd done.

Limping, she made it to the end of the street. Only silence and complete darkness met her there: The streetlights on that side had burned out. The wind began to moan. Dina felt cold. The same way she felt in her dream, the humid dark congealing like syrup around her as she ran, seeking recourse without her clothes and all the material things that made her powerful.

Looming to the left, where the thieves and her idol had vanished, rose the solid side of a church. A historical landmark, like so many in Logro, built in the days of robber barons and logging millionaires. It stood a pristine white in the darkness, its steeple reaching up toward the sky. It made no sense, but Dina knew, knew absolutely, that Gabi and friends had to have hidden in its shadows or in an archway, somewhere. There was no sound of a getaway car, and now no sight of them.

The church.

Dina had never particularly noticed it before. Most Sundays, if she did not have a tag sale to run or an auction to attend, she spent catching up on paperwork.

Now she wondered at the fact that, though the hour of midnight had passed, the church's interior showed signs of life. Its stained glass windows, done not in pictures but in abstract patterns of silver, gold, and copper, seemed to pulse and glitter with light from inside.

She looked for stairs or unguarded doors all along the building's side, then walked around to the front of the church. There she saw a sign. Not the wooden board or old-school light box she would have expected, but a digital display that proclaimed in fast-moving neon green letters: **IGLESIA DE GLORIOSO CONSECUCION...CHURCH OF GLORIOUS ATTAIN-MENT...**

A group of people stood in front of the steps leading to the church door. They all wore the casual yet expensive clothes of those who are rich enough to dress according to their whims no matter what the occasion.

A woman holding a monogrammed handkerchief stepped forward. "Glad you could make it, Dina." Mayor Bleeker smiled in welcome.

John Whitehead took her hand. "I'm a believer now, Dina. Go on in and see what wonderful things we can have if we only sacrifice. Wonderful things."

"But they *stole*." Dina shook her head. "They *stole* it. They stole *my* property!" Hot tears burned on her face. No one understood that there was nothing like the idol, that until it was safe with her again she could be sure of nothing in the universe.

Carlos Muratalla put his hand on her shoulder. "You'll see. We can get rid of all the dead weight in this town, make it into the city it *should* be."

Travis Lee nodded. "And all according to the ordinances!"

Muratalla gestured to the church doorway in invitation. "Let us show you."

Dina allowed him to guide her up the steps and inside. She glanced around, confused. The scene within did not look like any church she'd ever seen.

People from all areas of town sat on the floor, not even pews or chairs separating them, chanting a word Dina did not quite understand. Exactly as her dream had presaged.

At the front of the church stood a familiar religious accouterment: an altar, covered with a deep red cloth. And on the cloth, bathed in its own spotlight, high over the kneeling worshippers, stood the idol. It looked so glorious, so right and holy, that Dina forgot her anger, did not even remember Gabi's betrayal and the Ortegas' complicity. The jewels on the idol's sword and in its two-toned eyes gleamed majestically.

Dina moved down the center aisle until she could see what was happening around the altar. Below the idol, a small knot of people took turns throwing pieces of paper into a fire below its altar. Not just pieces of paper, Dina saw, but photographs, snapshots of family and friends. Some of the pictures looked old, dog-eared and sepia-toned, but most looked recent—candids of birthday parties and graduations and holiday celebrations.

And there in the very front, her hand protectively on the red altar covering, stood Alice Abernathy, beaming in approval just as she had in her mentoring days when Dina had been particularly clever in business. As each photograph turned to ashes she repeated as if saying a blessing, "This is the pledge of your sacrifice. This is the pledge of your sacrifice."

When someone ran out of pictures to throw in the fire, he or she would join those who chanted on the floor. Dina got closer to them, hoping she would catch the word they chanted. She noticed that each of them held a toy or a miniature of some kind. The incomprehensible word rose from their throats, a song, a heartbeat, a prayer.

While the ever-growing mob of worshippers chanted, Dina leaned to look closely first at one, and then another. A beefy man held a miniature red Ferrari. A middle-aged woman held an ad: before and after Botox. A young couple clutched a fistful of cash between them. And the chant grew louder, stronger, ringing with conviction.

Gabi stood a respectful distance from the altar, George Ortega at her side. His brothers, sister, Mom and Pop Ortega, and even Grandma Ortega, leaning on her walker. The entire family surrounded Gabi as she threw something in the fire. As the flames consumed the photo, Dina saw that it was a picture of Gabi and

Eric, obviously taken in happier times. Alice Abernathy stepped over to the Ortegas, acknowledging Eric. Dead, bloodied, broken-hearted Eric. "And this is the pledge of your sacrifice," she said, her hand extended in benediction.

Dina turned to Gabi, to Alice. "What is this? Why?"

Gabrielle lifted her hands in praise to the idol. "This god shows us our true desires. He helps us let go of our distractions."

She faced Dina. "Eric couldn't give me the kind of life I wanted. He had to go. And I guess he knew it."

Dina approached the altar, where the idol waited. "You know you can't have Him back," Alice said.

"But it's mine. It belongs to me," Dina said.

"No." Alice's eyes sparked with fanatical fire. "His name is Mammon. And He belongs to all of us."

Mammon? Dina looked around, at the crowded floor, at the colored windows, and tried to remember where she had heard the mysterious name. A dim memory appeared: A different church that overwhelmed her childhood self into silence, a place where the poor went to pray. A bearded priest who spoke the language Dina had known as a child. The priest trembled as he shook a black book—so enormous it had seemed to her at the time—proclaiming, "My friends, you cannot serve both God and Mammon."

The recollection seemed like part of another life, but as Dina turned to face the idol once more she realized that the priest had spoken the truth. The cosmic contest between two such powerful entities could only produce one winner. And really, was there even any contest between the unseen and the material, between some nebulous future glory and the lure of cash in hand?

As understanding came to Dina, she found that she finally understood the word being chanted, over and over and yet again: "More, more, more, more, more, more, more, more . . ." A hypnotic, a joyful refrain, full of sacred meaning.

Alice stepped toward her, a minister with a new lamb. "And you, Dina. Will you make a pledge of your sacrifice?"

Dina nodded. She knew the truth now. Carefully, she undid the beaded bracelet. Reverently, she laid it on the fire, watching its silk fastenings combust, the pretty beads grow shiny as they started to deform and melt.

Yes, Dina thought, *more. How can I get more?* Her business, for one thing. She'd have to start buying for less and selling for more. A lot more. She could fudge on the values of things. Plenty of people did it. Drove up demand, increased profits, brought up perceived value, and everybody won.

And Mother. Putting her in an expensive assisted-living facility had been a huge mistake. But having her home again? That would be impossible if Dina wanted to expand the business. Couldn't have an invalid and a nurse underfoot. She would find a cheaper alternative right away.

Looking from the idol's strange eyes to Alice's expression of serene satisfaction, to Gabi's stance of devotion, to the sublime loyalty of the Ortegas, the city council, and the other parishioners of the town of Logro, Dina saw that she had nothing to fear. All of them worshipped the same god.

Mammon was real. Anything was possible.

Dina gazed at the idol again, a receptacle glowing with its worshippers' desire. They would serve it and keep it with them always. And there would be plenty of what life had to offer for all of them.

EDDIE G. AT THE GATES OF HELL

R. B. PAYNE

Somewhere west of Santa Fe, the car's temperature gauge edged into the red and the rumble of the Ford Falcon's engine turned to a stutter. Eddie switched the ignition off and coasted to the dirt shoulder.

Route 66 in the summer of 1962 was a scorcher even in the early morning. Eddie watched the heat waves rising from the highway as the dust settled.

Not another car in sight.

Do it now, said the voice in his head.

Eddie fought the urge to reach below the driver's seat. Instead, he ripped the cellophane from a new pack of cigarettes.

"Momma, Baby Callie's got flies again!" said Tim from the backseat. Eddie adjusted the rearview mirror to look. Sure enough, Baby Callie was speckled with black flies.

"Shoo, shoo," Brenda said as she lifted Baby Callie to the front seat.

"Damn it, Tim, make yourself useful," said Eddie in his dad-voice. "I told you to keep those flies off your sister."

"Yes, Papa."

Eddie snapped a match with his thumbnail and lit a Winston.

Come on.

It will be easy.

Eddie ignored the voice and tossed the pack of cigarettes onto the dashboard.

Brenda dabbed sweat from her brow with a handkerchief. "You shouldn't talk like that to your boy, hon. He's only six, for heaven's sake."

"Almost seven, Mama," said Tim.

Eddie spit a fleck of tobacco out the window. Taking a drag on the cigarette, he exhaled a dense blue cloud. Baby Callie coughed and Brenda waved the smoke from the baby's face. In the rearview mirror, Eddie watched Tim as he caught flies one by one in cupped hands and released them out the window. The flies circled in the stifling heat and flew back inside the car.

That boy is so stupid he can't be yours.

Eddie glanced at Brenda.

She fucked somebody else, Eddie G.

Baby Callie cooed and Brenda nuzzled her. "Oh, pumpkin, you stink. You need a new diaper, don't you?"

Eddie flicked his cigarette butt out the window and stepped from the car. He raised the hood and tapped the radiator cap with his fingers.

Way too hot to let off steam.

Eddie circled the Ford and kicked each tire. With luck, he would get a fresh start in California. Everything he owned was crammed inside the car and he took inventory. A guidebook to Southern California real estate. Some pictures of his girlfriends. A box of dishes. Three suits for a traveling insurance salesman. A duffel bag of kid's clothing. Four nice ties and a pair of penny loafers. Three thousand two hundred and twenty-three dollars.

Two kids.

And a wife.

Eddie picked at his teeth with a fingernail as he walked to the edge of the dirt shoulder. A hundred yards away, a rock outcropping jutted on a sagebrush-covered hill.

You can hide the bodies there.

The voice was right, no one would know. It wasn't like Brenda had close relatives, just those hick cousins from Little Rock. Eddie pushed the thoughts aside and turned to get another smoke.

He hesitated, afraid.

Straddling the roof of the car was a giant fly. Its black, green, and blue metallic body intensified the heat from the blistering sun, and Eddie raised his arm to shield his face. The fly's long black legs clutched the trunk lid, and its middle legs clasped the Falcon's two front doors. The front legs, with hairs as thick as rope, clicked and clacked as the insect dripped white goo from its feelers onto the upraised hood of the car.

The fly's dark eyes glittered a thousand hexagons. Its bulbous abdomen heaved as its translucent wings beat in a blur. A high-pitched whine sliced into Eddie's ears, and although he knew it was impossible, he heard the fly say:

It's time to kill them, Eddie G.

Eddie started awake.

Slouched in the dirt, he rested against the shady side of the car. A handkerchief, dipped in water, cooled his forehead.

He climbed unsteadily to his feet.

The fly was gone.

"I was worried 'cause you was breathing so fast," said Brenda looking up from Baby Callie. "You got much too hot, I think."

A sharp pain pierced the backside of his eyes. He reached to the car to steady himself. A garbled conversation rambled somewhere in his head. In a moment, the voices quieted and he felt better.

Brenda leaned over the passenger seat and wrestled Baby Callie's diaper.

Eddie rubbed his forehead; he'd been out for a while. He grabbed a cigarette from the dashboard, popped a match with his thumbnail, and took a long drag. By now, the car's engine ought to be cool enough to get back on the road.

He squinted in the bright sunlight and looked for Tim, who was supposed to pee whenever they stopped. Apparently, he had wandered off to poke at roadside trash with a stick.

"Shake a leg, Tim," Eddie called.

"Hey, Dad. Look, a cowboy boot!"

Throwing his stick to the ground, Tim pulled a red and black boot from beneath some sagebrush.

"It's heavy, Dad!"

Tim clutched the boot and lugged it toward the car.

"Put that piece of crap down."

"Aw Dad, can't I keep it?"

Eddie grabbed Tim's arm. Tim squirmed and looked to his mom. Brenda cleared her throat but Eddie gave her a look that stopped her from saying anything.

"What did I say, Tim? What the fuck did I say?"

"You said to put it down, Papa."

Tim dropped the boot. It landed upright, then fell on its side.

Get the knife now, Eddie G.

Eddie shoved Tim. "If you're not going to pee, get in the damn car!" Tim scrambled into the backseat and Eddie slammed the door shut. Brenda lifted Baby Callie to her shoulder and grabbed the diaper bag.

"Aren't you done yet?" Eddie closed the car's hood gently. "We haven't got all day." Eddie watched Brenda struggle with the diaper bag and Baby Callie at the same time, but he didn't offer to help. Brenda shoved a soiled cloth diaper at him.

"Pail's in the back," she said and climbed into the front seat. She banged her door shut.

Eddie hefted the plastic bucket from the trunk and walked to the barbwire fence. On the other side was a ditch and he dumped the diaper pail. Puffing his cigarette, he watched as two ravens landed and pecked at the garbage.

Now you're being smart, said the voice.

On his way to the car, Eddie angrily kicked the cowboy boot. It *was* heavy and he watched bloody slime ooze into the sand as a pile of meat squirmed.

He already knew what it was.

A human heart filled with maggots.

His heart.

Wrapped in his lung tissue.

The first time the voice appeared it made a comment about Stella, the department's blonde secretary.

That dress makes her look like a whore.

For the longest time, Eddie paid no attention to the voice as he processed insurance applications from farmers and their wives, local businessmen on Main Street, and from the guys at the VFW and the barbershop.

But the voice wouldn't shut up.

Don't you wish you could fuck her?

Eddie knew the voice was right. She *was* fuckable.

After a few months, he learned to ignore the voice and that's when the red-skinned demon with the horns and the tail and the pitchfork appeared in his dreams.

Hey, Eddie G.

It's your pal, remember?

The demon always called him "Eddie G."

Edward Greene.

Eddie G.

He told himself it was no more than bad dreams or night sweats or too much tension at work or stress with the wife and kids and creditors. Maybe he needed to see a doctor. Instead, he found himself staring at the secretary's ass as she bent over to do the office filing.

You know, I can fix you up in Oklahoma, said the voice.

You like pretty girls, don't you?

On his next sales trip, Eddie got lucky with the Tulsa Regional Manager, a buxom divorcee with a hankering for necktie discipline.

The voice had delivered.

Now, it said, *you do something for me.*

But Eddie wasn't sure he could and the nightmares began. The demon came as a creature of fire with eyes black as night and a toothy grin that beamed when he tilted his head.

You owe me, Eddie G., it would say.

The demon would chase him through a maze or Eddie would open a refrigerator and it would crawl out. Once Eddie hacked a black panther to death before waking up, screaming. It didn't matter if he killed the demon, the next night it came again.

You promised.

Every night, like clockwork.

Sometimes it called itself Abaddon or Dasim or Putana. Other times it came as a gargoyle or a yellow-eyed beast with three heads. One night the demon tricked him and came as a Greek goddess and the wet dreams began.

Often, the demon appeared as a red-headed secretary that loved the whip. Sometimes, it was a whore from a bar down on River Road. Two or three times a night Eddie would find himself in an orgy filled with sex, torture, and debauchery. He would start from his sleep covered in puddles but feeling electric with stimulation.

Every night: pleasure and fear, over and over again.

Eddie had not slept well for a long time.

You've got to do something for me, the demon would say. Amazingly, Brenda never woke up, not even once. Eddie knew the power of the demon was that strong.

In the spring of 1960, the demon appeared at Eddie's insurance office. There was a knock on his door and the demon entered, dressed in a suit, his hair combed like an ordinary gentleman who said he wanted to talk about life insurance.

Eddie knew what he meant.

Eddie's life insurance.

Time to pay up, Eddie G. I have a deal for you.

Horns poked from the man's neatly combed hair and a tail twitched beneath his suit jacket.

Eddie listened. What choice did he have?

So, he killed that woman in Tulsa. He cut her into pieces and put her where no one would ever find her.

He left her in Hell.

Nice job, Eddie G.

That's how it all began, two years ago, last April.

Brenda twisted the dial and the sound from the car's AM radio went from a crackle to a hiss to a buzz. Finally, a station warbled into range and twangy songs poured through the dashboard speaker about cowboys, señoritas, and one about a burro named José.

Overhead, the sun grew hotter and the radio signal faded in and out as they drove through the low sandy hills of New Mexico.

In the backseat, Tim read a comic and munched a peanut butter and jelly sandwich. Baby Callie slept sprawled across a blanket on the vinyl seat. Tim waved his hand occasionally to disturb the flies that settled on her naked neck and legs. A scorching breeze blew through the open windows into the car.

"Sure wish we'd bought air conditioning," said Brenda, wiping her brow with a handkerchief.

Eddie was silent as the tires whined on the pavement. He checked the temperature gauge. The car was running hot, but that was to be expected in all this heat.

After a radio commercial for horse feed and a jingle for Martinized dry cleaning, the disc jockey came on with the *Lunchtime News*.

"Police in Santa Rosa have discovered the body of a decapitated young woman south of the railroad yards on Alameda de la Moscas. It may have been a train accident but the police are investigating . . ."

"That poor girl," said Brenda. "Isn't that the town where we spent last night?"

Eddie clicked the radio off.

"Hon, aren't you the least bit curious?"

"Nah," Eddie said snapping a match on his thumbnail and lighting a cigarette. "Not at all. Besides, the signal was getting weak."

But he knew all about it.

Such a pretty young girl.

Nine strokes.

He'd wanted a photo for his collection, but last night he had run out of film for his camera. So, he'd kept her head hidden in the diaper pail. Eddie sighed; unfortunately, another girl wasn't enough to square him with the demon.

His hand drifted below the driver's seat and he checked that the hunting knife was safely stowed.

Eddie Greene had been a good kid.

He had loved Siamese cats and comic books, got decent grades, and went to church every Sunday. Mom would dress him up in a clean white shirt and a black tie, and Dad would drop him off and pick him up. His parents weren't particularly religious, but they weren't agnostic either. They were struggling to make a living and Sunday mornings alone while Eddie was at church had always been a gift.

Eddie came to believe that there must be some higher power, however, that higher power didn't seem interested in a pimply faced kid in Chicago who lived on South Hartford Avenue in a run-down brick tenement.

Dad died of a heart attack the year Eddie graduated McCormick Middle School and his mother died of emphysema the day he graduated Central High. With no siblings, no relatives, and no prospects, he went to work at the local slaughterhouse where his dad had worked.

His first assignment was *Organ Man*.

Eddie's job was to make a long slice in the cow's carcass and remove the heart and lungs. They were steaming hot, bloody, and sometimes the heart was still beating. The organs were called "the pluck" because, well, his job was to pluck them out of the body as fast as he could. Nine quick strokes with a sharp blade and it was done.

Hearts and lungs were his speciality.

Eddie was good at his job. As the flies buzzed mercilessly, he would drop a heart and two lungs on a conveyer belt.

All day long.

Every six minutes.

With a strong work ethic, Eddie quickly caught the eye of management. Soon, he was promoted to *Stunner*, the best paying, but most unwanted, job at the slaughterhouse.

Because you had to look them in the eye.

The cows were herded in, lame and stiff from being hauled long distance in trucks. They were afraid and mooed uncontrollably as they were squashed and moved through the pens into the *Restrainer*. Once their necks were trapped, their heads couldn't move. Their big black eyes stared at Eddie and their wailing moos begged for mercy.

"Help me," the cow would say.

"I can't," he would answer in a sad voice.

Zap.

He'd smack the 300-volt stunner to their forehead and in a split second they'd kick and fall unconscious. A few moments later, hung upside down on an assembly line, their throats were slashed and they would bleed to death.

Here comes another one.

Help me.

Zap.

Help me.

Zap.

Help me.

Every six minutes.

All day long.

Somewhere west of Albuquerque, a billboard with a weathered painting of a dark cave and bolted oaken gates appeared on the horizon. As the car approached the sign, Eddie could make out faded letters that had once been bright red: MARV'S LAST CHANCE GAS and SEE THE ACTUAL GATES OF HELL!

"Papa, can we stop?" said Tim.

ONLY TWENTY MILES AHEAD!

A red-horned devil with cloven feet and a trident challenged: DON'T MISS SATAN'S SANCTUARY!

"Please!" Tim begged.

Despite the hundred-plus heat, a chill rippled up Eddie's spine.

The demon on the billboard was *his demon*.

"I think we should have a burger and a shake," said Brenda, winking at Tim. "It's past dinner time, after all."

Eddie checked the gas gauge, more than half a tank. He gripped the steering wheel and the Falcon sped up.

"I'm not stopping at any goddam tourist trap. I didn't stop for teepees or dinosaurs. We'll eat when we get to Gallup."

Tim flopped in disgust and pulled another comic book from a paper sack. He flipped through the pages, but in a moment, the lull of the road and the late afternoon heat put him to sleep.

Brenda stared at bleak desert and Eddie knew she was angry. In a moment, her head sagged; she had fallen asleep as well.

We had a deal, Eddie G., the voice said.

In the rearview mirror, a black dot appeared in the heat waves on the highway.

Another car, coming fast.

As the minutes passed, Eddie realized it wasn't a car approaching at all. It hovered above the road, a large blue, green, and black object with hexagon eyes.

He could hear the drone of its wings as darkness filled the rearview mirror. The car rocked as the insect landed on the roof and Eddie could hear the wind buffeting its body. A massive hair-covered leg clutched his doorsill, and then reached to Eddie. The fly's pulsating glands oozed a sticky substance that speckled him with whitish goo. A hooked hair-claw the size of a fist latched onto Eddie's face.

The fly leg burned, hot as hell, on his skin.

Eddie G., said the voice. *You belong to me.*

The long dark palpus of the fly wriggled through the open window, searching, until it wrapped around Eddie's throat. Eddie gagged as a wretched fluid sprayed across his face and he wanted to vomit. Something long and alive slid into his throat and he dry-heaved instead.

It's time.

A cloud of steam poured from beneath the hood. Eddie's eyes jerked to the Falcon's instrument panel. The temperature gauge rocketed to red. The car stammered, overheated, and lost power. On the horizon, Marv's Gates of Hell gas station came into view. Eddie threw the car into neutral and switched the engine off.

He'd coast the rest of the distance.

Brenda woke and looked around as she rubbed her eyes. "What's wrong?" she asked

It was then that Eddie noticed something *was* wrong.

There was no fly.

In fact, there was no evidence that there ever had been.

Tim's head poked above the backseat as the car bounced onto the weathered asphalt of Marv's Gates of Hell. The Falcon rolled onto the property and stopped next to a rusting Quonset hut.

"Yippee," Tim said as the Falcon came to a stop, and then he was quiet.

Eddie G. smiled.

A hot wind blew a tumbleweed across cracked asphalt. It bounced off a plywood-covered window before rolling into the gully. Marv's Gates of Hell was nothing more than an abandoned roadside attraction.

In 1953, nine years before, Eddie quit his job at the slaughterhouse because he couldn't take it any more.

He had learned that different cows spoke with distinctly different voices. Some were deep baritones. They would accuse him: "What kind of man are you?"

Eddie's answer was to hit them with the stunner.

Zap, and down they'd go.

Some would swear revenge in a high soprano squeal.

Zap, and down they'd go.

Some would beg for mercy in a rumbling bass voice.

Zap, and down they'd go.

All day long.

Every six minutes.

Over time, Eddie had grown impervious to their comments. His arm was strong and he could heft the stunner like the professional he was. On a typical day, he could stun most of the cows before they could even get a word out.

Zap, and down they'd go.

The cow that changed everything said: "Hey, boy! It's me. Your dad."

The cow was a sweet-looking, black-and-white Holstein.

"Bullshit," said Eddie aloud.

"Have you seen your mom, Eddie?" The cow twisted its restrained head to look at him. "I lost her in the herd."

"Shut up. You're just a fucking cow." Eddie said over the clanking of the machinery.

"I am now," the cow said. "But I wasn't always. Are you still living in the house on Hartford?"

Eddie wobbled, he felt dizzy as he stepped closer.

"I always meant to tell you," the cow said. "There's ten thousand dollars hidden behind the water heater in the basement. I always wanted you to go to college, Son."

Eddie aimed the stunner.

Do it now.

Zap, and the cow went down.

But later that night, the question nagged at him, and Eddie went to the basement. Behind the water heater, in a shoebox, he found ten grand. He never went back to his job, but whenever he thought of his mom and dad, he couldn't help but think of the slaughterhouse and what he had done.

As a graduate of the Chicago School of Insurance, Eddie went to work as an agent and soon met Brenda, a Southern girl living with an aunt for the summer.

Brenda and he were married and saved for a new home. They finally bought a small house in the suburbs, and it seemed like the good life would never end when Baby Tim came and, later, Baby Callie. But one day the voice came and Eddie knew he would never be free of the slaughterhouse.

A young blonde took a secretarial job and her desk was right outside his office door. She was wearing a dress sprinkled with a pattern of red flowers.

That dress makes her look like a whore, said the voice.

The dress was oddly translucent and so was her skin. He could see inside her.

Her heart was beating.

Her lungs expanded and contracted with each breath.

You've got to cut them out, the voice said.

It's your job.

Not long after, Eddie G. bought a hunting knife.

The sun was low on the horizon as dusk cast a smouldering glow of orange and red across the gas station. Eddie climbed from the car and raised the hood.

Way too hot to let off steam.

The car had come to a stop next to a Quonset hut that had been a garage. Out back, beyond a heap of rusting cars, was a boarded-up entrance to a mine. Eddie read the weathered sign.

THE GATES OF HELL.

Perfect, the voice said.

Eddie scanned the highway. Empty.

Tim clambered from the car, and Brenda struggled out with Baby Callie.

"Hey, look!" said Tim, pointing to the roof of the gas station.

Eddie glanced, and then stared. Atop the building was the roadside teaser: an oaken gate bound with sagging chains and a lock. Beckoning with an outstretched arm was Satan, complete with horns, spiked tail, and a trident. It was a mannequin from someplace like the Sears catalogue fitted out in a crappy Halloween costume.

Its eyes turned to greet him.

Welcome to hell, Eddie G.

Baby Callie was fussy and Brenda turned to Tim.

"Get Mama a bottle, hon."

Tim went to the trunk.

"It sure don't look like there's anybody here," said Brenda, glancing at the dirt and grime on the gas station window. Tim gave the bottle to Brenda who quieted Baby Callie with it. Tim ran off toward the abandoned building.

"Don't go far!" Brenda called to Tim. "How long do we have to wait?" she said to Eddie.

He took a deep breath and became the other.

"Not long," Eddie G. said as he fetched his knife.

The sun dipped below the horizon and the deserted Gates of Hell roadside attraction became a world of shadows.

Eddie G. lit a cigarette and pulled the knife from its sheath.

Eddie G. started working at the slaughterhouse about three weeks after Eddie Greene. It had been a particularly brutal day because of a new *Slicer*.

Slicing seemed like an easy job, but it actually required strength and precision. After being stunned and dangling upside down by a hoof, the cow's neck was sliced ear to ear—the carotid artery was laid open and the meat would bleed to death before reaching Eddie.

But not that day.

Most of the cows arrived at Eddie's work station still alive, hanging by a hoof, mooing in fear and writhing in pain, dripping blood from a poorly placed cut.

But Eddie had done his job anyway.

Nine quick strokes.

Starting the next morning, Eddie G. went to work whenever Edward Greene couldn't go through the slaughterhouse gates.

Eddie knew all about Eddie G. but he never told anyone.

Only the demon was wise to the switch.

Eddie G. was very professional and he learned what they both needed to know about knives and slaughtering. He knew about the tip, the bolster, the balance, the throw, the spine, the blade, the cutting edge, the handle, and the rear bolster.

Later he learned about the grind radius, the *ricasso*, the plunge, the rear quillon, and the hawk's bill.

Not to mention finger grooves and serrations.

And it didn't take Eddie G. long to master the pluck.

Slice the hide, cut the cartilage, crack the ribcage, two long hacking slices left, two right, one across the bottom, two across the top. Plop, a heart and two lungs drop onto an aluminum tray.

Nine cuts.

Eddie G. wiped the steel blade on his pant leg as Eddie fought the numbness that pushed at his mind.

Twenty-seven slices.

That's all.

Nine times three.

Brenda can't run; she's got the baby in her arms.

And no matter what, she'll never drop it.

She'll go to the ground clutching that damn baby.

Far away, Tim climbed to the roof of a rusty car. Brenda turned to say something, but couldn't get a word out when she saw the glint of the blade.

Eddie G. drove the knife deep.

Moments later, Eddie screamed when he saw what Eddie G. had done. The moon was rising and in its light, Brenda had let go of Baby Callie. Both lay on the ground, chests splayed open, their hearts and lungs piled sloppily next to them.

Warm and already covered in black flies.

Tim came running as fast as his legs could move. "What happened, Papa?" he called.

The sparkle of evening stars dotted the sky as Eddie G. stepped to the other side of the car to block Tim's view.

"Nothing," he said. "Come here."

"No," said Eddie, shoving Eddie G. aside.

You made the bargain, whispered the voice.

Now keep it.

Still holding the hunting knife, Eddie scooped Tim into his arms and ran with him toward the highway.

Maybe a car would stop and help.

Overhead, Eddie heard the familiar buzzing. Without looking up, he ran faster. Zig. Zag.

"What's wrong, Papa?" Tim was crying.

Won't somebody help me?

Anybody.

Something firm sent Eddie sprawling to the ground. Tim flew from his arms and rolled onto the asphalt, bloodied.

Panic swept across Eddie, he was trapped, helpless.

Save me.

The giant fly straddled him. As big as a car, it pinned him to the ground. The buzz of its wings was as loud as a jet engine as its hexagonal eyes bent close to Eddie's face.

There is no help, said the voice.

The palpus slid down Eddie's throat. The pressure was unbearable as it sucked his heart and lungs from his chest.

Eddie was empty.

The fly lifted into the sky and disappeared into the night as Eddie G. stood up and brushed the dirt from his pants.

Tim lay sobbing on the desolate highway, staring at his father. Eddie G. picked up the hunting knife where it had fallen.

"Come here, Tim," he said.

Even in the full moonlight, Eddie G. could barely see the dark hole that was the mine entrance.

No one will ever find them.

He popped the transmission into drive, flicked on the headlamps, and pulled onto Route 66. Not another car in sight. Surely he could make Los Angeles tomorrow. Eddie G. popped a match on his thumbnail and lit a Winston.

A lot of pretty girls in California, said the voice.

Eddie G. smiled at the thought. He liked plucking, especially from living things. Like cows. Like Brenda, Tim, and Baby Callie. Like all the others.

If only it could be every six minutes.

THE BEAR WHO SWALLOWED THE SKY

JASON M. LIGHT

I was in the graveyard when the storm hit, my face reddened with liquor and distressed Oklahoma soil, my blistered hands bleeding on the shovel handle, disturbing a grave that had been peaceful for over a century. Three feet down, three feet to go.

I had only been here once before, on Halloween night when I was a kid, and I didn't stay long because my friends and I spooked each other and split. But now was no time for fun and games. Now there was work to be done.

It was going well, too. Until the old man who kept watch came along, the one they called the Crypt Keeper. Till I saw him with my own eyes I wasn't convinced he was even real. Just some story someone made up to keep kids scared and out of places they shouldn't be. He looked frail, as if you could snap his limbs like they were dead branches. He had a creased face and what looked like empty sockets where his eyes should have been. He was brandishing his infamous shotgun, which till now I thought was just another part of the fairy tale. The fairy tale that said he was just as liable to shoot as he was to call your parents if he caught you trespassing.

He pulled a long drag on a foul-smelling cigarette, and when the cherry briefly lit up his face I was relieved to see there actually *were* eyes in those deep sockets. He tossed the butt into an empty grave nearby, the little bit of standing rainwater gathered there extinguishing whatever flame remained. Lightning reflected off the pool and a crash of thunder rippled across the sky, racing for the distance.

"What you doin' with that shovel?" he said. "*Chief.*"

I hated when people called me that. But he held the cards. I speared the shovel into the soft ground around the grave and raised my calloused hands, waiting for the blast. But it wasn't his shotgun that nearly knocked me over. It was the straight-line wind.

The day had started normal enough, with me standing behind my printing press, pouring red ink like so much wasted blood, pushing it to the corners of the screen with scrap stock cut from an abandoned job. I hadn't fucked up a job in years, and my worst mistake had cost the company just three hundred dollars. Which is nothing. That's babyshit compared to the screw-ups others have made. One time, a guy in the art department didn't notice that one of the sandwich photos in a color window cling we printed for a restaurant chain was black and white, and that cost us about thirty thousand bucks. The same guy made a forty thousand dollar gaffe just a couple of years ago. Put three *e*'s in the middle of the word *Cheese* and no one caught it till ten thousand pieces of material had been printed and shipped. And yet to this day he still gets free lunches with the boss and invited to matinee baseball games in the city during what are busy summer days for the rest of us.

"Hollowpeter!"

It was Todd, our production manager, standing on the loading dock that overlooked the downstairs production facility. He had little nicknames for everyone: Eric was Erica; Jeff was Bonehead; the other Jeff, Dumbass; Chuck became Chuckles; and Bob was Boob. We always had a Numbnuts, too, which was reserved for whatever newbie or temp whose name he didn't know yet. And, of course, there was Hollowpeter. Me. My name's Jay Hollowtree. It's an Indian name, a source of tremendous pride for me, but I guess Todd never saw it that way. It's okay. We called him Toad behind his back, and that always made us feel better.

"Boss wants to see ya." And then Toad was gone, off to give someone shit, probably. He was real good at that.

I shut off the press and scooped the ink back into the bucket from which it came.

My assistant, Chuck, who had been sitting at the end of the dryer belt where he checked the final prints for spots or bad registration, approached reluctantly.

"What's that about?" Chuck said.

"Cookie job, I 'magine," I said. I checked my appearance in the tiny mirror I'd pinned to the wall next to the head of the press. The company's owner, Sam, was cool about letting me keep my hair long, even when he made hippie white kids cut theirs to keep it out of the teeth and gears of presses and industrial material cutters. I just wanted to make sure it didn't look like hammered shit before I went to see him. Didn't want him to change his mind and make me get it trimmed.

"Oh," Chuck said solemnly, remembering the hell we'd been through the previous week, failing miserably to print a large photographic image of a chocolate chip cookie using a series of four-color dots. "Uh-oh."

"Yeah," I said. My heart raced in anticipation of explaining to Sam what had happened, how that job had gone so horribly wrong. "Go help out in finishing till I get back."

As Chuck bounded off toward the packing department, I envied him. He wasn't concerned with petty things like class jealousy or promotions or raises. He'd been employed three years longer than I but never showed the initiative to move up, had just kind of leveled off. I always wanted more. More money, more security, a better future for my family. I couldn't imagine not knowing or caring what life had in store.

The temperature in Sam's office was perfect as usual. Once, the air conditioning in the plant went out in the middle of July, and we were told it would take weeks to find someone to fix it, because every A/C guy in the city was booked. But when the front office unit went out a few minutes later, both were fixed before lunch. Funny how that works.

Sam was pretending to read some industry magazine when he saw me standing at the door, his feet proudly propped up on the desk so anyone walking by could get a good look at his overpriced designer shoes. He looked up, smiled, and waved me in. As if I should've just barged on in, as if he'd never made it clear he didn't like to be barged in on.

I went in and felt awkward as usual. Not sure what to do with my hands, whether to sit or stand. Sam always told me he didn't like an ass-kisser, but every time I saw him walk through the shop everyone rushed forward to kiss his ass and it looked to me like he ate that shit up.

"Thank you," I said quietly, stepping forward.

"Have a seat."

I sat.

"How are you, Jay?"

"Pretty good," I shrugged.

"You working on that political sign?"

"It'll be running like a scalded dog right after break."

The eclectic decorations lining the shelves and walls of Sam's office made me feel uneducated and as though I existed in some sort of culturally barren landscape. And I think Sam liked it that way. It made him feel important. That was okay, he *was* important. He was the boss. That was *his* scrawl at the bottom of our paychecks every two weeks.

"You see that piece," Sam said, nodding toward a new addition to the wall beside me.

"It's cool," I said, leaning back to check it out. I had no idea its significance. Just some pencil sketch of a sidewalk cafe with a signature scribbled across the bottom, framed in some shiny fake wood. Looked like something you'd run across at Hobby Lobby for a sawbuck.

"It's from Berlin."

"Oh."

"You know what that picture cost me, Jay?"

I shrugged. "Fifty bucks?" I thought I was *way* overestimating.

"Two hundred thousand dollars."

Was I supposed to laugh? Was he serious? Sam's humor was dry as Oklahoma red dirt and it was nigh impossible to tell when he was joking. Finally, I laughed. I had to. We hadn't had a raise in two years and he's spending almost a quarter of a million dollars on a doodle?

"Berlin's where Amy and I went right before the divorce," Sam said.

"Oh," I said. "I see."

We sat in silence for a few moments before Sam changed the subject. "How's Valerie, Jay? How're the hands?"

"She's great," I exaggerated. "She took the kids to the city this week. Red Earth Festival. Trying to sell some jewelry she made."

"Good for her."

"Some days are better than others," I said. "If her hands curl up, she has the kids there to help. I bet there's nothing this cool at Red Earth, though," I said, hooking a thumb at the pencil sketch.

"It's just a picture," Sam scoffed. "Just stuff. If this place burned down tomorrow I'd be more worried about *you*, Jay."

"Yeah?"

"I can't just worry about myself, Jay," Sam said. "I've got forty families out there to think about. The shop is old. The finishing department would go up like a book of matches if it ever caught fire."

He snapped his fingers. It sounded like an ember crackling. *Gone.*

"Let's hope we never have to worry about that."

The shop *was* old. Sam's father operated a garage out of the warehouse in the fifties, and it was something else for thirty years before that. Over the years Sam had added on two new sales buildings, but most of the production and all the fulfillment took place in the warehouse, which could be found in the shadow of Fort Slaughter's water tower.

The northern Oklahoma town was located on Highway 81 and was originally founded to help prevent hostile Indian tribes from raiding border settlements in nearby Kansas. The cavalry abandoned the fort shortly after statehood, and it's been in various states of disrepair ever since.

"Insurance went up again," Sam said gravely. He rubbed the vein that appeared on his elongated forehead whenever he was feeling stressed. "I want to do the right thing, Jay, but I'm not sure I can afford that anymore. They're making it impossible to provide good coverage."

"Oh." I thought of Valerie and her arthritis. What would become of the surgeries she still had scheduled? There were two more over the next six months, and who knows what after that.

"Property insurance is sailing, too," Sam said. He removed his designer-thin eyeglasses and kneaded his temples. "Especially after May third."

"I'll bet," I said, remembering the F5 tornado that had carved a jagged swatch out of the Oklahoma landscape that day in 1999.

"We're not covered for 'wind events.' So if something like that ever happens we'll need to burn the place down to make sure we get paid."

I smiled a little in case he was joking, then coughed quickly and covered my mouth in case he wasn't.

"And we're having a bad month, Jay," Sam said. He put his glasses back on and began sifting through a stack of papers and invoices on his desk. "What happened on the job for Mason and Moon?"

"Mason and Moon..." I said, unfamiliar with the name of the advertising agency for which we were supposed to produce the job. I knew jobs by the images I printed, not the company name at the top of the work order. Sam knew them by the people who wrote the checks.

"The cookie job, Jay," Sam said with a hint of impatience.

I took a deep breath. "Well, we've never done such a big process job before," I said. "At least, *I* haven't. And I'm still getting used to Wyatt. He's got some good ideas for the screens, but he's set in his ways. He doesn't like to compromise, even if it means doing something we've had success with here for years."

"Yeah," Sam said regretfully. "You know I like to hire green and train from the ground up. I went against my gut when I hired Wyatt. The way he played me, I should make him a salesman."

Wyatt was the screen maker. He'd been hired after the shop he'd worked for in New Orleans went out of business and he responded to an ad Sam ran in the back of a screen-printing magazine. Wyatt was a self-proclaimed wizard of process printing—creating a photographic image using a series of red, blue, yellow, and black dots—and somehow secured the position before he'd even set foot in Oklahoma.

"I told him every shop is different," I said. "Like you always say. There are variables here that he might not have had to deal with in Louisiana. The weather, for one."

"It's okay, Jay," Sam said. He was really doing a number on the vein now, and it was responding like an earthworm on his forehead. "Actually, no it's not. It's *not* okay. In all my years I've never had to tell a client we *couldn't do* something. Do you know how hard it was to make that call, Jay?"

"I can't imagine," I said. "No, sir."

"Normally it wouldn't be about the money but I don't mind telling you we lost our ass on this one. How many screens did we burn? *Forty?* For *four* colors?"

Sam punched some numbers into his calculator and zeroed it out angrily.

"Not to mention the ink we wasted, the blown material, the potential for future business we lost and, oh, God, the *man* hours. That's . . . that's where it gets dicey, Jay. We can recover the materials but there's fuck all we can do about the man hours."

I began to get a bad feeling about where this was going. Sam didn't cuss unless he was really upset.

"You didn't work Friday, right?"

"Not really, no," I said. "I left Friday morning about eight."

"And you'd worked all night?"

"Since Thursday morning at five."

Sam pulled my timecard out from a mountain of paperwork. "You worked sixty-eight hours in four days." The way he said it, it was as though he was accusing me of ripping him off intentionally.

"Yeah."

"Here's what I'm asking you to do for *me*, Jay," Sam said, rubbing the vein again. "I'm going to need you to take regular time for the hours you worked over forty, instead of time-and-a-half. That would help us. That would make this a *little* better."

I didn't say anything. I hadn't already spent that overtime money, but I'd sure counted on it. Putting Valerie and the kids up for four nights in Oklahoma City for the Red Earth Festival was going to break us without it. I didn't think she'd sell enough jewelry to even cover the gas it took to drive down there.

"I've already talked to the other guys, and they've all agreed, since we didn't produce the job, since we lost the customer and ate the materials . . . "

We ate the cookie job, I thought. Too bad we didn't print a nice pint of whiskey to wash it down with.

It was hard for me to imagine the other guys already agreeing to such a ridiculous—and probably illegal—proposal as stripping our overtime pay. But the more I thought about it, the more I understood. Wyatt was new, insecure in his position, willing to do anything it took to keep his job. And Chuck and Bob were both single and had roommates; the biggest stress in their lives was paying half the electric bill. I'm sure Sam hadn't had to remind them that he provided insurance and was looking out for all of our families. I'm sure they agreed to take regular time because they just didn't need the money and didn't want to rock the boat.

I had four kids whose mother was an out-of-work secretary with chronic arthritis and a passion for jewelry. Fortunately, she liked to make her own. Turquoise pieces with silver eagle feathers and other such emblems celebrating our native heritage. But it still wasn't a cheap hobby.

Before I could really give Sam an answer he smiled thinly and said, "I sure appreciate everything you do, Jay."

I stood to leave. Sam offered his hand and I took it, but instead of giving him my standard firm grip and single tomahawk chop, I laid a dead weight in his hand and slinked out the door, leaving any respect I'd once had for him behind.

When I returned to my press Wyatt was just delivering the screen for my next job. He regarded the simple image and smiled, shaking his head. "Don't you just love these one color political yard signs? I'll be here all night burning these screens. I've got this guy and all his opponents and five other counties to go yet. More *OT* for me!"

"You talk to Sam today?" I asked him.

"Nope. Not since Friday. He pissed about the cookie job?"

"A little," I replied reluctantly. I knew I shouldn't mention anything to Wyatt. Sam didn't like us talking about closed-door conversations from his office. That was something he always stressed. Still, he hadn't played by the rules and given us our deserved overtime pay, so why should I? "That's some bullshit about the overtime, huh?"

Wyatt looked perplexed. "What's that?"

"Sam stripping away our overtime pay on the cookie job, 'cause it didn't get done. He said you and Chuck and Bob already agreed to take regular pay."

"I don't know anything about *that*," Wyatt said. Then something dawned on him. "You weren't here Friday, were you?"

"No. I was gone before anyone got here."

"Yeah," Wyatt said. "Sam came down just before lunch that day and gave us all a C-note."

"A what?"

"A C-note, man," Wyatt said, smiling wide. "You know, a Benjamin. Hundred bucks. For the effort, man. Then he took us out to lunch."

"A hundred bucks?" I said.

"Yeah," Wyatt chuckled. "You didn't get a bonus?"

"A *bonus?*"

"Well, don't worry, man," Wyatt said. "It's probably 'cause you weren't here. You'll get it."

As Wyatt returned to the screen department, I simultaneously felt like screaming and fainting. I could feel and see nothing beyond the pinhole of light still barely penetrating my field of vision.

I somehow managed to collect myself and went back to work, but I finished the day in a stupor. I don't even remember the words on the jobs I printed, what colors they were, how many pieces of material they finished with. I don't remember delivering the pallet to the finishing department or caring if the product looked like shit or not. What difference did it make? Work my ass off and do it right and still get screwed, or fuck something up and maybe get a bonus and a free lunch and invited to a suite at the baseball game. I guess the only reason I didn't just go home is because I was an hourly employee and couldn't afford not to be on the clock. That, and I didn't like to screw other people who depended on me to do my job. If I didn't get the jobs printed, no one would be able to box them up and ship them out.

I was leaning against the wall outside shipping, smoking a cigarette when Chuck sidled up next to me and lit up, too. I drew a breath to ask about his bonus, but a growl of thunder interrupted me. The morning forecast had called for a slight chance of severe weather, but now a bunch of thunderheads were gathering in the west like a gang coming to a fight.

"I'm about tired of this shit," Chuck said, watching the skies. "Can't even watch TV anymore. Since that F5, every time it sprinkles they gotta freak out and tell you about it, interrupt your programs. Even when nothing's happening."

"Yeah," I said, mashing my smoke into the sidewalk. I knew he was talking about the weather, but I wasn't when I said, "I'm about sick of this shit, too."

I picked up a twelve pack of tall boys on the way home. Valerie knew I sometimes still stopped at the bar after a hard day's work and had one or two beers, but I didn't bring the habit home anymore. Not since the kids were born. And I knew I wouldn't have a problem downing every last one of them and sleeping off the evidence before they were due back from the Red Earth Festival.

The bad weather I had seen stacking up out west at work had slowly crawled across the horizon, gathering steam, darkening the day earlier than usual, and was practically on top of Fort Slaughter now. I sat down and turned on the weather wars being piped in from the Oklahoma City stations and finished my fifth beer. The buzz was officially on.

I drank another beer as I flipped between the channels. I had to laugh because none of them showed the weathermen from the waist down. Turned on as those assholes got every spring, they knew the FCC would come calling with obscenity charges if they did. It was like Elvis Presley on the Ed Sullivan show.

It wasn't until I heard hail pellets plinking down on the roof and wind whistling in around the beat weather stripping that I began surfing for some coverage closer to home. It was clear that the big network affiliates were fishing for ratings in Oklahoma City and didn't care what the fuck was going on near the Kansas border. I saw the swatches of red and green circulating over the Fort Slaughter area on the maps on the screen, and when the counties included in the subsequent tornado warning ran across the bottom like sports scores, I knew the town might be in trouble.

I found a radio and tuned it in to a station near Wichita. The signal was surprisingly strong, but interrupted too often by lightning strikes that grew quickly in frequency and whose accompanying thunder was louder and lasted longer each time.

The station was running a loop from the National Weather Service, the warnings issued by a computerized voice reading off a list of counties and watches and warnings. I heard the name of the county in which Fort Slaughter was located, and it occurred to me that it was the only warning we'd get; Fort Slaughter's beat emergency alarm had been inactive for years now, and because of my Indian heritage I knew exactly why it hadn't been fixed.

White Bear.

The old wives' tale that supposedly kept our town immune from being hit by a tornado. I wondered if that's the reason Sam thought he could skimp on his property insurance policy and keep what he saved to buy overpriced pieces of shit on his yearly jaunts to Europe.

As legend told it, Chief White Bear was born of the wife of a Kiowa chief imprisoned at Fort Slaughter for bragging about a wagon train massacre in 1871. During the birth, a tornado came screaming toward the settlement, visible only when lightning stabbed down from the heavens. But as the twister approached, a large black bear came out of the woods, the lightning reflecting its rain-slicked coat so it looked white. According to the fable, at the precise moment the baby was born, the bear opened its mouth and swallowed the tornado whole, saving the garrison. And to this day, it is believed that as long as Chief White Bear's grave is undisturbed, despite its location in the heart of Tornado Alley, a twister will never hit Fort Slaughter.

I don't remember how many more beers I drank before I ransacked the garage and found the shovel. I don't even remember driving to the graveyard, or if I'd run any stop signs or sideswiped any pedestrians or stray dogs in the process. The simple fact of the matter is I just didn't care.

I studied the three feet of mud piling up around my legs. I wondered if I'd done enough, or if I needed to dig all the way to the coffin and splinter it open. I had enough beers in my blood to believe the legend, to believe if I disturbed White Bear's grave I could unleash hell on what was left of the town.

The storm was on top of me now, thunder rolling and lightning stabbing down in every direction. I was so pissed off it never even occurred to me that I was digging a grave with a shovel that might as well be a lightning rod.

"What you doin' with that shovel?" the old man said between growls of thunder. "*Chief.*"

With the shotgun leveled at my heart, I speared the shovel into the ground and raised my hands. When a zipper of lightning traced behind the clouds, I wasn't sure if it was the weather or the sight of the shotgun that caused the short hairs on my arms and neck to stand at attention.

"Step away from the grave, Chief," he said, and now he was grinning a little. Like a mean son-of-a-bitch who had caught his wife in bed with another man and was looking forward to torturing them. "Slowly, no sudden moves or I shoot."

In an instant I was sobered up and regretted immediately what I'd done. Did I really want to destroy what was left of the town, including the shop where I'd made a living for so many years? Did I want to flatten my own home and the homes of my co-workers and friends? And what would they do for work if the shop were destroyed? All because my boss had screwed me over again? Would I find something better? Something that *paid* better? Some place where I could leave my hair long? Would I find a boss who wasn't a placating hypocrite? Weren't they all?

Thunder pealed from one end of the sky to the next and flashbulbs of lightning played behind the rotating clouds like a movie behind a curtain.

I sensed something behind me but did not want to move for fear of being shot. I did not want to test the old man's mettle. I'd already suspected he was just a myth, but he had proven real, and I'm sure rumors of his quick trigger finger were just as valid. But as the sensation grew stronger and I could actually hear something moving behind me, I could no longer justify not looking. What if it was something dangerous? A wish-boned tree trunk, split by a lightning strike, about to fall on my head? Or a second old watchman. An ambush.

I turned, but I'd only made it halfway around before the shotgun blast rang out. I dove for the ground, not sure if I'd made that decision or if the buckshot had made it for me.

I checked myself but felt no pain, no blood. Above me, something roared. Was it thunder? Or was it the sound of trees being uprooted from the earth, fed into the gaping maw of a funnel cloud? The sound grew louder before it ceased, bordering on deafening.

I cautiously raised my head and saw the bear. Swerving against a backdrop of swirling black clouds highlighted by intermittent flashes of lightning, stumbling toward me, roaring in pain, pawing at a star of crimson-matted hair on its side. I had just enough time to scramble away before the dying animal crashed down where I had lain.

I scurried rat-like to the old man, who was crouching, the tip of his shotgun smoldering like a cigarette. He had his head buried in his hands, and he was sobbing.

"I'm sorry!" he wailed. "I'm sorry!"

Suddenly I heard the sound of the trees in the forest beyond the graveyard crashing against one another like bowling pins, and whenever lightning charged the sky, I could just make out a funnel stabbing down on the other side of the woods. It was still in the distance, but I couldn't tell which way it was moving; it was impossible to judge by the wind, which was now swirling in every direction at once.

I imagined that what I was witnessing was no different than the storm that had descended upon Fort Slaughter all those years ago, when the legend of White Bear was born. I had to believe that the natural world had always acted by the same laws, that myths and legends were nothing more than hearsay told by one fallible man and passed on to the next fallible man in line, that it was more likely that someone had lied about the bear. Because that's what men did. If I needed any proof of that, all I had to do was think back to my meeting with Sam earlier in the day. *He'd* lied. And I'm sure it wasn't the first time.

There may indeed have been a different bear than the one the old man had just fatally wounded, who may indeed have stumbled onto the road and stood down that tornado like a gun-slinging outlaw at high noon. But *that* storm had just taken the bear and spared the town, had just randomly skipped over the town, like all the rest before and since. It really was that simple. Live around here long enough, legends and curses be damned, and you're likely to find a funnel cloud with your name on it.

I grabbed the old man, who was mumbling incoherently about White Bear, and dragged him to the empty grave where he'd discarded his cigarette. We splashed down into the hole and embraced, waiting for the impact of the tornado that was chewing up the woods, or an entirely different twister that might drop out of the growling black clouds at any moment.

"I'm sorry!" I read the old man's lips, but even though our noses were nearly touching, I could not hear his words over the clamor of the storm.

Hailstones crashed off our heads and disappeared into the mud around us like meteorites, throwing the standing rainwater back up into our faces.

The hole began to fill with storm debris. Leaves floated down softly around us as if in the middle of a peaceful fall morning, and jagged twigs tore at our skin like the diseased teeth of the living dead.

I poked my head out of the hole like a curious groundhog, and just as if I were hiding for six more weeks of winter, I scurried back into the relative safety of the grave when I saw that the tornado had hopped the woods and was spinning into one corner of the cemetery, heading straight for us.

Then it wasn't just leaves and twigs we had to dodge, but whole branches, chunks of tombstones, jagged shards of rotten caskets, and long-buried bones as the tornado unearthed the shallow graves.

When the eye of the funnel finally moved over our makeshift shelter, the suction pulled the old man away, and I watched him somersault through the air, dancing with debris. I was reminded of the Wizard of Oz, and I wondered if the other visions I saw were real or imagined. I saw Wyatt, a bunch of one-color political yard signs, their edges chewed up by the storm, and even pieces of the damned cookie job, cycling through the air like Toto and the Wicked Witch, all playing before my eyes on a gray, dreamy loop.

The shop was gone, its remains smoldering, and I wondered if Sam had done what he said he would do if a tornado ever flattened it. I wondered if he set it on fire to be sure the insurance would cover it.

Volunteer firemen stood in the middle of the field with limp fire hoses, shrugging their shoulders as they watched the ruins become ash. They didn't seem to mind that I was there, so near to the danger, probably obstructing any chance they had to make a difference. But then, they were just volunteers. What did they know about procedure? What did they care?

I saw Wyatt bounding across the field toward me, wearing a stuffed backpack that looked like it might explode. "Where you been, Jay? You missed all the excitement."

"You going somewhere, Wyatt?"

Wyatt shrugged and looked at the wreck. He shifted the weight on his back. "Back down south, I guess."

"Sam'll rebuild," I said.

Wyatt smirked. "Man, I ain't never seen no tornado. I don't think I wanna see another one. No thanks."

"Tornado caused this?"

"Craziest thing, it skipped right over the shop. Lightning hit the water tower, it caught fire and collapsed right on top of the warehouse."

Until he said it I hadn't noticed the water tower was missing on the horizon.

"That's why they're not putting it out," I realized.

"They're hamstrung," Wyatt shrugged. "All they could do was watch it burn."

"Did you ever hear the legend of White Bear, Wyatt?"

"No."

"Maybe you'll let me tell you about it sometime," I said. "If you ever make it back up here."

"Maybe," Wyatt said. "But there's a legend about New Orleans, too. You give a chick beads and she'll show you her tits. I like that one."

"It's a good one," I said. "Take it easy, Wyatt."

"Hey, they don't call it the Big Easy for nothin'!" he said and disappeared into the blackness that surrounded what was left of Fort Slaughter.

I wondered if I would really miss it all that much. I smiled at the idea that Sam was buried somewhere down there in the wreckage, his designer shoes, dulled by mud, sticking out from beneath his relocated shop.

I turned to walk away for the last time when something caught my eye, falling slowly from above. A flaming one hundred dollar bill fell at my feet, curling up into itself as the smoke it created raced back for the heavens.

I thought for a moment about saving it, and then I let it burn.

THE SVANCARA SUPPER SOCIETY

JOEY O'BRYAN

The total cost of a death row inmate's last meal may not exceed forty *reais*, a paltry sum in comparison to the ninety of the mid twenty-first century. Request Kobe beef, consider it your good fortune to receive the T-bone. A drowned Salisbury is more likely, though still preferable to the now ubiquitous protein loaf. For the majority of prisoners, such simplicity is sufficient, the difference between prime and canner as mysterious as Etruscan. The disenfranchised are, frankly, accustomed to the substandard and affectionate of the banal.

I am told the most requested last meal is a cheeseburger with french fries.

By far the most requested.

For those with a more developed palate, the decision isn't so easy. For a former taste researcher, it's overwhelming. My last meal. Day and night, I mentally catalog every last lukewarm, undercooked tray of food that has made its way through that little slot, recombining ingredients into a dish worthy of so singular an occasion.

A humble soufflé?

No, the prison kitchen will have all the ingredients except fresh nutmeg, and fresh nutmeg is essential.

Pommes Anna?

The potatoes will be sliced too thick and they won't leave it in the oven long enough. Prison chefs have been known to botch oatmeal. The recipe must be idiot proof.

Soon the time will come when I must choose or go without. A wizened death mask drawn over a skull glares, distorted from surrounding steel surfaces, taunting my indecision.

Can he truly be me?

Walls, floor, ceiling. No escape from what I have become. I shut my eyes but the stench of the toilet refuses to let me forget where I am: a gleaming Brazilian tomb, awaiting a lethal dose of a virus developed specifically to send prisoners out with tranquil expressions on our faces. The cramped dimensions of the room weren't humiliation enough, the architect had to position the cot beside the toilet. Designed for maximum psychological torment, I suppose.

I bring a hand to my nose, breathe through my mouth, and dream, desperately, of the Svancara Supper Society.

We were all aware of the laws we were breaking, yet we'd felt no remorse. Sinning with a clear conscience; a chief pleasure among Svancara's merry band of gastronomic outlaws.

We thought we were going to save the world.

No, really.

I first met Eva Svancara at an international symposium for food studies in Australia. Largest producer of food in the world and home to many like myself, operators on the periphery of the industry.

Half the planet was overweight, the other half skin-and-bone. Colonization on the moon and Mars had solved pressing overpopulation issues, but fear of famine still loomed large and neither world was suitable for extensive food production. Terraforming had a long way to go, assuming such a venture would prove successful at all.

Politicians assured the public that significant shortages were generations away. The right assumed much ado about nothing, the left lapsed into hysteria, the apolitical remained apathetic, religious factions prayed, and the good citizens of Starship Earth were yanked from one extreme to another.

Only agricultural and food scholars approached the dilemma with objectivity.

For our candor we would be, of course, marginalized.

"And how do you propose to reconfigure eating habits on such a scale, Dr. Berger?"

Svancara and I were settled at opposite ends of a crescent table. Between us, a handful of so-called peers. Before us, a horde of regressive thinkers. Government officials from all corners of the globe. Media. Sheep.

"The human tongue recognizes five taste qualities," I replied with barely concealed derision. "Bitter, Sweet, Sour, Salty, and Umami. Genetically reprogram which tastes appeal, we transform the way we eat and, simultaneously, the planet."

"What about a potential sixth quality," blurted a persistent voice from the back of the room, "and the developments in food production such a discovery might yield?"

"There is no sixth quality."

"The discovery of new taste receptors—"

"Does not equal the discovery of new tastes."

"Yet you yourself once campaigned for the recognition of a sixth quality," Mr. Persistent shot back. "Forgive me if I've misremembered the title . . ." He paused for effect, a masterful display of condescending delivery. "*Addicted to Adrenaline: The Sixth Quality and the Death Drive?*"

A ripple of nervous laughter throughout the hall.

"It was rightly acknowledged for what it was," I replied as coolly as possible. "The folly of youth."

"And yet you're still talking about altering human instinct, Dr. Berger. Surely you can see the potential for abuse—"

Svancara spoke up, cutting him off in mid-sentence.

"Such concerns," she stated with calm authority, "have yet to halt the development of new war weapons."

I liked her right away.

I wasn't alone. All were captivated as she went on, preaching of an endlessly regenerating supply of test tube meat produced for mass-market consumption, living up to her reputation as the rockstar visionary from Manhattan with ambition to burn.

Physically, she was not traditionally impressive—delicate, diminutive, with a wan complexion and all-too visible half-moons under her eyes—but the no-nonsense tenor of her voice compelled attention. The accent, a whiff of ambiguous European roots humbling otherwise perfect diction, also held intrigue.

The substance of her sermon was not novel: In vitro meat had been positioned by the scientific community as the most sensible response to the food supply conundrum for years. Still, she had a way of making one feel as if they were hearing the argument for the first time, an invaluable gift in these most desperate of days. The ease with which she glossed over the deficiencies of the cloning solution—public skepticism, health concerns, a limited repertoire of easily reproducible tissues—was impressive to witness.

I told her as much following the panel's conclusion.

She didn't think it much of a compliment.

"I sold them a bill of goods, is that what you mean?"

"I believe I said you were well-spoken."

"It's okay," she teased. "You want to change people. I want to give them what they want."

"What they want is an infinite all-you-can-eat buffet. Even cloned meat can't give them that."

As soon as I heard myself, I knew the jovial duelist I'd meant to affect rang condescending instead of clever. Her rebuttal was appropriately dismissive.

"Not yet."

Her lips curled into an awkward smile, conscious yet forgiving of my social inadequacies. My mind strained for an equally succinct response and came up wanting, unaccustomed to such unwavering confidence.

"Your paper on Adrenaline sounds . . ." She seemed to be seeking the least patronizing description. ". . . provocative. Is it available online?"

"In the IFT archives."

There was a subtle shift in her expression. Only then did I recognize my blunder. She'd presented an opportunity and I'd squandered it.

"Well," she sighed, "I shall have to run a search when I return to New York."

"Second stage of tests came back with only a thirty percent recognition factor . . ." I stammered, flailing to keep the conversation alive by, what, invalidating the single aspect of Edward Berger she found of note?

"Good day, Dr. Berger," she said, pleasant but definitive as she shook my hand and disappeared into the crowd.

A fumble, but I was, nevertheless, smitten.

It would be six years before our paths crossed again. The invitation was delivered by messenger.

The Svancara Supper Society
requests the pleasure of your company
on Friday evening the twenty-second of November
at half after seven o'clock
at forty-eight Nettlefold Street
in the city of Canberra

Sincerely,
Eva Svancara

While I was delighted to see the signature at the bottom of the card, I was surprised to learn of Svancara's return to Australia. The intervening years hadn't been kind to our field of research. FDA International had clamped down strident regulations in regard to food studies, claiming administration-monitored trials essential in maintaining safety standards. Given their ties to more than one food industry mogul, one could only assume the quote-unquote testing would be never-ending.

Grants dried up and we scientists were left with two unappealing choices: Work for the government or procure a new line of employment. I put my tail between my legs and accepted a position with central services, helping to engineer a more palatable nutrition paste for inner-city famine centers. Svancara faded from view with considerably more grace. Then again, the independently wealthy could afford integrity. For the rest of us, compromise was a way of life.

The gulf in social status was never more apparent than the monorail ride from Reid to Fraser Court, the walk from the station to Nettlefold. Forty-eight was an intimidating neo-brutalist eruption of angular concrete, redwood beams, and black glass. The sky hummed with wind and electricity, a harbinger of the monsoon season. Each year a little longer, a little wetter. Someday we too would become a canal city, provided the bushfires didn't get us first.

A twinge of anticipation as I climbed the stone steps and knocked. I'd met the woman once for five minutes six years ago and here I was anxious as a schoolboy.

The heavy double doors were answered by a lanky, tuxedoed Vietnamese servant with leathery skin and a poker face. I suspect he would have kept staring all night and never said a word had I not presented the invitation. The severe expression did not waver, but he turned to the side and extended an arm, beckoning me inside.

"Evening," I offered as I moved through the entryway. "I'm . . ."

The Servant closed the door and motioned to an open guestbook, seemingly in no mood for pleasantries, which, truthfully, agreed with my limited temperament. I noticed a pair of familiar names as I scrawled on a vacant line.

Albert Tsai of General Kwan's Freeze-Dried Vacupaks, excess astronaut sludge recycled for poverty row value seekers. Olivia Zell, formerly advancing our knowledge of food-based microorganisms, now reduced to helping Global Idaho engineer unnaturally large potatoes.

I caught sight of them across the crowded room as I took a tentative step into the parlor. One would never guess their downward spirals given the way they were laughing and carrying on. Their unabashed exuberance immediately set me on edge, as it is wont to do. The servant of course had already vanished, stranding me without so much as a *Mob, Edward; Edward, Mob.*

"Deaf, not rude."

I pivoted to face an oak of a man with wide shoulders distorting an ill-fitting suit. My guard instinctively went up. He must have misread it as confusion because he pitched his voice from mere shout to roar.

"HE'S DEAF—"

"I'm not."

The retort had come too quickly. There was a flash of irritation across his features, but it submerged as quickly as it had arisen. He grinned and offered his hand, jacket fluttering with the motion, affording a glimpse of an occupied shoulder holster.

I did my best not to stare.

"Jimmy Rapke," he drawled in a twang that marked him as a native. "How do you know Eva?"

"We met—"

"Edward Berger?" interrupted a rising voice.

Albert Tsai, en route.

"Edward . . ." moaned Rapke with seemingly sincere repentance. "I told you my name but didn't ask yours."

"It's alright."

"I've had too much to drink," Rapke apologized as he adjusted his waistline, revealing a badge clipped to his belt. Putting the pistol into context didn't necessarily ease my discomfort. He caught me looking and tapped the piece with his champagne flute.

"We enforce clean plates around here, Edward . . ." he deadpanned, mischief in his eyes. "People are starving a couple rail stops away, you know."

One, actually.

Albert, meanwhile, had arrived and was still talking. I hadn't heard a word he'd said, though I nodded and smiled as if I did. Each man had claimed an ear and pretended the other didn't exist. Tsai playing catch-up between shameless self-promotion, Rapke sketching out his first meeting with Svancara at a charity function.

"Say, do you know Herb Wakeman?" Albert asked as he pushed me toward an elderly chap in antique bifocals. "He's in gelatins over at Botello." No, I didn't know Herb Wakeman and I wouldn't know him any better after a five second shake-and-greet, but I was relieved to have left Rapke's orbit. I complimented Herb on his spectacles, which he said belonged to his great-great-grandfather. A whirlwind of faces passed in similarly superficial fashion, each making less of an impression than the last.

None belonged to Eva Svancara.

I felt like a stalker at a stalker party. Eva this, Svancara that. Soundbite crosschatter gradually made clear that these were monthly gatherings, which struck me as too much of a good thing. I was already exhausted and the night had barely begun. Many bemoaned their inability to share with friends and family, events apparently not to be discussed with anyone outside the circle. Even more off-putting was the almost religious fervor through which most seemed to view the proceedings.

"... counting the days ..."

"... pining for ..."

"... *live* for this ..."

I was beginning to wonder if attending had been such a prudent notion after all. Olivia was the only one to pick up on my tacit cynicism.

"You'll see."

The drumming of fingertips against glasses signaled a shift of priorities. The level of babble tapered off until a single enigmatic voice remained.

"If everyone will take their seats ..."

The years had been kind. She had gained a little weight and filled out in all the right places, choice of attire complementing newfound curves. I fell in line as everyone filtered past her through a blind doorway. Our eyes met and her mouth curved into that same strange smile from six years ago.

"Dr. Berger, so pleased you could make it."

We shook hands, her grip poised but firm.

"Edward, please."

"If you call me Eva."

Words still had a magical way of rolling off her tongue.

I followed her over the threshold. A spacious but minimalist dining room lay beyond, lengthy table formally laid with silverware, menu cards, and origami napkins. I came down sideways on my chair and nearly slipped off the edge, too busy watching Eva cross to the head of the table. Her body language was as self-assured as her speech. Limbs moving in smooth, clear lines; a being totally at ease inside her skin. It is a mystery to me how one comes to carry such certitude in their very bones, yet there is no denying the appeal of those who are uncompromisingly themselves.

Doors clattered to and fro as a pair of servers—the Vietnamese mute and his Amazonian right hand—delivered plates round the table. The first course, a bed of roughage speckled with pomegranate seeds and what appeared to be some sort of textured protein analogue.

Eva raised her wine toward the heavens.

"To tomorrow ..."

The room echoed the proclamation, as did I.

My gaze fell upon the menu card.

Asian Elephant
Bitter Greens Salad with Grilled Elephant
Boiled Elephant Soup with Onions
Roasted Elephant in Balsamic Vinegar
Elephant Dessert with Celery Stewed in Red Wine

The glass slipped from my hand, showering Chardonnay. My neighbors scooted backward to avoid the splash, servants racing to soak up the spill. Eva scrutinized me like an equation to be solved.

"Are you alright?"

I was not.

"Is this . . . some . . . some sort of . . ."

Eva gawked as I fought to articulate my distress.

"I'm sorry?" she replied with mock innocence.

"Elephants are endangered," I began to ramble. "More than endangered—they're practically nonexistent. Extinct in the wild as far back as I can remember."

She didn't deny it. On the contrary, the haughty self-satisfaction writ across her features all but confirmed it.

I pushed my chair back, rising to leave.

Across the table, Rapke stood in tandem. He unbuttoned his jacket, a reminder of the weapon within.

"House rules, Eddie."

I froze, gaze shifting between the crime on my plate, the bulge in the cop's jacket, and the siren presiding over it all.

"Rapke."

Her tone ground two syllables into a threat. Rapke fidgeted—embarrassed, flustered—then sat back down.

Eva's attention returned to me, impatience softening.

"One bite. If you still want to leave, no one will stop you."

I held her gaze, weighing my options. Rapke was still stewing, seemingly ready to pounce. If I refused her meager request, perhaps she would turn him loose.

I hoisted my utensils, speared a forkful.

Hesitated, then popped it into my mouth.

The flesh was surprisingly tender given the source, with a gamy texture akin to my memory of Alaskan moose. Greens heightened its earthy qualities, pomegranate bringing out a latent sweetness.

In a word, extraordinary.

I tried not to give myself away, but Eva was staring and had no doubt seen right through me. I summoned up all my willpower, set my utensils down, and turned to leave. Principle battled desire with every step. I hadn't tasted real meat in over a year and was desperate for another bite. All the more reason to go, and as fast as possible.

Albert groaned in exasperation.

"Edward, it's cloned."

I paused in mid-step.

Impossible.

A chorus of disapproval from the room.

"She puts all the newbies through this," Albert said, enduring jeers from around the table. Olivia gave him an affectionate punch to the shoulder. Eva simply shook her head, disappointed to have been robbed of the squirming spectacle that was my moral dilemma.

"The donor animal is alive and well on a wildlife sanctuary in Taipei," she confessed. "I have a mutually beneficial arrangement with the resident DNA archivist. Each dish is a hundred percent sustainable."

I found, almost unconsciously, my feet returning me to my place at the table. A rush of contradictory emotions as I settled back into my seat. Guilt begat skepticism trumped by curiosity. In vitro meat had never developed much further than chicken nuggets and fish sticks. Such a leap in taste and tissue diversity would amount to nothing less than a revolution in modern food engineering.

I paused to organize my thoughts. Not long enough given the plea that spilled from my lips.

"I want to see the lab."

Eva nodded, accommodating but still in charge.

"Between courses."

Eva pecked a code into a keypad and pressed her eye against a retinal scanner, triggering the intimidating growl of demagnetized bolts as the tungsten-carbide portal creaked lazily open. The laboratory stood in stark contrast to the rest of the dwelling, unsightly and cluttered. Smart boards twinkling border-to-border with incomprehensible facts and figures. The tortured buzz of pen PCs left on too long. Sheets of raw meat floating in vats of milky grey fluid. Whining mechanical limbs working flesh like taffy.

If the other rooms represented the self-conscious cool of Svancara's charismatic public persona, this one betrayed carefully camouflaged internal chaos.

"One hundred percent sustainable..." I wondered aloud, pondering the folds of tissue undulating above and below the fluid's opaque surface.

She was, as usual, way ahead of me.

"Mushrooms. Six varieties make up the growth media."

She was proud and had every right to be. Fungi-based mediums were not exactly an innovation, but even at the height of biomedical research, only cell cultures derived from animal blood had produced adequate results, which were laughable in comparison. The same was true of the animatronic appendages exercising cells into fully-developed muscle, far more sophisticated than the once *de rigeur* rolling mats that strained to fuse myofibers.

"Different tissues respond to different techniques," she continued. "Incubation periods, exercise regimen, fat content. Each requires a unique set of variations."

Her head came up, projecting to better address those loitering about the open portal.

"Informed feedback is crucial to the success of these experiments. That's the purpose of these little monthly meetings, of the Supper Society."

Her gaze came all the way back to me.

"My lab rats."

"Should've tasted the first pass on Elephant," Albert interjected with good humor. Eva was quick to correct him. "That was African Elephant, not Asian."

"Listen to 'em," Rapke chuckled. "Spoiled."

I had to agree. Even a tough, overcooked rendition of the first course would still have been a better meal than most would see in their lifetime. It was probably the best I'd had in a decade. We'd eaten the raw materials right out from under ourselves. These days you would have to be a wealthy man indeed to procure anything approaching equivalent merit, and perhaps not even then.

The next course was even better.

As was the one after that.

Svancara had evolved not only into a physiochemical trailblazer, but an epicurean wizard. She deflected my praise with uncharacteristic, and therefore trustworthy, humility, insisting necessity had forced her to learn her way around a kitchen.

Understandable. We would all be arrested were her laboratory discovered.

The risk seemed worth the reward. This was not merely great food with progressively like-minds, this was a chance to witness history in the making. Her plan to reintroduce the now passé concept of tissue engineering to world governments was practical and convincing. She had already done the hard work for the multinationals and the results would sell themselves to the public.

The latter point was beautifully illustrated by the arrival of dessert, the wonderful harmony between hearty flesh, celery snap, and tart Cabernet capping a spectacular evening in crowd-pleasing style.

A digestif, then a steady stream down the front steps. I allowed goodbyes to drag on past the limit of pleasant civility, carefully positioning myself as the last one out the door, lingering on the final step just long enough to let the sidewalk clear and arouse Eva's curiosity.

The door cracked back open. I turned to face her.

"How'd you do it?"

The distinctive smile widened, but was not forthcoming.

I pressed further.

"Double talk about engineering fat content might satisfy the others, but you and I know those techniques are not entirely new. Nor have they ever yielded a flavor profile analogous to the highest-grade organic meat."

For once she seemed at a loss for words, her features conflicted. The weight of secrets can be a heavy load, and I hoped she might trust me to shoulder a few.

A beat of contemplation before she broke the silence.

"Three million euros."

I wasn't following and felt foolish.

"Allied Science," she continued. "Three million euros. That is what they'll be paying for my paper. You will be receiving an acknowledgement in the text."

Now it was my turn to reflect.

"You fail to recognize the value of your own work," she elaborated. "It was your research that set me on the proper path."

My mind sped through a lifetime of theories and missed opportunities, struggling to put the pieces together.

She decided, mercifully, to help me along.

"Three words, one also a number."

I couldn't help but scoff.

The Sixth Quality.

"You're kidding."

She wasn't.

"It was nice to see you, Edward. I hope you'll be back next month."

The door closed.

First thing I did upon arriving home was search for that blasted paper. The failed ambition of that thesis had followed me for years. I'd been eager to sever ties with it.

Too eager, perhaps.

I wound up downloading *Addicted to Adrenaline* from the IFT server, just as I'd told Eva to do so long ago. I read and re-read it, searching for clues to justify Eva's cryptic promise of acknowledgement.

The text offered nothing beyond what I already knew.

The discovery of the TAS6R90 receptor had resurrected speculation regarding a potential sixth quality. I'd been in Korea researching my college thesis on the practices of underground dog meat dealers when the notion of a taste receptor for adrenaline first occurred to me. Beating dogs to death, without any Western pretense of so-called humane slaughter, was not uncommon. Most claimed the goal was to burst all blood vessels in the animal's body, turning the meat an appealing shade of deep red. Others insisted that violent, prolonged death resulted in increased levels of endorphins, transforming cheap protein into a superb aphrodisiac.

Tests on the dogs and those who consumed them soon steered me from endorphins to adrenaline.

It held an irresistible theoretical logic. Over the decades, demand for cheaper meat had shifted manufacturing priorities. Regulations were relaxed to fit more animals into less space, to be killed with the most cost-effective techniques available. The gist, basically, was that we had developed the TAS6R90 receptor in response to the heightened levels of adrenaline found in increasingly stressed slaughter animals.

The initial results were promising enough to inflate my ego past the point of caution. I abandoned the modest exposé I had been crafting in favor of a damn-the-torpedoes claim to the sixth quality. The paper caused a sensation on campus, then the elite of food science. They were a grand fifteen minutes, but with acclaim came funding, and with funding came professional facilities, and with professional facilities came that unfortunate thirty-percent recognition factor, and overnight Boy Genius became Overeager Hack.

For the first time in twenty-two years I found myself questioning that assessment. Might her accomplishments have been mine? It was infuriating to contemplate, so I did my best not to.

. . . counting the days . . .

. . . pining for . . .

. . . live for this . . .

It didn't take long to begin sympathizing with the antsy sentiments I'd disdained only a few nights before. Time literally crawled from November twenty-third to December twenty-second. There was hardly a single meal that wasn't dominated by fantasies of what Eva would next have in store. The reality of Humphead Parrotfish Sashimi more than delivered, yet the evening was over too soon, leaving another slog before the next fix. Even worse, every bite now carried a provocation, mysteries to be solved. I found myself letting flesh turn to mush in my mouth, as if hoping to discern its properties by osmosis. I would rush back to the flat afterward to weigh new observations against my bastard thesis, desperate to decipher Svancara's coy innuendo. The words on the screen, once mine, now refused to cooperate. Who could blame them? Given how quick I'd been to abandon my own ideas, the cold shoulder seemed a fitting response.

I thought of Amadeus and Salieri and felt far older than my years.

I began to spit chunks of Eva's miracle meat into my napkin whenever I could get away with it, spiriting it out of forty-eight for closer examination in a more controlled environment. Half-chewed bits of curried pygmy hog, braised Siberian husky, and steamed lowland gorilla.

I had to know how she'd done what she did.

What my work had to do with it.

One night a Yorkshire terrier accosted me on my stroll back to the Fraser Court platform, agog to get at my jacket pockets. That might have been the end of Edward Berger had his owner not yanked his leash and continued on.

I hoped reverse-engineering the genetic character of each sample would unravel the enigma of Eva's cloning approach. What little equipment I owned was dated and now served, for the lack of a better term, decorative purposes. I began to contrive excuses to stay after hours at central services, corporate resources allowing for a more thorough breakdown of each morsel.

Complicating my clandestine efforts was the new intern I'd been saddled with training.

Ignacio Castaneda was nineteen, a quick learner with an impressive GPA. He reminded me too much of myself at that age, a single-minded, self-proclaimed radical. His pet project involved manipulating bioactive proteins, hoping to reverse tissue decomposition. His endgame, widespread meat recycling.

"Obvious . . ." he was fond of saying.

What was obvious was my need for more stable influences.

I endeavored to avoid him, but he kept at my heels like a puppy. I had to be careful. The boy's enthusiasm could unmake me. Every night, I'd wave goodbye, head home, wait half an hour, then double back and set about playing with my samples. I set a limit of no more than two hours per night, after which I forwarded relevant data to a dummy e-ddress and purged all evidence from my workstation.

The wait between outings grew more unbearable as the new year wore on. Everyday breakfast, lunch, and dinner had become little more than fuel. There was no pleasure to take from food once you'd tasted what Dr. Svancara had to offer.

"I lost six pounds between my first and fourth visit," Albert admitted. "I dropped nine," Rapke laughed.

I'd lost twelve.

By the time monsoon season again approached, it was more like sixteen. Co-workers complimented my slimmer look. Some demanded my secret. Our supervisor had me drug tested. Outside, the skies darkened and the rain began to pound. On the plasma, Brisbane flooded. Less than a day's ride, yet I remained unmoved.

I poured myself into my extra-circular research, but found only aggravation. Of course I didn't have the luxury of comparing authentic Panda tissue with Eva's in vitro variant, but nothing overt distinguished her mirage from the genuine article.

I shuffled into our October congregation with all the enthusiasm of a pallbearer. The Supper Society had lost none its core appeal, mind you. On the contrary, Svancara's accomplishments in the lab and kitchen went from strength to strength. Fact was, for myself the evening had become a reminder of myriad failures. Had I any self-respect, I'd have stopped showing up long ago. I was jaded and everyone could see it.

Eva never blinked, even as my polite disaffection infected others. The collective mood had swung from "impressed" to "impress me." That initial rush of civil disobedience had, sadly, settled into routine.

Tonight's menu, however, promised novelty.

Svancara Special
. . . tappaiskeitto
. . . tartar with ginger and lemon juice
. . . oil-stewed with white truffles
. . . mango pie

"To tomorrow . . ." Eva intoned, glass held aloft.

I met her gaze as I lifted mine. Whatever surprises she had for us, her devilish expression revealed little beyond the usual unshakability.

We repeated her mantra, though many were still puzzling over their menu cards, Rapke struggling to pronounce the first course.

"Tapp-ai-ske-it-to," Eva offered, sounding it out as servers set bowls before us.

The broth was ruby red; onions, potatoes, and mystery meat bobbing round an auburn dumpling the size of a child's fist.

"It means Butcher's Soup," she continued. "Concocted by Finnish farmers to utilize scraps from the autumn slaughter."

I opened the dumpling with a spoon.

It bled.

"What's in it?" Herb asked as he pushed the contents of the soup around. Eva lifted her Bordeaux and put her nose in the glass, savoring the aroma before answering.

"Me."

The world froze, the single syllable stunning the room into reticent soul-searching. Svancara, meanwhile, had a sip of wine and thoughtfully examined the cork. None of us sure what to say or do. Eva had thrown down the gauntlet and we were flunking the challenge. She returned the cork to the tabletop, exhaling with a satisfied sigh.

Albert rose from his chair, breathing hard.

"This . . . this is too much . . ."

"Albert," she cooed as if comforting an infant. "It's cloned. Cultivated in a vat over the past thirty days. No different than the rabbit, the fawn, or anything else."

Albert faced the floor instead of Eva. I wondered if I'd appeared equally puny in my early moment of indecision.

"I want no part of this."

He turned toward the door. Rapke, in turn, slammed his revolver on the table. Eva snapped in his direction.

"Rapke!"

He ignored her, cocking the hammer. Gasps all around. Albert did not twitch. Fear had nailed him to the spot.

"Walk out that door, Al, you keep your mouth—"

"Rapke, leave him—"

The clatter of knife and fork silenced them both.

My bravado astonished even me. The spoonful of blood, dumpling, and human flesh in my mouth before I was conscious of having made the decision. It seemed not a choice at all in fact, but something beyond intellect, beyond morality.

Albert stared in disbelief. Others watched with morbid fascination, awaiting a verdict. Among them Eva, studying every subtlety of my expression with atypical unease.

She was exquisite.

The texture was somewhat coarse and the flavor tricky to pin down. There were hints of mild bitterness but she was generally savory, with notes of fully-developed veal and, kudos to Mr. Darwin, chimpanzee. Yet none seemed an apt description, so I chose to simply nod my approval.

Albert's face sank before he stormed out.

"The dough is made from blood and rye," Eva continued as she scooped a chunk of dumpling.

"Well done," I managed between bites.

She tasted herself and appeared pleased.

One by one, inhibitions faded and all followed suit. The superlatives began to fly as dishes came and went, adults reduced to giddy children, straining for worthy adjectives to describe this new, taboo sensation.

"A bit like beef."

"No, pork. Like pork but sweeter."

On it went, The Svancara Supper Society grasping at straws.

A lizard brain I had never known suddenly awakened to dominate my thoughts, an involuntary activation of primal, deep-rooted instincts. My gaze fell to Rapke's revolver, still on the table. I imagined closing the gap between us and atomizing his teeth with the butt of the weapon, forcing him at gunpoint to swallow the shards. I would then enjoy the rest of his tartar, as I'd reluctantly stashed away a good portion of mine for later analysis.

I wanted her secrets.

I wanted to bathe in her blood.

I wanted her to consume me as I had her.

So when she asked who might volunteer to be next month's meal, I didn't hesitate.

"I'll do it."

Our eyes met, but she was hard to read.

Herb chuckled, nervous. "You sound almost eager."

I glanced dismissively his way before returning to Svancara.

"Eva has done more than her fair share, I think you'll all agree. We're all past due to take on some of the burden."

"Hear, hear!" Olivia cheered as glasses were raised. I could've sworn a little color came into Svancara's cheeks.

"I'll ready the Basilisk."

I climbed into the unwieldy contraption known as the Basilisk, a form-fitting metal exoskeleton named after the mythological creature that turned its victims to stone. Designed to immobilize patients for unusually dangerous or convoluted medical procedures, this one was an obsolete model more readily available outside official government channels.

A hiss from twin leg-mounted tanks of compressed air as brace sections closed around me like a mechtronic iron maiden. Only my dangling right hand retained movement, everything else locked within the wiry frame.

"Ependymal cells are easier to manipulate," Eva explained as she double-checked the restraints, "and far safer to retrieve from the spine than the brain."

She picked up on my unspoken apprehension and patted my free hand.

"I'm still here, aren't I?"

She offered the wireless control module as a hologram flickered to life, detailing the extraction trajectory via animated model. In the event of a miscalculation, the odds of permanent paralysis were unlikely, but, nevertheless, I preferred the more experienced candidate.

"I'd rather you do it, if you don't mind."

She said nothing but a favorable shift in expression confirmed her approval. She stabbed a finger at the remote and the rig began to rotate, clanking along its tracks.

"Some believe there is a bone in the body that is indestructible," she mused. "Muslims call it *Ajbu al-Thanab*. Jews call it *Luz*. Scientists call it the *Coccyx*, the final segment of the vertebral column. Both religions contend that, from this single bone, God will resurrect the dead come Judgment Day."

The animated model turned as I did, lining up the base of my spine with an imposing retractable syringe.

"Ironic, no?"

I was surprised to hear someone of Eva's intellectual stature reflecting on so inane a subject. It had taken the better part of history to wrestle power from such fanatics.

"Surely you're not religious."

She held my gaze but, instead of responding, started to laugh. The bray of a banshee, most unbecoming.

"What?"

"You smell like dinner."

The exoskeleton shuddered as the rig came to a stop.

"Take a deep breath."

I did, trying not to sweat the sample in my pocket.

". . . and . . ."

Another whoosh of compressed air as the needle met flesh and set my back on fire.

". . . out."

I stumbled through my front door and hurried to secure the samples. This was as good as it was likely to get. Raw, not cooked. Not another exotic animal, but human. For once I would have comparison data to measure against. I couldn't risk even the slightest deterioration. I barely got the tissue into the regulator before I passed out on the couch.

When I awoke the next morning, my back was throbbing and my pants were wet with semen. The last time I could remember waking up in such a state, I'd been a teenager.

Details of the dream first proved elusive, echoes returning only amidst the ennui of the day job.

Eva and I, tangled in the writhing bodies of our monthly dinner companions. All nude, all taking bites from one another. I couldn't recall if Albert had been in the pile but he was certainly on the front page of the day's e-paper.

"Vacupak mogul Tsai injured in smash and grab!" bellowed the pulpy headline. I felt ill as I scanned the article. One eyewitness claimed the mugger flashed a badge as he approached Albert outside his building.

I had a suspicion I'd seen it too.

Albert would heal. He would live. He would also think long and hard before he said anything to anyone about The Svancara Supper Society.

We all would.

Therefore it was with renewed caution that I executed my nightly rounds. The additional glance over my shoulder, an extra hour between work and the return to work. Code-secured the laboratory door behind me once I arrived.

Quantitative analysis of average human protein characteristics with those of the sample finally yielded a discrepancy: unusually high levels of amino acids. Though I wasn't sure what to make of the revelation, it was a start.

From across the room, the sound of locks disengaging.

Whoever it was, they had an access code.

I scrambled to clean up the examination bay despite the door already sliding open. I managed to power down the holographic monitor and throw a sheet across the sample as Ignacio, of all people, swaggered inside. I could've strangled him.

"Castaneda?" I used only his last name to invoke the specter of authority. "What are you doing here?"

He seemed genuinely caught off-guard.

"Forgot my pod," he said as he swiped his media kit from a counter. "What are you . . ."

His voice trailed as he spied my workstation.

I'd been routing the data through my system and hadn't shut down. A scientist didn't need Ignacio's education to recognize a human DNA string at first sight, especially when you see one in a lab specializing in synthetics.

"What we got here, boss?"

He was headed for the examination bay.

"It's not your concern," I replied, blocking his path.

He paused, but held his ground.

I reinforced the advice with a threat.

"You can walk or I can invent a reason to have you thrown out."

He hardened, apparently not fond of ultimatums, then reached past and jerked the sheet away.

"That human?"

My guts boiled. The boy was forcing my hand.

"The end of your career, that's what it is."

He bobbed his head mournfully.

"You mean my big career in ghetto spam?" He grinned, cocky. "Probably be doin' me a favor . . ."

I probably would. Too bright for this dump and he knew it. He was more annoyance than threat. In a battle of his word against mine, I'd win. I could ruin the kid.

Lucky for him, I had a better idea.

It had been easier than expected to convince Eva to take on a new member. Albert's exit had left a vacant seat and I'd more than proved my loyalty with my enthusiastic DNA donation. Convincing Ignacio had taken no effort at all. A gamble on his ambition felt like a fairly safe roll of the dice. He'd been touting his Big Plans from the moment we met. Now he had a mentor and I an assistant. Together, we could bring back twice the samples for the next round of tests.

We'd already managed to identify the overabundant amino acid distinguishing Eva's sample: Tyrosine, one of the two amino acids that make up, yes, Adrenaline.

We were close.

The regulars shined to my young protégé right away, though Rapke subjected him to the usual passive-aggressive scare tactics. I thumped over my menu card as we made our way to the dining table. Eva offered an inquisitive glance and I explained myself.

"I want it to be a surprise."

Ignacio settled into Albert's old space a few chairs down, eyes wide as anime as he examined the menu.

"Not a word," I demanded.

Olivia raised her card and read aloud.

"Porcini encrusted—"

"Not a word!"

Laughter all around. It continued as Ignacio unfurled his napkin and sent his utensils to the floor, banging his head on the underside of the table as he bent to pick them up. The first course rolled out and we toasted the future. For the first time, it felt like an honest gesture.

Ignacio reappeared over the tabletop.

In one hand, a badge. The other, a revolver.

My mind locked up, unable to accept the image.

No, no, no, n

"FDA International! Hands on your heads!"

The weapon shifted my way.

"You too, boss."

I could only stare, bewildered.

"NOW! Don't make me—"

Rapke leapt up before he could finish and capsized the table, pinning Ignacio and several others beneath it. Wood splintered as Ignacio fired wild. Olivia's chest bloomed with red mist. Rapke drew his own gun and unloaded. From beneath the table, groans and screams and bubbling gore.

Far too much to belong to Ignacio alone.

Rapke spun, bludgeoning me with the pistol. I absorbed the abuse without complaint, lizard brain short-circuited by the messy reality of actual death. He might have beaten me to death had Eva not pulled him off.

"Stop!" she cried. "The gun was aimed his way, too!"

Rapke wasn't buying it. "He brought him here, Eva!"

I brought him, my responsibility.

The words out of my mouth were less damning.

"I didn't . . . I didn't know he . . ."

A plume of smoke as a tear gas grenade soared through the doorway, skipping across the dining room floor like a stone across a pond. A bean-bag projectile hammered Herb off his feet and flung his great-great-grandfather's frames to the floor, swiftly crushed beneath the heels of fleeing peers. An FDA tactical team emerged ghostlike from the fog, clad in body armor and firing non-lethal ammunition.

Until Rapke took a shot at them.

"Live rounds, live rounds!" sounded a panicked voice.

Switches were flipped, rifle barrels rotated, and bean bags became hot lead. The Vietnamese mute was shredded, corpse toppling a cart of meticulously prepared dishes. The Amazon went berserk, smashing an FDA trooper's head against a pillar. For her efforts, she received a backful of metal. I flattened to the floor, Eva waving me over from across the room.

"Move!"

I crawled toward her as she broke for the laboratory, trigger-happy Rapke laying down cover fire. He nearly killed Herb as he lagged to join us. Eva's fingers danced over the keypad. "We can get to the roof through the back."

She brought her eye to the scanner.

Blood spattered my face as a bullet pierced her shoulder.

Rapke pivoted and ended the offending shooter as the portal groaned open. I took Eva in my arms and dragged her toward the entrance. Rapke and Herb darted ahead, the former already working on getting the door closed.

"Move your ass, Eddie!" he roared as the portal whined and reversed direction. I was halfway through when another round tore her from my grasp, slamming us to the floor.

I landed inside. She, outside.

A groove of flesh had been shorn from my leg but I hadn't time to fret. Eva clutched my wrist. An FDA trooper had her feet. The portal would claim her unless one of us surrendered. I strengthened my grip and our eyes met.

"Tyrosine. It's the sixth quality, isn't it?"

She scoffed, amused.

"Eva, I have to kn—"

She smiled, let go and slid from my grasp.

The portal boomed shut between us.

Rapke was on me immediately. "Stupid cunt!" He hurled me from one end of the lab to the other. "You invited the fucking FDA!" He hauled me up and crushed my face against a second keypad, retinal scanner combo.

"Access denied," objected a stern recording.

Rapke dropped me and leveled his revolver. Herb tugged at his arm, begging him to cool down. I caught my breath. Pointed.

They turned to see the overhead vent.

Rapke probably would have shot me anyway had it not taken all three of us to wrench the grate off. No time to do it inconspicuously. Troopers would have the portal hacked in under five minutes.

We crawled inside. Herb first, Rapke second, me last. Air dissipated as dread solidified, the vice of claustrophobia instant and overpowering. Flimsy walls buckled about us, a cheap copper coffin that went on and on. I could hear Herb scampering like a rat in a maze, but there was no seeing around Rapke.

Our pace dwindled, the faraway murmur of FDA troopers through the portal spurring a terse inquiry from Rapke.

"What is it?"

"Good Lord . . ." was all the old man could squeak out, more to himself than us.

"What?!?" Rapke seethed a second time, in no mood to repeat himself. I felt the same anger but knew escalating the hysteria would accomplish nothing.

Rapke wasn't thinking that far ahead.

"Lemme see . . ."

The ruckus of wrestling bodies, then a terrible crash as both men plummeted out of sight, an empty square where a grate used to be. I braced myself for a collapse that never came. Once confident of the shaft's stability, I inched forward and peered over the edge. Herb and Rapke were sprawled below, moaning and trying to regain their senses.

They were better off without them.

Convulsing forms imprisoned within steel exoskeletons, all but their faces submerged beneath growth media.

More than an abattoir, this was a torture chamber.

I climbed down, approached a vat and took a wireless control module in hand. My fingers caressed the touch screen, triggering a Basilisk to ascend.

My clone shivered as it rose from murky fluid.

It was like looking into a mirror. If I were naked and whole sections of my body had been carved away, that is.

That it still lived was miraculous. The growth media had likely facilitated its regenerative abilities. It gazed my way with the blank-eyed innocence of a dumb animal.

I endeavored to hang on to what was left of my sanity.

Thumbed the touch-screen. Another Basilisk rose.

Eva's double was even worse off than mine, exposed innards sagging through gaps in her exoskeleton armor. Eva must've kept picking at herself throughout the month, not unlike the holiday turkey of old.

I collected Rapke's fallen weapon as he and Herb came to. On the other side of the wall, the racket of FDA troopers in the adjoining lab. They'd be in here before long. There was another exit at the far end of the room, but it too was secured by a keypad and retinal scan.

"I don't understand," Herb said, fighting back tears as he took in the surrounding horror show. "She didn't have to do this. We saw the lab, the process."

He broke down, losing it.

Rapke saw his gun in my hand and started toward me.

"Give it."

I aimed it instead.

He backed off. I got my breathing under control, building my courage. Turned, walked right up to my clone and put a bullet in his forehead.

I'd never been much of a shot and didn't want to miss.

I crossed the room to do the same for Eva's.

By now Herb was blubbering incomprehensibly.

Rapke retreated as a tear gas canister rattled through the shaft above and dropped from the open vent.

Out of time.

I unlocked a compressed air tank from one of the exoskeletons, rolled it against the rear door, hid behind a vat and fired.

The shot ricocheted off the floor.

I threw a look back at the vent. Herb had vanished into the expanding cloud. I could hear him choking. They knew we were armed and were letting it smoke up before coming in.

Rapke extended a hand toward me, eyes crazed.

"I won't miss . . ."

I couldn't trust him with the gun. I may have brought an undercover agent into our midst, but Rapke signed our death warrants when he murdered him in cold blood.

I tried not to think about that as I again drew a bead on the tank and pulled the trigger.

The explosion did what it was supposed to and little else. We ran past the blackened husk of the doorway and through a series of empty rooms to a staircase. Up we went, then out a window, across a few roofs and finally onto the street. Slowed our pace the more distance we put between us and them. Upon arriving at the Fraser Court platform, I again turned the revolver on my dinner companion.

"Take the next one."

He glared with wicked intent. I tried to reassure him.

"It's coming now, you'll be fine."

He remained unyielding, as did I.

The doors whisked shut, the issue of Jimmy Rapke shrinking to a speck as the train pulled from the platform.

I hid in a private restroom until the next stop, rinsing my wounded leg in the sink and sopping up blood with paper towels. Upon disembarking, I bought a razor from a convenience machine and a pair of pants off a homeless man. In a toilet stall, I bound the old pair around the clotting gash and slid into the new (well, newly acquired) pair. They reeked of liquor, but being mistaken for an alcoholic remained less problematic than a triage escapee.

I shaved my hair, beard, and mustache before venturing back into the station. Found an e-bank and withdrew the maximum amount. I would have to make it last. Every time I logged on, I would be tracked. Even if I could reach an airport, my photo would be in circulation. Security measures for rail travel were, thankfully, less rigorous. A low profile was my only salvation until I could arrange safe passage out of Australia.

I gifted my monorail pass to a couple of grateful backpackers—authorities would have a ball trying to keep up with them—and purchased in cash a one-way ticket to the Black Mountain.

End of the line.

My stomach ached as I settled in for the journey. I'd been so looking forward to tonight's meal, now I'd never look forward to another.

I tried to push such nihilism from my thoughts and laid my head against the window, praying the commotion emanating from my midsection was audible to no one else.

An eerie orange glow woke me as the train emerged from a tunnel, glass warm against my forehead.

Outside, flames for miles into the distance.

Windows shook as an aircraft swooped overhead, unleashing torrents of water. Below, ground units attacked the blaze with foam cannons.

An adjacent passenger glanced up from her media kit.

"Lightning strike."

I looked away to discourage further small talk.

If the bushfires don't get us first.

I eventually holed up in a decrepit hostel in the shadow of Telstra Tower and made no plans to come out. Paid extra for a private room, bath, and an ancient LCD, sliding bills beneath the door at the end of each week. My limited funds would go far here and people knew to mind their own business.

It was, under the circumstances, ideal.

I passed the days glued to the international news wire, of which the Svancara Supper Society was a constant fixture. Herb and the few surviving others were whisked one-by-one onto a transfer plane to the sunny prison state of São Paulo, where each would serve a twenty-year sentence for conspiracy against corporate standards.

Eva's case proved more complex. The prosecution sought the death penalty. The defense confused matters by igniting a global debate regarding the relative inhumanity of clones versus their value to society as test subjects. The trial could conceivably go on forever and the public was loving it. The more of Eva's *l'enfant terrible* charm they were exposed to, the less likely it became she would ever find herself on the murder gurney.

When asked by a reporter what drove her so far from the scientific mainstream, she blamed it on "the folly of youth."

Undoubtedly the high point of a very dark period.

Less inspirational was the fact that Jimmy Rapke was still at large, and authorities weren't any closer to apprehending him than they were me. This despite footage of my after-hours shenanigans at central services running in a loop. Agent Castaneda had apparently forgotten his media kit on several occasions, image sensor always conveniently directed toward my workstation.

He'd been recording me from day one.

Further contributing to my perpetually frayed nerves was ailing health. It seemed every morning I rose a couple pounds lighter, my body deteriorating at an alarming rate. I forced myself to eat, dishing out a couple more bills to have daily rations sent up, but rarely could I keep them down. Slept endlessly, pillow over my head to muffle the crackle of lightning strikes, the howling sirens of bushfire teams.

One afternoon, I stirred to an unwelcome visitor.

Leaning against the door, a grotesque wisp of a man. Bone, veins bulging beneath flaking skin. I might never have recognized him had he not opened his mouth.

"G'day, Eddie."

Rapke.

I reached for the nightstand, the revolver. It was now back in the possession of its rightful owner, quaking in his hand. He was on his last legs, even more so than myself.

"Do as I say, or I shoot."

I didn't bother to rise, exhausted.

"How'd you find me?"

He licked dry, cracked lips.

"I say to talk?"

He elaborated no further, motioning with the weapon.

I did as instructed, heading outside to a parked vehicle. The name on the registration sticker branded it stolen, Gungahlin license plate suggesting Rapke had been from one end of the line to the other.

A lesson learned too late, twice over: Underestimate the persistence of law enforcement at your peril.

He had me drive, gun never wavering. Such motivation wasn't necessary. I wasn't going to put up a fight. I was too tired to fight. All I wanted was rest. Should it be forever, I could live with that.

Pardon the expression.

The sun descended below the horizon as we veered off road, pushing deep into the bush. We finally idled into the middle of nowhere, where Rapke had improvised a threadbare camp consisting of not much more than a plastic tarp, sleeping bag and, ominously, roasting spit.

"Run, I'll put one in your back."

We stepped out together and ducked under the tarp. He motioned to a shallow pit beneath the spit, thick with ash and smoldering embers.

"Spark it."

Any doubts as to the fate Rapke had in mind for me were decisively laid to rest. Malnutrition may have sapped my will to resist, but pride was not yet spent. I imagined unzipping and extinguishing all potential combustion. Unfortunately there wasn't a drop of piss in my famished body, so I settled for the silent treatment, reclining onto the hard earth instead of getting to work.

Rapke exhaled in frustration, leveling the revolver.

Such a threat could carry no currency with a man who had accepted death. I was ready for the whole affair to end.

His features contorted with anger.

He stormed to the cot, dug inside the sleeping bag, retrieved a machete and, just like that, buried it my shoulder.

The bullet graze was a blessing by comparison.

By the time he yanked it out, I'm embarrassed to admit I'd screamed myself hoarse.

Magic hour clouds grumbled their disapproval.

Rapke withdrew, panting from the effort.

"Lots of ways to go. You might want to consider that."

I clutched my wound, determined not to give an inch.

"Stalling to get my adrenaline up?"

He glared, perplexed.

"What are you on about?"

I kept at him.

"How about you? Gun in your hand get your heart pumping?"

Rapke frowned with the realization that he was going to have to do his own dirty work. He tucked the gun in the front of his pants and heaved the machete, resigned if not especially enthusiastic. My feeling was not dissimilar. The blade whistled, my executioner flaring to blinding white. A distant crack. My eardrums popped.

I thought I was dead.

The tingle of static electricity convinced me otherwise.

Above, a supernova. I shielded my eyes as dusk became dawn, igniting the head of Rapke's matchstick frame. He radiated like a star atop a Christmas tree, lightning bolt twisting from the churning sky as if by divine intervention. The pistol in his pants detonated, taking most of his crotch with it. His pupils went next. What was left hit the dirt a smoking heap of charred flesh.

Twilight returned as thunder rumbled an epitaph.

Oh, what a difference a millisecond makes.

The reversal, of course, presented an enticing opportunity. Internal ethical debate was perfunctory at best. I bunched a sleeve over my hand for safety's sake, took the singed machete from Rapke's hand and slowly, surely sawed the cheek muscle from his face. He was, after all, already cooked. Allowing such a feast to go to waste would be pitiful considering the undernourished state of the world.

This is what I told myself.

I buried my face in the scorched delicacy. Texture was tough and stringy, a defect easily overlooked in light of the peculiar preparation. What was harder to ignore was the bland flavor profile. I hadn't counted on Supper Society quality, but this was below even central service standards.

Inexplicable.

I spit it out, then removed the other cheek.

It was, to my exasperation, equally unappealing. I forced it down as I set about severing a section of palm.

Hollow eye sockets snapped open as Rapke let loose an unholy wail, squealing like a freshly-sheared eunuch.

His revival seemed impossible but there was no denying the thrashing form beside me. Instinct took over, machete going up and down until the shrieking ceased or my arms gave out. Difficult to remember which came first. I slumped over—frenzied, winded—and admired my gory handiwork, shell-shocked at how far the lizard brain and I had traveled in so brief a time.

A spotlight washed over us.

Firefighters bounced from the slats of the arriving response unit, horrified faces commending me on sight.

Seven months later and half a world away, the last meal I'll ever eat slides into view.

Practical considerations had finally led me to the simplest of Italian dishes, bruschetta. I'd requested the ingredients be placed individually on a series of small plates, the excuse being that the bread would become limp were the tomatoes left sitting too long. I wasn't sure the prison chef would comply and worried he'd send garlic powder instead of the fresh stuff, but, to my surprise, everything was there awaiting assembly. Even the glass of white wine I never expected to see was passed through a half-opened door, though the "glass" was plastic and the color suspect.

If I'd surrendered the night the FDA raided forty-eight, I'd be out in twenty years instead of dead in one.

Best not to dwell on that.

I start soon as the door slams shut, clearing all plates from the metal tray. Stack the bread into small, four-inch pillars and balance the tray atop. Strip to my undergarments, tear my pants to shreds, push the material under the elevated tray and use contraband matches to set them ablaze. The fire eats hungrily through cheap single-ply fabric, heating up the underbelly of the metal tray.

From outside, a fist pounds.

"Berger, the hell you doin' in there?"

I pour the olive oil. It pops as it spreads across the tray. A handful of minced garlic follows.

"What's that smell?!"

On the other side of the door, the whirr of a retinal scan. Electronic chime signals positive identification. Rasp of the door sliding open.

Followed by the spine-straightening crunch of gears straining against the iron bar wedged between door and wall.

Where it once held my cot together, it now holds a fifty-pound steel door. My biceps were still sore from wrenching the bed apart. It'd taken longer than expected to disassemble without suspicion, but the bar was holding.

I would not make the same mistake a third time.

The weeks of worry are paying off, all is progressing as planned.

The grate drops. Eyes in the slot.

"Berger, listen—"

I tune him out, tying my shirt in a knot above the knee. Grip my shiv, hand-crafted from a mattress slat. Begin to sweat and, more disastrously, tremble.

Which are but two of the many reasons why carving a steak from my leg is so damned difficult.

"Christ . . ." comes a shaken voice from the other side of the door. I force him out of my consciousness, grind my teeth, and continue rocking the blade through flesh.

The rush of an acetylene torch blows a white-hot hole through the door.

I flinch, startled, and open a dam in my leg.

An artery, to be precise.

Blood pools fast beneath me. For a breath, every nerve goes stiff with shock. A shimmering ember cascades from the door into an open eye, stinging me back to the here and now. I jerk the tourniquet. Tight. The deluge becomes a trickle, but the tap is still flowing.

On the floor beside the shiv, a ragged cut of thigh.

It will have to suffice.

Whatever time was available to me has just been shortened considerably. Soon I may no longer possess the motor skills for a more controlled attempt. Oil crackles as I slap the fillet on the tray. The rising fumes smell, thankfully, sublime. I lean closer to drink them in and notice, vision shifting in and out of focus, plumes of smoke emanating from beneath the tray.

My blood is threatening to snuff out the cooking flame.

I whip around to snatch a sheet from the cot, go dizzy, and slide in the halo of red. I again catch sight of my reflection in the ceiling and, given my present state, I cannot help but recall my clone in Svancara's laboratory.

Though I've always considered superstition beneath me, it now seems, as much as it pains me to admit it, a premonition.

I suppose it isn't any less plausible than vengeful outback lightning or Svancara finding the secret to cell regeneration right where the Koran said it would be . . .

The Luz, Ajbu al-Thanab.

I struggle to regain practicality. Now is hardly the time to ponder the mysteries of the eternal. I gather the sheet, soak up the surrounding gore, and blow into the kindling, returning the fire to full strength. Right myself, flip the meat, retrieve my wine, and have a sip. It's from a box, as expected. I enjoy it for what it is and try to ignore the showering sparks as I watch my last meal sizzle on the makeshift grill.

Heartbeat hammers in concert with the inside of my skull. Everything below the waist turned cold, numb. My eyelids heavy. I will them open as her voice mingles with mine.

Not. Yet.

I move the steak from the tray to the molded plate, dot a few tomatoes across the top, and cut into it with my shiv and fork, my only hesitation is the memory of Rapke's curiously unsatisfying cheek meat.

I eat.

My gut reaction is that I taste not only as good as Svancara, I taste, perhaps, even better.

Therein lies an epiphany.

At first blush I credit the notion to the delirium of rapid blood loss, but it feels too much like truth to be denied. What if different amino acids are released in conjunction with different forms of duress? Running a marathon, you're pumping Adrenaline with higher concentrations of Phenylalanine. Facing a firing squad, Tyrosine.

Could I really have been so close, so long ago?

That's why Eva tortured those clones.

Why Koreans beat dogs before killing them.

Why Rapke tasted wrong—he never saw it coming.

Tyrosine, the sixth quality . . .

Fear.

Can't help but chuckle, cut short as a gob of chewed flesh falls from my lips, accompanied by a string of crimson saliva. What a fool I'd been. The world laughed, I'd surrendered, and it had taken Svancara's chutzpah to finish what I'd started. Her greatest strength, my greatest weakness; apparent from our first meeting.

The courage of conviction.

Hands move slowly as I slice another piece. Darkness floods in, contrasted by stars raining from the ever-widening gash in the cell door, horrified faces of authority agape on the opposite side.

I'll be dead before they can get to me.

Just as well. A magnificent exit compared to what the state had in store. No absurd *Deus ex Machina*, no lifetime in a government cage. I shall depart this dying world a proud soldier of The Svancara Supper Society, a gourmet samurai setting a defiant example via culinary *seppuku*. Svancara would hear of my fate and no doubt smile that crooked smile of hers. If only she could've consumed me as I'd consumed her. Alas, whatever strange thing had blossomed between us will remain forever unrequited.

I lift my tacky stemware of budget wine to her, if not in person then in spirit.

"To tomorrow . . ." I drool, resisting oblivion as I devour a final succulent bite of myself, the price of enlightenment a pittance beside its rewards.

THE CONTRIBUTORS

VINCE CHURCHILL has written two novels: *The Dead Shall Inherit The Earth* and *The Blackest Heart*. He has a Sunday column in the Jacksonville *Journal Courier* newspaper, and his "Splatter Pattern" column appears regularly for *The Hacker's Source* magazine. His short fiction has appeared in anthologies such as *The Undead*, *The Undead II*, *The Horror Library—Volume One*, and *The Beast Within*. He was also a list contributor in the recent *Book of Lists: Horror*. Vince's latest novella, *Condemned*, is set to appear in the *2nd Butcher Shop Quartet* anthology by Cutting Block Press later this year. His latest novel, *The Butcher Bride*, will be published by Black Bed Sheet Books by the end of 2009.

ARMAND CONSTANTINE is a writer of games, fiction, and film. His most recent game writing projects include Pandemic Studios' *Saboteur*, Bethesda Softworks' *Rogue Warrior*, and Ubisoft Montreal's *Far Cry 2*, for which he shares a nomination for the Game Developers Choice Award for Best Writing. Armand is a lifelong resident of Southern California and currently lives in Los Angeles. For more information about current and upcoming projects go to www.armandconstantine.com.

KELLY DUNN's obsession with madmen and monsters mysteriously led to a master's degree in English, a career in print and online journalism, teaching stints at ye olde university, and a sideline in professional stage acting. Her most recent short stories have materialized in such perfectly normal publications as *Aberrant Dreams* and *Necrotic Tissue*. Kelly was born, raised, and still lives in the shadow of Los Angeles, where her first novel is rising from the slab.

RICHARD GROVE trained primarily for the theater and has a long history as an actor. After graduating from the Yale School of Drama in 1983, he came to Los Angeles and worked in television and film. His most notable role was as Duke Henry the Red in Sam Raimi's *Army of Darkness*. More recently he has lent his voice talent to animated films and machinima. Although he's been a voracious reader his entire life, he's only recently turned his hand to writing fiction. With Lisa Morton, Richard co-authored the short story "Forces of Evil Starring Robert Fields" for *Midnight Premiere*. "Silver Needle" comes from his love of Halloween and his memories of trick or treating as a young boy growing up in Glendale, Arizona. Richard currently works as a book clerk at one of the best bookstores in Los Angeles: The Iliad Bookshop. Just look for him stocking books in the Horror/SciFi section.

DEL HOWISON—Along with being a writer, Del Howison is a former photo journalist and gas station pump jockey who is currently an editor, an actor in "C" horror movies, co-owner and operator of Dark Delicacies (America's only all-horror book and gift store—www.darkdel.com) and a trustee on the board of the Horror Writers Association. He also kisses his dogs on the lips. Basically he is a jerk of all trades and master of none.

JODI KAPLAN LESTER is an editor and transcriptionist. She has had the pleasure of editing or copy-editing the following books published by UglyTown: *An Occasional Dream* by Mike Lester, *Burn* by Sean Doolittle, *The Perpetrators* by Gary Phillips, and *Dark As Night* by Mark T. Conard. Jodi lives in Irvine, California, with her husband and animals.

JASON M. LIGHT is the author of five novels, including *Dust and Bones*, and short stories featured in publications such as *Whispers From the Shattered Forum* magazine and the anthology *Framed: A Gallery of Dark Delicacies*. He lives in downtown Oklahoma City.

LISA MAJEWSKI is a screenwriter and animal activist who graduated with honors from the USC School of Cinematic Arts. Frequently asked when her love for the macabre began, she replies, "At birth." Determined to help spread the darkness, she is now branching into horror fiction. Lisa resides in Los Angeles, where she celebrates Halloween 365 days a year.

MIKE McCARTY—Terror business veteran Mike McCarty has, hopefully, already been scaring the pants off of you with gruesome makeup fx in some of the top grossing horror films of the last decade. Now instead of splattery blood tubes and silicone body parts, he has chosen to do it with words as well. He lives in the frightening San Fernando Valley with his wife Grace and scary dog Mac. For more fright-filled information, go to www.mikemccarty.net on the terrifying interweb.

LISA MORTON has written some three-dozen works of short fiction, a trio of nonfiction books, and a number of largely forgettable movies and television series. She won the Bram Stoker Award for Short Fiction in 2006 and was a 2008 Black Quill nominee for *A Hallowe'en Anthology: Literary and Historical Writings Over the Centuries*. *The Lucid Dreaming*, her first novella, was recently published by Bad Moon Books, and her first novel, *The Castle of Los Angeles*, is forthcoming from Gray Friar Press. Also coming in fall of 2009 is a biography (co-written with Kent Adamson) of *Detour* star Ann Savage. She's never lived outside of California and can be found online at www.lisamorton.com.

JOEY O'BRYAN was born in Mississippi, raised in Texas, resides in Los Angeles, and keeps finding himself summoned to Hong Kong. One such occasion was to co-write *Fulltime Killer*, an award-winning action thriller directed by Johnnie To. After years of options, assignments, and hustling to get another movie off the runway, he got a short story published instead. "The Unlikely Redemption of Jared Pierce" appeared in the Stoker-nominated anthology *Dark Delicacies II: Fear*. He is currently dying from encouragement as various film projects inch toward production.

JOHN PALISANO creates stories. Tending toward the more exploratory and surreal in nature, he's recently been featured in the anthologies *Darkness On The Edge*, *The Beast Within*, *Harvest Hill*, and *Horror Library Volume III*. Additionally, John's odd films have played to festivals around the country. To watch the colors swirl, check out www.johnpalisano.com.

R. B. PAYNE believes that unbridled fear is the rocket fuel of evolution, synesthesia happens more often than we know, and there are humans walking among us. Richard's coffin of dirt from the old country is hidden in the hills above Los Angeles where he lives with his wife, a psychic blind cat, and a favorite guitar. Telepathic impulses are frequently recorded at www.rbpayne.com.

GEORGE WILLIS has a penchant for exotic travel and adventure—he's faced off against a knife-wielding thief in Morocco, leapt out of a perfectly good plane over the Mojave Desert, walked among wild lions and elephants in Zimbabwe, and has twice stood in the shadow of the Moon. When he's not wandering the Earth like Caine in *Kung Fu*, Mr. Willis enjoys writing. Currently he shares a home with a black cat that took up residence with him one Halloween.